THE SAINT

NANA MALONE

COPYRIGHT

This is a work of fiction. Names, characters, places, and incidents either are the product of the author's imagination or are used fictitiously, and any resemblance to actual persons living or dead, business establishments, events, or locales, is entirely coincidental.

The Saint, Book 3 in the Gentlemen Rogues Series

Cover Art by Najla Qambar

Alpha Reading: Suzi Vanderham

Edited by Angie Ramey

Proof Editing: Michele Ficht

Published in the United States of America

CHAPTER 1
KAYA

CHAOS HAD a way of finding you.

It didn't matter what you did to avoid it. It could ferret you out, glom onto you, and worm its way into your soul.

That was one lesson I'd learned when Mum disappeared.

If you were prone to chaos, you would never shake it.

Which was why I was currently hiding in the library stacks at my university. University of West London had a decent library. It wasn't enormous though, so hiding was only a temporary solution.

The journals and tomes stacked on ancient wood were only going to shield me for so long.

And sooner or later, I was going to need to either run or ovary up and deal with the situation.

This is what you get for not shooting him down hard when you sensed he'd started to develop feelings.

Admittedly, I'd had my hands full over the last few weeks with the anniversary of Mum's disappearance and critique week rapidly approaching for photography class.

My mind was a muddle of emotions, or I would have seen this coming.

I'd started to sense something was off with the Force for weeks. But I thought I could maneuver around it, pretend it wasn't happening. But now, here we were. Me, hiding in the stacks. Andrew, no doubt, using the Friends Locate app on our phones to find me.

I liked my privacy. Normally, I wouldn't like people knowing where I was all the time, but my past had taught me that maybe it would be a good idea if even just one person would come looking for me if I vanished off the face of the earth. I just never thought it would be used against me.

My only saving grace was that just like Andrew could see me, *I* could see *him*. He was along the other end cap by the far end of the stacks and closing in. I had to wait. Bide my time until he was *just* close enough.

This was dumb. I should be able to just tell him. To say the words.

You know full well you'll break his heart.

I didn't like lying. I didn't like hiding. Matter of fact, as an adult, it was very much my mantra to always tell the truth. Except in cases like this when I knew it would hurt someone. One of the few people I actually had in my life.

I didn't want to lose that.

I waited until he made it to the end stack and then turned toward me. And then I hit Location Off and bolted for the door. I would deal with this later.

Maybe I was wrong. Maybe this wasn't a thing. Maybe it was like all those stories that I'd concocted in my head about my parents when I'd been in care. Fantasies.

I bolted out the side door of the library, my heart rate not even ticking up, despite the adrenaline. My breathing was nice and steady and even. What was always interesting was that when I was in situations where I should be panicked or afraid, I never was. I always had this analytical approach to everything. Maybe that's why I was no good in relationships.

No, you're fine in relationships; you just don't want one.

Okay, there was that too. Relieved that I'd managed to escape without hurting Andrew today, I still knew that I had to come up with a proper plan of attack.

Andrew was a mate, but about a month ago I'd seen that look in his eyes. The one that told me he wanted something more.

Our friendship was important to me, and I didn't want to ruin it. I knew he wouldn't understand that I *couldn't* be with anyone or that it really had more to do with me than it did him. Even if he recovered quickly, our easy camaraderie would change.

I had done everything I could think of.

I'd made a point to refer to him as one of my best mates and point out that I was not looking for a relationship.

Our other best mate, Gemma Bloom, had also tried to dissuade him. And I thought maybe she'd gotten through to him, but apparently not.

Finally free of the library, I jogged down the main steps and headed to the cafe to meet Gemma, but suddenly, I stopped short.

Andrew.

How the fuck had he gotten out of the library quickly enough to meet me on the stairs?

The bright sunny smile he gave me made my stomach knot.

I was out of time.

"Hey, Kaya! Just the girl I was looking for. I was going to come and meet you and Gemma at the cafe after I retrieved my phone from my mate Carly. I left it in class and she grabbed it for me."

So, you've been avoiding a perfectly innocuous Carly in the library. Not Andrew.

"Oh, yeah? Unfortunately, I don't have a lot of time to chat today. I'm headed straight for the center."

I worked at a center for displaced women and children several hours a week. It was a temporary stop before we could find them more permanent placement. Unfortunately, it meant a lot of kids were displaced from school. And even if they did have work they could do, they didn't have their usual support networks.

My job was to provide some of that support. Helping kids with homework, playing video games, doing art projects. I loved it, but it took a lot of my time. Ruined a lot of nights out.

He licked his lips nervously. "Okay. I just wanted to ask you about my department's drinks meetup this Friday. I know you said you might come."

I tried not to grind my teeth. Saying I *might* go was being generous. I had said something along the lines of 'That sounds like fun.' I knew a myriad of ways to get out of things.

After all, I'd had lots of practice. I knew how to appear just available enough but never too available. Friendly, but not looking to make friends. I kept my circle small. These were tricks of the trade I'd learned young.

"Did I?"

He gave me a sheepish smile. "Okay, maybe not, but it'll be fun. And you never go out or do anything fun."

"Not true. You, Gems, and I went out on Wednesday. We had pizza and a pint, remember?"

"Yeah, but that was a study group thing."

Everyone had to take a basic coding class before they graduated. And Gemma and I had opted to take it this year, our second year, to try and get it out of the way. Andrew had taken the course the year before, so he had helped us.

"Andrew, I'm sorry I can't. I'm at the center on Friday."

His brows furrowed. "They can do without you for *one* night. Besides, I've already told everyone you're coming."

I hated being put on the spot. It was my least favorite thing. Growing up, I'd never been allowed to tell the truth. I'd learned to tell half-truths and sneak about. So as a grown-up, I learned to love the truth.

"Andrew, I'm sorry. Why don't you go with Gemma?" The two

of them would actually make a great couple. Someone like Gemma would be good for him. *Not* someone like me.

The furrow between his bushy brows sank even deeper. "Right. You know, for months I've been trying to work up the nerve to ask you out."

And there it was, the truth of it, right there on the steps of the library.

And I didn't want to look at it. "Andrew..."

"No, don't. You act like you like me, but you're just playing with me, aren't you?"

Remember, you don't want to hurt him.

I had to give myself that reminder because the sharper thought on my tongue would eviscerate him.

"Andrew, I've always been very clear with you that we're mates. I've always been very clear with you that I'm not looking for anything. *Any* kind of relationship, have I not?"

And yes, my tone was clipped. But it couldn't be helped. He was forcing my hand and bringing chaos with him.

I just wanted a simple, content life. Why was that so hard?

He shifted on his feet. "Kaya, I just —"

I shook my head. "Andrew, I don't want to hurt you. So I'm going to say this as directly as I can. We are *mates*. That's all we will ever be."

I could see the mutiny on his face even as I spoke. His pursed lips, usually in a smile for me, now a determined pout. "Well, you haven't even given us a chance."

"I'm going to ask you this, Andrew, and I want you to be honest with me. For the last year and a half, have we actually been mates, or were you just waiting to ask me out?"

He chewed his bottom lip. "It's not like that. I just... I just think we'd have fun and we'd make a great couple."

"And I think we make great friends. That's if you even want to be friends after this."

There was this thing about chaos. If it started to swirl around you, you could almost see the eye of the storm. That calm center where everything might be okay if everyone would just cooperate.

The problem was chaos itself. It would never let you get to the eye. That was the oasis that tempted you, pulled you in, and sucked you down.

Because once you were in the storm of chaos, there was no getting out.

"I just feel really misled, Kaya."

Misled?

I blinked at him once, and then twice, mentally watching our friendship disappear, as I inhaled deeply. "Why?"

"I feel like you put out a lot of signals that said you were interested. And I am—"

I shook my head. "I'm sorry, Andrew. I'm going to stop you right there. Have I ever said 'You know, Andrew, I quite fancy you. When are you going to ask me out?'"

He shook his head. "No, but—"

I lifted a hand to stop him. "And have I given you any indication that I don't know my own mind?"

Again, he shook his head. "It's just a drinks do, Kaya. You should just come."

If he was going to blow up our friendship, he was going to tell me the reason. "Why?" I was afraid I wasn't going to like this answer.

He shifted on his feet then. "I might've mentioned that we were going out."

And there it was in front of me. Chaos personified.

Before I could even dig into that kernel of shit, Gemma came bounding up the stairs. "There you are. I was at the cafe waiting on you." She gave Andrew a sunny smile. "What are you doing here so early? You don't have a class until, what? One, right?"

Andrew flushed. "I have to go," he grunted.

Gemma tossed up her hands. "Was it something I said?"

I ran a hand through my tangled curls. "No, it was something *I* said. You know how you warned him not to ask me out? Well, he did."

Gemma cursed under her breath. "Oh, for fuck's sake. And let me guess, he gave you that bullshit line about how you've been giving him *signals*."

My eyes went wide. "You knew he was going to do that?"

She winced. "He's been saying it for weeks. How you were totally giving him clear-cut signals you wanted him to ask you out. I didn't know he was dumb enough to believe that bullshit."

I joined her jogging down the stairs my backpack flopping against my back as we went. "Well, now he's annoyed. Can you believe he had the nerve to suggest *I* had somehow been the reason he misconstrued everything? And he admitted that he'd just been waiting to ask me out this whole time."

Gemma covered her face with her hands. "Oh, Jesus. He's like every bad date on Bumble and Hinge right in front of our faces."

"All this time, he was just thinking about how best he could get into my knickers?"

"I'm so sorry. To be fair, I *do* think he has been your friend. I just also think you're the prettiest girl to ever speak to him, so in his head he's worked it up to be a thing. God, I'm sure that was just so awkward."

"It was awkward at *best*. Just horrible. And the worst thing was there I was in the stacks with nowhere to go."

"The stacks?"

"Long story." I summed it up for her.

"Well, the good news is it's out in the open. That's if you even want to be friends with him anymore."

"I'm not even sure how I feel about the whole thing. On the one hand, it's *Andrew*. On the other hand, did you know he told his entire department that we were dating?"

Gemma stopped in the middle of the walkway and grabbed me by the arm. For a little thing, she was fiercely strong. "Stop it. He did *not*!"

"He told me he did. Tried to use that as a good reason why I should go out with him."

"Bloody Andrew."

"Yeah, bloody Andrew indeed. I'll deal with him another time. I just have enough time to grab a smoothie on the way to the center."

"Oh, blasted. I wanted to talk to you about my Professor Hottie project."

Professor Hottie was none other than *the* Xander Chase. He was hands-down the best-looking professor we had. Everyone had a crush on him. He was married of course. Didn't stop anyone from dreaming though. His wife was this amazing West End actress, Imani Chase. They were actually really cute together. And stupid in love. Gemma and I were both photojournalism majors, and Xander's class was a tough one.

"I'm happy to help you scope out locations. I got my project done early." For her photo project, she had asked to photograph me. I had said no, but we'd brainstormed another idea for her project, and I was her location scout.

Gemma danced on the balls of her feet, and I could tell there was something she was holding back. "That's just it. I don't need you."

"Well, that's all well and good. One friend who needs me too much and another who doesn't need me at all. I'm doing just great, " I joked.

Gemma rolled her eyes. "Will you stop it. Have you heard of the tycoon, Connor Phelps?"

"Should I have?" I asked as I placed my smoothie order.

"I suppose not. He's huge in finance. Also stupid wealthy and very good-looking. When I narrowed down the parameters of my project, I realized that I could do a profile on him, complete with photos. Which would cover me for both my writing assignment and my photography assignment."

"Okay, fine. I forgive you just this once for not needing me to model for you." I pursed my lips and struck what I thought was a model pose.

She laughed as we collected my smoothie and she took a sip of her energy drink. "You can scout for me another time. In the *meantime*, what are we going to do about your Andrew problem?"

I didn't want to think about it. "You know I hate chaos."

"Oh, I know," she said with rolled eyes.

"This is just so messy. And the last thing I want."

"I get you. But you can't avoid him forever. And from the looks of it, that did not work out well today."

Fair point there. "Well, I very much doubt he's speaking to me right now, so it might not even matter."

"Look I'm going to say this, and I don't want you thinking that I'm taking his side."

I lifted a brow. "If you take his side, I swear to God, Gems..."

"I'm not. And to be fair, all the bad decisions he made, I told him not to. So he made his own choices. That's not your fault, and you shouldn't have to pay for that. What I will say is that you don't date *anyone*, Kaya. *Ever*. Not that Andrew should take that as a hint or some declaration that you're holding out for him to ask you out. But the only time in the last two years we've known each other that you went out on a date was so Andrew *wouldn't* ask you out. Not that it's any of my business. Even though we're besties. You can tell me if you like girls or are asexual or something."

I lifted my brow. "Thank you for the approval. I once did have a crush on Lizzie Dubois, but I discovered Henry Cavill shortly after that. And that was the end of poor Lizzie," I said with a smirk.

"Fair. Henry Cavill will make anyone salivate."

"Right?"

"You never date *anyone* though. And I just wondered maybe if you were worried about telling me something."

"Trust me, if there was something to tell you, I would. And I wouldn't be ashamed to be into women or asexual. Sadly, I crave the devil's eggplant. Just not *Andrew's* eggplant."

She howled with laughter. "Eww, Andrew's eggplant."

I held up my hands. "For all I know he has a very nice eggplant. I just don't really want to know."

"I just don't like seeing you closed off."

"I don't need a relationship to make my life complete," I muttered.

"Of course you don't. But I also don't want to see you *avoiding* relationships like you're hiding."

That direct hit made my lips pucker. Sometimes Gemma was an easy friend. And by that I meant she didn't dig too deep, didn't try to unearth any scars. But every now and again she saw too clearly, and that made me nervous.

"Not hiding. Just not really focused on that right now."

"Fine, I'll stop harassing you." She started riffling for something in her bag. "Where did I put my bloody headphones?"

As she looked, out fell two notebooks, a pencil, and a magazine. I helped her dive for a wayward pen and the magazine that nearly toppled off the cafe table. I froze when I saw it.

Staring back at me was someone I hadn't seen in five years.

The last person to see my mother alive before she vanished.

Connor Lohman.

KAYA

My home was normally a place of refuge. I loved my flat. It was the first place I ever lived where I was completely in control.

After my mother disappeared five years ago, I had been sent into care. Luckily for me, it had only been a couple of foster homes.

The first one was a disaster. Pure chaos. But not chaos filled with love. Just chaos and fear. The second one was a great family with three other kids. It was safe. I was fed and even cared for. But so much chaos with people and noise. There were still moments these days when I marveled at the silence in my flat.

To keep the place a refuge, I rarely invited people over. And honestly, by 'people' I meant Gemma. Even Andrew hadn't seen my flat. What was interesting was that Gemma seemed to understand once she learned a little bit about how I'd grown up.

Granted, she thinks you were always in care.

Another half-truth.

She assumed. I just hadn't corrected her.

But now my refuge had an intruder. Chaos in the form of Connor Lohman, now Phelps.

After I made my excuses to Gemma, I'd gotten the hell off campus and then done something I never did. I called off work. Luckily, another girl owed me for a double shift I'd taken last week. I hated to do it, but there was no way I could focus on the kids today.

Connor Lohman was on the cover of a magazine. But he was going by Connor Phelps now. I stared at my computer screen.

It was him all right. My brain did the work of matching the face to the one of the man driving the car my mother had climbed into five years ago when she disappeared.

The familiar knot of worry and guilt threaded through my gut. My mother was smart. She was capable. For fifteen years she'd kept me alive and hidden. And then one day she'd walked away.

You know full well she would never leave you by choice.

Something had happened to her. And I'd been young without any resources, so I'd done the one thing she always forbade me from doing; I walked into a police station and told them my mother hadn't come home.

When I was growing up, my mother was always going on and on about how we had to stay hidden. At the time it had made sense. There were bad people chasing her. *Chasing us.*

But as I got older, I realized that was just the chaos of the things that she brought about. I'd never witnessed anyone chasing us. All I'd witnessed was having to move every year. A new name, a new identity. More than once I'd moaned about how I was sick of it and just wanted a normal life.

But now that I had my normal life, I could feel the edges fraying.

I could patch it. Stop the madness. I didn't *need* to pull on that string. I could just snip it and put a bit of glue down. I didn't need to unravel it.

You don't, but you will.

I would. Because chaos was my constant companion.

It didn't matter how much I thought I could outrun it. It didn't matter that I thought I had found peace. None of it mattered. The eye of the storm was an illusion.

Connor Lohman, aka Connor Phelps, or whatever his name was, he was the one responsible for what happened to my mother. And I owed it to her to question him.

But as I stared at the news article, I could see the truth. Connor Phelps was no two-bit thug. He was a financier. At least according to this article.

I needed a way to get close to him, and I intended to get my answers by any means necessary.

CHAPTER 2
KAYA

For years, I'd wondered about my mother's sanity. The shadows she always saw, the fear she always lived in. I hadn't thought it was a real thing because I hadn't seen it.

But as it turned out, the boogeyman was real.

So what are you going to do about it?

At the very least, I had to talk to Connor. Find out what he knew. I had to try. But how the hell was I going to get to someone like him? I knew that he was surrounded at all times by security and yes-men. People who, for the right price, would say what he wanted to hear. I needed a way around them. A way to make this work.

What the hell are you going to do? You know who he is, and ostensibly where he might be. And how will you get to him? Men like that have dragon-guarded moats.

I stared at the article again. The kind of man he was, the circles he ran in, his access to money, it was all evident.

I did not have the kind of money or power it was going to take to get access to a man like that, so I needed to be smart. I scanned the article again, praying for something to jump out of it. A miracle.

Or you can leave it. Do nothing. Stay in your normal life.

I frowned at that. There *was* no normal life. There was no *unseeing* what I had already seen.

For years, I hadn't believed my mother, but she'd been telling the truth about dangers in the world and the people who didn't care who they hurt to get where they needed to be.

Connor Lohman was one of them. The last I had seen of him, he'd been a low-life thug. And in the five years since, he'd turned himself into a scrubbed-up money man. How did that happen?

Then I saw my opening. Like most other philanthropists, he liked to splash his money around because it made him look good. The Almed Fund for Children was having a gala, and sure enough, Connor Lohman was a benefactor.

Of course, he was.

The question was, how the hell did I get access to something like that? The article held some information about how to donate to the all-important cause, and I recognized a name. Jennifer Cormack.

I knew her. She often helped with events for the center. So was this one of those few times in my life that I had a string to pull?

Sometimes we have to do what we have to do.

Jennifer answered on the first ring. "Kaya, hi. How are you? Is there a meeting at the center I'm late for?"

"No. Actually, I'm calling about something else if you have a moment."

"Of course, how can I help?"

I was playing with fire. I knew that. But this was about my mother. I hadn't even looked for her beyond checking homeless shelters. Not in a proper way. I'd believed she left me behind. But what if she hadn't? What if I'd been blinded by that belief and gotten it wrong? Now was the time to make it right.

"I see you're holding an auction for the Almed Fund, and I'd love to participate. Maybe I can help with the auction." That should be easy.

She squealed in delight, and I could picture her flouncy blond hair and perma-pink cheeks. "Oh my gosh, I love everything about this. You do realize you'll be auctioning a date with yourself, right?"

What? No. I'd thought I could organize.

My stomach sank. It didn't matter, because I needed access to Connor Lohman, and that was where he was going to be. "Sign me up. Can't wait to auction myself off."

———

KAYA

Two weeks later, I realized I'd miscalculated.

When I had seen the article about the charity auction, I'd assumed I could get a spare moment to speak to him. That would have been simple. But oh no. In fifteen minutes, I was going on the auction block.

No matter. I could adjust. I had to adjust. I *would* adjust. He was my first lead in five years.

In this room stood the wealthiest of London's elite. The problem with this crowd was they were so incestuous it was easy to spot anyone who didn't belong.

The impostors, the interlopers. Like me.

But I was good at blending. My entire purpose in life was to hide in plain sight, and I had gotten really good at it.

But moments like this, where I was out in the open for everyone to see, made me twitchy and edgy.

I could fake the confidence and belonging with the best of them though. But knowing I needed to look as bored as the rest of the socialites and actually *maintaining* my cool were two different things.

I had been waiting all night for this. Hell, I'd been waiting weeks for tonight.

The last man to see my mother alive was there, and I wasn't leaving until I talked to him.

Damn my mother and her secrets. I'd had to untangle the web of secrecy she left behind. She'd gone to meet Connor Lohman about his boss, and he was going to give her everything, fully grass on everyone.

She'd left me at home alone that night, and she'd never come home. I was fifteen.

He knew something. If Connor hadn't just been the mealy-mouthed middleman, I would have suspected he'd done something to her. Hell, maybe he had walked her right into a trap. But Mum was too smart for him, and he was afraid of her for some reason. But he had to at least know what had happened to her. All I needed was to talk to him.

I'd given him a bright sunny smile, cocking my head at an angle so that the hair I dropped over my face covered half of it. Hopefully, the most anyone would ever get of me for facial recognition, if that was even going to be a problem, was my profile.

One quick glance told me exactly where he was. *Showtime.*

I sauntered over to the bar with a smile. Just close enough that he might notice me and, very likely, the daring dip of the back of my dress. But not so close that I was all up in his face. Not obvious. I kept telling myself to breathe deep and not blow this. What would my mother do? That was the question I kept asking with every step of this ridiculous adventure. Whose bright idea was this?

Yours.

Right. The bartender approached with a grin. "Hello, beautiful. I'm Tucker. I can serve you tonight. What would you like?"

I took note of Connor's gimlet. "I'll have what he's having."

Connor turned. His head angled, a smile already on his lips. He scanned my body first, his smile growing wider. And then his grin froze in place when he reached my face. What the hell was that

supposed to mean? It was sort of recognition, but it was also...
fear?

That wasn't right.

I forced myself to smile back. "Hello."

He seemed to shake off the stun of seeing me. "You have good taste in drinks."

"I do, don't I?"

His gaze searched my face again. "Have we met?"

"No, I've not had the pleasure. I'm Kaya Sinclair."

The fake name was the one my mother had used often in many of the places we'd gone. Sometimes we'd been the Sinclairs, sometimes the Freemans. We always kept our first names though. Especially when I was small. She made it easy for me to remember if someone was using my actual name. But Reynolds was my real surname. I wasn't giving this geezer access to it.

"Well, a beautiful name for a beautiful woman."

It was only then that I noticed the men that were in close proximity to him. He called one over and muttered something to him. And then the three men that I'd seen in their dark suits and wired communication devices all but vanished into the crowd. Then he moved a little closer. "Now, what is a beautiful woman like you doing at a place like this alone?"

"Oh, you know, we all do things for charity."

"Yes, we do. You know, I'm sorry, but I could swear I have seen you before."

"I'm already speaking to you. You can drop the line."

His gaze ran over my body again. "Maybe you just have one of those faces."

I shrugged because no one had ever said that to me before. Suddenly, Connor's men were back, but they seemed to have multiplied. I counted six in the crowd. "Your friends, they're creepy."

Connor laughed as he glanced around and shook his head

slightly. "Well, you can't be too careful these days. In my life, I've just learned to be cautious."

"Well, if you're overly cautious, how on earth do you have any fun?" I tried not to gag on the words as I flirted with him, but I knew it was important to keep his attention.

Tucker served my gimlet, and I took a sip, forcing my face into utter neutrality. I moaned a little to try and indicate bliss, but God, it tasted like shoe polish.

"A woman with good taste in drinks. I like it."

"Well, I learned to appreciate certain things in life."

As Connor flirted more, I moved closer and closer to him, occasionally lightly touching his arm, gauging interest. The crowd started to move toward the larger ballroom, and he inclined his head. "Might I escort you inside?"

"Oh, I'm sorry, I have to decline. I would like some time to talk to you later though. Perhaps we can have another drink, somewhere more... private?"

He took my hand and then bowed forward and kissed it. "I was certainly hoping you would say something like that. What do you say the two of us actually skip this whole thing? I've already written a check. I don't have to be here."

I smiled at him. "I would love that. However, I did already promise I'd take part in the auction."

His eyes went wide. "You're up for auction?"

I gave him a flirty shrug. "Yes. It's for charity, so I agreed."

"Well, in that case, I will certainly bid on you. And immediately after, I'll get to enjoy some time with you for the evening."

"That sounds perfect." I said it with the kind of smile I hoped that the seductresses in James Bond films would use instead of the tight revulsion with which I felt then. I saw Jennifer waving me over, and I sighed. It was showtime. But at least now I had whet his appetite.

After this auction, I was going to get alone time with Connor Lohman, and then I would get my questions answered.

Jennifer, wearing a black sheath cocktail dress, her blond hair coiled into curls on top of her head, smiled as she reached the podium. "Now, ladies and gentlemen, I know that you have been waiting ever so patiently for the final lot of the evening in our bachelorette auction. Well, the wait is over."

I tried to remind myself that women did this all the time. They talked to nasty, disgusting men to secure their safety, to secure their futures, hell, even just a drink. Sometimes even health insurance. I could do this. We were just going to have a conversation without his babysitters.

But now, I must auction. Whose bright idea was this?

Yours.

God, what if people bid on me? That would be awful. But what if no one bid on me? That would be equally as awful, and I wasn't sure which one I preferred.

Jennifer gave an introduction and gestured toward me, and I sighed deeply. It was showtime.

I walked onto the stage and there was discreet clapping, hooting, and hollering. Some of the organizers that helped at the center were behind it, trying to make me feel better, no doubt.

Jennifer detailed my accomplishments and explained that I was a student who had, thus far, been unlucky in love and mostly spent my time volunteering with underprivileged youth. Then she opened the bidding.

I tried to not take myself seriously, so I gave her a little curtsy and did a little twirl. The girls over at the bar hooted and hollered again. And then to my horror, or my relief, I wasn't sure which, Connor Lohman/Phelps bid on me.

I gave him a wan smile and tried to push down my shudder of revulsion because... gross.

But then I saw someone else with a paddle in the air. I turned and my gaze locked on moss green eyes. I did a quick scan of the bloke's face too. It was... holy shit. There was an aura of intensity about him. Even though his smile was flirty, there was something about him that screamed *I am a deadly predator.*

He was a smorgasbord for the eyes. I couldn't figure out what part of him to look at first. The body, the hair, the eyes. All broad shouldered like a swimmer with an insane wingspan.

He was handsome in that way that was striking, where you were sort of compelled to look at his face and you couldn't look away. His jaw was stubbled, and heat flooded my veins as I wondered all the places that stubble could abrade the skin.

What? No. Oh, hell no. I didn't date. I didn't do relationships. And the one or two hookups I'd ever had were lackluster at best. Awkward and embarrassing or worse. Why was I having sudden horny feelings for someone I didn't even know?

He was very pretty. A carved jawline that made him look sexy and roguish. A sharp Roman nose that looked like perhaps it had been broken once before but expertly put back together by a very good plastic surgeon. He looked young. Under thirty definitely.

His hair was slightly longer on top, expertly styled with gel to look slightly haphazard but not too much. In a word, he was gorgeous.

And he knew it.

But worse, it was as if my pussy had called out to me, wanting to finally be put into action.

Oh God. Not on the stage. I resolutely snapped my gaze away from him. And when the hooting and hollering began again when Connor upped his bid, I laughed and shook my head.

Apparently, the laugh worked because suddenly more hands went up, and I flushed. This was horrible and embarrassing.

All the while, Jennifer was going on and on about how amazing I was. How athletic, my history of martial arts, and I wanted to be ill.

Had I really put all of that on the auction form? It had asked for hobbies.

Then she said that I read, and she highlighted my favorite romance novels. That got several hands up. *Bloody hell.*

When the price went up past five thousand quid, I laughed nervously. What in the world?

Finally, the bloke with the green eyes and jaw that looked like it had been chiseled called out, "Ten thousand pounds."

My gaze snapped back to him, and he grinned, his smirk melting that whole core of ice somewhere deep inside me, making me throb.

No, no, no. Which was the worst bet? Connor or this guy?

This guy, definitely. You need Connor.

I did need Connor.

My decision made for me, I sent Connor a pleading look.

He smirked at me and then the other bloke, as he called out, "Fifteen thousand pounds."

My jaw dropped. I thought he'd bid by a few quid only. I mean, what was a few bob? But five thousand? Jesus, this was getting out of hand. I mean exactly what did they think I was going to do on this date?

I certainly was not going to fuck Connor.

But you will be locked in a room with him. So there's that.

Fuck.

Well, I would deal with that when I came to it. Besides, I could grab a weapon, right? I saw some knives on the table that would make excellent defense weapons.

You really did not think this through very well.

Okay, fine. I'd walked into this auction situation not having thought it through.

After Connor's latest bid, a hush fell over the room. Everyone whispered and tittered around. There was a dark-skinned black woman sitting on the other side of Mr. Green Eyes, between him and another man who was equally good-looking. He had dark curly hair, and he looked familiar. Why did he look familiar? Maybe he was an actor or something. But he was jaw-dropping.

That bloke leaned over and kissed her shoulder, and she smiled up at him. Her smile was incandescent. They were in love. And then they whispered something about Green Eyes because he turned to look at them and just shook his head and kept his paddle up.

Connor too. Finally, Jennifer called out, "Gentlemen, I thank you for a very interesting evening. We are up to fifty-thousand pounds. Do I hear fifty-one?"

Connor kept his paddle up. The beautiful woman sandwiched between the two men lifted her brows, her dark skin glowing under the light in the ballroom. She was beautiful. It was as if several models had turned up from fashion week just for this auction. Green Eyes was about to put up his paddle again, but then she shook her head and whispered again. He sighed, and then gave me a look that said he was sorry and disappointed.

Jennifer glanced from him to Connor and back to Green Eyes again. "We are currently at fifty-one thousand. Do we have any other takers at fifty-two?"

When Green Eyes shook his head, she banged the gavel down. "And we have closed the bidding at fifty-one-thousand pounds. Mr. Phelps, we are beyond thrilled by your most generous donation." Everyone clapped. I did a little curtsy, and then I waved at Jennifer, who indicated she'd be right down at the bottom of the stairs to tell me where I was supposed to go meet Connor.

When she joined me, I was searching the crowd, hoping I could just grab Connor without even having to go to a room with him, but I knew that I needed the privacy. "Come with me. You'll wait over here for Mr. Phelps."

"So just like that, I'm being handed off as a prize?"

"Oh, I know, auctions are a little déclassé and problematic. I get it. But they're fun. And for the Almed Fund, that's fifty-one-thousand pounds. Not that Mr. Phelps didn't already give a generous donation. But this is even more. We will gladly take it."

"All in the name of charity, I suppose."

"See, you get it. Just wait here ten minutes. Mr. Phelps should be right by."

The moment she was gone, I started pacing. I could just wait for him to show up, but what if he didn't?

Maybe it was better to be proactive.

I opened a door, and there were people bustling about, jogging somewhere. There was a woman all dressed in black and she had an earpiece in, just like Jennifer did. "I'm sorry, I've been waiting for Mr. Phelps. Can you tell me if he has a room assigned back here?"

"Yeah, it's just down there. Turn left at the end of the hall."

"Thank you, I really appreciate it."

She nodded and then headed off. Clearly, something was going on with the event. As I marched down the hall, nobody seemed to notice me or tried to stop and ask me where the hell I was going. When I arrived at the door she'd indicated, I took a deep breath. I could do this. Where was his security anyway?

Maybe they weren't allowed backstage. But that seemed unusual. I knocked on the door, and I could hear some muffled noises in the background. "I got tired of waiting for you. Are you in there?"

I hoped that sounded seductive, although I was pretty sure I sounded tight and anxious. I knocked again, and when I tried the door handle, it swung open. But it wasn't Connor Phelps who opened it. It was the other green-eyed bloke. "Oh, I'm sorry. I was told that this was Mr. Phelps's room. Is he here?"

Green Eyes grinned at me and then braced his arms on the door frame. "I'm the only one here, sweetheart. This is my room. No Mr. Phelps."

I laughed. "Oh, come on, where is he?"

I'd noted the tie that Connor had been wearing earlier, black with subtle gray polka dots on it. It was on the dressing table. "That's his tie. Where is he?"

He shrugged. "Sorry. I don't know what to say. I'm the only one here. I hate to break it to you, but I'm your date."

CHAPTER 3
SAINT

HE WASN'T SUPPOSED to fight back.

The assignment was meant to be easy. Pick up Lohman, interrogate him, and take him back to Rogues Division for processing. For years, Connor Lohman had been a midlevel enforcer for Antonio Igno, embedded deep in the organization. He knew where lots of bodies were buried.

A few years ago he'd leveled up, making it to adviser status. But the only way to do that was with blood or intel. And Lohman was notoriously squeamish. So what intel had gotten him even closer to the emperor?

We were going to find out. One more step in capturing Igno. The Rogues Division was a top-secret, highly-classified, *I'd tell you but I'd have to kill you* kind of organization. The kind of organization the government pretended not to love having at its disposal.

We chased down the scum of the earth and brought them to justice. Scum like Connor Lohman. The fire that burned in my gut just thinking of his name was a constant companion. Because of him and the people he worked for, my fiancée was gone. An innocent bystander in Igno's games.

Sure, I liked taking out the trash, but this was bigger than that. Lohman owed me vengeance.

That was why this charity auction was so perfect. I could grab the mark without anyone being the wiser. Except his security had put up a fight. And now the woman with the smile bright enough to chase shadows from your soul was here to find her winner.

My gaze slipped over her slight frame. She was delicate, maybe five foot three without the heels. Slender, she wore her hair in a style that covered half her face in soft waves. Her skin was the color of sand during sunset. At first glance, I thought maybe she was biracial or Latin.

One thing I knew for sure, her dark eyes could capture the soul. They had me pinned against our escape door unable to move as she stared at me.

Her eyes went wide with alarm. "Where is Connor?"

How easy was she going to be to convince? My main directive was to maintain cover while my team got out. "It's Jasper if you must know, but everybody calls me Saint. I'm your guy. Why are you looking for Connor? After all, I won you. Okay to be fair, Conner sold me his bid before he left."

She blinked rapidly. Obviously trying to think on her feet.

"Um, we just hit it off earlier before the auction, so I wanted to say goodbye." Her brows furrowed. "What are *you* doing in his suite?"

It was my turn to tap dance. "Just warning him to stay away from my prize."

The arsehole billionaire was a thing, right?

Unlike him, I'd been smart enough to bring people who knew what the fuck they were doing.

The sprite in front of me gave no fucks about any of that though. "I'm no one's prize."

In my earpiece, one of my best mates, Lachlan, chuckled. "I feel like you're going to have to level up your game. You're crashing and burning here, mate."

I clenched my jaw, wishing I could remove the earpiece. Unfortunately, I needed it to be in contact with them to make sure they got Lohman out of there. Which meant keeping this one distracted.

I finally tore my gaze away from her eyes, breaking the spell she had on me. My gaze ran over the rest of her face. Delicate bone structure, full lips. A slightly flat button nose with a low bridge. There was something inherently sensual about the set of her lips. She could go easily from being the bloody girl next door to a vamped vixen. Tonight, with the red lipstick, she was all vamp. And she was giving my dick all kinds of bad ideas.

The fuck was that about? We were on mission. No reason for my dick to sit up and pay attention.

You can't live like a monk forever.

I wasn't. I argued with my subconscious. But when I gave it thought, I hadn't been with anyone since Elise, three years ago.

I deliberately held up my badge. "Last I checked, I just paid a pretty penny for the pleasure of your company. Okay, to be truthful. Conner sold me his bid before he left."

Her gaze narrowed on my face. "For *charity*. I'm not actually yours. You do understand that, right?"

I lifted my brow. "Oh, I beg to differ. You and I had a whole exchange while you were on stage. You are mine."

Fire sparked in her eyes. "You will have to try harder than that. I'm sure putting real effort in is a foreign concept."

I had to laugh at that. "Are you always such a pain in the arse?"

In my ear, Rook chuckled. "So yeah, the best way to a woman's heart is to antagonize her."

I wanted to tell them to shut the fuck up. They were going to ruin this.

The sprite in the short dress with cleavage that made my mouth water strode up to me and tried to push past me through the door. "Tell me where he is."

I stayed her with a hand in the crook of her elbow. "Easy does it. Where are you going?"

She yanked back her arm. "To talk to Connor. We have things to discuss."

I chuckled low, unwilling to back down. "I already told you no."

She was wilier than I thought though, and she ducked under my arm and yanked open the back door. I chased after her, looping an arm around her waist before she could duck into the back hallway.

"What's happening back there? What's all the commotion?"

I dragged her back away from where she might see anything. "I see you don't listen so well. Are you always so stubborn?"

Her brows furrowed. "What's going on back there? I heard groaning."

I forced my face to go completely neutral. Putting me undercover was difficult. Everything I felt, usually about someone being an idiot, was written all over my face. Saffron, Lachlan's fiancée, liked to call it my resting asshole face. It kept me from lying effectively even when I had to.

"Look, we clearly got off on the wrong foot. But let me introduce myself again. Hi. I'm Jasper Saint. And you are?"

She pressed her lips firmly together, and I wondered if she would answer me. But then she squared her shoulders. "I'm Kaya Sinclair. But I don't care about niceties. I want to know what's going on."

"I just want to get to know you better." My dick agreed wholeheartedly. "Why are you so pressed for Connor?"

"It's not your business."

"We could make it my business."

Stall better, you twat. The team still needs three minutes.

"Tell me what you need from him."

She shook her head. "What is your deal anyway? Why do you want us to go on a date so bad?"

"Because you're a beautiful woman. And I just won a chance to make you smile."

"Nice try. Not interested."

"Pretty sure you are. Otherwise you wouldn't still be here."

She threw her hands up. "Jesus Christ I did not—"

The publicist and the organizer of the event strolled in, both of them looking giddy. The organizer said, "There you are, Mr. Saint. Miss Sinclair, is it? We are so excited about your donation. The two of you certainly make a beautifully stunning couple."

I grinned at Kaya, and she scowled at me. "What's the problem?" I asked. Given her reaction to me while she was on stage, shouldn't she be happier she wasn't stuck with Lohman?

"You're passable looking, but you are arrogant and a pain in my arse."

The publicist looked around. "Excuse me? Is there a problem?"

Kaya turned to her. "Can I pull out of this date? I'd like to exchange this one for one who is less of a pain. Or maybe back out entirely?"

The publicist frowned and shook her head. "No. We've got photographers waiting. It's good coverage for us. This event and the romance of it all really helps with donations."

Damn her for pulling on my do-the-right-thing strings. But at least it would give my team time to secure Lohman. "Please make this quick. I'm sure Miss Sinclair has things she would rather be doing," I said with a wry smile for Kaya.

The publicist clapped her hands. "Excellent, now if the two of you would just step this way."

Kaya frowned, and we both said at the same time, "Why?"

The publicist widened her large hazel eyes. "Because the two of you are expected on the dance floor for a photo op. All our other couples I've already done theirs. Just you two remain."

CHAPTER 4
KAYA

This was *not* part of the plan. Dancing in Jasper Saint's arms was not why I was there.

I should be chasing Connor. He knew something. He *had* to.

Jasper bloody Saint. What kind of arsehole name was that? Dripping of old money, no skill set, and a lack of morals. Funny though, he didn't reek of nepotism and elitism.

He smelled good. Like sandalwood and vanilla with something a little woodsy. There was a very small part of me that wanted to lean in and inhale.

Inhale? What the hell is wrong with you?

Oh right, you know what's wrong with you. How long has it been since anyone has touched you? Held you? Kissed you?

Let's be real, those kisses were far and few between, not to mention lackluster and uninteresting.

Jasper Saint didn't look like his kisses would be uninteresting at all. I dared a look up at his face, just a quick glance. Once my gaze tipped up to do my surreptitious exploration, I realized that he was watching me with those intense eyes. Now that I was up close I could see they were a deep moss green. The sheer force of his attention made something low in my belly pulse and ache.

There was a challenge in his gaze. Like he was daring me to stare back. So I did. Why should he be the only one getting an eyeful? The way he held me, close but not too close, made me so aware of the heat of his body wrapping around me, caressing me. Not tight enough to scare me, but definitely a presence. Surrounded on all sides.

His level of intensity was intoxicating, thick and heavy, and it lulled you into complacency by making you feel warm and safe. But that was a lie. There was no place warm and safe. And that security certainly couldn't be found in the arms of someone else.

Even though I knew that, the temptation to lean in was so strong. And I couldn't help the long slow exhale as his fingertips gently traced along my spine, coaxing the calm into me. Letting the tension out. Giving me the cocoon of calm I craved.

I felt weak. I should not be enjoying this. I didn't know this bloke, but I knew he was keeping me from Connor.

His fingers trailed sensually over my back, just the soothing I needed. Also, with his height and the broad set of his shoulders, for the first time in a long time, I felt safe. Secure.

That's the complacency talking. And that's going to get you killed.

I quickly squared my shoulders and lifted my head. "Why are you so insistent on this date?"

He crooked his brow and gave me a sardonic smirk. "Think of me as a rule follower. I paid for the pleasure of your time. And you're a beautiful woman, so it should be obvious."

I shook my head. "I don't believe you. Someone like you wouldn't be swayed by a harried publicist telling you to dance with a perfect stranger. So why? Is it the fact that I don't want you as my date that's making you all the more interested?"

His low chuckle rolled over me like warm whiskey on a cold night. "You think so little of me. You don't even know the first thing about me."

Staring defiantly up at his impertinent gaze, I huffed out, "Don't I though? This is about your ego. You can't fathom that a woman doesn't want to date you. And to be fair, most of the women you run into are probably desperate to climb into bed with you for your fortune if the press release before the auction is to be believed. I'm sorry your ego was bruised, but I have zero desire to date you."

"Oh, really? You recognize that puts you in the minority, right?"

I had no doubt. Yeah, he definitely had the kind of looks that could make women push their best friend down the stairs to get to him. As in, 'Sorry girl, there are no friends in love and war. He's mine now.' And he was wealthy. I didn't know the contents of his bank accounts yet, but you could tell by the way he carried himself and the way he wore his suit like a second skin. He was comfortable in a tux. Comfortable in a way that said he'd selected this one specifically because of its expertly tailored fit. It made him look like a billion dollars even if it was a lie. "Your money and your wealth don't make you the least bit appealing to me."

Liar.

He chuckled low. "Let me guess. You're alone here tonight. Not a lot of friends. Prefer a nice quiet life with zero excitement?"

That smarted. "You think you know me so well?"

"Oh, I see you, Sprite."

I scratched my nose at that. "Sprite?"

"That's how you look to me. There is something delicate about you."

If that comeback didn't get my hackles up, nothing would. "I'm *not* delicate."

"Sure you're not. And as beautiful as you look in a cocktail dress, I can somehow picture you with a short Pixie cut giving someone a proper what-for. To me, that screams Sprite."

"Fine. Now I'll just call you Basil."

He chuckled again, this time the motion giving him a slight crease at his eyes. "Oh, yeah? What the hell is that supposed to mean, love?"

"Like in old books. You're the guy everyone loves to hate. You have it all. The money, the house, the name. All of it without even trying or a sad day to show for it."

"You think you see me so well, Sprite?"

I gave him a sharp nod. "One hundred percent. You're clearly gorgeous, but you're typical. You're rich and think that makes you worthy. It doesn't. Especially since it does nothing to improve your personality."

"Wow, tell me how you really feel, why don't you?"

Over his shoulder, I spotted one of Connor's men, the same one who had been staring at me earlier.

My back went rigid as my heart rate kicked in, and I turned, attempting to flee.

Saint held my hand tight. "Where the hell are you going? They haven't even taken our pictures yet."

"Sorry, handsome, I have somewhere to be."

I glanced over his shoulder again and tried to take my hand out of his. He finally glanced over his shoulder and saw the hulking brute coming our way, and he stopped fighting me. But he didn't let me go. Instead, he allowed me to tug him through the crowd and said, "Clearly we are going on an adventure. So, Kaya, tell me where we're going?"

"Where *I'm* going, you mean. Goddammit, let me go."

"Is that geezer chasing you?"

"That is none of your business."

"Seems like my business if you're dragging me along with you."

I tried to shake his hand away again. "I don't want you with me. For fuck's sake, why are you so irritating?"

"You know, you're not the first woman to say that to me."

"Shocker." I dragged him out into the hall where there were more people. But as I glanced around, all I saw were threats. Anyone in a tux could be after me.

Where had it all gone wrong tonight?

Maybe walking into the open where Connor Lohman's men could get a good look at you was the first bad move.

Coming here had been a risk. But how had they figured me out so quickly?

Doesn't matter now. Run.

Through the crowd, I tried to lose Saint, but he was surprisingly agile. When we reached the end of the hallway and I was trying to go right, he immediately took me left into a small alcove . "Hey, stop moving."

My eyes went wide at him. "What the hell are you doing? I need to get out of here."

"I get that. Something is clearly wrong. Why don't you tell me what it is and I can help you."

I laughed. "Sorry, billionaire, as helpful as you could be, you can't save me from this shit show about to start. I need to go."

Pushing further against the wall he used his big body to cover mine.

"You could talk to me. Everyone needs a friend sometimes. Are you in trouble?"

I blinked rapidly, looking into the cool green of his eyes. I was stuck. I did not have any other options. And he was offering help.

Just once in my life I wanted to be able to trust someone. To get help when I needed it. But I still knew deep down that trusting the wrong person could get me killed. Help from Saint was not going to be an option. I shook my head. "No, I got this."

His smirk was borderline insulting. "Are you sure about that? Currently you're running from a charity ballroom. Tell me Kaya, who is after you? I can help more than you know."

Maybe he can help. Maybe for once you don't need to do everything on your own.

And I was tempted. So very tempted to just reach out and take the help as it was being offered. But I knew how that would end up. Owed favors. And you never knew people's motivations for wanting to help you.

"Come on. Out with it, Kaya."

"Would you be quiet and let me think for just a moment?"

I angled my head to peek around the alcove we were tucked in, and I could see the bald head of one of the men searching the crowd for me. Over Saint's shoulder I could see the other hallway with two dark-haired men looking for someone. It had to be me.

All this time I had lived quietly. Been nondescript. Lived a perfectly bland life. Then one night, the *one frigging night* I stand out into the light from the shadows, this happens.

She was right all along.

My mother hadn't made up the threats that constantly plagued us. There had been a point in my teen years when I was convinced she'd made it all up. That there was no danger. She wasn't being chased.

And thinking back to that, I'd been a teenager desperate for a solid foundation. A place to call home. I'd said some things that I could never take back. Calling into judgment her abilities as a mother. And all that time she had not been lying. That boogeyman in the dark was here now. He was hunting me. And I had seconds to make the right decision.

Saint switched our hold as he pulled us from the alcove and turned us down a darkened corridor, once again tucking me away from prying eyes. "Talk to me," he begged. "You clearly need help, and if you would just tell me what's happening, I could help you. If you're in some kind of trouble, you need to say so. Clearly you can't run from them in a cocktail dress in heels. You're in trouble. Let me—"

Again, over Saint's shoulder I could see the tall man checking the alcove where we'd previously been hidden. *Shit. Shit. Shit.* He was absolutely looking for me, and I was out of options. There was nowhere to hide. All because I'd come looking for Connor Lohman. Because I hadn't been able to resist the urge to speak to him. One little misstep and I had led him and his men straight to me.

My gaze met Saint's. "What are the chances you won't take this the wrong way?"

His brow furrowed. "What do you mean the wrong w—"

I didn't wait for the rest of his question. I just pulled him close, angled my head, and planted my lips over his, slipping my hands into his hair and tugging him forward so that his whole body covered mine. I knew this way we would look like a passionate couple that had slipped away for some much needed alone time.

I knew we would be instantly dismissed, hiding in plain sight.

What I did not know was the way the electrical charge would shoot up my spine, sending bursts of awareness and tingles to every single nerve ending, making me pulse all over, particularly between my thighs.

What I did not know was that despite the sardonic twist of his lips, I could never have guessed that Jasper Saint knew how to kiss like an absolute pro.

After a shocked gasp, he growled low in the back of his throat, dug his strong hands into my hair, fisting it ever so gently, then adjusted my head just so and dove in with licks into my mouth and the scraping of teeth. He backed me up to make sure I felt the full press of his thick erection.

There was no thinking now, only feeling and a desperate scramble for purchase. But there was none to be had. Just a straight down tumble into the abyss of lust and desire. Holy fucking Christ, the man could give lessons.

Suddenly, he pulled back, his body still covering mine. "Fuck me."

Instead of shooting back a biting retort about how no one would be fucking anyone else, all I did was sway into him and inhale deeply. His scent wrapped around me, giving me that same cocooning sense of peace.

It took several moments before my brain cleared and I shook my head.

Jesus, Mary, and all the shepherds, what this guy was doing to me I couldn't afford to let happen.

I took one unstable step backward, and Jasper was right there, leading with his lips as if he meant to kiss me again. And if I was being really fucking honest, I totally wanted to let him.

But you know better.

Yes, I did know better. I took one more wobbly step backward.

I shook my head, and lifting my chin, I met his gaze. "Thank you for the distraction. But it's time I got going." And then with a quick glance around to make sure none of the goons were even searching in this direction, I sidestepped Saint's underarm, and went out the exit.

Straight into a shadowy hulk.

CHAPTER 5
KAYA

THE SCREAM CAUGHT in my throat as the handsome man with the silvery gaze and the dark lock of hair falling on his brow righted me. "All right, miss?"

Like a fool, all I was able to do was nod, and the moment he released me, I ran. I had a car waiting two blocks down, but I didn't trust it any longer. Mere steps from my exit and the hulk who had turned to watch me, I paused only long enough to rip my shoes off my feet, lift my dress, and off I went. I ran straight home like the devil was chasing me.

I couldn't think. I couldn't breathe. Everything I had worked for my whole life was over. The last five years. The comfort I had found was shattered into a million pieces.

And it was all his fault.

Connor Lohman.

Well, and Jasper Saint's too. Actually, come to think of it. This was *all* Jasper Saint's fault, damn it. If he hadn't interfered, maybe I would have already found her or be on my way to finding her with something useful Connor would have coughed up. But now I didn't know any more than I did the moment I saw Connor's photo on the cover of that magazine. Stupid, good-looking Jasper Saint.

So you noticed he was good-looking, huh?

I did more than notice, thank you very much, conscience. A simple kiss at the end. Yes, it had been a means to an end, but it was so much *more* than simple. I hadn't accounted for the searing electricity of those tantalizing lips. That zapping shock, jolting my body and liquefying my insides.

And I could still feel the subtle press of his fingertips on my spine. It wasn't that he pressed hard; it was more about the intimacy of the way he had touched me. Like I was something delicate. Something precious to be held.

Stop getting carried away, Kaya! This is not a romantic encounter to be daydreaming over. Because of him, because of them both, you are now exposed. You cannot stay here.

My stomach knotted. I hadn't had to do a runner in five long years. Five years of waking up with a routine. Five years of normalcy, of not looking over my shoulder. Now in one night, trying to live a full life like everyone else was gone.

Rising panic threatened to overtake me. I had worked hard for this life. The fear, the warring feelings of what to do and where to go next, and especially the anger, all those emotions were like an almost forgotten memory I just couldn't shake. First my mother was taken from me, and now I was back in a race to protect myself.

Connor's men had been searching for me. Connor wasn't even sure he recognized me when we spoke. Where had I gone wrong?

Your first mistake was going to that event. You know the rules.

Growing up, my mother had a set of rules for our survival. Among them, lay low. Don't draw any attention to yourself. Which included not standing out in a crowd too much but standing out a little so people remembered that you were there. She always insisted that I participate a little bit but never excel too much. A concept that was very confusing as a child.

She always encouraged me to make at least one friend, so if anyone was asked, they'd say, 'Yes of course she had a friend. She talked to so-and-so often.' But that friendship was never meant to be *true* friendship. It was a surface connection where I mostly let the other person talk about themselves.

Yes, it was lonely. But this was about survival. And as I stared at the flat that I had made my home, the walls that I had painted and negotiated with the landlord about, the paintings I had put on the walls, I let myself shed a silent tear.

You can cry when you're safe again. Get a move on.

I knew what to do. My mother taught me well. However, before I scrubbed this place of my existence, there was something I just had to see for myself.

I ran to my laptop, dragged it over to the couch, and pulled up a program I hadn't used in about a year. My mother had relied on her contacts when I was a kid. People she knew who would let us know when people were after us. Now I had the internet and a single programming class that came in super handy in a time like this. I was no super-spy hacker girl, but a simple script could do what I needed. I did a search for my name, Kaya Reynolds. The search on my name, my real, given name, had one hit with a time stamp of about an hour ago.

Fuck me.

I was in the process of slamming my laptop shut when I paused and did one more search. *Jasper Saint, let's find out a little more about you, stud.* I knew I was out of time, but I quickly scanned the pages and pages of information that populated about Jasper and his family. Billionaires, philanthropists. Jasper had gone into Her Majesty's service and left with accolades and lots of medals. He took over the family's tech firm two years ago. Bullshit, bullshit, more bullshit... This thing read like a press release.

One piece of information that I did yield was where his offices were. Sadly, there was nothing saying whether he was married or had any children.

What you're saying is, the man is single.

No, brain! That was not what I was saying. What I was saying was nobody would notice if he went missing, either. Because I knew one thing from tonight; Jasper Saint was mixed up with all the commotion somehow. I didn't know how or why. All I knew was that he had deliberately stopped me getting to Connor. I needed answers out of him and soon.

Protocol for situations like this was to run and run fast. Mom had always insisted that once a year we would scrub our place and then head off to Spain, France, Italy, Croatia, didn't matter the destination. One time we even went as far as Australia. The motus operandi was leave on the old papers and come back on a new ID. Move to a new village and live there for a bit with a nice, quiet, boring, average life. Not too average but average enough so we weren't noticed. What I should do was pick a spot on the map I'd never been to. Maybe Mauritius was nice this time of year.

When she vanished, my mother hadn't touched our go funds. Money she left in the walls of our old house. I hadn't touched a dime of it. When I was put into care, I asked my social worker for one thing: my own bank account. I had a small part-time job, so I had an excuse for a bank account, and I asked her to take me to the bank where I walked right in and opened a safe deposit box. I'd left the bulk of the money in there. I'd have to collect that tomorrow.

Connor Lohman had taken my mother. And Jasper Saint was keeping me from Connor. So he would be the one who would answer my questions. Before I disappeared, I was going to pay him a visit and force him to tell me what he knew.

My first step was to march over to my living room wall and pull down my Z Con print. The landscape of Table Mountain in South Africa was gorgeous, and I absolutely loved this print. I would have to buy another because nothing this big could come with me today.

I took the painting off the wall and then opened the safe behind the print. Mum always said to keep some cash and passports on you for a quick move.

After all this time, I guessed she was right.

Within thirty minutes I'd changed my clothes and packed my

favorite items into a bag. The few personal items I had, including my mother's prized ring that she carried with her everywhere, all shoved into an easy-to-carry bookbag and a small suitcase. I was ready to go. A glance back at my flat showed a cheery space. One I was going to miss after finally having a home for so long. Just as I was about to unlock the door, there was a sharp knock.

When I glanced through the peephole, my heart stopped.

"Whoa, what are you doing here Gemma? It's late. "

"I had to find out if something happened. You missed class this afternoon and our meeting at the café."

I hadn't bloody texted her. I'd completely forgotten. I'd been too busy getting ready for seeing Conner, and I hadn't given a single thought to go to class or that Gemma might be waiting.

"Um, sorry, I had some things I had to take care of at the center."

"Well, it doesn't matter. I brought Pimms, and we missed *The Bachelorette*, but it's dvr'd. We can still watch if you're up for it. We don't have class tomorrow. We can stay up past our bedtime."

I frowned at her. "*The Bachelorette*?"

She laughed like I was joking. "Yes, honey, *The Bachelorette*. Just that show we've been watching together for well over two years now. What is wrong with you tonight?"

Right, *The Bachelorette*. It was a long-standing tradition. "Fuck. Sorry. Like I said, busy day. Listen, can we reschedule?"

I was blocking the door, but Gemma just barged right in. For a little thing, she was surprisingly strong. And I didn't want to hurt her. "What the hell is going on?" she asked.

"Come right in, why don't you?"

"Yeah, thanks. I think I will. What is happening? You're acting weird. You never miss class. N-E-V-E-R! What is happening with you?" She saw my bags by the door and frowned at me. "You're going somewhere?"

"Gems, it's not what it seems like."

"Yes, by all means, tell me what's happening. Cause you know what I think it looks like? It looks like you are going somewhere and weren't planning on telling your best friend."

"Listen, my foster mother needs some help with something, and—"

Gemma crossed her arms. "I don't fucking believe you. You and I are going to sit down right here, right now, and you're going to tell me everything. Something's been going on with you for ages, and you're not saying a word. Tell me. Did Andrew say something? Do you not feel safe with him?"

"Andrew? He's the least of my problems right now."

Her voice went soft, and she took my hand and said, "If you're in trouble or something, just tell me. Talk to me."

"I don't have time for this. Honestly, I just—"

"Well, make time, because I'm not leaving here until you do."

I watched her face. She wasn't kidding. She really had zero intention of leaving until I told her what the hell was going on.

How much could I tell her?

"Okay, but not here, all right? Let's at least get as far away from here as possible."

She frowned. "Are you in some kind of trouble?"

I thought about the men chasing me. All the things my mother had said, the ways I'd resented the chaos that came with her and her ramblings.

I was worried and scared.

"Honestly, I'm not sure. So let's keep moving."

By the time we grabbed my bag and I'd walked her home four blocks on the outside of campus, I had told her everything I could say about the last twenty-four hours and what little I could share about Mum.

When I was done, she stared at me for a solid minute. "Holy shiiiit."

"Yes, indeed. So you see, that's why I've got to get out of town for a little bit, and that's why it's probably safer that you not tell Andrew or anyone else."

She waved a hand. "Oh, of course, I'm not telling Andrew. He couldn't handle this if he knew. Also, you need help."

"I don't want you to help me. It'll get dangerous for you."

"Whatever. You know I'm not going to listen. You can't do this on your own, so I'm going to help you whether you like it or not."

"Gems, I don't want you involved."

"Tough. If you're involved, I'm involved. Now, lucky for you, if you want access to Jasper Saint, I have a cousin who works for a cleaning crew who contract with the All Saints offices on the South Bank, so you have an in."

I stared at her. "Gems, why are you doing this?"

She cocked her head and blinked wide blue eyes at me owlishly. "Because I'm your friend. Because you need help. Because I love you. Letting people help you isn't a death sentence, I promise. I know you think it's messy. I know you think emotions are a problem, but they aren't always. So for once in your relationship with me, let me help you. Besides, how else are you planning to get this done?"

CHAPTER 6
SAINT

We had bloody done it. Fucking A.

After everything, we'd gotten him. Connor Lohman was a slippery cunt.

Thanks to the right funding, a decently sharp mind, a little luck, and a lot of cunning, Connor Lohman had become Connor Phelps. He was no more just a thug working for Antonio Igno. He had put on a bit of polish. He'd learned to insulate himself. Made it hard to get close. The auction had been our one shot. And even then, we'd been told to handle it with kid gloves because of Phelps's reputation as a philanthropist.

Oh, is that what you call trussing him up like a Christmas goose and shoving him in the back of a truck?

Honestly, we'd barely touched him.

Okay, I'd touched him a little. And maybe, just maybe, King had to talk me down from touching him too much. Repeatedly.

Our intel said Connor had been the bagman who paid the bomber that had killed my fiancée, Elise, three years ago.

We had been planning our wedding. Young, in love, and thinking the whole world was our bloody fucking oyster.

My family actually loved her. The Cochrans were old friends.

Asking her to marry me was the one thing I had done to make my father happy. She'd been supportive when I said I wanted to do something different and wanted to go into the Queen's service. She said she'd wait for me, and our wedding would be after my tour.

But that never happened.

Because she betrayed you...with your father.

I tried to shove the thought aside. I had nowhere to put that anger, the hurt the pain. We'd cared about each other once and she'd died without me by her side. All alone, thanks to a fucking car bomb.

I'd come home straight away, but there had been nothing to bury. All I had was an urn full of ashes and memories of me not being there for her when she needed me the most.

I might not be able to do anything with the sick cocktail of betrayal roiling in my gut, but I could channel that pain and put the wankers responsible for her death in the ground.

Easy does it. No way in hell will Gabe let you kill him.

Gabriel Webb was director of operations of the Rogues Division. And for all intents and purposes, my boss. He'd been the one to recruit me, to tell me about this shadow world we were all living in. He trained me and promised me vengeance.

And by vengeance you mean prison, right?

Yeah, sure. That's what I meant.

My only concern was doing right by Elise. Knowing that she had died all alone without me there, even years later it still dug deep into my soul.

My family had tried suggesting that maybe it was time for me to move on. But I couldn't. Antonio Igno had taken something from me. I would not stop until I took everything from him.

I was going to start with questioning Lohman. The only way this interview was going to stop would be with me getting answers or him losing consciousness. The good thing about people passing out during interrogations was that you could always find fun ways to revive them.

Getting a bit dark there so soon? Don't lose yourself, mate.

I promptly shut down that automatic inclination toward decency. The part Elise had always said she loved about me.

Elise said a lot of things. Many of them not true. Like she loved me. Like I was her everything. Like she would wait for me to get back.

Maybe so, but her death and the circumstances surrounding it had changed me. Sure, I knew how to put on the show of being Jasper Saint. Matter of fact, it was easy. I was good at manufacturing the façade, and no one had seen through it for years. No one had seen the hollowness. Everyone just assumed I was getting over it, moving forward. But I wasn't.

Are you sure Elise was the only thing on your mind when you kissed that woman tonight?

My brain conjured up images of Kaya. Her flawless, brown skin, the way her soft curls swept forward and framed her face. The flashing fire in her eyes. The feel of her tongue against my lips.

It made me wonder if the rest of her body was soft like her lips, begging for a taste from my tongue.

I could still feel them beneath mine. The soft texture of her curls in my hands as I gave them a soft tug. The shocked gasp she made at the back of her throat before she opened to me automatically.

One fucking kiss.

I met a woman at a charity auction, and now I was having visions of her. What kind of crazy thing did they put in our drinks for me to be feeling like this? I needed to regroup and figure out the next steps for Lohman, not focus on her damn pouty mouth.

Connor's men had been chasing us. Correction, they had been chasing *her* without any knowledge of who I was. So just who the fuck was she? What kind of trouble was she in for them to hunt her? She'd seemed hell bent and determined to catch up with Lohman after the auction. The question was, what the fuck did she want with him?

Are you sure that's the question? Not what would she sound like moaning your name?

My cock started to twitch, and I scowled down at my body.

Shut it down, asshole, we don't have time for that shit.

Damn thing jolted again as if in mutiny.

Sure, she was beautiful. Stunning really. Whether it was her perfume or hair products, the smell of hibiscus had taken over my brain. I swear I could smell it even as we drove back in the truck with Connor to the compound.

I scrubbed a hand over my face and tried to shake the memory of her in my arms. I did not have fucking time for this. Nor did I want this overwhelming feeling of longing that kissing Kaya brought to my mind. I still hadn't figured out my shit with Elise being gone, and I knew better than to think about someone else who couldn't rely on me right now. Anyone who got close to me, actually really close to me, ended up dead. So yeah, Kaya whatever-the-fuck-her-last-name-was should steer far away from Jasper Saint. Despite my fervent last thought, the odd mixture of grief and desire was still weighing heavily on my chest.

Still irritated at myself, I stepped off the elevator to find my mates standing on the other side, arms crossed. Lachlan smirked as he studied me up and down. "Just so you all know, while the rest of us were fighting with Connor's men, this one was snogging some bird."

Westin chuckled. "Well, isn't that a fine how do you do? I didn't even get a chance to meet anyone to kiss, let alone see Saint's new woman. I was busy getting this." He pointed at his left eye. I could see the shadow of a bruise there. "One of Connor's men tried to get the drop on me. I'll have you know it was a close fight. No one even offered to kissed me afterward."

I rolled my eyes. "Don't you wankers have something better to do than take the piss? We were chased after by those fuckers, too. And now I have an interrogation to get on with."

Lachlan stepped up and patted my shoulder, saying, "Sorry,

mate. We're up first because we did the real work today. You, on the other hand, are the sorry bastard who gets to go see Gabe. He wants a word."

I lifted my brows in shock. "There's no fucking way he would let you idiots talk to Connor. That arsehole is mine to break."

The team just shrugged at me and started to walk away, leaving Lachlan behind.

"We just work here. Why don't you go see Gabe? Tell him all about the beautiful woman you were wrapped around after the auction. I'm sure he's very curious." And then he stroked at his stubbled jaw as if giving it a second thought. "Come to think of it, Saffron was saying that he hasn't ventured out on a date in a while. Maybe you shouldn't lead with the chase. Start by regaling him with stories of the gorgeous woman you were snogging. Probably the most action he's had in a year. Make a big point out of that to him, too. I'm sure he'll appreciate it!"

"Wanker," I grumbled at him under my breath. I knew they were just giving me shit, but still, this was over the top.

Lachlan chuckled. "What? I'm just saying. Maybe you guys can bond over your utter lack of game?"

I opted to try and ignore his prattling. "No one is talking to Lohman without me."

Rook happily chimed in from down the hall. "Don't be jealous, love."

Under normal circumstances, I liked the kid. He was smart and a quick fucking study. Not formally trained, but anything you gave him didn't take long for him to master. He was some kind of genius with computers, had a photographic memory, the whole bloody lot. But knowing he was going to get a crack at Lohman before I did set my fucking teeth on edge.

"Just you hold the fuck up until I'm done with Gabe."

Lachlan frowned. "Don't worry, you'll get a chance. Or is there something else you're not telling me?"

I didn't take the bait, especially not with Rook listening. There was a lot Lachlan didn't know about me, and now hardly felt like the right time to get into all that. "Fine. I'll go see Gabe now while you go have all my fun, you wankers."

I'd been looking forward to this moment for three years. They had better leave me something to work with.

Knowing that I was thwarted put me in an even shittier mood.

And the worst part was I could still fucking taste that woman as I stomped toward Gabe's office for our *chat*.

Her taste was like the finest whiskey. Biting at first, overconfident, but then it had a mellow, smoky quality to it. The type of drink that settled into crevices you didn't even know you had and warmed them up. A long slow burn. Infiltrating like an assassin. Before you knew it, you stood up and were punch drunk from having one sip too many.

Back up the stairs I opened the door to the main offices. Gabe Webb was in there with his sister, both of them staring at something on the monitor.

Saffron saw me first and gave me a wide smile, her ebony skin impeccable as always with a flawless bone structure. Some days working with her was like having a bloody supermodel or something as a manager. Only difference was that Saffron Abbot was no supermodel. In hand-to-hand, she could still take me down in a flash. Perhaps not as easily as when I first arrived, but she could still take me out for damn certain if she was inclined to fight dirty. Which she always was.

I didn't let that get to my ego though. The woman had been training since she was able to walk since both of her parents were agents. They'd been preparing her for this career forever.

"Hey, Saint. Lock tell you to come on up?"

I nodded. "Yeah, he and Rook found me as I was headed to interrogation. What's the holdup?"

Her dark eyes studied mine, and I knew the moment she saw it — the frenetic energy. The desperation to not be here but instead be in interrogation getting my answers. Getting my revenge.

Saffron walked over and squeezed my bicep gently. "Lachlan and Westin will soften him up for you. They're just going to ask him a couple of questions. They'll leave all the revenge for you, I promise."

I shifted on my feet, uncomfortable under her gaze. She saw way too much. She tended to see through my easy-breezy affability to the real me hidden below, and I didn't know what to do with that feeling. Sometimes I would catch her just staring at me, as if waiting for me to peel off the fake skin and show her the real me. I never did. I couldn't do it. Not with Saff. Not with anyone.

She gave me a nod and then turned back to her brother, bidding him farewell.

When Gabe looked up from his desk, his gaze was different from his sister's. I still remember Lock being confused as to how they were related. I might have kept their actual relationship a secret from him for longer than I should have, just to watch him squirm. He was so stupidly in love with Saffron but wouldn't do anything proper about it, so I gave him the nudge he needed. Jealousy was a great motivator. So I'd let him think that she and Gabe had a thing going on as opposed to telling him that they were adopted siblings. My bad.

Gabe's green eyes met mine gravely. "Saint, take a seat."

I stood stubbornly. "While I do respect you Gabe, we both know I should be the one interrogating that trash."

"Oh, believe me, you wouldn't be in here unless it was important."

I scrubbed a hand over my face and tried to let his words settle over me. "What's going on?"

Hitting a couple of keys on his laptop, the screen changed to a close up picture of Kaya. For the second time that night, my breath whooshed out like I was gut punched. Good Lord, she was beautiful.

"What about her?" I asked. "She wasn't a problem tonight. She was the one Connor bid on. She tried to see him after, but we didn't let it happen. We still got out in time within mission parameters and protocols."

"Relax, Jasper. I'm not about to lay into you about going off script."

Funny, because staying on the script was Gabe's favorite game. However, I tended to do the things that worked but at times went against protocol.

"So what's the problem then, sir?"

"Well, it seemed Connor's men were after her tonight."

A tingle of unease wrapped around my spine.

"Someone *was* after her. No idea why. She made it out the door and off premises with no one chasing her, so maybe they were just looking for Lohman and not Kaya."

Gabe watched me carefully with shrewd eyes, especially since I'd called her Kaya, not just the female or the woman. Solemnly, he stated, "No. They were after her. Her name is Kaya Reynolds."

Icy dread gripped my gut. She'd given me a fake surname of course.

Another woman you should have saved.

"According to fresh intel, there's been a bounty put on her head. For a million quid. I need you to go undercover right now to protect her."

What the fuck? "Me? Why?"

"She's a person of interest. Her fingerprints popped tonight on a mission for Oversight."

My brain knew that this was a bad idea based on the hairs standing up on my arms at the mere thought of being close to her again. The scent of her hair, the supple feel of her lips, the temptation of Kaya was so strong, and I knew I couldn't give into it. This was too dangerous for my heart and soul to be that close to her again. My dick liked what Gabe was saying, but it wasn't like he could report for duty alone.

Why the hell did Gabe want me when we had any number of great agents who could protect Kaya? I had unfinished business waiting in one of our interrogation rooms. Nothing was important enough to push that to the back burner.

"We just got Lohman. I haven't even had a chance to interrogate him yet. He's going to have intel, which means I'm going to have to go right back out. What's so special about her anyway?"

Gabe pressed his lips together. "She's important to Rogues."

Was that it? I knew Gabe's secrets had secrets.

Any desire I felt for her froze to icicles. I hated secrets.

Lohman wanted her, so *we* wanted her.

I shouldn't care. I really shouldn't give two shits. I did not fucking have time for this, knowing that Elise's killer was sitting in this building.

"What did she want with Lohman?" I asked Gabe pointedly.

"That's just it; we don't know. We need to track her down and put you on her patrol. I need my best on this, Saint."

I stared at her picture on the monitor, which was a bad move as the icicles that had formed melted with the desire I felt for her. "Like I said, I want to stay on Lohman. You're going to need to send someone else, sir."

Gabe pressed his lips together and just stared at me like he couldn't figure out why I was bailing on this woman's protection detail. "If you're sure."

Oh, I was fucking sure. Given my body's completely inappropriate response to her, I should stay the fuck away. I already had one innocent soul on my conscience. I didn't need another.

I was never going near that woman again.

CHAPTER 7
SAINT

OUTSIDE THE DOOR of the interrogation room, my phone rang, delaying me again. Who the fuck? I dragged it out, scowling at the screen.

Adrianna.

My twin sister's timing was impeccable.

I answered tersely. "Can this wait?"

Her voice was clipped and tart. "No, this cannot wait, Jasper. Where are you?"

"I'm busy."

There was a beat of silence. She knew where I was. She knew not to say it though, because the whole Rogues thing would send up a million flags. Who the fuck knew who the hell was listening in at any given time if it wasn't a secure line?

And then there was the whole *if I tell you about the Rogues, I'll have to kill you* thing.

I didn't love the secrecy, but after the military, my family was used to it. "Is there something urgent, or are you just calling me to bust my balls?"

"Eww, I would rather not think about your balls, baby brother."

"Baby brother by only three bloody minutes."

She laughed. "Listen, we need to do something about Dad."

I froze, my gut clenching. The mere mention of my father could sour my whole mood. "I told you I'm handling it."

"Well, you need to handle it a bit faster. He's trying to get board support to call for a vote of no confidence on you. You know what happens after that, right? He will try and appeal his ousting, so we need you to actually pretend to give a fuck."

I did not have time for this right now.

"I *do* give a fuck."

"Then why aren't you taking the stipulations Grandad laid out seriously?"

"I am. My hands are just a little bit tied right now, okay?"

"What are you doing that could be more important than this?"

I sighed. There was no way she would ever let me just sit still and live. "We've got him, Adrianna. After all these years, we have the wanker. I saw a hole in his security. We finally have him."

My sister was silent for second. "Seriously, you have him?"

"Yes. Which is what I'm trying to attend to right now. I need to get off the phone with you."

There was another beat of silence. "I know this is important for you. It's something you've been trying to resolve since you came back. Are you sure that you want to do this?"

I hated that she knew me so well, that she could always feel what I was feeling. I hated that she never let me shy away from any of those feelings. I loved my sister, but goddamn, when she wanted to make a point, she was relentless. "It's fine, Adrianna. I'm fine."

She sighed. "Well, I can't change your mind. But let me just remind you that Elise brought all this on herself. You aren't at fault."

The pain twisted in my chest. "It doesn't matter. She was still mine to protect, and I failed. So I'm going to bring them to justice, and then I'm going to move on with my fucking life."

"You say that, Jasper, but can you actually move on? Especially if you do what I think you are doing. Will it ever be enough?"

It was a good question. Could I move on from this? Could I walk away, let it go, and go back to my normal life? Not if you considered dear old Dad.

"Love, I have to go."

"Fine, but call me back. You know what the terms say."

"Bloody hell, I can't focus on that right now."

"I know that your other *career* is important. And trust me, I understand what you do for the world. I do. I am immensely proud of you for it. At the same time, we have a business to run. You know that. And if we cannot run it together, someone else will be happy to step in and run it for us. So I need your focus and attention. We need to deal with this now."

I scrubbed a hand over my face. She was right of course. Adrianna was always right. She really relished being right, and it was irritating to say the least. "I hear you. I understand you, and I am working on it."

"Work faster. We don't have a lot of time, and eventually, you're going to have to make choices. Tough decisions on which world you want both feet in at the same time. You understand that, right?"

"I'm not an idiot. Of course, I understand."

"All right, fine, I will lay off because you clearly don't want to talk about this."

"No, I don't." I felt like shit. She was telling the truth and she was protecting me. Which was a lot more than I could say for other people. "Sorry. I'm being a wanker. A complete twat, I know."

"Well, I'm glad you're aware of this fact that hasn't changed since your birth."

I laughed. "Let me take care of this, and then I'll come home and you and I can make a plan."

"Do you at least even have prospects?"

I hated that word, *prospects*. "When you say *prospects*, what do you mean?"

"I swear to God, Jasper Saint, you have to take this seriously."

"Relax, I am taking it seriously. It'll be fine. Okay?"

"It had better be. I'm not letting that monster take over our whole lives again. You know what happens when he's in charge."

Our father was a tyrant who had tormented us. Him back in charge of the company was going to be bad for all three of us, me, Adrianna, and Trevor.

"I know and I'm on it. I swear to you, I will find a wife or die trying before the term is up. Okay?"

"Thank you, and goodbye, little brother."

I hung up with my sister and stared at the interrogation room door.

This was it. I was going to take all my frustrations out on Connor Lohman. He was going to give me the information I needed. But I knew his type, and it was unlikely he would volunteer anything. I would have to apply pressure. A fuck ton of pressure. But I was more than happy to do whatever was necessary.

I was just stepping in the door of the interrogation room as Connor raised his head and smirked. "Please tell me you're the good cop."

"I'm sorry to disappoint you."

"All right. Well, I've had nothing but bad cops so far. The angry terse ones."

I just lifted a brow, closely watching him.

Connor continued. "I also had the pretty-boy type who looked like he was having fun, at least."

Again, I said nothing.

"Ah, are you the silent one? Waiting for me to make a mistake? Waiting for me to say something I shouldn't?" He shrugged and sat back. "You can wait all you want. I'm not going to. I haven't spilled in all these years, and I ain't fucking spilling a word to you lot today. Besides you can't hold me. I won't be here long."

I took a deep breath, marched over to the table, and sat. He was handcuffed, but still, I didn't trust the bastard. There were safety measures in place though, and a taser was underneath the table. One press and he would get a nice jolt. After some twat had almost gotten his hands on Saff, Gabe got extra worried and had the button installed in all the interrogation rooms. Because once was enough, even though the fucker who'd tried a move on Saffron got a bloody nose via an elbow to the face. That woman was fierce.

"At least tell me what you know about *her* death?"

I placed the file in front of him and opened up to the pictures of the bomb site. I kept my gaze on him, watching for tics, an overly calm demeanor, anything really. I watched for it all. Something to tell me what part he'd played in her death.

"I don't know what the fuck you're on about. I don't know that bird."

"Yes, you do."

"No, I don't."

I flipped around one of the images. "Take a closer look, Connor. What do you know about her?"

This time, he winced. I knew which photo it was, as I'd stared at it a thousand times over these last three years. The charred remains of the woman I would have married.

"This is ridiculous. I'm a billionaire. I didn't have anything to do with this, and I don't fucking have to answer any of your questions."

"Yes, you do. I'm just looking for you to tell me the truth. Now, go on and tell me, what do you know?"

"You can ask me the same questions Saturday through Sunday. I'll give you the same response. I don't know the woman."

"Stop lying, Connor. You know how this goes. Just say a few words, and it'll be a lot easier for you."

"Mate, I don't know what you want me to say."

I flipped over another photo, and Elise's beautiful face came up. Her smile was wide, and her eyes were bright and full of hope.

She usually wore her hair short, but in this photo it cascaded past her shoulders, with a dark and lustrous curl. "Her. This woman was blown up in a car bomb. A car bomb either put there by you or one of your minions."

"I sympathize with you, but I really don't know what you're on about."

"Sure you do?"

This time there was something in Connor's eyes. A doubletake. And I knew he recognized her face. "I'm not telling you anything. Do you know who the fuck I am?"

"Yes, which is why you're here. Connor *Lohman*, midlevel enforcer for Antonio Igno. But something happened five years ago to change your luck. Before that, you couldn't even get a free email address. And then suddenly you were Connor Phelps, globetrotting financier. Can you tell me how that happened?"

"Turns out I have a way with numbers."

"And a way of bullshitting. Just tell me how you did it, Connor. No one moves up that fast. No one makes changes that quickly. I want to know your secret. But it will be a secret just between us since we're mates and all."

Connor sat back and shook his head. "We're not fucking mates, and nothing fucking happened."

"You don't have to talk to *me*. Obviously, we have a whole team of people who make it their business to get people like you to talk. I'm only here because of this woman, and you know what happened to her, *mate*." My fingers tapped Elise's image. "Elise Cochran. She's what matters here. I want to know your involvement in her murder."

Connor looked at the photo again. "Who was she to you? Was she your bird or something?" Looking up at me and my intense stare, he kept going. "What you don't seem to understand is that sometimes bad things happen to good people. They get caught in the crosshairs. All because of their associations. I don't know your friend. But she did look like a fine piece of—"

I had Connor's lapels in my hands so fast he didn't see me coming. "Start talking, asshole." I was glad I'd locked the door so it would take the other agents on watch duty a moment to get in.

"Ah, I see she *did* mean something to you. All I can say is I've seen her photo before. No need to get all testy." He laughed. "But I have to say you're the stupidest son of a bitch I've ever met. You don't even know what you have in your hands right now."

I frowned at that. "What?"

"Did you have fun at the auction last night?"

I puzzled at his question. "The auction? What the fuck does that matter?"

He grappled and tried to shove away from me. I released him and he plopped back into his seat. "You don't even get it. You and your merry band ain't got a fucking clue. You're trying to call the shots, but you don't even know what kind of game you're playing. Look at the players on the board, shithead. Stop fucking around with pawns when you could have the king."

"What do you mean by that?"

Connor shook his head. "No, I'm not talking. If you don't know what you have, I'm not telling you. But you keep coming in here asking me questions. I'll wait." He glanced around. "This place is real nice. Not dark and dingy enough to give me the real heebie-jeebies or *I'm going to die today* feels. It's clean, doesn't smell bad, and there's not standing water and electrodes everywhere. No Albanians named Boris who like to pull out people's fingernails. That tells me you're part of the government, which means you're not going to kill me. So I'm just going to sit here and keep my fucking mouth shut."

I lifted a brow. "You want to be in a place that's filthy and smells bad? That can be arranged."

"Yeah, then maybe I'll talk to you. But this is child's play. You don't scare me. Especially when you're an idiot. The whole lot of you. I am not going to do the work for you when you don't even know what you have right at your fingertips. You're here asking questions about the past, but not even the right ones. You had a fucking raven in your hands, and you didn't even know it."

I glowered at him. What the fuck was he talking about? A raven?

———

SAINT

Later that night, I was still mulling over the raven question.

Since it was a mission day, I was staying on Rogue's campus for the night in the bungalow I'd been assigned to with Lachlan. Lachlan on the other hand was staying on site with Saffron, so I had the place to myself. After a long shower, I crashed, too bloody knackered to think. My mind had different plans as visions of Kaya Reynolds played in the forefront.

She needs someone to protect her, and you bitched out of duty.

No. Gabe would make sure she had the protection she needed. She didn't need me around, and Gabe sure as hell didn't need me distracted on duty.

As I drifted off, trying to force my brain to quiet, I couldn't get the image and taste of Kaya's soft lips out of my brain. Only fits of sleep happened, not the kind of rest I needed to interrogate Connor again.

I groaned as the phone on my nightstand buzzed somewhere around 6:30 in the morning. I'd not had nearly enough sleep for a call this early, but when I saw who was calling, I picked up immediately. "Are you letting me back at Lohman?"

Gabe's voice was croaky, but clear. "The asset you refused to protect is in the process of breaking into All Saints Tech."

CHAPTER 8
SAINT

THAT ICY, clawing feeling in my gut wasn't fear. Of course not. I wasn't afraid of this woman, especially since I had only met her once. I knew next to nothing about her.

Except how she tastes. And the amazing little throaty growling sound she makes when you take away something she enjoys.

Just the thought of our kiss and the sound she made when I pulled back made my cock stiffen and throb. I ground my teeth, thinking about the way she moaned, the way her lips felt against mine.

I had to get this shit under control before I had to face off with her. This situation was dire. She was on my fucking doorstep. How did she even know where to find me? Who was this girl, and what the fuck did she want from me? Besides to make life a living hell.

Is that what you call kissing her? That was not the impression you gave.

My conscience and I needed to have a talking to when this was all said and done.

Thanks to the Rogues helicopter, I was on the roof of my building in less than fifteen minutes after Gabe's call. I was out on the helipad, yanking open the rooftop door in no time.

I asked Reed Daniels, one of our comms guys, "Tell me something good mate, where the fuck is she now?"

"She's made it down the hall from the server room. Best I can tell, she is in a broom closet."

What the fuck would she be doing in a broom closet? "Wait. Do you think she has a blueprint of the building already? If so, she knows there are vents connecting rooms all around the building. You don't think she's small enough to fit through them, do you?"

Shocked at that idea, Daniels started clicking faster on his keypad. "No, that's gotta be impossible. A child could barely fit through those vents."

Fucking hell, she was going to hurt herself. She was coming after me for some reason, and I was worried for her safety? What a knob I was. But what if Gabe was right and she was in trouble?

And you refused to help her.

I did not refuse. I just had more pressing concerns about getting answers from Connor Lohman. Besides, Gabe would have someone else covering her. It just wouldn't be me who was responsible for her safety.

I jogged down the three flights of stairs to the seventeenth floor, and my first stop was the server room, making sure that she hadn't made a mess there. Any breach of the server room should set off silent alarms everywhere, but it paid to be sure. All of our games and apps, everything was stored there. While everything was backed up, there was still damage that could be done.

I continued the search for Kaya near the supply closet. Talking to Daniels on the comm set in my ear, I asked, "Do you see her?"

"She should be right there. You should be looking straight at her."

All I saw was our normal janitor pushing a cart of cleaning supplies down at the other end of the hall. He wore overalls as his uniform, and they were baggy on him. Lumbering away slowly, Anton had a slight hitch in his gait, as always. My gaze went down to his trainers. He always wore these orthopedic beige ones all the time. But these trainers were bright blue.

Shit.

I spoke into the comm. "I think I have her."

The moment I spoke, the janitor froze and slowly turned. Except our friendly custodian wasn't Anton at all. It was her—Kaya Reynolds.

Her eyes went wide as mine narrowed. She took off running, headed for the service stairs. With a groan, I took off after her. It was too early for this kind of chase. What the fuck was she doing to me?

Thank goodness it was still early enough that there were few people on this level. Anyone who was here was likely in the gym or the spa facilities downstairs. Nobody would be working this early. Except maybe Trevor, but even he didn't come in this early. *Usually.* I was sure today he would show up just in the middle of this rundown.

"Tell me where she is Daniels!" I shouted in my comms.

"She's taking the service stairs, and she's already down one floor."

I knew how to cut her off. Instead of going directly for her, I went for the freight elevator that would take me to the fourteenth floor. I could swing back up the stairs and catch her in the middle. Swiping my card, I got lucky, and it was only one floor above me.

I jumped in the oversized elevator and back out almost immediately on the fourteenth floor, sprinting along the corridor, hopefully parallel to her. "Keep talking to me, Daniels. I need you to tell me where she is at all times."

"Looks like she's right on top of you."

Good. That meant I was right. She was going to change her clothes and make it look like she was one of the employees. Blend in one way or the other. Not bad Kaya, not bad at all.

"Did she make it into the server room?" Daniels asked.

"Not as far as I can tell, unless she had some way of shutting down the alarms from inside the room, and I don't see that happening. This all was probably a calculated risk for her to see if she could make it there."

"Yeah, but what could she be after?"

"That, my friend, is up to you to find out."

When I hit the south stairs, I took them two at a time up one floor. But I was too late. She was already coming out of the corridor, hair pulled high into a ponytail, a bouncing corkscrew of curls, and she had her workout gear on. God, she looked good.

When Kaya heard the stairway door click, she turned and smirked at me.

Jesus, you're in so much trouble with this one.

And she headed right back for the service stairs. This time I followed her. For every step she took, I took three. I was gaining quickly on her until she hopped the railing down to the next level.

"Jesus fucking Christ, woman. You're going to break your neck."

She didn't even slow down to acknowledge me. Just kept moving.

Kaya hit the bottom floor, her hand on the exit door, just as I was making it down the last steps. I called out, "Wait."

Again, she didn't listen. The door exited into a hallway, and she was already sprinting toward the parking garage. But I had anticipated that and took the short cut through the building that she didn't know about and met her on the parking deck.

I reached out, wrapped an arm around her waist, and dragged her body against mine.

"Let me go, arsehole!"

"You break into *my* place of work to do God knows what, and you think I'm going to let you go? Hell, no."

She struggled against me to get away, but I had her locked in my arms. Backing us up against the corner of the concrete walls, I whispered to her, "You're going to stop moving right now. I don't want to hurt you or for you to hurt yourself. I want you completely intact when I call the police."

Her eyes went wide, and she cried, "You can't prove anything."

"I've got you on cameras, darling."

"Are you sure you do?"

"I've also caught you red-handed."

"Unless I escape?"

The fire sparked in her eyes, and I could feel it straight down deep into my bones. The heat, the electricity, the burning need, and I swallowed hard against it. This was not what I needed right this minute.

A car drove slowly by as if looking for a parking spot, although there were many. With a sharp inhale, she ducked and turned her head into my chest immediately.

"Are you in trouble?"

When the car rolled away, she turned her gaze back to me, chin lifted, eyes still sparking. "I'm fine. No thanks to you."

"What the fuck is that supposed to mean? I met you last night. And so far, you have already proven to be a handful. We're going back to the offices to sort this out. Let's go."

"Me? A handful? Because of you, my whole life, everything I've worked toward, is over. No flat, no more school, no more volunteering. You stuck your goon squad on me, and I have to get out of here."

I blinked slowly. Was she mad? "What goons?"

"You and Connor are working together. His men last night. That car now. Why did you come after me yourself just now? You could have just had one of them grab me."

"I came after you myself because I got a security alert. Also, I'm not currently in possession of goons, let alone a squad of them. Why don't you tell me what's really going on here? Who are you?"

"I already told you. My name is Kaya."

"Right. Why are men chasing you?"

"You tell me why! All I wanted to do was have a conversation with Connor last night. Instead, you stopped that from happening and men started chasing me. Now I'm not safe to go back home or school or anywhere."

I gritted my teeth. "So what made you break into my office?"

"Well, I can't get to Connor. You're protecting him. So you are the next best thing."

"What were you going to do in the server room?"

She licked her lips and glowered at a spot just over my shoulder.

I took her chin between my forefinger and thumb, gently but with enough pressure to force her head to align to mine.

"Okay, Sprite. You either talk to me, or you talk to the police. It's up to you. I can have my security guys take you to the station. Take your pick."

"I'm not talking to you."

"That's a very poor choice as clearly you're in some kind of trouble."

"Because of you."

"I don't know how many times I have to tell you this, love, but I don't know your friend Connor. I'm sorry he is such a hard man to find for someone who clearly needs to talk with him. As for people chasing you, that's an actual fucking problem."

"Yeah, tell me about it."

I could see her fear even though she was trying to play it tough. She was scared. It showed in her eyes. They were a little too alert, a little too wide. Way too assessing with her gaze rapidly staring back and forth between me and our surroundings.

From my peripheral vision, I could see the slow headlights of a car coming our way again and deliberately shifted her further into the shadows. I frowned as I watched them approach. This wasn't one of our security cars. This was a nondescript, dark sedan with two men in the front.

I glowered down at her. "Friends of yours, I assume?"

"No. I'm leaving."

"Not without—" I didn't get the *me* part out as bullets ricocheted off the concrete wall to my left.

Tires squealed to a stop as I grabbed her wrist and took off between two parked cars. As we crouched down to hide, I turned to her. "We've got to get to the lower level and get out of here."

"I was trying to do that when you stopped me, arsehole!"

I pulled on her wrist again and moved down the aisle of cars just as the two goons stepped out of their vehicle and start looking around.

"Look, Kaya, we've got to move toward that outer door. There's a small set of fire stairs that leads to the street level. On the count of three, run to it and go to the right at the bottom of the steps. There's a coffee shop with a side door we can hide in."

"I'm not hiding anywhere with you—" She sucked in a breath of shock when a shot rang off the column next to us. "I'm running! I'm running!" she shouted and took off toward the door.

"Who are these guys?" I shouted to Kaya.

"I don't know! I thought they were with you!"

With the car almost on my heels, she flung open the exit door. The metal of the door deflected another shot. We were either really lucky or those lads really needed weapons training.

"To the right!" I shouted as she jumped the rail again, escaping to the pavement. Just as I hit the concrete, the screech of tires told me we were out of time.

Exiting the ramp, the goons turned to the left away from us, but they were going too fast, jumping onto the curb and hitting a parked car in the process.

I turned to see Kaya, wide eyed with her hand on the door to the coffee shop. "Get in here!" she yelled as she motioned to me.

Inside, with my back against the solid door, I grab her tight in an embrace. "Why are you constantly trying to get me killed?"

"I'm not. I thought they were friends of yours." Kaya said.

Was she serious? "I keep trying to tell you if you would just listen. I was minding my business and tried to get a date with a girl. She took off running, and I followed as we got chased. Why would *I* be chased, twice now mind you, and shot at by my very own goon squad?"

She bit on her plump bottom lip. "Not your goon squad, then?"

I threw my hands up. "I don't even have a goon squad. Just a few blokes who work security for my company and don't even report directly to me."

The strong defiant woman I'd seen just a second ago had disappeared. Fear had taken over and was coming off her in waves. Kaya wasn't just afraid; it was something deeper. A hopelessness no one should ever have to face.

"Listen, what was it that you said about not being safe to go home?"

She shook her head. "Nothing. I don't need your help."

"Well, being shot at says differently."

"I can take care of myself."

"Do you really have to fight me on everything?"

She tilted her chin up, and for a moment I thought she was going to say yes. Just to take the piss. But surprisingly, she didn't. Instead, she pressed her lips together firmly and glowered.

I pulled out my phone and she stiffened again. "Relax. I'm just going to make a call, okay?"

"Why should I trust you?"

My gaze slid over her face, and I knew she was ready to run like a scared rabbit all over again. I really didn't have it in me to chase her again. "Of course, you can't just trust me, but you don't really have a choice now, do you?"

"Just promise me you're not the bad guy in my story."

"I can't make too many promises, but what I can absolutely guarantee is I am not the person actively trying to hurt you. Now, before we both get too frazzled to make decisions, let's get you somewhere safer."

"I don't know you from Adam. How do I know you aren't going to lock me up in your dungeon or whatever?"

I rolled my eyes. "Oh, for fuck's sake, one billionaire in one movie happened to have a sex dungeon, and the world thinks we *all* have them."

Her lips twitched in utter amusement. "So you saw that movie, did you?"

I lifted my brow and couldn't help a smirk. "I may have heard about it. The point is, for now, the safest place for you is with me."

She continued to glower at me with suspicion. "I don't need a handout. I just need to get away from here for a little bit."

"We need to get you a safe place to lay low."

She shook her head vehemently. "But—"

I stared at her and she stopped her rambling. "Sprite, if you do not shut that gorgeous mouth of yours, I'm going to shut it for you."

Her brows knitted together. "If you think I'm going to let you manhandle me—"

"Manhandle? And what, kiss you? Isn't that how you shut me up last night?"

Her eyes widened in embarrassment as she stared back at me, her gaze drifting down to my lips as I said, "Oooooh, right. You kissed me because you were hiding. Very clever, Sprite."

I watched the pink flush creep up her neck under her tawny skin, making her look more bronze. Like she'd been kissed by a little sunshine.

Clearing her throat, she said, "You were a decent distraction."

"Right. Decent. We'll circle back to that later."

Her voice went soft as she straightened. "Why are you helping me?"

"Because you need it. And you were desperate enough to break into my offices and I'd like to know why."

"Why were you in the room Connor was supposed to be in last night?"

"I was assigned that room," I lied smoothly.

Her gaze searched mine. "Really?"

"Really."

She blew out a breath. "I nearly got you run over by a car." Her voice shook, and I knew she was going into shock.

"You know, that's not even the worst date I've had this year."

Again, there was a perfect quirk to her lips as she smiled up at me. My eyes were glued to the plump softness of them. I wanted to taste her again. See if she tasted the same. I sucked in a deep breath and held out my hand. And when she reluctantly grabbed it, I pulled her with me.

"My car is back at the office. I'll drive you to my flat. You'll stay with me."

CHAPTER 9
KAYA

BLOODY HELL. So this was how the other half lived.

Jasper Saint's penthouse was spectacular. I had never been to a place like this before. One wall was floor-to-ceiling glass. Freaking glass! That required a level of confidence in yourself I'd never seen the likes of before. No doubt there was probably something fancy that made it so other people couldn't look in, but if you looked as hot as Jasper did, maybe not.

The floors were a light hardwood. Everything was modern, fresh, and clean. There was some clutter, like papers and mail on the coffee table, but mostly things were neat and it was furnished in a muted neutral tone. A little color wouldn't kill him. The place looked barely lived in.

This isn't your house.

Nope. No, it was not. This was *his* house, the rich billionaire. I had zero business even having an opinion, let alone coming up with ideas of how to redecorate. What the hell was I thinking? As I spun around, I couldn't help whistling low. "Nice digs."

He nodded with a shrug. "It does the trick."

"You have a penthouse in central London, and you shrug about it."

"None of it matters. What matters is you're okay. Are you hurt?"

I frowned at that. "No, I'm not hurt. I just..." I frowned as I thought about it. What the hell was I doing with my life? Twenty-four hours ago, I'd had a perfectly nice flat. I was a student. And now, everything was up in the air.

You can't go back to your life.

That was true, but could I stay here? There were men who had legitimately tried to hurt me today. Men I'd never seen before. To make matters worse, all the times my mother had spoken about the invisible boogeyman, I had doubted her. In the last five years, I had started to wonder if anyone had been chasing us because I had been completely safe. But now I knew she wasn't kidding. Our lives hadn't been a joke when we were running.

As I stared out of Saint's massive windows overlooking the South Bank, the London city lights twinkling in greeting, I realized I wasn't ever going back to my life. At least not how I knew it. Not after they'd chased me this morning. Was this place even safe? Fuck, I was tired of thinking about it all.

Saint disappeared for a moment and came back with a bottle of water. He held it out to me, and I took it gratefully. When I uncapped it, I noticed the label. *Pierre Lucian.* I had once asked them for sponsorship for the center. I knew how much their bottles were. Nearly twenty quid... for *water.* I was breathing that rarefied air now.

"I think it's probably better if you stay here for a while."

"I'll get out of your hair just as soon as I figure out what to do next."

He sighed and then crossed his arms. I tried not to think about what that did to his suit jacket, the navy fabric pooling over his arms and shoulders. "Do you have anywhere to go right now?"

I licked my lips and shifted from foot to foot. "My flat, I guess."

"And where's your flat?"

"In Ealing, near uni."

"You can't go back there. Not now, and probably not for a while. Do you have a flatmate or something? Someone who will worry about you?"

I shook my head. "No, and I already scrubbed my place."

He frowned. "What do you mean, *scrubbed* it?"

"It's a long story, but no one who goes looking for me there will find anything about me."

He nodded slowly. "Stay here. Stay off the streets. You need a place to lie low for a moment, and we have to figure out who the fuck is chasing you, and obviously they're not looking for you to have a nice, safe chat. For now, you lay low. Do you work?"

I frowned at him. "I'm a university student. I work at a subsidy shelter called The Ealing Center."

He nodded. "Call them and tell them you're not going to be in for a couple of weeks."

"They need me," I sputtered.

"They'll have to do without you for a while."

I wanted to argue, but he was right. I was in over my head and I needed a moment to think.

"I was wrong about you, okay? I can admit that."

His grin flashed, and my knickers threatened to disintegrate. "You're a charitable woman. Any idea why people are chasing you? Anything you can think of?"

My brain ran it all over. This all started when I approached Connor. "That bloke Connor, he knew my mother. He was the last person to see her alive. Before I approached him to talk, I was completely normal. Nobody shot at me, not a single car chase. Everything changed after we spoke at the bar."

His brow furrowed. "Is there a reason you might be a threat to them?"

"I'm just a girl looking for her mum."

His voice was soft when he asked, "When was the last time you saw her?"

"Five years ago."

"Kaya..." His voice trailed off, and I could hear his disbelief and reluctance. I could almost hear him say 'Five years is a long time.'

I shook my head. I knew what he was going to say, what most people said when I told them the first time. The same thing they'd said back then when I'd asked the police if they were looking for her.

"I know it's been five years, but if he can tell me something, anything, I want to know."

"You need to be careful."

"You don't think I know that? I was being careful. Besides, how was I to know Mum wasn't making it all up the whole time?" I uncapped the bottle and sat on his couch, staring down at the floor as all the tension poured out of me. "When I was a kid, I believed everything she said. But then once I was in the foster care system after she disappeared, I wondered if she was just mentally ill. Unable to hold down a job and maybe that's why we moved all the time. Every place we went she always seemed to know the shady characters. Someone to get us new ID and someone to get her an under-the-table job. She lived in fear, always diligent against an invisible boogeyman. I just thought maybe she made it up. But now..." I let my voice trail off. "Now I can see that she was telling the truth all along."

Saint sighed. He walked over to the entertainment center and grabbed the remote, turning the TV on before he handed it to me. "Try to relax, watch some television, and raid the pantry. I need to go into the office again and sort a few things out. Housekeeping doesn't come until tomorrow, so no one should be here throughout the day. Don't answer the door for anyone. If you need anything, pick up the phone on the wall and it goes straight to Nigel at the front door. I'll let him know to get you anything you need."

"I'll need my backpack and suitcase."

"And pray tell, where might I find those for you?"

I winced. "Um, in the supply closet at your company."

To his credit, all he did was lift a brow. "Right. When I come back later tonight, we're going to have a conversation, Sprite. You will let me know all about how and why you thought breaking into All Saints Tech was a good idea."

"To be fair, I wasn't trying to break in, per se. I came in with the cleaning crew, hoping to find out more about you and your connection with Connor. But considering those guys tried to kill you too, I don't really think you're working with Connor."

"Clocked that finally, have you?"

"Sorry. What was I supposed to think?"

He shook his head. "I don't have time for this conversation right now. You just stay here. Stay out of trouble. And try to eat something."

He kept talking, but my gaze was focused on the television. I frowned at the familiar sights of Ealing and the school campus and the stone road from my flat. Then I recognized the building itself. Smoke was billowing out of my building at the end of the road.

The reporter stood away from it all as the camera panned back to his face, and he said, "Gas explosion."

The bottom of my stomach fell out and goosebumps lifted on my forearms. My heart beat a hummingbird tattoo against my ribs and the room started to spin.

Saint noticed my face. "What's wrong?"

All I could do was point at the television. "That's my flat."

He frowned and turned around. "What?"

"My flat. It just blew up in a gas explosion."

I could see it in the set of his shoulders. He didn't believe anything about that, and neither did I.

"My flat, my home, the only place I've ever had on my own. Those men are trying to *kill* me."

"It's okay, Kaya. I've got you Sprite." He wrapped his arms around me then. Strong. Solid.

I held myself stiffly, the shock of the truth of the whole thing settling in. Last night I told myself that I could go back to my life. I could return. That everything that had happened in the last twenty-four hours was only temporary. But I was just lying to myself. The truth was, I had nowhere to go.

And then suddenly, my truth became Saint's arms. The smell of sandalwood and something clean and earthy wrapped around me, making me feel cocooned and safe. He smoothed a hand down my back.

"You're going to be okay. You're safe here." He stepped back, his arms on my shoulders. "But I need you to stay here. I don't want you to leave, okay? I just want to make sure you're safe. If you still want to leave tonight when I get back, I'll take you wherever you want to go. But for now, just stay put for me, all right?"

"No one helps a stranger like this for no reason."

"You've never met me before."

There was a knock at the door and Saint frowned. I might not entirely trust him, but I knew for now he'd keep me safe so I tucked myself behind him.

It was a survivor's move.

You're starting to trust him.

No. No, I was not.

I watched warily as he sauntered to the door, feeling like I was perched on a razor's edge. He used a panel near the door to verify who it was, and I watched as even more tension dumped on his shoulders.

He yanked the door open and crossed his arms. "What the fuck are you doing here?"

Someone on the other side of the door whom I couldn't see said, "Hey boss. Just reporting for duty."

Boss? I poked my head around Saint's broad shoulders and my gaze landed on another stunning looker of a man. Dark blond hair, dazzling blue eyes, with a scruff dusting his jaw. He was also built tall and lean like Saint. "Who do we have here, boss?"

I flushed at having been caught being nosy. "I'm Kaya. Nice to meet you."

The bloke smirked at me. "Hello, beautiful, I'm Westin. I'm a member of Saint's security team."

Of course he had a security team. "Oh, uh, nice to meet you."

"You said Kaya? That's a beautiful name for a beautiful woman."

"You need something, *Westin*?" Saint's voice was all growl and gravel.

Westin grinned at me again. "Just letting you know I was on duty and would handle any security you need from now until you return this evening."

"Goodbye, Rook," Saint muttered and slammed the door.

"He seemed...nice." I murmured.

"You don't go near him with a ten foot pole, you hear me?"

CHAPTER 10
SAINT

Rogues agents had already been over Kaya's flat, but I had to see the wreckage for myself. I'd called it in as soon as I found Kaya some clothes to change into. The question of how they found her was next on the list of unknowns. Last night potentially made sense. Lohman recognized her and sent heavy hitters in to grab her. But today, this morning, didn't make any logical sense. Was she being tracked? Who knew where she was? And what did they want?

You would know for yourself if you were the one protecting her from the start.

I'd somehow thought after our harrowing adventure, I'd be assigned to Kaya.

But you refused, you twat.

And now bloody Westin was there. And every cell in my body hated the idea. Rook was a decent fighter, but we didn't need him.

He was also stupid attractive, and she seemed to like it. Yeah, fine, it made my chest tight to think about him being the one to guard her. But I had bigger fish to fry because when I was done here, I planned to talk to Lohman again. The important thing was we had the bastard, and now it was just a matter of getting answers out of him. Then using that intel to capture Antonio Igno.

Kaya was only a distraction to the mission.

The sooner I could get her situated, the better off we all would be in getting the case closed. The problem was how long we could keep her sitting tight and complying with orders.

She had a life. Things she wanted to do. Things I was sure she needed to get back to.

You heard the girl, she can't go back to her life.

Why did that sound so ominous? I'd already had Maureen order some clothes for her as all she had in the backpack were a few changes of clothes and her laptop, which I'd had my men clone. So far, they'd found nothing on that or her phone. I picked up some items I thought she could use, and then I stopped at the Italian place four blocks from the office on the South Bank. It was a hole-in-the-wall place that a guy named Luigi Franco had owned for years. My father started taking me there when I was a kid, and I figured she was hungry.

So much for the woman being a thorn in your side.

Fine. She was a thorn, but she still needed to eat.

Security at the front desk give me an odd look when I entered carrying all the bags. "How's it Nigel? Anyone go up to see her?"

He shook his head. "When the packages came in that Maureen sent over, she came down and got them herself. Hasn't left since."

"Thanks."

In the elevator, I shifted from foot to foot nervously. I could feel the tightness coiling in my chest. It wasn't until she finally released the lock and I saw her smiling face that some of that tightness uncoiled. She was okay. "Hey."

She smiled up at me. "Hey yourself."

I held up the bag of food. "I brought you something to eat."

She looked bemused and then stepped aside to let me in. "Thank you, but Westin already got me food when he stopped to check on me."

The fuck? "Well, that was *nice* of him," I said through clenched teeth.

Her smile was bright. "Yeah, he's lovely."

I might have growled a little when I asked, "How lovely?"

Of course the twat was friendly with his too perfect hair and too perfect smile. Stepping past her, I said, "I'll put this in the fridge for you."

"I appreciate it. You've done a lot for me. I'm not sure how I'll be able to pay you back."

The fact that she thought she had to pay me back irritated the hell out of me. "You don't need to do anything. Just lay low, be safe, and that's all we're going to worry about right now."

She tucked her hands in the back pockets of her jeans. She looked every bit the co-ed now, curls loose and free, bouncing around her shoulders. I wanted to wrap one of those silken curls around my finger and tug just a bit.

But that would be creepy, you git…

"You have everything you need?" I tried to change the path of my thoughts.

"Honestly, thank you for everything. You didn't have to do any of this."

I pierced her with a studious look. "You and I both know I did. I couldn't just leave you. You were likely to get yourself killed."

The tip of her tongue peeked out to moisten her lower lip, and I bit back a moan. That was the last imagery I needed in my head.

"Look while I appreciate everything you did and are doing, I'll be out of your hair in a couple of days. I just need to sort out accommodations and make sure they're safe."

The hell? Where did she think she was going? "Do you know who's chasing you?"

"No but—"

"And do you know what they want?" I prompted.

"Again, no, but I can't—"

"And do you know if it's even safe to leave here for anywhere on the planet?"

She sighed then acquiesced. "No."

"So again, where the fuck would you go?"

She pressed her lips together in a firm line. "I'm not a prisoner. I can go when I want."

She has you there.

"Yep, anytime you want. There's the door, and you obviously know how to use it. Just tell me all the details of who's chasing you, and I'll be the first one driving you to wherever you need to go. Until then, use your head, woman."

She narrowed her gaze mutinously, but she knew I had a point.

"Also, I've dealt with the police."

Her eyes went wide. "I'm not really fond of the police."

"This is my shocked face. Can you tell? After all you said today about having to go on the lam, I took care of it. You can relax, they won't come looking for you. I answered their questions and handed them the shell casings found in the garage. And they have the evidence to play with in their little labs. You're clear."

"My, you are a regular fairy godfather, aren't you?"

There was a hint of a smile playing on her lips, and I couldn't stop staring. I did not have time for this... *thing* between us. I needed to get back to Rogues Division. But somehow, I couldn't make myself walk away when she smiled like that. I wanted to stay. I felt a need to make sure she was all right. And being here caused an ache in the center of my chest to return.

Just as fast as I came into the flat, I started my exit. "I'm off. Stay inside. I'll be back later."

"Wait! Where are you going?" The lonely plea in her voice nearly had me stopping.

But I couldn't very well tell her where I was going. "I have errands. I'll check on you before I go to bed."

I turned to leave, and her voice was quiet. "Hey, thank you. I mean that. You saved my life today even after I tried to make yours more difficult."

Every cell in my body said stay. Hold her. Comfort her in some way. But the only way I wanted to comfort her right now was to take her lips with mine again.

So to be wise, I deliberately kept my back turned, and gave her brief nod before practically running out my front door.

With each step, I had to fight the pull. The gravity of her allure was almost too strong, making me want to turn back. I had felt it last night, but now, seeing her in my place, that primal urge clawed its way to the surface.

I stopped down the hall by the elevator and knocked on Rook's door.

The fucker answered with a sly grin. "Saint. What brings you round to my door, mate?"

"What's up is you're off duty. She's staying with me, so I'll be primary."

What the fuck was I doing?

I hardly registered the words until they were out of my mouth. I didn't want this. The kid was just as good as anyone else, though personally, I preferred Lachlan. He was nice and attached, practically married and desperately in love with Saffron. He would have made a great bodyguard for Kaya.

Rook laughed. "What are you on about mate? I haven't been pulled. This is the assignment. Besides, she likes me. I can tell," he said with a wink.

The fuck did he just say? "Excuse me?"

He gave me a sunny smile and nodded. "Well, the way I figure it, she's going to need round the clock watching, so I might as well do it from bed."

Was pretty boy's smile inviting my fist? His obvious glee at this bright idea made me want to knock him into next week. "No. Not a good idea."

He frowned. "What? Why not? She likes me. She's well fit. Seems sweet. I might like her."

I glowered at him. "Keep your eyes on the fucking ball instead of her arse. Matter of fact, don't think about her at all. You're done here."

Rook narrowed his eyes. "I knew you liked her. Listen, I know you've got the most experience and all on account of your age. I'm just a rookie in the ranks of Rogues. But we don't have to let this be a thing between us. Let the best man win."

I leaned in so that he would hear me clearly, but I was very careful not to touch him. "I will say this once and only once. You touch what's mine and *I. Will. End. You.* Is that bloody clear?"

With a cocky smile, he nodded, and I turned and strode off. He thought this was a game. She needed protection. And I was going to make sure she got it starting right fucking now.

From *me*, not from Rook, and I had a wild idea how to go about it.

CHAPTER 11
SAINT

Drastic was the wrong word. Insane was probably a better one. But still, I kept mulling options over and over in my head, and I kept coming up with the same conclusion. Kaya needed coverage that would keep somebody from making big moves against her. In a span of forty-eight hours, she'd gone from your average university student to being actively hunted. Okay, not average. I'd done the research. Her grades were exemplary, and the work she'd done at the center was above excellent. Everyone had great things to say about how much they loved her, how great she was with the kids.

Then there was that face.

She was a stunner. Those big eyes and lips that look like she was Grade A at sucking cock. No wonder Lohman had been watching her during the auction. But there had been nothing that stood out about her history that deemed she was a threat. What the fuck was I missing here?

Yes, she'd been in care. Even her foster parents had had great things to say about her. In the report I'd seen, they'd even tried to adopt her, but she'd stopped that herself. The only notes in her file being that she thought she was too old for adoption. And then she'd lived a quiet life. The landlord loved her as she paid her rent ahead of schedule. No trouble. She only asked him once if she could put nails in the walls to hang up paintings. So how did that girl go from that quiet boring life to this? Hiding away in my penthouse with men trying to kill her?

Were they trying to kill her? Or are they trying to grab her?

The more I thought about the movements in the garage, the more I got the distinct impression they were gunning for me. Which meant I was the assassination target and the goal was to take her.

Shit. This girl needed coverage. Because whether it was Connor's men, or worse, Igno's men, Kaya was in trouble.

Just like Elise had once been.

I wasn't due back on the Rogues campus for two more days. But the situation called for an unscheduled visit. One, I wanted to take another go at Connor and see what the interrogation turned up. Two, I needed to talk to Gabe, because for this plan to take hold, he was going to need to be in on it and pull back Rook, the wanker.

What I wanted to do was go straight to Connor. But I knew Kaya was the pressing issue, so I went to Gabe's office first. Surprisingly, his office was open and Saff was sitting on the corner of her brother's desk, long legs dangling, barely touching the floor. And Gabe was... what?

Playing darts.

Saff leaned forward and rolled several darts between her fingers.

Gabe muttered, "I can feel you staring. It's distracting."

"Who me?" Saff asked innocently. "I'm not doing anything. You said you were stressed out and needed a game. I brought you the game, and now you don't like it because you're losing."

"I'm *not* losing. This is strategy."

Saff rolled her eyes and flicked some of her braids over her shoulder. That was when she saw me. She waved at me with a wide grin. "Hey, Saint."

She said my name just as Gabe fired a dart, going just wide of his likely target.

He cursed under his breath. "See? You're distracting me."

She rolled her eyes and hopped down. "Fine. I'm going to take a picture of this just in case you pull the darts out before we reconvene."

"We don't need to reconvene. Aren't we working?"

"Oh no, we're going to finish this game. And I can't have you pretending that you didn't know where your darts were."

Saff took a picture and then sauntered out.

I did like her a lot. God, she was good for King. Just the kind of anchor he needed.

"What do you want?"

Saff wasn't kidding. Gabe was grumpy about something, and he was about to get a whole hell of a lot grumpier. "I wanted to talk to you about the Kaya Reynolds situation."

"The fire? Yeah, I saw that. I have someone looking into it. Luckily, she wasn't there. Do you have information on why she was at All Saints Tech?"

I winced. "Would you believe she was looking for Lohman?"

"The fuck, how did she connect you two?"

"She caught me in Lohman's greenroom at the auction and I had to improvise. She's a sharp one and didn't buy the ruse."

Gabe's eyes narrowed on me. "Correct me if I'm wrong, but isn't it your job to sell the lie?"

My lips still burned with the imprint of hers. Oh, I'd sold it.

"She was at All Saints trying to get information on me. I chased her. She ran. And then this funny thing happened. A couple of goons tried to snatch her off the street. When I got in the way, they tried to shoot me and run me over."

Gabe eased into the chair behind the massive oak desk. "I saw the report, the recovery team hasn't pulled anything back yet. She give any indication as to why she's a target?"

"No, but the distinct impression I got was that they were

aiming to *take* her, not to hurt her. I shrugged. "I don't know. All I know is that she's in trouble. A lot of it. She needs more coverage than just bodyguards. She needs public coverage."

Gabe rubbed his jaw. "We don't know anything about her. We're not bringing her to Rogues."

"No, I'm not talking about that. She needs powerful coverage, but she's the kind of girl who will take off. If you don't want her in the wind, I have an idea."

Gabe sat back and rubbed his jaw. "Why do I get the impression you're about to pitch me a very bad idea."

"She needs public protection from someone powerful enough to make it stick. Someone Lohman and Igno and the lot is not going to touch. Or at least think twice about."

"Okay, but these are men who aren't afraid of a lot of people."

"I have a plan though.

He watched me warily. "All right, I'm listening."

"I need to marry her."

Gabe's eyes went wide and his jaw went slack before he regained full composure. "What?"

"I need to marry her, or at least make it look like I'm marrying her."

Gabe stared at me blankly for a long moment. The tiny scar on his brow somehow more prominent. "So, let me get this straight. Your bright idea after Igno and his men took Elise from you is to marry *this* woman?"

"When you say it like that, it sounds like a shit idea. But it's a good plan."

Gabe asked, "Do you think your name is enough to make these men back down?"

"I don't know, but I need to try, because if this isn't Igno and it's someone else, the Saint name is enough. Plus, I can keep her close and find out exactly what Connor wants with her. When I questioned him about her, he didn't seem all too eager to talk except in riddles. He said, 'You don't even know what you have.'

Wouldn't say what their connection was or why she wanted to speak to him. She sought him because she thinks he has information about her mother. But her mother vanished five years ago when Connor was still an enforcer. Even if he does know something, he probably won't be helpful to her."

"Saint, this is out there. Even for you."

"I just want to buy her some coverage. She's the kind of woman who instead of walking will do a full sprint if she's spooked."

For a long moment, Gabe studied me. "Obviously, there will be no fraternization. If we're doing this, keep it clean. I don't want to answer questions from Oversight just because you want to wet your dick."

There was no problem there. I had no intention of ever touching her again. Elise had left me scarred. Staying away was wise. "That's not what this is."

Liar.

Gabe nodded. "All right, fine. Make it happen. Rook stays in play though."

I halted before turning to walk away. "What?"

"Rook, he stays in play. Because after all, the great Jasper Saint would certainly have a full security detail on his new fiancée, now wouldn't he?"

I cursed under my breath. "Son of a cunt."

Looked like I wouldn't be getting rid of Rook after all.

———

KAYA

"Well, say something." Saint said as he stared at me.

I stared back. There was no way. There was no fucking way. He was kidding, right? He had to be kidding because he had not just said what I thought he'd said.

I was seated on his plush sofa in the middle of his penthouse flat, and he was sitting next to me saying ridiculous things. But somehow he looked at me like I was being the crazy person.

"You've got to give me something, Kaya."

"Jasper Saint. Did you just say you wanted me to marry you?"

He winced. Of course he'd wince. This whole thing was ridiculous.

"Yes. For all intents and purposes, I am asking you to marry me. Sort of."

I couldn't help it, the nervous bubble of laughter just tripped out of my mouth without me even thinking. "You're insane! That's what this is you've lost your ever-loving mind. Why would I say yes to marrying you? I'm not even sure I like you. Not to mention, why the hell should we be talking about marriage forty-eight hours after meeting?"

"This plan, the whole thing... Well, it's about giving you coverage and safety. And for what it's worth, I didn't really set out to marry you either, but after watching men chase you through a gala, trying to run you over, and consequently me as well, both of us being shot at, and then, presumably, those very same men blowing up your flat, at least this way you'd have some kind of protection."

Fuck. My home. I'd been trying very hard not to think about my flat.

"Right. So, I'm in trouble. I know it. You know it. Everyone knows it. But again, why would I marry you?"

"Because of my name. The Saint name is a very powerful one, and at the very least it will buy you time to figure out how to live your life safely."

All I could do was stare at him.

Two days ago, I was convinced he was working with Connor Lohman. Convinced. I had bet the farm on it. But I'd been wrong, because if he was working with Lohman, I would have been dead by now. I ran my hands through my hair, my curls, essentially a rat's nest forming a fuzzy afro halo around my face. I probably needed a good deep conditioner, and my products. Jesus, how was this my life?

"How would this even work? I have no clue how getting married to you protects me."

"Well, for starters, we wouldn't actually have to get married. We just need to make enough noise about you being my fiancée. We make a big and splashy announcement that will give them pause before coming for you again. No one would try killing you with a marriage to a Saint on the line. There's more of a ransom concern, but again, they'd have to get to you. There wouldn't be any more subversive attacks."

"Can you guarantee that?"

"No, I can't. But the Saint name would make someone pause. Especially if that someone didn't know that we were affiliated or connected before."

I narrowed my gaze at him. He was saying things that sort of made sense, but why? "I don't get it. What does your name have to do with my safety?"

I mean, I knew that All Saints Tech was a big company, family owned with a shit ton of money. I knew that Jasper Saint had lost his fiancée, but what was I missing from what he was sitting here and trying to tell me?

Saint stood up and rocked back on his heels, his hands in his pockets, shirt sleeves rolled up, tie off, and he looked... delicious. Like, the real him was more casual than the suited and booted look. But he also looked sort of contrite, like he was sorry for something. Clearing his throat, he said "Three years ago, my fiancée died in a car accident. Except it wasn't an accident. My father very famously went on live telly and told the world that he would pay anything for information on the people who killed her."

I blinked slowly. "I remember something about that."

"For the most part, it was my father dealing with his grief of losing Elise, except... not so much as a father-in-law would have acted. I discovered that while I was shipped out on military appointment, they had a relationship." His eyes met mine, and I could see all the betrayal and pain in their green depths. His voice was steady but heavy with the weight of what he was telling me.

"But not everyone knows that. My father became ruthless in his pursuit of her killers. Any lead we had, he followed it up and met it with vengeance. He hit fast. He hit hard. He hit finances. To my knowledge, he didn't kill anyone, but there are criminal organizations that are missing some serious money. Father made sure that anyone who had even a touch point to legitimate businesses lost all their access and all their power. So, these days, word on the street is it's not a good idea to mess with a Saint."

I stared at him in disbelief. "But doesn't that open you up to vulnerability and vengeance?"

He gave me one of his panty-melting sheepish smiles. "No. There's something to be said for the fear it instills when you're working with billions and not millions."

I blinked at that statement. "Ah, okay then."

"Besides, we don't actually have to get married. Like you said, we don't know each other."

"I said I'm not even sure I like you."

He lifted a brow. "That's impossible. Everyone likes me."

"No, not everyone."

He shrugged. "Give it a chance. I know there are lots of women who would agree that I'm very likable."

"Oh yeah, speaking of the women in your past is making this whole let's-get-married thing seem like a fantastic idea."

"Look, I know it's sudden and it's jarring. I don't even know if you have a boyfriend, or girlfriend, or someone significant. But my name can provide you with protection."

"And if I take your protection, how long does it last?"

"This will save your life. Once word is out that we're engaged, I can openly provide security for you. The twat down the hall is more than just a friend. He is part of a private security company."

"But why would you do this for me? You don't know me at all, and now you are jumping at the chance to marry me?"

"You needed a friend." The smile that lit up his face at being my friend suddenly closed down and his jaw clenched. In a cold tone, Saint stated, "And let's remember that they also attacked me. Someone should answer for that."

Saint talking about being friends and his protective nature over me was breaking me down. "I just want to go back to my life. I had a job. I had friends. I had a life. I had school. I don't have that anymore."

Sitting down on the couch close to me, he reached out and took my hand in his. "You can't go back to your life exactly as it was. Not right now. Maybe in a couple of months, love. But in the mean-time, we can keep you safe and you can still do some things."

"I assume I'm not supposed to tell anyone."

"Absolutely not."

I shook my head. "I only have Gemma, and she needs to know,"

"It's not wise."

"I'm grateful. I am. But she's all I have. And I need to go to school. It grounds me. And I have some things that are nonnego-tiable. I'm looking for my mother. I need help with that, and I need to be able to search for her."

He worked his jaw. "That's not wise either. Like I said, give it a couple of—"

I shook my head vehemently. "Like I said, I'm grateful, but that's something I need, and I'm going to do it anyway."

He sighed. "Okay, as long as you don't do anything reckless, I'll help you. And before you can argue, you are staying here. We'll work it out. While you're under my protection, you're mine. No one touches what's mine."

A shiver ran up my spine at the determined look in his eyes. He was serious. He was willing to put his life on hold to save mine. And I was just desperate enough to let him.

CHAPTER 12
SAINT

Lachlan and I were putting the new Rogues potentials through some training as we sat in the woods just off campus, picking them off with paint guns.

He turned from his perch and asked me, "So, are we going to talk about this whole getting-married thing?"

I should have known he wouldn't let me get away with not talking about it. "What? *You're* getting married. What's the big deal?"

"Well, the big deal is I love Saffron. Do you love this random woman? What's her name? Kaya?"

I glowered at him. "Spit it out. What are you trying to say?"

He casually picked off another recruit who was moving in the opposite direction from the target. Pink paint splatted on his arse as he careened into a bush. "Okay, look. I'm all for doing the right thing, protecting the asset. Which, by the way, you should have said yes to the *first* time."

Of course Lock would get in a dig. I'd fucked up. I should have just taken the goddamn assignment the first time Gabe offered it to me. Now I had to fucking contend with Rook as well.

"I have my reasons."

Lock grinned. "Oh, you mean like All Saints reasons? Like she's saving your arse?"

I blinked at him. "How the fuck do you know that?"

"Mate, you have a lot of conversations with your sister in the bungalow. She's been berating you for months."

"Fuck."

"Are you going to tell Kaya that's why you're marrying her? To save your own skin?"

Why did he have to say it like that? I narrowed my gaze at one of the recruits who was trying to outsmart the others, following along their chosen route but staying hidden. He hadn't broken any rules yet, so I let him carry on before turning back to Lock. "I'm not *actually* going to marry her. This is just to buy time."

Lock laughed. "How is this going to work?"

"Look, we're just going to go through all the pomp and circumstance and do the dance. And then, while we're getting ready to get married, I'll be looking for a way out. There's a loophole in the clause. I just haven't found it yet. I have no intention of getting married to her. But my name does provide protection. *And* it buys me time. Two birds, one stone."

Lock shook his head. "And you don't want to tell her all this?"

"No, it's too complicated. I can tell she trusts nobody. She'll run, which will get her killed."

He shook his head at me. "I don't know, mate. This just seems like you're playing with fire. Maybe you should just tell her."

He didn't get it. "No. She's skittish as it is. Besides, Gabe already cleared it."

Lock laughed. "Are you fucking kidding me? Look, Gabe and I have reached a détente, but do you think I don't know that he will do everything in his power to attain his goals? He's not above using a twenty-year-old uni student. If he wanted you to protect her in the first place, he has a reason. And you're just playing right into his hands."

Lock did see Gabe clearly. Gabe was ruthless. When it came to missions and the safety of his agents, he would do anything. But he was also ruthless. He would use someone to his advantage if he needed to. He was probably using Kaya, and I had no idea why. The problem was I needed her. At least to buy time. There was an even exchange.

Except she doesn't know anything about it.

"I have it under control."

"So you don't actually want her? I've seen her, mate. She's bloody fit."

"Of course not," I lied smoothly. "Besides, even if I did want her, which I don't, I'm perfectly capable of keeping my hands to myself."

Lachlan laughed. "Famous last words. I've said them myself."

———

CHAPTER 13
KAYA

"Xander, oh my God, oh my God, right there. Xander. Fuck."

"That's it, Imani. One more. Let me feel your tight pussy squeezing around me one more time."

I shifted uncomfortably on my feet, trying to pretend I couldn't hear the sounds coming out of my professor's office. There were rumors, of course. We'd all heard them. Hell, we'd all heard the moans coming from his classroom. And there was the way that he constantly looked at his wife like he wanted to eat her, or well... *eat* her. But I never thought *I* would be a witness.

Next to me, Saint slouched in his chair, head leaned back against the wood paneling with a dirty smirk on his face. "Well then, he certainly is... *thorough.*"

Deep in my core, something clenched at the way he said *thorough.* Fuck me. Jasper Saint was probably very... *thorough.*

I jerked my face away, focusing on the wood floor then the announcements posted along the hall on corkboards. The advert for an easy internship with pleas to call. Abandoned posters for past department parties.

Anything to avoid looking at Saint. I couldn't think if I did. Those were not the kind of thoughts I should be having. Nope. Uh-uh. I should focus on other things. Except he was looking at me, and I could remember the feel of his lips on mine, the tease, the temptation, the sinful deliciousness of it. And that was just a teaser. A taste. Imagining if he kissed me for real, like he meant it, like we had all the time in the world and he'd lay out a full seduction, and I'd be toast.

He would absolutely be *thorough.*

I shifted in my seat.

"Are you all right?" he asked. "You look slightly flushed."

"You can't tell that."

"Yes, I can. Just here." His thumb reached out and dusted my cheek lightly.

I froze, because even though I basically now lived with him, he never touched me. Which was probably for the best because I would explode into a puddle of need.

Five minutes later, when the door to Xander's office was finally yanked open, Imani Chase came stumbling out.

I'd seen her earlier today when she'd dropped Xander off for work. Her hair had been in a braided bun. Now her braids swung free over her shoulder, completely loose except part of them in the back was secured by a ponytail holder, so maybe he'd ripped them down. Which was hot. Jesus.

When she saw us outside waiting, her lips parted in surprise, but then she gave us a broad smile and a shrug and kept marching. That was the full confidence of a woman who had been thoroughly dicked and didn't give a fuck who knew about it.

Xander poked his head out of his office, and he too seemed surprised. "Oh, you're early."

I shook my head. "We were on time. You're late."

Xander's brow lifted, and he grinned at me when his gaze fell on Saint. "Well, ah, come in."

As he walked in, Saint leaned into me and said, "Tough little Sprite."

I ignored him and sat on the couch that was wedged in the corner of Xander's office.

This was a larger office than the one he had last year but was no less cluttered. Stacks of books and photography equipment and photos on the wall. Some he'd taken, some from his protégé, Abby Chase. Abby had married his brother. Some were from another photographer, Z Con. All brilliant. Beautiful. Stunning in different ways. Saint chose to stand by the door.

"Kaya, what can I do for you, and who's the bodyguard?"

Saint smiled. "Funny you should mention bodyguard."

I rolled my eyes. We did not have time for this. I couldn't just sit in Saint's penthouse not doing anything. I needed to come to school, so we needed to make this work. "This is my, um..." I didn't get to finish because Saint interrupted.

"Fiancé."

Xander's eyes went wide as he looked Saint up and down.

I understood the look. He wasn't even thirty, but Saint had this mature, world-weary look about him that was hard to catalog. Even though he looked barely older than me.

Then Xander's gaze flickered to mine again. "Okay, are you dropping my class?"

Saint lifted a brow. "We have a security concern."

Xander blinked once then twice. "Why? What's the problem?"

Suddenly, Xander had gone from devil-may-care, young, hot professor to *I could burn down the world if necessary.*

There was something very appealing about that. I could see why half the girls in class swooned in his presence. He had a certain appeal. I couldn't deny that.

"There's been a threat against Kaya. I have a security team for her. We've talked to the administration, but Kaya wanted to clear it with you."

Xander's gaze narrowed and he shrugged. "Of course. What's the level of threat?"

Saint shrugged back. "Right now, probably a three, but it's enough that we want to be careful."

"Of course. Are you sure maybe you don't want to pick up again next semester?"

I sat forward then. "No. Absolutely not."

Saint just pursed his lips, as if to say, *I tried to tell her, but she won't listen.*

"I'm sorry, Saint, but I can't just be locked in your penthouse all damn day. I need to go on with my life, engaged or not."

Saint sighed and gave Xander an exasperated look.

Xander just smiled. "Oh, I see. It's fine by me. You can have as many men as you need. They just can't be disruptive to class."

Saint nodded. "Of course not. Probably just a man inside posing as a student and one outside as a deterrent."

Xander nodded. "Fair enough. And Kaya, I know the syllabus tells you the upcoming assignments, but I'll give you the additional details in advance so you can coordinate with your security team for your safety."

"Oh my God, that would be brilliant. Thank you. That's wicked."

Xander nodded. "I understand a thing or two about security myself. Is there anything else?"

Jasper gave him a smile that was more teeth than anything else. "Yeah, just one more thing. She's the most important person in the world to me. I will do anything to protect her."

"Of course, she is. She's a dedicated student. Brilliant, actually."

I could see Saint's frustration when he lifted his brow. "What I mean to say is, hands off. She's mine."

Xander sat back with one quirked brow. And then he did the unexpected thing. He laughed. A full, raucous belly laugh. "I don't shag my students."

Saint rolled his eyes. "Oh, let me guess. The woman who left is a *former* student?"

Xander kept laughing. "Oh, this is even better. No, the woman who just left is my *wife*."

And I couldn't help but wonder what it would take to put that look of astonished bewilderment on Saint's face and keep it there.

KAYA

While the decision to accept the proposal made sense to me. It took Gemma a little convincing when I met her at the campus café like everything was in fact normal. Even though things were far from normal, given my casually dressed armed guard at the next table over.

I'd dropped the marriage bomb as soon as she sat down, but her brain was in full does-not-compute mode.

"Explain this to me again like I'm in primary. You're going to do what now?"

I sighed, desperate for her to catch up so I could get a little help processing how I felt about all of this. "I'm going to get married, Gemma."

"The hell you are. What are you *really* doing?"

I took a casual sip of my smoothie as if it was perfectly normal that I'd be telling my best mate about my impending nuptials at school.

"I'm getting married to Jasper Saint."

Gemma laughed, throwing her head back. "Oh, come on. The billionaire? You're marrying him? But you broke into All Saints. Is this some sort of *I caught you, now you have to marry me before I expose you* situations like in my Mafia romance novels?"

"I'm serious. And no he's not forcing me. He's offering me his name as protection. Don't be so dramatic. Whoever is after me, whatever I did, they are going to have a hell of a time getting past all the security. The Saints are powerful. It would be like picking a fight with Goliath."

Gemma was silent for a minute. "Hmmm. Actually, it does sort of make sense."

I frowned at that. "What do you mean, 'It makes sense?' Has everyone around me lost their mind? I expected you to be all, 'This is insane. Come stay with me. I'll smuggle you out of the country.' But you're saying marrying a flipping billionaire I met two days ago makes sense?"

She shrugged as she sucked on her smoothie. "All I'm saying is that it totally makes sense. Is it crazy? Yes. But at the end of the day, he's filthy bloody rich. If anyone fucks with you, they fuck with him. They could easily disappear a university student. I mean, a lovelorn Andrew and I would miss you and be really fucking pissed you were gone. But he'll have the power and juice to turn over every stone looking for you. It's actually the perfect level of crazy ideas, but only if you go splashy and make it public."

"Oh God, you sound like him."

"Why? What did he say?"

I rubbed my temple, trying to force myself to calm down. I would not have a panic attack in the café with my fellow students watching.

"He just said that we're going to have to announce it publicly on television. That way, it will get whoever's coming after me to back off. At least for the time being that should work."

"I mean, look, I'm all for practicality, I am, but sometimes you need the fantastical."

"I am spinning, Gems. Spinning. A week ago, I was in classes and life was normal. But now everything is flipped upside down."

"Listen." She had her best friend voice on, the one where she was going to fix everything. "Your name is going to be Saint. Or at the very least, your fiancé's name will be Saint. The university will make you any accommodation you need, and I'm pretty sure that he will make sure that you're covered and protected."

"But the center... my life."

"Well, your life has to be on hold for the time being. Although, the other upside to all of this is he can help you find your mum."

"That's part of our deal. I just... I'm not sure how much to trust him. With my safety yes, but... It just feels like Mum should be my thing."

"Honey, asking for help is not a bad thing. I promise."

That made my stomach turn. Because Saint finding everything out, including how I'd lived before, always on the run, would make me more vulnerable to him. And while I had told him a little bit, he didn't know the whole picture. I'd never let anyone in that far, not even Gemma. "Oh God, Gems, this is... I don't like being backed into a corner."

"You aren't being backed into a corner. This is a lifeline."

"Easy for you to say. It feels like I'm a sitting duck."

"Maybe, but now you're a sitting duck with a hell of a lot of protection surrounding you."

"Right. I suppose I should be grateful for that."

"Yes. In the meantime, when I went to class the other day, Andrew asked about you."

I groaned. "Right. I forgot about all that mess with him wanting to ask me out. How is he now?"

"Oh, he's not good. Pining over you like a rejected puppy dog. He wants to know why you haven't been around the last couple of days. He even popped by my place. I think he assumed you'd be with me after the thing with your flat. I said that you just have a lot going on personally. He looked a little sad that he wasn't in the know, but it's probably better that way."

"Yeah, absolutely better that way. He's too much to handle on top of everything else."

Except an incoming text told me I'd be dealing with him sooner rather than later.

Andrew: *We need to talk.*

CHAPTER 14
SAINT

"SO JUST LIKE THAT, SHE AGREED?"

I winced at my brother's question.

Trevor was popping wheelies in his chair which he knew irritated the fuck out of me. And I resisted the urge to stop him from doing it. He did it to annoy me, but I assumed it was fun. I couldn't turn off the gene that made me want to look after him. Didn't matter that he was a grown man.

"She didn't quite *agree*, but it's happening."

Adrianna kicked off her shoes and hopped off my desk. She treated my office as if it was her sitting room. I tried to ignore them both as I poured myself a sparkling water. I really wanted scotch, but if I was going to need to iron out my relationship with Kaya later this afternoon and what it meant to All Saints, then I was going to need all my wits about me. "What do you mean she didn't quite agree? Is there anything you won't do to keep the old man away from us?"

"Hardy har," I said with a rolled eye. "You're hilarious. Honestly. Remind me again why I bend over backward trying to save you two?"

Trevor smirked. "No one asked to be saved."

I pointed at my sister. "She did. *She* asked to be saved."

Trevor shrugged. "It's not my fault that you can't resist her. It's that twin bond and all."

"So who's the woman?" Adrianna asked as she tucked her feet under her on my soft gray leather couch. I supposed with the sunshine streaming through the floor-to-ceiling glass, my office did resemble a sitting room.

"Someone who needs help. It's an advantageous relationship."

Adrianna's sharp gaze focused in on me with all the intensity of a hawk suddenly aware of a delicious morsel. "You didn't tell her, did you?"

Fuck.

I rocked back on my feet as I slipped my hands into my pockets. "No. I didn't."

Trevor chuckled and spun his wheelchair around. "Oh my God. You're an idiot."

Adrianna shook her head. "Oh, this is such bollocks. She's going to leave. And we don't have time to find someone else."

"We have plenty of time. She's not going to leave. She needs my help. You worry too much."

My sister threw up her hands. "Except she doesn't know *she's* helping *you*. What is wrong with men? Do you people grow up missing that gene that makes all these little connections?"

"It's fine. Besides, she has a lot on her plate. The less she has to think about this, the better. Also, work made it pretty clear. They don't want her read in."

Trevor just kept laughing. My sister though, she looked furious. "One of these days, you're going to twist yourself into a pretzel trying to be everything for Rogues and everything for us and everything for the board members. You will need to make a choice about what you want and what you need to be. But it's like you've already made your mind up."

"I have. I'm getting fake married to her. Don't worry. While I buy us some time with the engagement, you two are going to be finding a way out of this. There's no way we're handing this company back to Dad."

———

KAYA

After the café with Gemma, I'd stopped by the center to do my leave paperwork which had taken a couple of hours. By the time Saint's car took me back to the original scene of my B&E, it was late afternoon. All Saints Technologies.

I supposed I should be happy I was walking in the front doors this time. The driver came and opened the door for me, and I thanked him as I smoothed my hands down my skirt. Simple but elegant, it was one of the items of clothing the mysterious Maureen had picked up for me. A designer label I didn't recognize since, for the most part, I dressed like a student at all times. From the items Maureen had delivered, I was able to pair it together with simple flats and a fun blouse with little pineapples on it. A silky material that made the little ruffled cap sleeves stand out. When I walked into the building, I saw the familiar face of Westin smiling at me.

"There you are," he said with a grin.

"What are you doing here?"

"Well, that's a fine how do you do, neighbor," he said with a quick flash of a grin, making a dimple peek out. This man was dangerous. Flashing his dimples left and right. How many women had swooned at him today already? Just here in the lobby there were several women who stopped and stared.

"You should probably stop doing that. Someone is going to walk into a glass door or something."

Westin's brow puckered. "What?"

"The smiling dimple thingy. It's unnecessary with me."

He chuckled low then whispered conspiratorially, "What

smiling dimple thing?"

I gestured in the vague vicinity of his face. "That one. What are you doing here?"

"I think Saint told you I work security. Those men following you all day work with me."

I blinked slowly. "He said that, but you're too young to be doing something so dangerous."

He shrugged. "Let's just say I am precocious. Right now, it's just me with a few friends, but lucky for you, I live down the hall. I told Saint I'd meet you here today."

"Right. So, you're my armored tank?"

He gave me a wink and a nod. "Walk softly and carry a big stick. I'm your big stick."

If only his charms worked like Saint's did.

He led me to security, where a grizzled, elderly Black man gave me a badge and a smile that made his dark eyes crease at the corners, reminding me of my own grandfather.

"Guess this is it. I'm officially part of the family now?"

"Saint has a thing about people in trouble. He's willing to do everything in his power to protect you. That's who he is."

"It's not exactly the vision I had of a billionaire."

Westin choked. "Yeah well, he's not your typical Bruce Wayne, but close enough in this situation."

"That's exactly what I was picturing. Well, without the bat costume anyway."

Westin winked at me as he led me to the elevators. "Well, maybe ask him if he's into kinky shit. He might wear one for you."

My face flamed, and Westin just chuckled as he pressed the button for the twentieth floor. "Do you think he's crazy for doing all this ,Westin?"

"Well, it's not my job to have an opinion. It is my job to make sure you stay safe."

A young red head at reception sent a dazzling smile to Westin and then she sent me a far less cheery one. "Can I help you?"

"Um, yes, I'm here to see Maureen Flanaghan."

The girl frowned again. "And who should I say is calling?"

I'd been waiting for this question. I knew there was a specific format that Saint wanted me to follow. Something he wanted me to say to antagonize the gossip mongers and get them talking immediately. I took a deep breath, lifted my chin, smiled at the girl, and said, "I'm Kaya Reynolds. I'm Jasper Saint's fiancée."

Interestingly enough, nobody blinked. Had he already told people? Was it common knowledge and now I'd walked in here and everybody was going to be scrutinizing me?

But no one looked at me. No one paid me any mind as I was going to the elevator and escorted upstairs.

It was interesting seeing the glass and chrome of All Saints in the broad light of day. Well, the gray of day. Light drizzle did its best to annoy the cement and glass exterior of the building. It wasn't even real rain. It was somewhere between a mist and actual condensation.

Just enough to make my hair curl and make it look frizzy, but not enough to actually make all of it wet. Annoying.

In the elevator, the security guard who had escorted me hulked next to me like a giant. He looked Scottish. I don't even know why I said Scottish because he hadn't really spoken. His name was Thomas, and he had been called over to show me the way. But he looked like he would have a brogue. And if he had a full beard, I could picture him in a kilt.

I was shown to the twentieth floor, and he used a special passkey to make the back doors of the elevator open. I stumbled with surprise and turned to find myself across from the offices of Jasper Saint.

"Oh, okay. Thank you."

He gave me a terse nod and waited for me to exit. When I walked in, a pleasant looking brunette assistant waved me in. "You must be Kaya Reynolds."

"Yes. That's me."

"Everyone's in here waiting for you."

I blinked slowly. "Everyone?"

"Yes, for the meeting."

I racked my brain. Had Jasper said it was a meeting? He just said come by the office. There's paperwork to sign. He hadn't said anything about a meeting.

My shoulders immediately stiffened as I prepared myself to be ambushed.

The assistant knocked on the door, and when Jasper's voice rang out, she opened it and showed me the way in.

Jasper was in there with two women and a man in a wheel-chair. The man in the wheelchair looked shockingly like Jasper. Same shit-eating grin. Not that Jasper spent a lot of time grinning at me, but I recognized it. I'd seen it the night of the auction. His eyes were more of a sea green, and his gaze perused me apprecia-tively. "Oh, well done, brother."

I smiled bemusedly at him. "Well, if I'm going to be assessed, I'd like to know who by."

The bloke threw his head back and laughed, clapping. "Oh, I do like her." He turned his attention to me. "I'm Trevor. Jasper's better-looking younger brother."

I went over and shook his hand, which was firm and strong. "Hi, I'm Kaya."

"I know."

"I guess the news is out."

He grinned. "I am delighted to have a new sister. This will be entertaining as hell."

I lifted my brow, unsure of what he meant by that.

One of the women stood. She was tall and willowy and stun-ning with a set of eyes that matched Jasper's. Her skin was that kind of alabaster tone that you read about in romance novels, the ones without any melanin in them. It was smooth and clear. And she had fine features. She was beautiful. But she didn't look much like Jasper except for the eyes. It was all topped with a widows peak and inky jet black hair that fell in that just blown out look over her shoulders. "I'm Adrianna. I'm Jasper's twin sister."

I lifted my brows. "Twins?"

"Oh yes, twins. Keep that in mind for any extracurricular activities. The twin bond is a real thing. You and I are going to get very close indeed."

Jasper groaned. "Oh, for fuck's sake, Adrianna. Stop fucking with her."

Adrianna laughed and then came over and wrapped me in a hug. "Sorry. I am fucking with you. Welcome to the family."

"Oh, okay."

She grinned. And I could see it then. It was in her smile. When she smiled, she looked like him.

And then there was another woman. She had a no-nonsense look about her. Her suit was just this side of edgy. Maybe a little too sexy. The dress was cut with hints of cutouts, but the cutouts were different colors. It was excellently tailored to her silhouette. She was about average height, wore emerald green, and she was gorgeous. It brought out the vivid blue of her eyes. Her hair was wild and curling and red, and she had freckles all over every inch of her face and her arms. "Hi, I'm Maureen Flanagan. I am Jasper's right hand, and I will be managing your transition."

When she came over and shook my hand, I took it while trying to appear placid and perfectly content and not at all panicked at the word *transition*. "What do you mean by transition?"

She was acting as if this was a job interview.

Jasper gestured for me to sit on the couch in the center of the room when he strolled over to join me. Trevor was popping wheelies by the window. Adrianna kicked off her shoes and hopped on Jasper's desk. It was a move that looked like she was very used to doing it. Maureen sat at Jasper's desk, and Jasper joined me on the couch. "There are just some things we need to talk about. So as my fiancée, obviously you get the protection that you need."

My heart started beating so fast I couldn't even process the words he was saying. Because this was so much more than he made it out to be. They were talking transitions. The fuck?

"I'm sorry. I don't understand. Don't I just have to like sign papers and a prenup or something? I'm happy to do that, but you're talking about transitions and my role, and I'm not sure what that means."

Adrianna rolled her eyes. "Oh my gosh, Jasper. It's like you didn't fucking tell her."

Jasper winced. "It's not quite so simple."

"What does that mean?" My sister had no plans on making this easy.

"It means that there will be people very interested in our relationship. If reporters approach you, just say no comment. If anyone suddenly befriends you and wants to know every detail of our lives, you just say no comment or you can't talk about it. Keep to old friends. And don't talk about us or the relationship. Don't talk about All Saints. It's all right here in the document."

Maureen stood and walked over carrying what looked like a giant tome. "These are the papers you'll need to sign."

I stared at the thick stack. "You're kidding. I get it. Secrecy is important, but Gemma already knows. She's the only one though. And she's not talking."

Everyone exchanged glances. But Maureen simply nodded. "In that case, then this is the one to sign. It allows for a confidant. The rest is mostly prenup. Just outlining that everyone walks out with what they came in with."

"Fine. I don't want your money. I'll sign whatever."

He frowned. "You'll want a solicitor to look over it."

"No, I don't care."

Maureen's brows popped, and she placed her freckled hand on mine. "Love, he's right. To protect you, you want to make sure—"

I shook my head and interrupted her. "I'm sorry. Honestly, I know you probably planned a whole spiel. But I don't want anything from him. I only agreed to marry him because I'm desperate. I don't want his money. I don't want any of this. Your company's safe from me."

Adrianna and Trevor exchange glances with Jasper.

Trevor grinned at me, and Adrianna had her head cocked as if assessing me anew. Finally his sister spoke. "I know I said I liked you before. I think I'm half in love with you now. But still you should probably really read the contract."

"What does it say in here?"

Jasper looked at me. "It is a prenup. It outlines what is All Saints property, how press will be handled, what charities we contribute to, what charities we *don't* contribute to, and the status of your relationships."

My brow furrowed. "Relationships?"

"Yes. Obviously since this isn't real, you'll want to... or maybe you won't want to... but it covers how you conduct your relationships. You know, dating and such."

When he said the word *dating*, it came out through gritted teeth. And I blinked rapidly. "What? I don't want to date anyone. And how long do you think this is going to be for? This is only temporary. Right?"

The siblings again exchanged a glance. But none of them said anything.

Maureen started talking again. "So I'll handle the press inquiries. You'll have to make an announcement, obviously. I'll have a speech writer prepare some remarks. It'll be something very simple. How excited you are to be part of the Saint family. You know, the basics. And then we'll get you going with a wardrobe. Anything gifted to you is yours to keep, of course, so choose wisely."

Again, lots of talking.

Everyone acted as if this was completely normal. But I just stared at Jasper. When his gaze met mine, we locked in, and I couldn't even hear Maureen as she talked and prattled on about clauses for exit, et cetera, et cetera, et cetera. I put up a hand. "I'm so sorry to interrupt again. Honestly, I am. Except why all of this? Why can't we just say, 'hey we're engaged,' act madly in love, and I live with you. So it's fine. And then we'll quietly break up in a couple of months when these idiots stop chasing me."

Adrianna clapped. "Oh my God. I'm keeping her. Yes, I like you very much. And while it would make sense to do that, and be very practical, we are Saints. And we make things far too complicated for our own good. And you'll be a breath of fresh air. But in the meantime, basically, Saint here gives you security and treats you like his wife. But then he is hands off. You see my younger brother isn't so good with relationships anyway."

I blinked in surprise. "I'm sure he does just fine. I'm not worried. I'm ready to sign when you are."

"Okay, fine. That's enough grilling you two. Leave my fiancée alone," Saint growled.

Adrianna grinned. "See, Jasper, was that so hard? She's ready to sign. Let's get the show on the road. Because I'm sure you two have other things you want to do. Whatever platonic things people do in that penthouse of yours."

Heat crept up my neck. Because while Jasper Saint hadn't touched me, not since the night of the auction, it didn't mean I hadn't fantasized about touching *him*. Which now was obviously never going to happen. But I said nothing.

"Like I said, I will sign on the dotted line. Married before twenty-one. Lucky me."

Saint's brows popped. "Your birthday is coming?"

"Yeah. In two weeks."

"Noted. You're sure you want to do this?"

Was I sure? Hell no. But I needed this. "I'm sure."

So when Maureen came over and presented me with the tablet for signatures, I took a deep breath and signed. Whatever feelings I was currently feeling for Jasper were going to be ignored. I could do it. No way in hell was I ever, ever acting on it.

CHAPTER 15
KAYA

IN THE LAST FORTY-EIGHT HOURS, I had officially become a crazy person. That was literally the only explanation for this shit that was about to take place right now.

Two weeks ago I was a normal girl, catching the bus, spending too much money on wine, and nursing an unhealthy addiction to *Love Island*. But now I was leaving campus, coming down the stone stairs of uni with my driver waiting and my capable armed guard flanking me.

Before I even made it down the stairs, one of the back doors of the car opened and out stepped my future husband, looking every bit the billionaire playboy. He wore a suit complete with vest, crisp white shirt, and a green-striped tie that brought out his eyes. He looked good enough to eat.

Which was a problem because he was *not* on the menu. I was so blown away by his presence that I couldn't help but hesitate just for a moment. He watched me with a smirk on his face, but the moment I paused he frowned and stood to full attention. The look in his gaze said it all.

If I ran, he would hunt me down. I could see it in the way his body weight shifted forward to the balls of his feet. There was no running from him. Which was an insane thought anyway. Why would I run? He was the only thing keeping me safe right now.

And somehow tomorrow night, I had to go on stage in front of a room full of people I didn't know from Adam and proclaim that he was my fiancé. Not just any fiancé off the street. Billionaire, Jasper Saint. I was losing my mind. How had this become my life?

"Are you okay?" Jasper's gaze roamed over me with concern as I approached.

I gave him a nod, and he opened the door to let me in to the back seat. When he joined me inside I took a deep breath. "So tomorrow's the big announcement."

"That's the plan. I promise it'll be mostly painless, so try not to look like I'm walking you to the guillotine, okay?"

"Said the lion to the mouse," I whispered.

He cleared his throat and pulled something out of his pocket. "We should take care of one detail though."

My gaze fell to the pale blue ring box in his hand, and my heart squeezed. The seat in the back of the Tesla suddenly felt too small.

His gaze lifted to mine. "You don't have to panic."

"Who's panicked?" I said in a high-pitched voice with rapid glances between Saint's face and the box. "I'm not panicked."

He chuckled low. "You look panicked, Sprite. And when I asked you before, I should have led with this."

"Oh, look at you, being all chivalrous," I said, still not taking my eyes off that blasted box. "Are you sure we have to make a big announcement? Maybe we can make it quietly."

He shrugged. "It's convenient and expeditious. The sooner we can get the Saint name connected to you, the better off you will be in the long run. Speaking of your security, how did things work out with Rourke's team today?"

"It was fine. He just walked around the building a lot and put two other men on me for my afternoon classes."

"He was supposed to give me a report today."

I nodded. "Yeah, an assessment of the security measures or something?"

"Something like that. He didn't bother you or anything like that, did he?"

I looked into his green eyes, trying to assess what Saint was hinting at, and he frowned back at me as I said suspiciously, "No, was he supposed to? Was it part of his job description to peeve me off?"

"No. I just know Rourke can be annoying sometimes."

"He was a perfect gentleman."

Saint's brow furrowed even more.

"Honestly, there's no need for all this frowning at me. I mean, he kept flashing that fucking dimple of his everywhere, and it legitimately made all the ladies' knickers melt in the entire building. Other than that, no problems."

He lifted a brow. "His smile melts knickers, does it?"

There was a kind of edge to his voice, and I studied him. That brief desire I'd seen in his eyes was back, and I wanted to melt under that look. Longing bubbled up inside me with the thought he might be jealous over someone like me.

He made it clear that's not what this is.

Still, with a tease in my voice, I asked, "I thought Westin was your friend?"

"He is. But Rourke is too good-looking for his own damned good."

I lifted my brows in shock at his statement. "Is this jealousy, Jasper? That's a little out of place in this relationship, don't you think?"

That's it, pretend. He'll never notice your drooling that way.

He chuckled and rolled his eyes. "Just wanted to make sure he treated you well. If he was a right gentleman all day, then there's no problem."

I grinned at him. "Right gentleman, of course. No really, he was great. I'm just amused, at your attitude."

"Everything will be fine as long as *you* don't start noticing Rourke and his smile, Sprite. We're getting married after all."

I had to laugh at that. "You're funny when you are a little green with jealousy, Mr. Saint." I changed the subject. "So who will I be meeting at the engagement party?"

"Well, you've met Adrianna and Trevor already."

And I liked them immensely. "Will I meet your mum?"

His jaw went tight. "Mum's gone."

Shit. Way to step on that landmine. "I'm so sorry."

His brows lifted. "Oh, she's not dead. She just fucked off to live with a shaman in Bali. We see her at Christmastime."

I blinked slowly as the relief washed through me. "Really? From your reaction, I honestly thought she was gone, Jasper."

He grinned and winked. "Sorry. She's fine. Just can't stand to be on the same continent as my father."

"Will he be there?"

"Like a bad penny."

"But he doesn't know this is fake between us?" I asked.

He shook his head vehemently. "No, and he can never know. He's not to be trusted with that information. Ever."

I dragged in a breath. Okay then. Don't tell dear old Dad."

"To be safe, assume you can't tell anyone who was not in the room with us yesterday afternoon. You should bring your friend to the event. The one I hear you talking on the phone to. It would probably be nice to see a friendly face."

"Okay. I think I can manage that."

"Relax. For tonight, you just have to look adoring, I suppose."

"Right, adoring. Well, tell me something I should keep in mind while I think adoring thoughts about you."

He chuckled, and the warmth of it slipped in my veins. I liked hearing him laugh, and being the one to make him laugh was even better. "Well, I did save you from potential kidnappers, so, you know..."

I barked out a loud laugh at the cute way he shrugged out his statement. "Fine, you did manage to save me from... Well, a very unpleasant situation."

"You mean that's not enough to make you adore me? What's a bloke have to do nowadays?"

I rolled my eyes, unable to stop smiling at his questions. "I mean, you're not bad. You do knight in shining armor well enough."

"Not bad? Not bad?" He asked, his voice teasing. He looked so young when he teased me.

He looked down at the blue box in his hands. "Hopefully this cements me in the knight-in-shining-armor category." He held up the ring box and I sucked in a breath, getting nervous and flustered all over again.

I knew this was just part of the charade. Wasn't it normal for a ring to be involved in an engagement? "So, Mr. Saint, do all billionaires just have an engagement ring on standby?"

He shook his head, losing some of that jovial spirit he'd had a moment ago. "No, actually I didn't."

He opened the box, and inside sat the most gorgeous princess cut diamond, but not so big as to be ostentatious. It was set in a white gold band with the tiniest diamonds all around it.

"Oh wow, Jasper. It's beautiful."

"I'm glad you like it. Hope it's not too small or too big. I went with two carats. I wasn't sure of your style or anything, but when I popped into the jewelers and saw this, I don't know... It looked like you."

My eyes went wide. Had he really taken the time? "You picked this out yourself?"

"Well, if you want something done right, you might as well do it yourself."

I gazed at the delicate ring. "Right. I'll remember that."

Holding my hand, he slid the ring on my finger ever so gently. I couldn't believe it fit so well as it sparkled up at me. We both just gazed down at the ring until he quietly said, "Perfect fit."

I stared down at my new ring. I knew this wasn't real. I knew that this was pretend. I even understood *why* we were pretending. But there was that little part of my heart that couldn't help but believe in this fairy tale. Who knew I was an inner romantic? "It's really a shame that men don't get rings too. Not engagement ones anyway."

He shrugged. "I've never been one for flash anyway. One ring is enough," he said as he held up his left hand, showing off the signet ring there.

I leaned in closer. "That's so interesting. My mom had one like that. Hers had some kind of bird on it though. Yours is a cross."

He stared at me long and hard for a moment but then shook his head as if a trance was broken. "Are you ready to do this? To tell the whole world that you're my fiancé?"

Looking back up at him with all the confidence I could muster, "Absolutely. Tomorrow night we'll dazzle the world."

Except, when I slid my hand into his, the prickle of awareness up my arm wasn't about being dazzled. It was a plain, clear, vibrant warning that I was in too deep.

———

SAINT

The nightmare was the same. Always the same. Me somewhere dark. Hot, exhausted, covered in mortar shells and dirt and dust. Being rushed to the med bay to be checked out because I'd been knocked out by an explosion. Coming to and getting the phone call. Elise was dead.

As usual it woke me with a start. I was sweating, my T-shirt drenched. I dragged the sheets off me and sat up in the bed. I'd been having the dream more frequently, especially when I was exhausted and not paying enough attention to my health. And there had been a lot of that lately.

But my brain was registering something different this time. It wasn't until I pushed out of bed, padded over to the bureau, and pulled out a new T-shirt and boxers when I realized that in the dream, I hadn't gotten a call about Elise. I had gotten a call about Kaya.

"Motherfucker."

You want to keep her.

No. I do not want to keep her. This whole bloody arrangement was temporary. This was just anxiety. It would pass.

I tugged open my bedroom door and padded down toward the kitchen.

It was only natural that I hesitated at her door. I didn't knock. Just a mere silent pause.

That was all.

Sure, you tell yourself that.

Okay fine, so I had stopped for a moment. To what? See if she was awake?

No. I wasn't doing that. I had to keep a barrier between the two of us. I had a job to do, and the job was to protect her. That was all. Nothing else.

In the kitchen I grabbed a glass of water and leaned my forehead against the upper counters as I tried to force deep calming breaths. My subconscious, however, was having a bloody field day. Happy to point out that when I had an Elise nightmare, I was always able to go straight back to bed. When I had an Elise nightmare, I didn't have the shakes or the sweats and I was able to shake it right away. But this time it felt real. The cramp around my heart, the pain in my gut, it was all real. My brain really thought I'd lost her. And I was... devastated.

I scrubbed a hand down my face and drained the glass of water, and when I turned, I gasped and stumbled back, the counter digging into my ass. "Jesus fucking Christ. What the fuck are you doing?"

Kaya's eyes were wide. "I thought I heard something outside my door, and I saw the light so I—"

I forced several quick sharp breaths. "Sorry. I just needed water."

She was standing too damn close, and she smelled so sweet, tempting me into the things I knew I should not do.

"Are you sure you're okay?"

I licked my bottom lip, watching her watching me. And suddenly, I could not remember anything about why it was so important that I not fucking touch her. There was a reason, but it was one I had a hard time remembering because my gaze was focused on her lips and her scent was wrapping around me like a python, refusing to release me.

"Jasper?"

My name on her lips was a whisper and a caress. And when I didn't answer, she tried again.

"Saint?"

I wasn't sure why, but *Saint* sounded somehow more sexual, like she was suddenly more aware of me as a man standing in front of her ready to lose absolute control.

"You should go to bed, Kaya."

"Well, I was in bed, but... Are you okay?"

I tried to say yes. I tried to speak. But that feral, desperate part of me that remembered how she tasted, how she sounded, how she smelled, was taking over, and it was hard to form coherent thought. Whatever the hell I said came out sounding sort of a cross between grunt and growl. "I said go to bed."

"What's wrong with you?"

She wanted to fucking know what was wrong with me? I stepped forward until there was barely a breath between us, and I loomed over her.

Kaya tilted her head up, glowering up at me and telling me silently she did not appreciate my heavy handedness. Her annoyed frown told me that I was going to get a proper what for.

But instead, her lips parted and I watched as she swallowed hard.

"I feel like I told you to do something, and I need you to do it," I growled.

"Why are you being like this?"

When she didn't budge, I chuckled harshly. "Because I'm trying to be a fucking gentleman. And you being this close right now is making it fucking impossible. Can't you feel how impossible you're making it?"

Her eyes went wide and flickered from my face to my rather impressive erection that was now pressing into her.

She didn't move.

She just stared. Which of course made it worse because then my fucking cock was all manner of insistent.

Inside. Her. Now. The fuck are you waiting for? She wants to lick me. Suck me.

I wanted to be buried so far up her cunt that our bodies fused. But oh no. Fucking no. I'd given my word. And she had no idea she was helping me with our arrangement, and even I wasn't that much of a prick. "Kaya, for fuck's sake, I'm fucking begging you. Turn around and go to bed."

But Kaya kept staring down at my cock and inhaled a deep breath, which made her rub up against me.

With a groan my hands reached up to her hips and tightened. "Kaya, I already told you. Fucking go to bed." I knew I was done for. Before this whole mess was over, Kaya Reynolds was going to own my soul. But that sure as fuck didn't mean I wasn't going to stop fighting it.

She dragged in another deep breath, forcing her to move against my erection.

I groaned. "What the fuck are you doing, Kaya?"

Finally, her head jerked up. Her eyes were wide, and she blinked rapidly before taking a harsh step back. "Oh fuck. I'm going to bed."

"Yes, you are. Run along, little Sprite."

She stared at me for a long hard moment and then did as she was told for once. I wished I could say that I stopped us, that I saved us. But the truth was that running was the smartest thing she'd done since I met her.

Problem was, now that I'd seen her stare at my cock like she wanted to swallow me all the way down, all I could think about was making her absolutely mine.

CHAPTER 16
SAINT

NEWS TRAVELED FAST, as I had known it would. My father wasted no time barging into my office, probably because he knew there was no way he was going to be able to barge on to the Rogues campus, not without someone having something to say about it.

"You're bloody getting married?"

"Honestly, I don't know why I'm surprised anymore by how quickly the gossip spreads." I had told my staff a million times over that my father no longer sat on the board and was no longer the head of All Saints Technologies, and they *seemed* to listen.

But my father had run this place for two decades, so sometimes it was hard to get them to comply with simple instructions. Things like *don't let him past security* or *don't tell him anything*. The past-security thing needed some working on, obviously, but I was glad he'd gotten the gossip this time.

"What is it you want, Dad?"

"Who the bloody hell are you marrying? You need to have a prenup."

I sat back, steepled my hands, and watched him as he blustered and paced.

"Do you really know this girl? She could be using you for your money."

You mean like Elise?

I bit back that retort which pained me like a twisted knife in the gut. I did not need to watch the man whom she'd preferred over me bluster around, acting as if he'd actually loved her. I'd known him long enough to know that he wasn't capable of love, let alone for Elise. After all, if he was capable of love, how could he have betrayed his oldest son like that?

All while I was away serving queen and country.

"Is there an actual question in there, Father? Or did you just wish to barge in here and complain?"

"Who is she?"

"No one you need to ever meet."

"Where does she come from?"

"Again, none of your business. All you need to know is that I plan on announcing our engagement tonight, at the Wandsworth Benefit Center."

"Wandsworth is one of *my* charities. You would hijack that for your own selfish purposes?"

"Well, it's one of your *legacy* charities, but it's mine now, remember? You are no longer a board member of All Saints Tech."

"Oh yes, son. So you keep reminding me. My point is, who is she? And why does she want into our family? You've made drastic mistakes before."

I pushed to my feet. "No, old man, you made the mistakes. You tried to pawn them off on me as just minor errors in judgment. Remember what you said, Father? '*I made a mistake. It wasn't something I should have done. I'm sorry I had to do that to prove her unworthy of you, son.*' Some made up song and dance." I strode around my desk to stand before him. "Speak the truth. When you promised me to her parents and encouraged us to date and me to propose, you bloody knew her father was in bed with the mob. You knew and you still dragged me into that. Then you doubled down and didn't just bet your son, but the company your father-in-law built. What kind of man does that?"

His face went red as he flustered at my statement. The thing that really got me was that I looked like him. Spitting image. He was all silver now with old age, but we were carbon copies. Every time I looked in the mirror, I saw the man I hated. Which was a real motherfucker.

"You can't mean to go through with this, Jasper. I forbid you doing something so rash! You can't know anything about this woman. I mean, who is she? Where does she come from?"

"We already settled that. *You. Don't. Know. Her.* Given our history, that's perfect news to my ears."

"I know you're still smarting from what happened with Elise. I understand. I hurt you and I deserve your derision for that. The board ousted me after I went off the rails due to her death."

"Not death. Murder. Make sure you use the correct word."

He swallowed hard, his eyes not quite meeting mine. "Have you found him?"

"You see Dad, how this works is that I don't tell you anything about what I do with Rogues. You don't get to ask about Elise's case. And I'm not looking for you to have closure. I'm looking for me so I can move on with my fucking life. A life that you're not part of. And you know, a fiancée that I can almost guarantee will not come close to shagging you."

He frowned. "What you are saying is you have failed to make progress."

"I don't care if you think I haven't made progress. I don't need to answer questions from the man who fucked around with my first fiancée while I was deployed. What I *am* telling you is stay away from my current fiancée. She's not your type. She's too smart for you, a little too aware of bullshit."

He sighed. "Will you ever forgive me?"

I shook my head. "No. No I will not. Is there something else you needed to discuss? Because I have work to do."

I deliberately sat down again, waiting for my words to sink in. *I had work to do, not him.* I couldn't count the number of times he'd dismissed me out of this very office as if I was unimportant, but now I had parroted the words back to him.

"I see."

"You should see. Kaya has a strength of character I've never seen, and I am proud to have her standing next to me in front of everyone tonight. So again, just stay away from her. Otherwise, the thing with you and Elise will become public knowledge. And when it does, those few charities and patronages that you're holding onto will be gone too. You will no longer be one of the most powerful men in Britain. I swear before God."

He sniffed. "You're hurting. I know and understand that. But this girl you want to marry out of the blue *will* be investigated. I won't leave a single stone unturned. If you won't look into her and protect yourself and this company, I will. This is still my family, and I'm still the head of it."

I shook my head. "You're the only one who thinks that. Adrianna and Trevor certainly don't. And well, you know how I feel about you. You'd better behave tonight at the event. If you don't, I will make sure you pay the price."

———

Saint

Later that night at the bar, Lachlan had somehow managed to find me. "You look nervous, mate."

Looking over his shoulder, I asked "Where's Saff?"

King grinned at me. "No, no, no my friend. My wife isn't going to save your arse from the round of questions I have for you."

"Must we do this? Must you interrogate me about this whole thing?"

"Remember that time when I had my head up my arse and couldn't figure things out with Saffron?"

Did I remember? Hell, it was only a couple of months ago. They'd had a rocky start. "Go on then. Say what you have to say."

"I am not going to say anything." He took a sip of his scotch. "Okay, maybe I'm going to say one little thing. When Saff told me this was your plan, I thought you were insane."

"This is insane."

Lock grinned at me. "Okay, good, so you do know that it's insane. Glad I'm not the only one."

"Mate, I know."

"I mean, especially with everything else you have going on. We've got Lohman in custody, and our interrogators haven't gotten shite from him."

"I'm completely aware of that."

"You haven't been back to see him?"

I shook my head. "Nope."

"Because you are now planning this extravagant wedding and long-term marriage?"

"We're not actually going to get married. We just need to take the heat off her. I mean, it's not a terrible plan. Just having a powerful name and making her someone who's not anonymous will make things a lot easier."

"I know what you're driving at. And that way if she's at the company, we've got eyes on her at all times and protection is easy."

"Yeah, I thought it was brilliant."

King rolled his eyes. "Mate, don't get cocky."

I laughed. "She's just a kid. All she wants is her life back."

King's gaze slid over the crowd until it landed on my fiancée with her tanned skin glowing under the lights of the chandelier. Saffron was there too, looking every bit the fashion model, also wearing black, but in a silky material. And then there was Tabatha, wearing bright white and daring the world to spill red wine on her. King said, "I mean, she may be young, but she is definitely no kid and she's not ugly."

"I'm aware she's not ugly. And okay, maybe *kid* is the wrong term. Just a little younger than what I should be dating. But she's got sass and intelligence, mate."

"And she still has no idea how you're benefiting from the arrangement?"

I shook my head. "No. There's no reason for her to. In the meantime, I'm working on trying to figure out exactly what's going on with her. She doesn't trust me, nor should she. But at the very least, I can keep her safe." I could feel the burn of King's gaze on my profile. "Do you have something else to say?"

"Oh no, not me. I don't know anything."

"Just spill it."

"Obviously, unless it's mission protocol, don't tell her who you really are outside of the billionaire leader of All Saints Technologies."

"It's not and I won't. Right now I'm just trying to keep my family from fucking this up."

"Speaking of the old man, what did he have to say about Kaya?"

"Nothing good. Right now, I'm just hoping he lays low and doesn't say anything to piss her off or make her run."

"In that case, you should probably go get her before he catches up to her."

He angled his head toward the west doors, and I could see the old man was making a beeline straight for her. Lock didn't need to tell me twice. I drained the rest of my scotch and marched straight to Kaya.

Saffron saw me approaching and lifted her brows, angling herself just in front of Kaya as if I was coming to hurt her. But no, I was coming to use my body to physically protect her from that bastard.

"Darling?" I reached for Kaya's hand and intertwined our fingers, ignoring the heat of electricity that skipped over me. Kaya's eyes went wide, but she didn't shake me loose. She schooled her expression quickly and replace it with one of adoration.

Pulling her close so only she could hear me, I said, "Prepare yourself for my dear old dad."

When my father approached, Saffron really did protect Kaya this time with her body. "Excuse me, can I help you?"

My father stopped just short of walking straight into Saffron. "What the hell is your problem, girl?"

"Well, first of all, you walked into me, so I think the proper phrasing you're looking for is *I'm so sorry*."

His brows lifted and he turned beet red.

I swallowed a chuckle. Saffron was not the one to fuck with.

Tabatha eyed my father up and down. "Oh, so this is what you're going to look like eventually, Saint. But somehow I don't think you'll be nearly as ugly."

My father whipped around, glowering at her. Tabatha just stood there, her hair pulled up into some kind of swooping side bang thing and a ponytail that had loose curls. She looked elegant but still young. "Just who do you think—"

I stepped forward before he could insult my friends further. "Is there something you want, Dad?"

"Well, I'm here to meet my future daughter-in-law."

Kaya squeezed my hand. "Sir, it's lovely to meet you. I'm Kaya Reynolds."

My father eyed her up and down, and I prayed to God he was not going to say something sexist or racist because with him you never fucking knew.

"So, this is the whore who's after my family's money?"

Kaya lifted her brow. "Well, Jasper, when you mentioned he was a bit of a dick, you weren't kidding."

I grinned at Kaya then. "Darling, meet my father. You never have to speak to him again."

Dad continued to leer at her. "He's already had one engagement and he failed at that. She wanted an improved version, so I had to show her the upgrade. Isn't that right son? And you have never let me forget it."

Kaya just shrugged. "I recognize that says a lot more about you and his former fiancée than it does about Jasper."

All the old man could do was glower at her.

Kaya one. Father zero.

Apparently, my siblings also saw my father barging in.

It took Trevor a little longer to get to us, but Adrianna marched straight for him. "Dad, why don't you leave Jasper and Kaya alone?" She turned to Kaya with a wide smile. "It's lovely to see you again. I'm so sorry I was preoccupied earlier this evening." She took Kaya's hands in both of hers and then leaned in to give her a kiss on the cheek. I could tell Adrianna whispered something to her, but I couldn't hear what it was.

My sister stepped back to make room for Trevor. "And you remember Trevor."

Trevor rolled up, dressed to the nines in his tuxedo, and he reached forward with a hand to take hers. "You have to forgive my father for his rudeness. I think I speak for Adrianna when I say we are thrilled. Jasper could use some happiness."

Kaya gave Trevor a wide smile. "Thank you again for welcoming me into your family. I don't have a lot of family of my own, so this means a lot." She was really playing the part.

I'd been so busy worrying about protecting her from my father that I didn't see how easily and effortlessly she could charm my siblings. Adrianna turned to me and gave me a knowing look that said *oh boy, I love this one*. Trevor wheeled around, giving me a head nod and a wink. I'd be hearing a lot from him later about this. My father, once he saw that my brother and sister were supporting me, didn't bother excusing himself and just marched off.

I turned to my fake fiancée. "Now that the disaster is over, are you ready to announce this thing and let the whole world know that you're mine to protect?"

CHAPTER 17
SAINT

She was tense. I could feel it in the car.

I had driven us for ease and convenience, but it kept me from being able to study her face properly.

"Are you okay?"

"Yeah, I'm fine. It's just—I can't believe we just got on stage and announced our engagement. That was a shit show."

My lips twitched. "Yeah, you could say that. The good news is, it'll give us plenty of press."

"Yes, the whole world knows that I'm your fiancée now. And I'm engaged to someone I barely know."

"It's only temporary. This isn't ideal, obviously."

"Right, obviously," she murmured.

"I'm sorry if my father was difficult to deal with."

She licked her lips, and like a fool, my vision trapped the soft pink tip of her tongue. The pull deep in my groin had me swallowing hard.

"Your father is a real dick."

The laugh that escaped was genuine and quick. "Did he talk to you again?"

"Just once. But Adrianna stepped in and saved the day."

"Yeah, she's good like that."

"I like her and Trevor a lot, actually. They were really nice, considering they don't know me, and well, me being your official marriage of convenience. Except this arrangement doesn't seem all that convenient for you."

"Don't worry about if it's convenient for me or not. For now, all you need to know is that you are protected."

You're lying to her.

Yes, I was lying. But at the end of the day, this was never going to come to fruition. My lawyers were already on it. I was never going to have to marry her. We were just going to have a nice long engagement. One where she'd be safe and I could get my father off my back.

"Why does he hate you so much?"

The question was unexpected. It made me stop and think for a moment. "Well, when Mum was still around, he was a real dick. Kind of like he is now, really. Expert, next level prick, he is. She took my side always. And when it came down to assigning her shares of the company, she gave them to me. I think he thought that she'd give up the fight along with her seat on the board, but instead, she handed them over to me. Or maybe he thought that she would give up her shares to all three of us, not just me. I don't know. Either way, he was less than pleased, and I wasn't even here for all of it. I was deployed, so Adrianna and Trevor had to deal with most of his bullshit, but there were many, many calls when I was stationed with my team. Lots of video calls with the lawyer."

"I'm really sorry. All of this is about greed?"

"Yes, and no. He thinks I forced my mother. But he's the parent and should have acted like one. Instead, he's been trying to mess everything up. It's who he's been my whole life."

"And your mother, she had shares in the company?"

I smiled thinking about it. "Well, it was actually her parents' company in the beginning. My grandfather retired because he wanted to enjoy time with my grandmother. The two of them were madly in love. When Mum married Dad, Dad was the COO. After they were married, he took over as CEO after my grandfather's retirement. He took his seat on the Board and rebranded the company as All Saints Technologies. But then there were problems. He couldn't keep his stick in his pants."

She winced.

"It's all ancient history though. It's fine."

"Well, I mean, ancient history or not, I do need to know about it since I'm going to fictitiously become part of the family, right?"

I slid a glance at her, and I could see that her lips were curled in a small smile. "Yes, fictitiously part of the family."

I pulled into the garage and found my spot right next to the elevators. "Look, all you have to know is you're safe now. No one's going to touch you."

"Are you sure? And why are you doing this again? This isn't your fight."

"Well, you see, there was this beautiful woman. She broke into my office. I chased her. She ran. She's got secrets and she needs help. And I'm categorically incapable of not helping someone. That's why."

She searched my gaze. "I don't believe you, but that's okay. Because I do need your help. And I don't have anywhere to go, so I am accepting this help. You can tell me when you start to trust me. I just want to crash in the meantime."

"Yeah, let's get you upstairs."

Upstairs. The other night, I had dumped her in the guest room. I hadn't had to think about it. But now, we'd told the world we were engaged, and what the fuck did that mean?

It didn't have to mean anything.

Once we were upstairs in the hallway to the flat, she nodded her head down the way toward the Rook's flat. "So what's the deal with him anyway? Is he just going to keep following me around?"

"That's the basic idea."

"And you trust him?"

I ground my teeth. "Yes. Why, is there a problem with him?"

"No. He's funny, charming, really nice. He looks young though. Shouldn't you have like an old security guard that's been here since you were a child or something? Don't all billionaires have one of those?"

I chuckled softly as I led her into the penthouse. "Yes, I did have one of those, actually. He's just too old to do the stuff now."

She rolled her eyes and laughed. "All right, fair enough."

"Is Rourke a problem? I'll replace him if he is." Gabe wouldn't like it, but if he bothered her at all, I would make sure he didn't get a second chance.

She chewed her bottom lip as if she was afraid to ask me something. "There's something I need to go get. Something of my mother's. I might not have access to Connor, and I have no idea where he's gone, but if there are people looking for me, they are probably looking for these papers as well. I'll need to go through them and see if I can find any answers."

My brow furrowed. "What papers?"

"My mother had all these files. I just shoved them in a box that I left at my last foster home. I didn't want to think about them, but they might have a clue as to where my mother is."

I frowned. "If you tell me where they are, I'll send someone to retrieve them."

"No, my foster mother doesn't like strangers, and she'd roll the fucking door closed before they could even get a hold of them. I need to go myself."

"I don't like it."

"Trust me, I don't like it either, but I don't really have a choice. If I want to find my mother, I need those papers. So we're going to have to figure out a way to deal with that."

CHAPTER 18
KAYA

I DOUBLE-CHECKED my camera bag again. There was nothing worse than being out in the wild, when you felt prepared, you looked good, you were ready to roll, and then you didn't have a lens you needed.

When I'd scrubbed my apartment I grabbed a few pairs of clothes and my camera bag. So I had most of the things I needed. I did have some storage at school, which had been helpful to store the majority of my lenses, and I'd collected those after my meeting with Xander.

Saint came out of the main bedroom, barefoot and dressed casually. Had I ever seen him in jeans and a plain white T-shirt?

There was something so appealing about it. He looked good. Good enough to eat. Jesus. Why on earth did I ever agree to stay with him again? I didn't talk to men as good-looking as he was. Never. Ever. On purpose. Mostly because people tended to look at them and I was trying to be inconspicuous.

But Saint had become the man I could no longer avoid. I'd tried ever since our big announcement two days ago. I kept to myself. I'd done a lot of schoolwork because, let's face it, I had needed to catch up after all the excitement. But I had been able to mostly stay out of his way and I'd been in the library a lot.

All with an armed escort. But after forty-eight hours, he'd caught me off guard. "Where the hell do you think you're going?"

I lifted a brow. "Good morning to you too. Are you always grouchy or do you just need coffee?"

He sighed. "Sorry. Let's try that again. Good morning. Where are you off to? I thought we'd spend the day together."

I lifted my brow. "Why?"

"You know, things that couples do. Publicly so we're seen."

Of course, publicly. This wasn't about spending any time with me at all.

"I need to shoot today."

"Shoot?"

"I'm a photo journalism major, remember? Surely the giant camera bag has not escaped your attention. And I know you've probably had your men check me out."

He grinned at that. "I did know you were a photojournalism major. I just guess I don't really know what that means."

"You know, people that go to interesting places and report on things. I like to write, and I like to capture stories. Seemed like a good fit. Besides, that way I guess I can be somewhat anonymous."

He studied me carefully. "It's always about staying anonymous, isn't it?"

"Usually, yeah. Anyway, I need to get some shots for this assignment for Xander. You met him. He's a giant pain in the ass."

"I have some of his photos. Maybe you saw the one in my office?"

"Oh, I saw it. He's exceptional. But then of course he'd be the first one to tell you that."

Saint grinned at that. "He's a character. I like him."

"You haven't even seen just how much of a character he can be. But the one side that we all try to avoid is his bad side. I have a critique coming up, so I need to go shoot."

"Okay, I'm coming with."

I laughed. "Why? I'll have security. I'm not going to ditch them or anything."

"Like I said, it's important we be seen together and also, I'm curious. About you, what you do, how you do it. Do you mind?"

Did I mind? How the hell was I supposed to answer that?

For starters Saint was... well, Saint. I found it easier to refer to him in my brain as Saint because when I referred to him as Jasper, it somehow felt intimate. And that was worrying. So I told myself to call him Saint. But the other thing was, even in his casual attire, he still looked like something out of a Calvin Klein advert.

Maybe Levi's. Honestly, it was distracting. People looked when you were walking with someone like him. Stubble dusted his jaw. His hair looked like he'd only just raked his hand through it with a little bit of gel. He looked disheveled and sexy and like he was going to toss somebody in bed and spend a very thorough lazy day making sure that they were completely boneless.

"You would hate it. It's just boring walking around, you know. And I've got security. You don't have to worry. I'm not going to do anything dumb. We told the whole world that I'm your fiancée, so I won't do anything stupid like making out with any hot blokes, all right? You don't have to babysit me."

His brow furrowed, and he shoved his hands in his pockets as he rocked back and forth and gave me a sheepish smile. "Honestly, I just wanted to get to know you better. For all intents and purposes, we are flat mates now, and it's my first day off in a while. I thought it would be... nice."

Oh, fuck me. He was trying to be nice. "Ah fuck, I'm sorry. I just don't want you to feel obligated. You've already done so much."

"It's no big deal if you would rather be by yourself."

"No, no, of course not. I'm happy for the company, honestly." I rushed to add, "Please, join me. Okay?"

"If you're sure."

"Yeah. It's just an assignment to capture joy in the city, and since the sun is actually out, I can capture joy in any park."

"Do I have time for coffee?

"I'm losing light. We'll grab coffee on the way."

"Oh Lord. You do drive a hard bargain."

Saint, as it turned out, was true to his word. As we walked and talked, exploring South Bank and then heading into central London with our massive bodyguards in tow, he chatted with me easily. Well, more easily after he had coffee.

We walked around Covent Garden and Soho acting goofy, playing around.

That's when I realized that Saint was really only a few years older than I was. Between his bespoke suits and his determination to fix everything for everyone, he always seemed older. But today he was practically boyish. Kind of a dick at times, arrogant, bossy certainly, but there was an inherent joyfulness about him.

When I finished shooting, we packed up my camera bag, and he handed it to one of the guys to take back to the car.

When my hands were free, he took one of mine in his and pulled me along. "Come on. We're off to the cafe."

We found this little tucked-away nook in the middle of Covent Garden, and I was shocked to find that it wasn't overrun by pedestrians and tourists.

When we sat down, he winked at me. "You are about to have the best scone of your life."

"Oh, I doubt that."

"No. It's vegan and I'm—"

I held up a hand. "Stop it right now. You are ruining this scone for me."

"No. Trust me."

"I don't know, Saint."

"Seriously, trust me. It's banana oat. It's like a scone and a banana muffin combined."

I leaned forward. "Okay, tell me more."

He laughed. "You just have to have it for yourself."

It seemed so normal to have a scone and tea on Sunday mid-morning while I strolled around with my boyfriend.

Except, he wasn't my boyfriend, was he?

He's your fake fiancé. Whatever.

When he leaned over across the wrought iron table outside the cafe and cupped my face, I stilled, the shock of it making my stomach flip. "Hold still. You've got crumbs all over you."

And when he was done, he quickly but gently dusted a finger over my lips.

"There, all set."

"Thanks."

His gaze focused on my lips. God, why did he have to look at me like that? Like I was good enough to eat. This was dangerous territory, and we were playing with fire. And since that was the case, he should leave me the hell alone. Because I was weak. I think we'd already established that.

His gaze flickered away and back again. And then he did the one thing I did not expect. He leaned forward and kissed me.

———

SAINT

Rookie mistake.

I should have just kissed her on the cheek. Anything other than putting my lips to hers and getting that electric shock once again. She tasted of strawberries and cream which was the jam and the clotted cream and herself. Since the kiss was for the paparazzo I saw lurking in the shop across the way from us, I didn't dare deepen it. When I pulled back, Kaya's eyes opened slowly and I could see the confusion in them.

I angled my head to the right. "We've got a paparazzo there. That'll make for a beautiful photo."

And I swear to God. I could almost see disappointment on her face. No, it was something else. She looked irritated.

"Next time, before you kiss me, could you warn me that you're going to do it just so I can have the right response and not slap you or something?"

"You would slap me for kissing you?"

That was when her gaze went deadly serious. "Well, I mean, we've both been very clear this is for show only. So if you start making out with me, it's confusing."

I winced. She was hurt. And confused.

You're a twat.

"Come on. Finish your scone." The only option I had was to change the subject. Because she was right. It was confusing for me, too. I had been very clear that we were not doing this. Hell, I was still clear. And I had my orders.

Your orders are stupid.

Stupid or not, they were still my orders, so I was obliged to follow them. I might not always like them, but I had a duty.

What about a duty to me, my dick moaned.

The fucker didn't get a say.

"Sorry. We'll have to do a few of these. Go out, have dinner, look the part."

She took a deep breath and sat back, a small frown creasing the center of her forehead.

"What is it?"

" I thought we were actually getting to know each other here. Becoming friends, you know, since you are protecting me and all that. It would be nice to get along. To be friends. I thought that's what you wanted. And then you tell me that we've got paparazzi watching so you kiss me. I don't like it."

Fuck. I wasn't sure why, but she was mad. Very, very mad.

"Kaya, I'm sorry. I thought that after you signed all the paper-work the other day you understood."

I watched her press her lips together and then take a long, deep breath as if she was looking for just the right thing to say. "Yes. But maybe your sister, Adrianna's right, you know nothing about women, or at the very least this one. When someone says they want to be my friend, want to spend time with me, I expect that to be genuine, not because they're getting something out of it."

Ah fuck. She started to push to her feet, and I reached for her hand. "I'm sorry, Kaya. I didn't communicate that to you very effectively."

"You did not. Hence, my surprise and confusion."

Why the fuck was she confused? "I'm sorry. I should have made it clearer that we needed some exposure, okay? It just seemed like a perfect moment, and I went for it. I won't touch you again."

She sighed. "It's not about the touching. It's about the ineffective communication, you twat."

It was my turn to frown. "Ineffective communication?"

She threw up her hands. "See, your intended thing of the paparazzi catching the perfect picture is about to fail because you're pissing me off. If you look at a woman like you want to kiss her, and then you do kiss her, but then you pull back and tell her, 'Oh, it was all for show,' she's going to be upset about it."

I frowned. "You understood, Kaya. We're not doing this."

"Yes, I understood. But, you blathering idiot, you *kissed* me. So yes, it's confusing."

And then I understood. I'd been signaling it for several days. The want, the need. And let's face it, I wanted her to look. I wanted her to see it.

Kaya was on her feet, already marching toward the other table where the guards were. "I'd like to go home."

Fuck. I ran after her. "Kaya. Kaya! Hold on. I'm sorry. I fucked up."

"Look, Jasper, it's already confusing enough. Let's not make it worse. I get it now. We're friends. Nothing more. Every time you give me that look, I'll know that you don't mean it."

"That's not what I said. Of course, I—"

She was already turning on her heel and stalking away from me.

"What the fuck, Kaya?"

"I'm exhausted. I'd like to get back."

I'd ruined the perfect day, and I needed to catch up to her and make it up before I ruined the day forever. But before I could catch her, my phone rang. "Trevor. Mate, what is it? I'm in the middle of something today."

"Sorry to be a party pooper on your one day off, but we have problems."

"What do you mean?"

"Dad is running around telling anyone who will listen that your newly announced engagement will never last. And that is all the publicity that we're getting out of it so far."

"I'm going to fucking kill him."

CHAPTER 19
KAYA

IT HAD BEEN YEARS. Five to be exact. Five years since the nightmares began. I hadn't had one in a long time, but after the fight with Saint, when I was tense and vulnerable, it happened again. It was always the same, me running after that car as if I could stop the nightmare from happening.

But as I chased after my mother's car, it stopped, screeched, reversed, and came for me. Then I had to run faster and further than I'd ever run in my life. As this car did a doughnut and proceeded to chase after me, I could see my mother in the car, beating on the driver. And all I could do as the car narrowly missed me was scream and cry, like someone weak. I had no tools, no way to protect myself. I could see my mother screaming from the car. "Fight back. Fight back."

As if I knew what to do.

Sure, she'd put me in self-defense classes and martial arts, but there wasn't anything I could do against an enemy like that, against someone who was hell bent on killing me. And so, in my dreamland, as men came for me, chasing, clawing, grabbing at me, I was defenseless. No one could save me, and I was going to die.

And so I did the only thing I could do. I ran. Panting away, my heart feeling like it was going to explode in my chest. I screamed as loudly as I could, begging someone to hear me, begging someone to save me. But nobody came. There was no one coming to save me. I was alone. Completely, unequivocally alone. She had abandoned me.

No, she didn't. You abandoned her. When she needed you, where were you?

My gut clenched. I'd been right here, fighting for my life, fighting to forget, praying for normalcy instead of doing what she taught me. How on earth had I assumed that she had left me behind?

My mother had not walked away from me. How had I not seen this before? For years it had felt like she'd abandoned me. Walked away. Left me alone to survive. But that wasn't true, was it? I'd been the one to abandon her.

Suddenly there were arms on my shoulders, pulling me out of the abyss, arms too strong to fight against, determined to save me. Someone had come. Who?

"Kaya, Kaya, wake up. You're having a night terror. Kaya, listen to me. Follow my voice. You are safe. I have you."

Then his arms wrapped around me, the warmth of him seeping into my whole body, chasing away the chill and the depth of my despair. With a gasp, I woke up, the tentacles of the nightmare still trying to reach me, still trying to pull me under. But the arms around me were too strong, refusing to let me go, demanding that I pay attention and wake up from the nightmare.

Slowly I blinked awake to find Saint, his smell surrounding me everywhere. Smoky sandalwood. It kept me safe from harm. Just like he'd done from the moment I met him.

He pulled back, wiping the slick curls that had escaped my silk bonnet. "Hey, are you okay? You're having one hell of a nightmare."

"I'm sorry. I'm sorry. I didn't mean to wake you."

"Wake me? Are you insane? I've never seen anything like that before. You were thrashing and I couldn't wake you."

I swallowed hard. "I'm okay now."

His fingertips traced my face, and automatically, I leaned in like a fool. Normally, I never let anyone touch me. I didn't like it. It made me feel uncomfortable and hemmed in. People expected things when they touched you. A response, an emotion, things I kept locked away. Things that were safer for me not to feel. Except, with Saint, I did. I leaned into the caress, chasing the warmth of him. Just for a moment, because I knew eventually, he too would expect something, right?

But I wanted more of his touch. I leaned forward, closing the space between us to a mere inch, and I could feel his breath shuddering in and out.

"Kaya, you need to go back to sleep."

We sat still like that for a long time, our gazes searching one another's faces. We were so close that our breaths already mingled, the tense desire swirling around. I couldn't say who moved first.

When he groaned against my lips, I knew it was a bad idea. This kiss was setting the stage for something that I was not ready for. Something that would require trust and letting someone see me.

But I didn't care. All I wanted was more of his scent, more of his arms, more of his safety. For a moment, his hands tightened on my hips hard and he groaned. But just as quickly, the heat that slipped around me was gone, replaced by the cold ache of a chill, and Saint was three feet away, standing above me in boxers with his arms crossed.

"Kaya, it's not a good idea. Especially not when you're chasing off nightmares like that."

A different kind of heat snaked up my body. Embarrassment. Humiliation. "I'm sorry. It won't happen again." Fucking hell. What was wrong with me?

He watched me long and hard, and I could feel the heat of his gaze, but I refused to meet his eyes.

"Do you want to talk about it?"

"No, I don't."

"All right, I'm going back to my room."

I lifted my gaze, catching the glimpse of his bare feet. They were big with a smattering of hair on his ankles that wound around his strong calves and over the expansive muscles on his thighs. I drank him in, taking my snapshot before we would both be on lockdown again.

I stopped at his boxers, and I could see the enormous bulge. Holy fuck.

He cleared his throat. "Go back to sleep, Kaya." And then he turned and was gone.

I knew I'd said that it wouldn't happen again, but I knew without a doubt that before my fake engagement to Jasper Saint was done, I was going to break that promise. And I was going to beg him. Beg him to have me.

———

Saint

I could still feel the burning imprint of her lips on mine.

Fucking hell.

Sure, I'd told her to go to bed, but there was no way I could sleep after that. Besides, it was four in the morning. Perfectly rational time to start working out. When I went back to my room, I leaned against the door as if holding back the driving need to run to her, to feel her desperation and desire mingled with mine.

There was no holding it back. It was like the night at the auction. And now she was here under my roof. Good luck resisting her now.

You should probably have thought of that before you decided to marry her.

Fucking hell.

I marched into my expansive closet. I had some Rogues gear in it and plenty of suits, but at least I had workout gear. I shoved on a pair of shorts and a T-shirt, grabbed some socks and a pair of trainers, and then marched down the hall to my private gym.

The whole time I was trying to shake off the need and desire, my brain tried to latch on her dream. What had she been shouting? 'Fight back. Fight back.'

What the hell had happened to her? Who was she supposed to be fighting back against?

Once I was in the gym and knew I was alone, I shut the door and jumped on the bike. I hit the com unit and dialed the special code on my phone. Gabe answered right away.

"What is it, Saint? What the fuck are you doing awake?"

"I'm off sleep. I never sleep." I'd expected to get an automated response, not actually speak to him. "I'm just calling for an update on Lohman."

"He's still tight lipped, offering nothing. Interrogators can't get through to him. He doesn't care about anything. We're bringing in a specialist, so if you want to take another crack at him, you'll want to do it this week."

I did want another crack at him. The last time hadn't gone well. He'd been the one to get inside my head.

He said you don't even know what you have.

And what did I have? What did *he* know I had?

"Yeah, I'll take another run at him. Not until tomorrow though. I need to get Kaya settled. She had some nightmare and she's on edge. She said she wanted to go and find something of her mother's. I'm not sure what she's talking about."

Gabe was silent for a moment. "Of her mother's?"

"Yeah, I got the impression it was some files. She's looking for her mum, but I don't really understand why the gap. She made it sound like the files aren't readily accessible."

I could hear Gabe's deep sigh. "You do that. We'll handle Lohman."

"No, I need to talk to him."

Gabe's voice was clipped when he spoke again. "Ever since you started this mission, you haven't listened when I've given you a direct order. Can you explain to me why that is?"

I frowned. Gabe and I had no problems with each other. It wasn't like him and Lock. Lock was tied up with Saff, and Saff and her brother had lots of issues. They fought less now, although there were still times when they really did go after it. I could hear them clear across campus sometimes when they disagreed. But I'd never had a problem with him. I was a soldier at heart. I followed orders all the time, but right now I just had my hackles up.

"Listen to me," Gabe said. "Lohman's under your skin. What you get won't be useful, and that'll make you far less useful to me."

"It was something he said earlier that's bothering me. That I didn't even know what I have. I need to know what he meant by that. And what does Lohman know about me anyway?"

"It could have to do with Elise. It could have something to do with your father. We don't fucking know."

"Well, my father could still do damage."

"Not officially. You are the CEO of All Saints Tech now. That's all that matters."

"It's eating at me, Gabe. I don't even know what I have. What the fuck?"

He sighed. "If you think talking to him again is actually going to get you answers, fine. But while I truly think having an emotional outlet is a good idea, beating on a prisoner, is not ideal. Besides, if I didn't let Saff get on Webster, you can't touch Lohman."

"He's responsible for what happened to Elise."

And then Gabe said the one thing that I didn't want to face. The one thing that I knew deep down but hadn't examined. "No, a bomb was set for retaliation for debts unpaid. Elise got caught in the crossfire. That's what happened. Yes, Lohman is responsible, and yes, he is the monster we chased. But it was your father who got entangled into a bad business deal with Igno. Whatever the hell that side deal was, it nearly got him killed. Now that he's out of All Saints, Igno has no leg up. Don't go inviting trouble."

I didn't want to hear what he had to say. "I'm not inviting trouble. He and I just have to have a conversation. He knows something."

"Fucking hell, Saint, you need to listen. Hands off Connor Lohman. We have our hands full. If you want to question Lohman about why his men were after the girl, then that's great. The problem is, if you speak to him, you show your cards. He'll know the girl is important to you."

"It's not like he can get intel to Igno. We have him on lockdown."

"You think we can keep him here forever? No. We will hand him over at some point. And until we have the girl locked down, I trust no one. So if you can question him without giving up our position, fine. But don't let him get in your head."

I wasn't going to let him get in my head. He owed me blood though. And I intended to collect.

CHAPTER 20
KAYA

During the drive to East London, I fidgeted. When I had said I wanted to get my mother's papers, I hadn't quite anticipated that Saint would insist on coming with me. I didn't want him to come. I didn't want him to see who I'd been, where I'd come from.

Walthamstow was an East London suburb. Not posh, not fancy. And at the time, I had been thrilled to have some place to call home. Before Mum disappeared, I had lived in North London up near Angel.

East London still had that slightly gritty rock-n-roll feel about it, where in any moment, something could pop up that would remind you that you are still in the poor London that taxi drivers still can't go to.

But hooray for gentrification, because on Sunday mornings, most of East London was full of prams and new parents discussing the best preschools. When we pulled up to the house, a swamp of memories overwhelmed me. For three years, the Cortez family had provided me a home. For three years, they clothed me, fed me, and did their level best to love me, even when I didn't want to be loved. They had gone out of their way to make me feel like I was one of theirs. And I should have been grateful. I had nowhere else to go, no one to count on, and they saw to it that I did. But I still felt like no matter what I did, no one could see me properly.

"How are you doing?" Saint asked. "You've been tense the whole way here."

"I'm sorry. Honestly, like I said, you didn't have to do this. Drive me all this way. I would have figured this out."

"Right, just like you figure everything out."

"Yes. There's nothing wrong with that. I'm self-sufficient."

"Yes, I know."

"I'm just saying, I don't like having to ask for help. It hurts me."

"Fine. Fair enough. But I'm here, so take the help, okay?"

"I'm taking the help."

"So where are these files?"

I winced because I knew what I was going to have to do. "Um, about the files. I buried them out by the shed."

To his credit, he didn't even blink. "You buried them?"

"Yes, by the shed. It seemed like a good idea at the time."

"Of course, it did. By the shed. Excellent. All right, well, let's go."

But he headed for the front door. What was he doing?

"Where are you going?"

"To the front door. Where else am I supposed to go?"

"Not the front door, that's for damn sure."

"You're telling me you lived here for three years."

I nodded. "Yes."

"Okay, but you have no intention of going inside?"

"Correct."

"That's weird."

"It's not weird. My foster mother, she's lovely. Honestly. But she comes with baggage and I don't... I *can't* do baggage right now."

"So you intend to just sneak around back and dig up this box."

"Yes, you say that like it's a bad thing."

"And you say that like it's normal."

"I'm not normal. I could have told you that."

He shook his head. "Jesus, what the hell have I gotten myself into?"

"You insisted on helping."

His brow furrowed. "Fine. I'm helping but this feels wrong."

"Don't worry. No one goes to the backyard."

We walked around the side of the house to the garden, and I was happy to see that my foster mum had listened when I told her to get a gate up. I went over and punched in a code then smiled to myself. Four, three, two, one. It was the only way the kids would all remember without her having to change it all the time.

"Are you sure you really did grow up here?"

"You think I'm lying?"

"It is a bit shady."

I sighed. "You know what, leave it. I don't need your help."

"We both know that's not true."

"You know, I already regret telling you anything."

His chuckle was low. "Well, when we are at our lowest, sometimes we need help."

"Yeah, but sometimes help comes back to bite us on the arse."

"If I bite you on the arse, you'll know."

Heat suffused my skin. I knew he didn't mean it like *that*, but still, there was that growl in his voice, and it felt like he'd meant it that way. I knew better, but my body apparently did not. Damn it.

He eyed me suspiciously. "What's wrong?"

"Nothing. Nothing's wrong, okay?"

"Where is it?"

"It's here by the shed. Might as well get this over with."

"So what was it like growing up here?"

I sighed because I knew how this was going to go. He wanted to talk this through, but honestly, it was the last thing I wanted. "It was fine. Just chaotic."

"What do you mean by chaotic?"

I turned around. "Can we not do this right now?"

"Fair enough."

"Thank you."

"But maybe you can tell me something about yourself later. Like if you're still in touch with the family."

"Yeah. My foster mother and sisters were lovely. Young though. They still call for... you know, help sometimes."

"But you're a student."

"Yeah, but I have a job. It's just for little shit. You know, baubles and candies and that sort of thing. I'm happy to do it."

"But you don't see them often."

I shook my head. "No, I don't."

I marched to the side of the shed and grabbed one of the shovels that was hanging on the deck.

Saint held out his hand. "Give me that."

"I can shovel myself."

"Right, sure you can." But still, he shrugged off his coat, handing it over and putting his palm back out for the shovel. His shirt sleeves were rolled up, exposing his forearms, and he looked delectable. Good enough to eat.

He already made it clear that he's not interested, so back the fuck off.

Right. My raging libido had unfortunately been woken up. Stupid kiss.

I was going to have to put that bitch to sleep again.

Good luck with that while you're living with him.

He shoveled, making quick work of the job, and had quite a pile of dirt before long. The plastic covering that I'd put the box into was still intact. The files looked intact as well.

"Yeah, that's it."

"Well, that wasn't too hard."

"Not if—"

Suddenly, my foster mother called out, "Is someone there?"

"Fuck, she wasn't supposed to be here." *Fuck. Fuck. Fuck.* I turned to Saint. "Behave."

He frowned. "What do you mean?"

I didn't have time to answer him, but I called out. "It's me, Kaya." And then I stepped out, leaving Saint to put the shovel down and wrap our contraband in his jacket. Luckily, he hadn't gotten too much dirt on him.

"Oh my God, Kaya, what are you doing back there?"

"Well, it didn't look like anyone was home, so I let myself into the garden. I'm just trying to climb in the treehouse."

"You should have called, you know?"

I sighed. I knew what I had to do. Throw myself on the altar, otherwise there would be a lot more to explain. "I wanted to surprise you and introduce you to my fiancé."

CHAPTER 21
SAINT

Kaya was so tense. Everything about her was tight. Fraught. She did not want to do this. Why was that? She'd said her foster mother was kind, but was that a lie? Was that just some bullshit she told herself?

You don't know her. She doesn't need saving in everything.

I smiled wanly at the woman in front of me, bringing every bit of my charm to the forefront. "Lydia, I'm so happy to meet you. Kaya was looking for the spare key."

Kaya just blinked owlishly at me, asking for help, but not really asking.

Lydia tsked. "Love, we always keep the key in the shed. Have you forgotten?"

Kaya blinked again, as if trying to find me in her stupor. "Sorry, I must have forgotten. I don't know where my mind was."

Lydia stepped back, making room for us to come in. "Well, I'm glad you're here. I just got back from the shops, so at the very least, let me make you a cuppa. Are you hungry?"

Kaya gave a shake of her head, and I smiled. "Here, why don't you let me help you with the tea. If you have a biscuit, too, I wouldn't say no."

Lydia gave me a smile. "Ah, a man after my own heart. You got a good one, Kaya. Engaged you say. How did that happen? I want to know every detail."

This woman was warm. Kind. Kaya tried to shy away from it. "Oh, you know. He asked and I said yes. Not a big deal."

She stopped. "That's our Kaya for you. I'm sure you already know this. She's not the type for too much fuss and emotion. Did you know for the three years we had her, I kept trying to get this girl to celebrate her birthday, but she wouldn't. When I tried to give her a surprise party, Lord, we could tell she was so unhappy." Lydia tsked again.

Next to me, Kaya sank into one of the well-maintained kitchen chairs around a small dinette. "Lydia, we don't have to do this."

"Oh, but we do. You're getting married." Lydia put the rest of the things from the shop in the fridge and the cupboard. "Now, let me just get the kettle."

"Oh, I don't mind. I'll do it." I offered. I made it to the kettle before she could. And then she sat back, getting a good look at me, assessing me, seeing if I was really into her foster daughter.

I gave her a wave and she just chuckled. "Oh, I like this one. You know, all those years you never brought anyone home, I just figured maybe you didn't like the lads."

Kaya groaned. "Lydia, please don't."

"What? I'm cool. You have a couple of foster brothers who are LGBTQ, you know?"

Kaya looked like she wanted to crawl into a hole and die. "I know."

"Well, I'm glad, you know. We would have been happy either way just to see you making friends, dating, that sort of thing."

Kaya groaned. "Right. I was mostly just trying to keep my head down."

"I know you weren't happy with your first family, but I hope we made you happy here."

Kaya's face softened, the corners of her lips tipping up slightly.

"Of course, you did, Lydia. I'm really grateful to you guys. How are the kids? Mark and Mary, I talked to them two weeks ago. Did she get the books she needed?"

"Oh that girl, she's supposed to be reading chemistry, but now she thinks she wants to go into politics. Can you imagine? I'd spend less money if she just made up her damn mind. You see what I'm saying?"

I laughed. "How many children do you have?"

It seemed like a safe question to ask. She could talk about her children, while I tried to get Kaya to calm down. She looked like she was about to scream and run away.

"Oh, my kids are my jewels. Let's see, biologically, I've got Karen and Kevin. But then the doctor said we couldn't have anymore, so we started fostering. Then we adopted Maya. She's off to uni now. Actually, she's doing her masters. She's a bit older. Kaya here, we fostered her until she was ready for college, you know. She just needed an environment that was safe and secure. Which I hope we gave her. And now we have Mark and Mary and Henry."

I smiled at her while I leaned toward the counter. I felt too big for this kitchen, so I tried to make myself as small as humanly possible, trying not to bump anything. Finally, Lydia just gave up and sat down with Kaya at the table. "I wish you'd told me you were coming. I would have baked."

Kaya smiled softly. "Lydia is a great baker."

"I make a cherry pie that will make you weep. You haven't been home in a long time, Kaya."

I could see it in her eyes then. The confusion at the use of the word *home*. But she recovered quickly and said, "I'm sorry. I'm just so busy at school, you know."

"Yeah, I know. I also know that there's a part of you that saw this as another temporary stop. But once you're family, you're always family."

Kaya smiled. "I know, that's why I brought Saint home to meet you."

"Now what kind of name is Saint?"

I choked a laugh. "Actually, that's my surname. My first name is Jasper."

"That sounds nice. Good to meet you, Jasper."

Kaya said, "He runs a tech company."

Lydia's eyes widened. "Oh, well that is fantastic. Like you do things with apps and things, right?"

I laughed softly. "Something like that. I enjoy it."

"That's sounds fascinating. My Henry, one of the fosters, is into tech. I think he's studying IT or something. You know, my eyes sort of glaze over a little bit when he talks about that stuff, but he looks so excited, so I guess he really enjoys it."

"Good for him."

"Well, you know, if he happens to need a job or something, I'll tell him to come and look for his new brother-in-law."

I smiled warmly. "Just have him chat to his sister and I'll look after him."

I supposed I would have to, because Kaya was, for all intents and purposes, my soon-to-be wife.

"Why don't you tell me more about what Kaya was like?" I asked.

Kaya kept giving me a look that said *Shut the fuck up. What the fuck are you doing?* At least that's what I think her look said. For the moment, it just looked murderous. Which was fine. Besides, it's not like she'd told me much about herself.

"Oh, you know, kind of like she is now. Quiet. Holds everything close to the vest. Almost as if she's waiting for disaster at every turn. I kept trying to tell her that nothing bad was going to happen. But she doesn't listen, do you, love?"

Kaya gave me a wan smile. "Saint doesn't think I listen either."

"She doesn't. It's incredibly frustrating. How do you deal with that?"

Lydia laughed. "But she's smarter than she looks, that one. Did she tell you that she has a photographic memory? Or is she keeping that from you too?"

My gaze snapped to Kaya's. "What?"

"It's not a big deal."

"You have a photographic memory? I would say that's a pretty big deal. I'll never win an argument again."

"That's not how it works. Not for me anyway. Anything I read, I remember. But I don't always know what I'm looking for, so sometimes I have to reference it and I need a cue."

"That is very handy."

"Yeah, it's great for school."

"It will probably make you a great photographer too."

"Yes."

Lydia's eyes lifted. "Um, you're still going to continue school, aren't you, Kaya?"

Kaya had been very concerned about not going back to her life and school. "I know how important that is to Kaya. I want her to continue, of course."

"Well that's good. I wouldn't want you losing your head over a man, and then forget that you have dreams. It happens to too many women. I believe in you."

"Thanks, Lydia."

"I just want you to be happy. You were always so self-contained, you know?"

"I'm just shy, Lydia. I was happy here."

Lydia reached and patted her arm. "Happy is not the right word, love. You were never really happy. But you were content. And sometimes that's all we can give you. So I'm happy that even for a little while, we made you content."

Kaya's eyes were sad. "I know that you think I was ungrateful, but I know what you did for me. You gave me a home when I didn't have one. I was completely alone, and you made sure that I didn't feel that way. So I am grateful. That's why I always volunteered to watch the kids if you needed. I wanted you to know that what you are doing, it mattered to me."

Lydia's eyes filled with unshed tears. And she flapped her hands, trying to dry them out.

I watched Kaya carefully. This girl had been all alone. Not an ounce of family. She'd found a temporary one here. I could see it. The way she thought she had to pay them back. She wouldn't have to pay me back. That was for sure.

"Oh honey, that makes me really happy to hear that. Sometimes with you kids we never know if we've done the right thing. I suppose that's parenting."

Lydia tucked a lock of blond and gray hair behind her ear before she lifted her gaze to meet mine. "Saint, tell me you're going to let my baby wait a little bit before you start filling her with babies of her own. Our Kaya has her whole life to live. She can't let a man keep her from all of that, you know?"

"Oh, I am, of course. I would never dream of keeping Kaya from all the things she's meant to do."

Lydia laughed. "Oh no, I'm teasing. You look well-to-do. You can certainly find something to kill the boredom."

I coughed a laugh then. "Yes, ma'am."

"Don't you ma'am me."

Kaya just looked like she wanted to crawl inside a hole and die. "All right, Lydia, I think we're going to go. This conversation has taken an awkward enough turn."

Lydia tried to halt her. "Oh no, don't. Michael and I will make dinner tonight. Please, stay till then."

Kaya shook her head. "No, I can't. We can't. I just wanted to see you and tell you the good news."

Lydia watched Kaya carefully. "Are you sure? There's nothing else you needed?"

Kaya shook her head. "No."

Lydia stood then. "Well, I know I'm not your mum, but I hope I helped make a difference for you. Truly, I appreciate that you came all this way just to tell me your news in person."

We stayed for another ten minutes to have our tea, because you could tell that even though Lydia had given a home to so many kids, too many of them didn't come home often enough for her liking. And she was very happy to see Kaya.

When we climbed in the car, I grinned at her. "She was lovely. Why on earth were you trying to avoid talking to her?"

But she remained silent and appeared to not hear my question at all.

As we drove away, I kept glancing at the stoic young woman deep in thought next to me. Just when I thought it would be a quiet ride back, Kaya blurted out, "When are we going to talk about the kiss?"

———

Kaya

"Fuck me." Saint sputtered out as he slammed the brakes hard enough to make me jolt forward in my seat. "Kaya?"

Yes. Explain Kaya. This should be great.

"After all the things Lydia brought up tonight, you and I should probably have the kiss conversation if we are going to do this pretend marriage thing."

"It was the grandbabies comment, wasn't it? Why are mum's always pushing for that?" he muttered.

"Listen I have no expectations. I know this isn't real. Sorry I brought it up."

Saint reached out and took my hand. Warm tingles raced along my arm like they always seemed to do when we touched. "I'm here to help you. Let's get through that step first." But he left his hand in mine all the way back to the penthouse.

When we were back just inside the penthouse door, files clutched under my arm, I barely touched his elbow to stop him.

Looking at the floor for a beat I let my gaze go from my hand up to his eyes. "I want you to know that I am grateful for everything. You didn't need to do any of this for me. Thank you."

I figured that I should stop there before I said anything wild or crazy.

With an adorable shoulder shrug, he ran a hand over the scruff beginning to build on his face. "You don't have to thank me, Kaya. You were in trouble. What was a decent bloke supposed to do?"

"I know a lot of decent people who wouldn't have done anything. I haven't gotten many people shot at in my lifetime."

He chuckled low. "You know what? I'd like to not repeat that."

"Not my fault. How was I supposed to know they had guns?" Sliding into the ease of humor that flowed between us, it always seemed easier than being sincere. I couldn't fully break that wall with him. He sure seemed like he wanted to hide behind the laughter, too.

Staring up at Saint's bright green eyes as he looked back at me with care, I wondered what I was supposed to do with all this emotion flowing through me. This connection we created when we were this close. An incessant buzzing formed deep inside me that hummed with anticipation. It terrified me. I wasn't sure what I should do next. Part of me wanted to run into my room far away from him and that pull.

I ran away from my feelings a lot. It was easier and safer than dealing with the heartache that came with deeper feelings. But I didn't want to run this time, so I stepped forward and wrapped my arms around Saint, folder and all.

Completely awkward. Unquestionably not my best move to just reach out and grab Saint in a hug. But the well of emotion after going back to my foster home was too much. Having this protector of a man step up, walk inside, and see part of me no one else did was overwhelming. Then seeing Lydia's response. The woman who had known me for years, looked after me, taken care of me, had felt that distance, one that I'd put there for her own safety. If I couldn't let her understand how I felt for all these years, I could try to let Saint know how much this all meant to me.

I kept on hugging him. This probably wasn't even a good idea, considering that I kissed him the other night after my nightmare and he had essentially run away. But the way his arms snapped around my body so fast and drew me in shocked me and I dropped the files.

You know this isn't completely horrible for him.

His deep inhale told me that he was trying to breathe me in. I felt like he was trying to consume me, to meld our bodies together until I could feel him in my soul. The more we stood together in this embrace, the more I wanted to lean into it, to feel it. Letting myself relish the feeling of being held. It was like Gemma was always saying; I held myself too tight, too stiffly. I needed to let people in. How long had it been since I'd let someone just hold me like this?

Those thoughts started me spiraling. I tried to pull back, becoming uncomfortable with the level of emotion I was displaying.

Just let yourself be hugged and don't shrug it off before it gets good.

When Saint did pull back, it wasn't quick. He didn't step away from me. He pulled back just enough that there were mere inches between us, and I lifted my head. At five-three, I wasn't particularly tall. But he was tall. Six foot two? Six foot three? It was enough that I had to crank my neck just to meet his gaze.

"Kaya." His voice was a whisper and a question I had no idea how to answer. How was I supposed to respond?

But then he groaned, his hands tightening on my biceps before he dragged me to him again and slammed his lips over mine.

Holy shit.

Heat and ecstasy and adrenaline made for a heady cocktail in my blood. I must have swayed because he wrapped his arms tighter around me. The drug of his kisses shut down all brain function so all I could focus on were his lips and his tongue and the sparking electricity jumping all over my skin.

Suddenly I heard a low, keening sound. Was that me? Was I the one making that sound of desperation? With a grunt, he picked me up easily like I weighed nothing. One hand on my back and one on my arse, the motion bringing our lips closer together, easier to connect. *God yes. More.* I wrapped my legs around his waist in this moment of pure bliss.

He slid his hands into my hair, fisting my tight curls. I was in Saint's arms and could quite possibly stay in them forever without a care about anything else.

I cried out when my back hit the wall "Jasper!"

"Need more," Saint panted as he adjusted his hips. And before I knew it... holy shit!

The full length of him, hot, insistent, was pressing into my center. And all I could do was exhale a shuddering breath at the stab of desire that threatened to make me implode.

This kind of kiss wasn't a run of the mill kiss brought on by a sentimental hug. This was a Leonidas and Gorgo, return-of-the-conquering-hero kind of kiss. This was what it felt like to be claimed. This kind of annihilating kiss was pure sensation, need, and full-on desperation.

I slid my hands into his hair, tugging and pulling him closer, wiggling my hips, trying to get that deeper connection. He growled at my movements, dragging his lips from mine, dropping his forehead to mine. Ragged breaths kept propelling out of his lungs and I matched him chest fall to chest fall. We stood there like that for a long moment, my legs wrapped around him, fingers in each other's hair, my vision unfocused as I tried to lift my lids.

What the fuck just happened?

Saint eased back, his motion pulling me back from the wall. I loosened my legs, and he helped ease me back to the floor. Standing there glancing from my eyes to my lips, he cleared his throat. "You never have to go out of your way to say thank you again, Kaya."

I should say something. Except I had no words because someone had stolen my last brain cell. It wasn't my fault. Honestly, it wasn't.

When he spoke again, his voice was firmer, more in control. "Back to what you said in the car. I'll make an addendum to the contract."

"Is that necessary?"

He took a half step toward me and then growled. "After that? Fuck yes, we need the paperwork." Then he forced himself to take a step back. "Considering the things I'm wanting to do to you right now, yes. It's one hundred percent necessary. I'm going to have it drafted, and then you are going to sign it. And just so we're both clear, no way in hell is this relationship going to stay platonic."

CHAPTER 22
SAINT

I DIDN'T EVEN LOOK BACK at her as I stormed into my room and headed straight to the bathroom. I deliberately avoided looking at the bed. I needed to wash her off me or my cock would be harder than steel the rest of the night.

I was in a burning inferno of my own making.

The kiss had been unplanned. I hadn't expected her to hug me. I hadn't expected her to wrap her arms around me like I was the sole person keeping her alive. How was I supposed to prepare for the tectonic plate shifting of my soul when she hugged me like that?

There was something grounding about someone counting on you, depending on you. It added to your purpose, that sense of responsibility. It didn't weigh me down like I thought it would. I don't think Elise ever depended on me for anything. No matter how I felt toward her, she could always stand on her own two feet without interference from me. But now, to see someone so open with how they were feeling. Fucking hell. It was torture.

Torture because I had no idea what to fucking do or what she was feeling. She'd just hugged me. I, in return, had ground my dick into her. Bloody brilliant. She'd been grateful that I had been there for her as she went through the difficult times and retrieved her mother's things. The whole evening turned into a mess when we got caught, but she'd taken that like a champ. Squared her shoulders, been ready and willing to deal.

I admired that about her. Even when something was terrifying, she got on with it. I could probably use more of that in my life.

And then she hugged you. And you liked it... a little too much.

I could still feel her breasts plastered against my chest. Her arms were surprisingly strong as they wrapped around me. Her body tight as she silently begged me not to reject her. I could feel her tentativeness in every touch. All of the *is this okay* questions surfacing with every hitch of her breath.

Little did she know I was the one who was desperate to give in despite the promise I'd made. I was serious about the contract. It would help me stall, but I had no intention of getting married. I still had several aces to play. I just had to hold on.

But there's no resisting her.

I shut out the truth and lied to myself as I hid from her in the shower. My cock insistently bobbed as if to ask, 'Why are we resisting her again?'

Because she's too vulnerable. And how about you are still fucking lying to her.

Son of a bitch, this conscience of mine was going to drive me to drink.

Tugging off my shoes at the bathroom door, I kicked them aside. I shook off my shirt, getting stuck at my sleeves and angrily tugging off my cufflinks. I could not move quickly enough. The sooner I did this, the better off I would be. The freer I would be of her scent, because if I let it linger, it would drive me insane. Slowly. Deliberately.

Coconut and lime wrapped up into one delectable dessert that was her.

I turned the water on and stripped off my trousers and boxers. My dick was making its ever happy appearance, bobbing straight up to my stomach, glowering at me for letting her go in the first place. "Mate, you know why we can't do that."

He just bobbed back at me as if to indicate that he had no idea why the fuck we could not.

Bollocks, could you die from blue balls? It had to be a viable cause of death.

The water was automatically set to warm, but I turned it to icy cold. Every cell in my body rejected the idea. Despite my body's protest, I had to go with ice, otherwise I would have fever dreams of *her*. I wanted her. I was about to break every promise I'd made. I was weak at the core of it. From the moment I met her at the auction, I'd wanted to inhale her. She'd worn that black low-cut dress, the sassy lift of her brow when I stopped her from coming in the room. Goddamn it. I wanted everything from her.

This was a terrible combination of need and lust. I had too much baggage, and she needed someone who wasn't trying to fucking take advantage of her desperate situation.

Maybe taking advantage isn't a bad thing since she seemed as into it as you did.

All my brain wanted to do was rationalize and negotiate with all matters concerning Kaya. She'd wanted a hug, and I'd had no business kissing her.

Just thinking about the way her tongue met mine and the way she'd wrapped herself around me, rocking her hips over the length of me, and the way I'd picked her up, slamming her against the wall, locking into her.

For fuck's sake, I was throbbing hard all over again. My cock looked furious now. Less happy go lucky *let's get up to some no good*, and more like angry *fuck you for taking me away from the thing that I need to survive*. How did I get to this point with a woman I'd met less than two weeks ago?

I stepped under the spray, gritting my teeth as the icy pinpricks of water tapped a merry tune on my skin. A jolly, happy jig that stung with every drop. When I dunked my head under the hard pelts of water, I cursed under my breath. But it did the job as all I could feel now was a full body shiver.

Only then did I feel relaxed enough to slowly turn the heat up, warming myself slowly, praying to God I hadn't frozen my cock off. I glanced down and he was still there. And what do you know, still at half-mast.

I washed my hair quickly. More of a slap and slather situation honestly. I wasn't trying to do a good job, but rather scrub that delicious scent away. I'd be able to breathe and rationalize if I could just get her scent off me. I'd seen some of the darkest hell holes in the world. Why was it *this* woman sent me reeling?

Yes, she was beautiful. Bright. Sunny when she wanted to be, but vulnerable in that aching way where you knew she was untouchable. There was something remote about her that made me want to know everything about her. The more I thought about her, the more I remembered the slide of her tongue, the hitch of her breath, her gasp of surprise, and the way her hands had delved into my hair, pulling and tugging, dragging me closer.

And of course, the rock of her hips.

Fuuuuuck.

The rush of heat to my groin was warning me I turned that warm water on far too quickly. The ache of my balls told me there was only one way to take care of this particular problem. But I knew the truth. Once I answered this question, it would be one I would have to answer over and over again, and it would be a poor facsimile for the real thing.

And would once with her ever be enough?

But the pain and throb would not dissipate. With a curse, I slammed a hand against the glass tile on the shower, and with a pump of the soap, I reached for the base of my cock and groaned as I fisted myself. I was nearly choking on my own tongue just thinking about her.

I squeezed at the base with a slow slide up to the tip, circling the head, and I shivered, nearly giving out. I squeezed my eyes shut, willing myself to not picture Kaya, not picture her delicate long fingers wrapping around me. Her big brown eyes gazing up at me, silently asking if this was right. If this was how I liked it.

I told myself not to picture Kaya's pink tongue peeking out to lick her bottom lip as she stroked, watching me in fascination.

I choked a cry as I imagined her lowering herself to her knees.

This imagery was not helpful. But Kaya was sinking so far under my skin she was all I could think about.

You might as well give in.

I knew how it would feel. But when I was around her, it would be all I could think about. Her taste, her desperation to taste me, how those two things mingled and merged together in my brain. But that small, dark part of my brain had taken over, and shower Kaya was on her knees, her curls springing around her shoulders and down her back. Dark eyes blinking up at me. Lashes wet from the spray. Her bronze skin highlighted by the water. Fucking hell. Kaya Reynolds was a sex kitten without even trying.

As I stroked down again, I pictured her smooth tongue peeking out to lick the tip, and I ground my teeth against the rush of heat that coiled in my spine in no time at all.

Fuck, fuck, fuuuuck

I could see it all play out right here with the water cascading over her imaginary body. Shower Kaya's hands on my base as her heavenly red lips wrapped around me, sliding down, her tongue gently suckling and swallowing. My thick cock hitting the back of her throat and that light gagging noise that she would make. Drawing back, making a second attempt, Kaya taking me deeper, deeper, swallowing just a little, to give me that feeling of suction.

I could see myself dropping my hands on her delicate hair while attempting to pull her off my dick. I could see the determination in her eyes as she gave me a little shake of her head, taking me deeper, gagging just a little bit more, and then pulling back. Inhaling a deep breath before sliding right back down, using her hands to aid her.

I could see the hint of a smile in her eyes as she stroked me up and down like that. Her gaze never leaving mine like the dirty, dirty girl she was just for me. I could see myself trying to warn her. "K-Kaya... I'm going to—"

But instead of pulling back, instead of letting the jets of cum hit those voluptuous tits, she only took me deeper. All the way down. Not letting me pull out and away, but swallowing all of me. Taking it all as I fucked her mouth and I blew. The peculiar tension of the last few days all poured out of me. Excitement, worry, concern, need, electricity. The sum total equaling absolute desperation. Thoughts and visions of her rocketing into my life so quickly caused me to gasp and grunt, and I dropped my head against the tile as my whole body jerked with jets and jets of cum exploding forth.

The throes of my bliss just etched her face further into my mind. All I saw was shower Kaya with a smug, self-satisfied expression as she continued to stroke me even as I begged and tried to back away. No, she wouldn't allow that as she continued the onslaught of pressure on my cock, because that was her way. Stubborn, with just a little bit of evil inside her.

Holy fucking shit. The water sluiced down my back as my legs shook, and I sighed against the shower wall, knowing I was in so much trouble.

Because this was all over. I was going to end up inside Kaya Reynolds.

She was already inside my heart I'd thought was made of stone.

Kaya

"Saint has a brother right? Because a girl could get used to this view, Kaya."

I laughed. "He does. Trevor. You met him at the engagement

announcement. And as for the view, it's nice. But remember, Gemma, it's not mine and none of this is real."

She merely lifted her brows and gave me a smirk. I knew despite what I told her and my protests, she very much thought that Saint and I were going to be a thing. "Trevor. Right. But that man is a good time for *now*. You can see it in his smile."

"You're right I think. But this will never be my life."

"Never say never. Besides, you're having sex dreams about him."

I smacked her arm. "Gemma! No, I'm not." I glanced around quickly, wondering if there were listening devices in here. "Shut up, What if the walls have ears?"

"Ooh, kinky."

"Gems!"

"Fine, but let's talk about the sexy stuff. He's hot. You're smokin' hot. What's the problem with a little one-on-one time? You are about to marry the bloke."

"It's a little awkward. I nearly got him killed and everything is complicated."

"No honey, my darling girl, *you* are making things complicated. I mean, you know he's thinking about it. Where did he back you up to ravish you? I want to visualize properly."

I dropped my head into my hands and plopped down to the floor next to the couch where I'd laid out Mum's paperwork I'd dug up. "Right there, by the door."

Gemma glanced over then gave me a wicked grin. "Was it hot as hell like in the movies?"

Heat suffused my face, and I was glad, thanks to my brown skin, she wouldn't really be able to tell. "That's not the point. We aren't talking about hot or not hot. We need to be going over these papers."

"How long do we have before your hottie comes back?"

I snorted a laugh. "Oh, do you mean Saint or Westin?"

"How is it that it takes attempted maiming for your love life to pick up?"

All I could do was laugh, because she wasn't wrong. How in the hell did my life have two hot guys in it when before all I had was Andrew following me like a puppy? Saint was built like a Roman statue and I'm pretty sure the chisel marks were visible if you removed his shirt.

Westin was handsome. Okay, fine, he was beautiful. That devil-may-care smile was the kind of thing that probably melted panties from here to Cornwall.

"I mean, when I say well fit, it doesn't even begin to cover it," Gemma continued. "Saint is beyond fit. And beautiful doesn't even begin to cover it for Westin. Let me know when you let Westin off the hook, I'd like to mend his broken heart."

"You are horrible! Why did I bring you over here?"

Gemma joined me on the floor, sitting cross legged, and she picked up a file. "If you're not going to shag the billionaire, which," she glanced around, "you totally should, because who has ever backed you into a wall and wanted to bang you? He wants to work on a contract that covers sex, Kaya! If I don't know anything else, I know that's fucking hot. If you're not going to shag him, fine, I won't make you. But at least give up Westin because I'm using that man's arse in my wank bank."

I laughed and threw my head back, realizing that for the first time in over two weeks, I was actually relaxed and having fun. If I closed my eyes and didn't look too closely, I could almost pretend everything was okay. I could pretend that this was normal, that we were just having a girl's day, that no one was chasing me.

But I knew somewhere behind the laughter was constant danger. I shoved it down though. My best mate was here. Today I didn't have to worry about anything, and tomorrow would come soon enough. I didn't need to invite trouble; it had already found me.

"Here, you take this pile and see what you can find."

Gemma nodded, grabbed her hair and tucked it up into a pile on the nape of her neck with a pen. "I'm on it. I still think it's really cute how he went to see your foster mum with you."

"That's not exactly how it was meant to go."

"Oh, come on, let it just be adorable like it is Kaya. He helped you. He charmed Lydia. Technically he really is angling for best boyfriend ever."

"Except he's *not* my boyfriend. He's the man pretending to be my fiancé so that gangsters or whoever the hell don't try to kill me."

"You know, you have a way of ruining my fun. Can't you let me live vicariously through you?"

"I'm rolling my eyes loudly at you, Gems."

For the next hour, we dug through the paperwork. There was information on school records and such. There was also information on banks where she had safe deposit boxes stashed. Other files showing things I didn't quite understand. Something called the *Dove* and then a set of files called *Ravens* were in this section. Then Mum had just stacks and stacks of maps. To me, it looked like schematics to buildings and layouts of towns.

Some of the images were difficult to follow. Why would Mum have pages that looked like they were in codes? I needed to suss out what it all meant for the bigger picture.

What had she really been running from?

An hour and a half in, Gemma whistled loudly, waving a piece of paper in the air. "Oh boy, I think I've finally got something."

I glanced up. "What do you have?"

"It's a property deed in the name Cass Reynolds. That's your mum, right?"

I frowned. She'd used her middle name. Her full name was Keilani Cassandra Reynolds. But using the name Cass, I would have just ignored it. This felt like something big. I leaned over. "Where's the property?"

Gemma grinned at me. "Croatia. You know, I've always wanted to go to Croatia."

"I can't just go to Croatia. Let's look up the property online."

Gemma nodded. "To Home Search International." She put on incognito browser mode and typed in the address. Google maps was oh so bloody helpful.

"Okay, here it is, located in the village of Petina, near Zagreb, the capital of Croatia. The property is near the city, but more like in one of the neighborhoods. Looks like a house." Then she went to Home Search. "I don't know about you, but I think this place looks kept up. Don't you agree?"

It wasn't listed for sale, but you could see photos of the property. There was something old-world looking about the architecture. Lots of arches in the doorways and in the gate. Pristine too, as if someone had been there recently to keep it up. Stark white paint, manicured lawn and perfectly painted flower boxes. The house was a mile from the center of the small town of Petina.

My stomach cramped as I stared at the house. This was the kind of place mum said we should have someday. Some place safe where we could be ourselves and no one would come looking for us. Had she found this on her own and just left me behind to enjoy it?

I knew in my heart of hearts that didn't sound right. Truly I did, but it was so hard to ignore that feeling of being abandoned. Watching her go away in that car all those years ago... Was it to leave me behind for her perfect life? The whole situation made my guts twist in agony.

"I... I really don't know what to think."

"Well, you know, the only way we're going to find out is if we go to Croatia and see it."

"I can't just go to Croatia."

"Sure, you can. You know, there are these things called planes. You can buy a ticket."

I blinked rapidly. "No, I have school and..." I heard myself making excuses. I'd committed to finding her, and I could work on my next photo assignment in Croatia.

"I can see your mind turning," Gemma said. "Don't focus on what's on hold. How about we focus on the fact that Croatia isn't far away? That's a weekend girls' getaway. Something we can plan out tonight, be there tomorrow, and then be on a plane back tomorrow night or the day after."

"I-I don't know."

Gemma turned, put the file down, and took my hand. "I know it's scary, but it's a real lead. One that doesn't involve you being chased by scary men. We're just going to go have a look at this property. Take a couple of photos of the location and be on a plane right back."

"Well, what about Saint?"

"Well, nobody has told you that you are a penthouse prisoner, correct?"

I shook my head. She had a point there. I was not a prisoner. At least I shouldn't be.

"You just tell him the truth that you are spending the weekend with me."

"Gems, we can't just take off."

"Who says?"

"I don't know. Me. I say it. We have classes, and Saint's hired me to work, and you have your own things."

"I have things, yes. But I am also your bestie, so I'm coming. And chillax. I know we have classes. But it's Thursday, which means tomorrow is Friday, so we could be on a plane tomorrow night. And since you're not a prisoner, you don't actually have to tell your very beautiful, very sexy fiancé that you're leaving the country. We'd just say nothing and go. Don't you know the rules of a relationship? Sin now and ask for forgiveness later."

I had to laugh, because this, one hundred percent, sounded like something only a best friend would say. "You are going to get me into so much trouble."

"Only if you get caught. But chances are, you won't get caught. We'll go in, have lunch in Croatia, and come back home in no time. And if you are feeling extra guilty when you are at my house, you can leave a note there, because if he goes looking for you there, then it wasn't an actual lie."

I shook my head. "How have I not noticed how diabolical you are?"

"Because you weren't looking at what was in front of you the whole time, my darling. Now, what the hell does one wear to Croatia?"

"I have to tell him something. I can't just vanish."

She rolled her eyes. "The real question is, does it matter?"

"No, love, the real question is, what's he going to do when he finds out I'm gone?"

Gemma winked. "Well, that spot on the wall says your punishment could be something really fun."

CHAPTER 23
SAINT

THERE WAS nothing I loved more than Saturday morning meetings. Didn't everyone love waking up and sitting in a conference room instead of being comfy at home?

As Mitch Foxton, our CTO, ran through the latest apps, where they were in the marketplace, and what their earnings were, all I kept thinking about was Kaya. These were important numbers, things I should pay attention to, things I should care about for our business. Yet my mind kept going back to the bomb I'd dropped on Kaya about wanting to amend our contract. And then I'd resolutely ignored her.

I was being a prat. I knew it.

Shit or get off the pot, mate.

Kaya left to stay at Gemma's last night and Ryan and Jason were following along but staying out of sight. She needed some kind of normalcy after this week. I'd been an absolute wanker thinking that ignoring her was the best course of action.

Things had been busy. As my Rogues team prepped Lohman for transport, I had tried and failed again to get more answers out of him.

So much for keeping promises. This was turning into a disaster.

I had to surreptitiously crack my neck and not pay attention to that voice, the one that told me I hadn't done enough. It was just simply easier to stop looking, stop caring. Elise was still dead. Lohman still knew something about it, and I was taking the easy way out. This entire narrative I created in my head wasn't helpful.

Across the table, my brother cocked his head. When I frowned at him, he mouthed, "What the fuck is wrong with you?"

Was something wrong with me? Fuck, I didn't know.

At that moment I realized that the whole table was staring at me. *Fuck.*

I'd missed the entire discussion, let alone that someone had asked me a question.

"I'm sorry, Mitch. Repeat it, please?"

He repeated his question, and I gave him the answer easily enough to hear, but it was clear to everyone that I wasn't paying attention. Adrianna slid her glance to Mitch then to me. "I think maybe we've gone far enough today. Let's reconvene on Monday early." She was saving me a Sunday. I could kiss her. "There's still a lot to do, but let's just let it rest for a few days."

When the meeting broke up, Trevor pushed back from the table and rolled over to my side. "Daydreaming, big brother? Spill everything. Are you having fun playing penthouse fun times with your fiancée?"

I groaned as I scowled at him. "You twat. Your love of gossip is unbecoming."

He laughed. "When did you get boring? Cause I'm certain your Friday night wasn't as good as mine. Happy to report back all about mine. I went out with Felicia last night, and I have to tell you, she is very, very good at sucking—"

Adrianna clapped her hands over her ears. "Blah-blah-blah, Jesus Christ, you are so gross, Trevor. Jasper, tell him to shut up."

I rolled my eyes. "Give it a rest. Both of you. You're giving me a headache."

Adrianna sat on the edge of the table next to my seat. She slipped off her Louis Vuittons and rubbed her arches. "You are clearly distracted, baby brother. What's wrong with you?"

"I'll call Mitch later to apologize."

"You're doing no such thing. He doesn't have to forgive you because you're the boss. But Trevor is on point. You are distracted. We need your attention. Are things still busy at Rogues?"

I frowned. "No, I'm just... I don't know."

Trevor grinned. "Adrianna, you're missing the point. He is very much into his new flat mate. You know, the one pretending she's going to marry him. This whole thing is supposed to be pretend, but he's gone and got feelings, don't you see."

I scowled. "Must you, really?"

"What? I'm just laying it out how I see it. Am I wrong?"

I rubbed my temple. "None of your business, you slag." To which Trevor just leaned back in his wheelchair and laughed.

Sometimes they irritated me to no end. I loved them immensely, but goddamn. "Can you two just stop with me, please?"

"Trouble in paradise so soon, old boy?"

Adrianna shot Trevor a look before she turned to me with concern in her eyes. "Are you sure, Jasper?"

"Oh Jesus. She's fine. All right you two? Everything is just peachy keen, okay? She's just at her friend's this weekend, and I don't know. I just wanted to know if she's safe."

"You know she's safe. Security would have alerted you. So what's the real problem?"

"I don't know. I just have a weird feeling."

Adrianna glanced at me and asked sheepishly, "For once, is Trevor right? Do you have a crush on your fiancée?"

"Oh, for fuck's sake."

They both howled with laughter.

"You know, I never really did like either of you."

I shoved back from the table and then intentionally left my seat pulled out to make an obstacle for that twat Trevor.

"She's fit, obviously. And yes, she's beautiful. But it's fine. We just have to work out a couple of things."

Adrianna sat back, crossing her feet at the ankles and swinging them back and forth. "Okay, so obviously, I'm going to ask the question. Have you told her the truth yet?"

I crossed my arms as I sauntered to the window. "I'm not sure what you mean."

My sister rolled her eyes. "Mate, you have to tell her all of it."

"It doesn't matter. In a month's time I'll at least secure our position with the company, she'll be safe and free to go on her way, and then there won't be anything to tell her."

Adrianna tossed her head back and laughed. "Sweetheart, you like her. I can tell you like her. Moreover, Father can tell you like her. So what's the problem? She likes you too. I can tell. I'm a woman. I know these things. I might find you immensely irritating, but she is fantastic, and seeing how she looks at you, makes it real."

That was just the problem. I wanted it to be too real. But there were things I had to do. Things that were unfinished.

"It's too complicated. She needs protection. I'm trying to give it to her."

Yeah, you want to protect her with your dick.

Adrianna lifted a brow. "Jesus fucking Christ. You would ruin everything. You are so stuck in the past with Elise and Father. You have a real chance at actually having something and look at you fucking it up. Just call the girl. You know, take her on a date. Take security and take her out. Woo her. Move on from Elise. Make this real and maybe you don't have to tell her anything. Don't lie, hide, and try not to move forward. That's not fair for her, and it sucks for you."

I did not want to think about this. "I cannot believe I'm having this conversation with you two."

Why was this so fucking difficult?

I just wanted to get one more go at Lohman, wanted to get a better lead on who was coming for her. I wanted to cement our relationship better.

"Maybe." I sighed. "Fine, already. I'll talk to her."

Even Trevor had advice for me. "Mate, I hate to say it, but Adrianna is right. You're so stuck on Elise and righting some imaginary wrong. You weren't the one who wronged her. She wronged all of us. The people she was involved with, dragging Dad into it too, it was just a mess. You weren't here. You were doing the queen's work. Fair enough, but had you been here, it would have been even uglier because she would have dragged you and Dad down with her. She was bad news from the get-go."

"Then how the fuck did I not see that?" I whirled at my siblings. "I should have known. I should have seen it all coming at us."

Trevor shrugged. "I actually thought she was kind of like that airline hostess from three months ago who was married. Remember that ordeal I had? How was I supposed to know her husband was going to come looking for me? I will say though, being in this chair certainly saved my life. He didn't actually believe that I could shag the shit out of his wife." He winked and spun around in a swivel. "Little did he know the things I can get up to in this chair."

My lips twitched and I shook my head. "Mate, you are so fucking wrong."

"My point is... Actually, I don't have a point. I just wanted you to know that I shagged a fucking fit airline hostess in this chair. You should have seen her tits bouncing with every rock of this thing."

Adrianna gagged. "I hate you so much."

Trevor winked at her. "You love me because you have to. But it's still fun to tick you off."

"You're obviously itchy and antsy and want to see her Jasper, so just see her. Let go of Elise. If you'd focus on who the world thinks you're going to marry, you might actually find happiness. Yes, you could save her arse, too, and you both would be the better for it."

I groaned. "Fine. I'm going to see her now. She's with her friend, but I'll go pick her up for brunch and talk to her."

I hit my quick dial on Rook's number. He answered right away.

"Mate, who do you have on Kaya? I'm headed over to Gemma's. I want to take her to brunch. How long since they've checked in?"

"Mate, I've been trying to reach you for the last thirty minutes."

"Sorry. I was in weekly meeting. What's wrong?"

"It's Kaya. She and that mate of hers have done a runner."

***

Kaya

"Come on," Gemma said. "We're going to go knock on the door."

I had said I wanted to do this, right? But standing there, now I wasn't so sure. My feet were planted and rooted to the pavement.

The neighborhood was residential. Somewhere in the distance, children played and laughed. Cars drove by. People speaking Croatian. Some English. I heard a couple of passersby speaking French too. We were at the address in my mother's papers. The one that maybe led to nowhere had actually led to somewhere in Croatia, and now I couldn't move forward.

If I opened that door and she was there, I'd know I'd been abandoned. If I didn't open the door, she was still just missing and could come back at any time. I could step forward to see if this was my destiny, or I could move backward, run away, and hide. I was locked in place, not knowing what to do.

Gemma put her hand on my shoulder. "Hey, we don't have to do this. We can turn around and go back to the hotel."

I slid her a glance. "I'm not afraid."

"Honey, even with all that gorgeous brown skin of yours, I can see you're flushed. And you've got that wild look in your eye like you want to run. It's okay to run. You've seen it. You've been here. You can come back any time you want. Ask questions later."

"Are you really going to let me run?"

She shrugged. "Yeah, we will find a taxi, I'll put you inside it, and you don't have to do this. On the other hand, my arse *is* going to that door and I *am* going to do this. But I have a feeling if that is in fact your mother in there, or someone who knows her, they won't talk to me. But I am hellbent on figuring out what the fuck is going on for you. You can come or you can go home."

I blinked at her. And then despite myself, the laugh came bubbling up. Slightly nervous and teetering, but it was still a laugh, because Gemma knew how to do that. How had I lied to her for the last couple of years since she walked into my mess of a life? How had I not taken full advantage of this level of friendship?

"So it's like that, huh?"

"It is like that. I love you so much. I will fucking do this without you."

"But isn't it my mum?"

"Yes, but you're being a little petty-arse bitch, and we don't have time for that."

"Wow. I hope someone gives you a motivational speaker job right away."

"Funny. I do love you so much, but let's get on with it. We didn't come all this way for nothing, and we aren't getting any younger."

"You're like a drill sergeant. Did you know that?"

She shrugged. "Yes, you are not the first person to tell me this."

She laughed, wrapped her arms around me and gave me a tight squeeze, and then pinched me and shoved me forward.

Maybe we don't like her after all.

She winked at me when I turned back to her, and I took another step forward. I unlocked the gate and walked through. I could see that the patio grass in front was well maintained. It was beautifully managed, no weeds in the little lawn, and there were red begonias and purple irises in the corner. Someone loved this house. Someone took care of it. The question was, who?

I walked up to the front door and rang the bell. All the while my heart beat so fast, sweat leaking in my palms and fear creeping through me, tainting every part of my mind. Telling me to run, telling me that I had no business here. Telling me that she would know I hadn't looked hard enough for her and that she would hate me.

I stood at the solid wood door waiting.

Right behind me, I could feel Gemma shifting from foot to foot in the nervous way she often did when she was impatient, which was almost all the time.

After five minutes, no one came to the door. Gemma went to the side of the house and tried to peer in the windows, but she shrugged. "There're some sheer curtains in there. Not a lot of furniture, but you know, there's a couch and it's empty."

As I stood there, I heard singing coming from the other side of the house. Someone humming something that sounded like a lullaby. I listened to the tune and for some reason I hummed along. Like at some point in my life I had heard it many times and knew every note. A middle-aged woman came from around the house and smiled at me. She started speaking French, which I barely understood from the basic French courses I took at school.

"I think you are asking if I need help? Sorry, pardon, my name... umm... *Je m'appelle* Kaya Reynolds. *Je cherche pour quelqu'un.*" I fumbled for the right words in French, so I switched to English. "But I don't think they live here."

At the sound of my name, her eyes went wide. And then she clapped her hands and switched to English. "Ah yes, I'm Magda, and I've been waiting long time for you."

I blinked in surprise. "What?"

"I have something for you."

"Do I know you?"

"Oh no, darling. I knew your mother."

Knew.

Past tense.

The pain zapped through me. I wished she hadn't said it like that. Why couldn't I be strong when the news finally hit? But my knees crumbled, and I almost sank to the ground. Then she reached for me.

"Oh my darling, your mother was here six months ago. She was fine then. What I meant to say, is that I'm her friend but I don't see her often. I'm sorry I was so insensitive. I shouldn't have worried you."

"What? My mother... She's alive?"

The woman's eyes went wide. "Yes, of course she is."

Panic laced through my body, and I started to hyperventilate. Air swooshing in and out of my lungs, none of it hitting where I needed it. It was swooshing in too fast, and God, I couldn't fucking breathe.

All this time. Where the hell was she now?

She'd been alive six months ago. My mother had been here.

Why didn't she come for me?

"I don't understand. If you've seen her recently, then why didn't she come back for me?"

She waved me over. "Why don't you come in? We'll go in through the back. I don't use the main house often as I live in the caretaker's quarters back there."

"You take care of the house?"

"Yes. Come in and I'll explain everything, or as much as I can."

Then she walked, expecting us to follow. Gemma nodded that I should follow her, and she was right behind me. At least, I wasn't doing this on my own. As I followed Magda to the back, I could see the caretaker's cottage she pointed out, but she led me to the back stairs of the main house and then picked up a key from the stone as if it was the most natural thing in the world and opened the door. Inside, the house was cute. Unused, but clearly aired out and pristine. The furnishings were modern. Bright and all white. Open and spacious; the kind of thing my mother always loved.

I could see bits and pieces of her. The art on the walls, the little tchotchkes. There was a lot of my mother in here. I had more surprises when I turned to the bookshelf. There were photos of me at all stages of my childhood, as a baby, a toddler, and even in secondary when I had been awkward and sullen at best. Candid shots of me showing all the different moments of a past that was slowly fading from my memories. Moments when I was smiling, moments when I was happy, relaxed, or even pensive. How were they all here when we always got rid of everything each time we moved? None of this made any sense to the reality I had lived.

"Where did all of this come from?"

Magda put the kettle on. "Your mother said this house was meant for you and her. But the last time she came, she said it still wasn't safe but that one day, she wanted it to be perfect for you. Every time she came, she brought something for your room."

I blinked rapidly. "My room?"

"Yes. It's just down the hall."

I shook my head. "I don't know what's happening..." My voice trailed as everything started to spin.

Gemma was right there, directing me into a seat. She didn't stop pushing me down until my butt hit the soft cushion.

"Breathe." She turned to Magda. "Water. She needs a glass of water." Magda immediately went to the faucet and brought a glass over. "Drink this. Slowly," Gemma said in her drill sergeant tone that I was so grateful for at this moment.

"You're telling me my mother has been alive this whole time?"

Magda nodded slowly. "I'm sorry. I don't know why she wouldn't tell you that she's been very much alive."

"All this time."

"Sorry. This is probably all bewildering for you."

"Yeah, you could say that. So you just take care of the house?"

"Yes. Your mother hired me seven years ago."

I blinked up at her rapidly. "Seven years? Where was I?"

"I don't know. She could only stay overnight though. She said her daughter was busy at a school competition."

In a snap, that memory was at the forefront of my mind. Debate Club. One of the few things she'd let me participate in. I had worried for months about how to ask her about it. I wasn't certain I'd be allowed to go. And all this time, she'd been looking for an escape. "So she just came here, to what?"

"To hire me to fulfill her very specific instructions for renovations and preparations. She very much intended that this be a safe haven for you both."

My stomach cramped. "A safe haven?"

"Hold on, she left something behind." She went to one of the paintings in the living room and moved it to the side, and I could see there was a safe behind it. She tapped in a few numbers, and it opened. I couldn't see much of anything as it was too dark. Reaching inside she pulled out an object that looked like a wooden carving or something.

"Another clue to follow? Didn't she leave a letter or something?"

"Your mother is very private. Always has been. All I was told was that you must have that key and to protect it."

Gemma reached over and fingered the key as she glanced at the script on it and frowned. "I'm sorry, but this explains nothing. You've told us nothing. All you've done is give her a wooden key. You just reached into a safe she can't even access."

Magda smiled. "It's your house. You have access to everything.

There's a file I can provide you with if you wish to stay with pass codes to the safes."

"Did you just say safes?"

"Yes, there are two more. One in the floorboard in your bedroom, and one in the main bedroom's closet."

"Safes? Why are there multiple safes in a single house?"

"I'm sorry. I really do wish I knew more."

Magda turned to the stove where the kettle was whistling, and she continued to hum the song from the garden earlier. I recognized that I had heard it before.

"For the girl to shine, even she must be pruned. For even a diamond began as coal."

"That song you were singing, what is it?"

"I don't know it by heart, but it was something your mother always sang. She said it was a lullaby. Other than that, I don't know what it is. It just seems comforting, so I sing it."

It was melodic and achingly familiar, like I should know it, like I should understand it. So why didn't I?

For the girl to shine, even she must be pruned. For even a diamond began as a coal.

Over tea, I tried to ask Magda more questions, attempting to get more clarity about my mother. Who she was, or if there was anything she said.

"Are you planning on staying?" Magda asked. "Your room is ready. You and your friend, you can stay."

But I knew I couldn't. Not until I understood more.

"She's not coming back, is she?"

Magda gave me a soft smile. "The last time she saw me, she said that she wouldn't be here for a long time. And that if you came without her, I was to give you that key."

The tears that had been banked all this time started to burn the backs of my eyes, and I wanted to cry, but I wasn't going to. My mother was alive. She'd been here. And I was going to find her.

CHAPTER 24
SAINT

"You had one fucking job."

Rook glowered at me. "Listen, how the fuck was I supposed to know she was going to do a runner?"

"*You. Lost. Her.* Explain to me how the fuck you lost my fiancée!"

The muscle in his jaw worked. "We both know she's not really your fiancée, but I'll let it slide. I put a man on her outside Gemma's apartment. How was I supposed to anticipate she was going to do a runner at the exact moment of shift change?"

"For fuck's sake, Rook, this isn't your first day on the job."

A flush crept up his neck. He knew he'd fucked up. There was no point in me riding his arse any further because Gabe was going to rip him apart. But still, Kaya was gone and it was all his fucking fault.

She was out there alone and completely unsafe. She could be hurt. I wondered if this was what it felt like to care about people. Maybe it was the reason I felt like I was coming unglued right now. Maybe I hadn't really bothered giving a shit about anyone before now.

Caring was too fucking hard. Life wasn't supposed to be this difficult. All we had to do was stash her, and we couldn't even manage that. Gabe was going to kill us.

"Look," Rook said, "we will get her back."

"How?" We were already on the airstrip, heading toward the hangar and waiting for a direction to go. "Explain to me how the fuck we're going to get her back?"

"I tagged her. It'll ping the satellite wherever the fuck they are."

"Are you sure that shit will work?"

"A hundred percent," he said. "I may have fucked up here, but with that tech, I don't think they're capable of disappearing completely. We'll get her back."

I frowned at him. "*I* will get her back. You just stay out of my way."

Rook laughed. "Oi, mate, I see how you look at her. Especially her arse. I must say it's a very nice arse. I also noticed how quick you were to jump in and offer to be her fiancé for cover. I see what you're doing. And she's smart, she'll see it too."

"Shut your shitty face."

"What, are you going to make me?"

"I mean it. Shut your pie hole. You don't know a single bloody thing."

"I think I do. You want her. But here's the thing; she's also checking me out. She likes what she sees. And there's not a damn thing I can do about that if she decides she likes me better than you."

What I wanted to do was lunge at him, put my hands around his neck and squeeze. It was his fault that she was gone. Except, why didn't she just call me when she was planning something?

As we pulled up to the hangar, he whistled low. "I found them."

"Where the fuck are they?"

"Croatia."

I frowned. "What the fuck is she doing in Croatia? Did someone take her?"

Rook shook his head. "No. I went over every piece of video footage after we realized they were gone. No one took her. She went on her own. The videos showed Kaya and Gemma, each with one small bag, enough for overnight, or at least it looked like it. No one took them unless her friend isn't who she says she is."

My stomach cramped again. I thought back to meeting Gemma at the gala-turned-engagement party. She was nice. Bubbly. Did she have another motive? She seemed to really care about Kaya. She even tried to threaten me if I hurt her friend. People don't go to those lengths if they're just pretending to be concerned. So what was the angle here?

"I swear to bloody God, Rook, just fucking find her."

"Right, but aren't you asking yourself what the fuck she's doing in Croatia?"

"I'm asking myself a lot of things. Most importantly, is she safe and how do I get away with killing you if she isn't?"

Rook groaned. "I fucked up, all right? I know I fucked up. I'm working on it. We'll get Kaya back, damn it."

I sighed. "She's our mission, mate. It's our job to protect her. We need to get her back because we can't lose her, too."

He sighed as he studied me. "You are so obvious, mate. Will you just take a moment and admit to me, let alone yourself, that you want her?"

I scowled at him. "Don't start with me on this shit, too. I see the way you look at her."

"Well, she's fit. I'm definitely going to look. I'm a male, alive and kicking, you know. "

"I prefer you don't look in my presence."

He chuckled low. "If you want her, then do something about it. Or I will."

I narrowed my gaze at him. "She's not looking at you, Rook."

"Are you sure about that? I see her checking out my arse. I have a very fine arse, indeed. You know, kind of like Captain America's arse. I am England's arse."

"You most certainly are *an* arse."

Rook's brow furrowed. "Oh, did you just try and take the piss? It didn't land mate. I'm so sorry."

"I'll show you land." I shoved him toward the plane. "Get on the plane. We need to find her."

The next three hours were tense and tight. It was all I could do to not jump out of my skin as I waited, so I tried to focus on the task at hand. When we landed in Zagreb, there was a car already waiting to take us to the smaller town of Petina, fifteen kilometers away.

Westin was on his computer in no time, hooking up to our Rogues comm team. We pinpointed an area where the signal on the tracker was the strongest. Driving into a residential area, we pulled up to the location just as Kaya and Gemma were leaving a house. An elderly woman, probably in her early sixties, gave them both a hug and waved them off.

Who the fuck was that?

I took the photos while Rook was trying to run facial recognition. "What do you want us to do, boss? Stay? Investigate?"

My gut twisted. We could stay. It would probably be wise to get information from the woman, but I was too worried about Kaya. "No, follow."

"Yes, boss. Whatever you say."

I could have sworn I saw him smirk. Unfortunately, it looked like Kaya and Gemma were headed back toward Zagreb. That didn't make any sense unless they were already going back to their hotel. Were they going to meet someone, or was something else happening? What the fuck was going on here?

About five minutes from the center of downtown, Rook frowned. "We have company. Or rather, the girls have company."

I could see a dark sedan, trailing. Watching them.

"How do you want to handle this?" Rook asked.

"Fuck, let me think. She doesn't know we're following her.

They're not taking any precautions, so they don't know they're about to get ambushed. Where's the car?"

"Two cars back now. We're going to have to make a move if we want to deal with them."

In my comms, I spoke to the other Rogues in our follow car. "Car two, black sedan out back." And then I rattled off the plates. "Cut them off."

In thirty seconds, I could hear the revving of an engine and screeching tires. They'd blocked the car. Or tried to. But then the sedan whipped around them and was still behind us, only four cars between us now.

"Fuck."

From the passenger seat, Rook nodded.

"Yeah. But hang on to your hat. We're going to make this very difficult."

As the car approached, I waited. The light above was turning yellow, and the sedan was trying to beat it. But before it could, I pulled the emergency brake and spun, hitting the car as it approached on my left, and hitting another, making sure to stay locked with that one.

When the light turned red, we could see that Kaya's car had turned right down the road. The black sedan still tried to lunge forward, but I'd kept the spin going just long enough until I hit a hydrant and pinned them in.

When I turned to Rook, he stared at me. "Are you completely insane?"

"The question you should be asking is, who the fuck are these idiots? And why are they following Kaya?"

———

KAYA

I wasn't exactly *sneaking* back home. I was merely returning from being out with a friend... stealthily.

You're totally sneaking back home, and it's not even your home.

Ugh. I hated my brain. My mind was a soupy sea of questions, worry, considerations, and more questions. My mother was alive, or at least she had been as recently as six months ago. So what the hell had happened to her? She'd built a whole house for me, in a place that I had never even known existed. How was I supposed to confront that? Would she have ever let me know she was alive if I hadn't come looking?

As my brain tried to sort out all of the questions rolling around in my head, I was doubly distracted. Saint had been on me to get back to class, back to meeting at least one of my life's goals. I had to study as I had a major fucking exam waiting for me.

And you have a wedding to get ready for.

A fake wedding to my very fake fiancé. I wasn't really going through with marrying him.

When I entered the building, Westin Rourke met me. He nodded at the two security guys who'd dropped me off after Gemma and I snuck back into her apartment. He said, "I'll take it from here, mates. Nice weekend, Kaya?"

I tried to give him an unaffected smile. "Yeah, it was lovely, thank you for asking. Yours?"

"Oh, you know, chasing down a few things here there and everywhere. Nothing really eventful."

"That's good. Glad you had fun." I hated to lie.

As we stepped into the elevator and he typed in the security code for the penthouse level, he turned to me. "So, the whole wedding to Saint thing, how do you feel about it?"

I blinked rapidly. "Excuse me?"

"You and Saint, you're not like a real thing, right?"

I knew he was aware that this whole thing was fake. It was just jarring to hear him talking about it. "Of course. I mean, you know we're just pretending for the time being while you guys look for whoever is after me."

"That's perfect. Just swell. That means I can take you to dinner."

"What?"

"You know, a date. Surely you've had dates before. I could cook, we'd talk about things while Saint's not around, that whole thing?"

What the fuck am I supposed to say here?

He was attractive and kind. And there was nothing wrong about it. Saint had said he wanted this whole thing to be more than platonic, but he'd done absolutely nothing about it and was still a little distant, so there was no problem with me going on a date with Westin. "I, um, sure. Dinner sometime."

He grinned and winked at me. "Perfect. Tuesday sound good?"

"Uh, yeah."

"Excellent. I'll come by at seven. Saint's got the nicer kitchen, and I've been dying to get my hands on some of his knives."

"Really, you can cook?"

"Oh ,yeah. My last name might be Rourke, but I have an Italian grandmother. She taught me how to cook everything from scratch. From noodles to her secret sauce. You're going to love it."

I laughed at his enthusiasm. He really was like a big kid with that adorable dimple. There was a little boy still inside. Maybe I was playing with fire and this was a bad idea for reasons I might not even be able to articulate right now.

But you have to eat.

And between classes and everything, I couldn't just sit around waiting for Saint to talk to me, to pay attention to me, to tell me something vital. No. I was going to have this date. There was nothing wrong with it.

But when we reached the penthouse and Westin walked me in, I found Saint waiting in the foyer for me like a father staying up all night for his daughter coming home from a date.

Unease rolled over me. Something was wrong. There was something tense around his mouth and his eyes.

"Hey, Kaya."

"Jasper."

Westin cocked his head at that. "She calls you Jasper, huh?"

I wasn't entirely unaware. I neither liked nor hated his name. But I knew that it had the most delicious effect on him when I used it. It made him narrow his eyes ever so slightly and focus his gaze on me, making me hot and prickly all over my skin. I liked it, so I kept doing it. "Is there something I'm supposed to call you besides Jasper?"

The look, as focused as it had been, was gone in a second. "Everyone else calls me Saint."

"Well, I am your fiancé, right? So I should probably call you Jasper."

Westin grinned then. "I'll leave you two to it. See you tomorrow, Kaya."

"Yeah, bye." I wanted to call out, 'Oh no wait, don't leave me with him.' But that was ridiculous. It wasn't like I was afraid to be with him. And I knew he wasn't going to hurt me. He just looked... I don't know, intense.

"Good weekend?"

"Yeah, how about you?"

He stared at me, as if he was waiting for something.

He knows.

But how could he know? How? We'd slipped out and back in through the backdoor of Gemma's place. It wasn't really a backdoor even. She and her flat mate found a connector with another flat that had a side door to street parking on the other side of the building. They barely used it. As far as other people were concerned, we'd been in her flat the whole time. If Saint knew I had taken off to Croatia, he didn't say anything. "Everything okay?" I asked. "You seem tense."

"Do I now? I wonder why that is? Did you and Gemma get up to anything special over the weekend?"

Oh fuck, oh fuck, oh holy fuck. He knows.

I would not panic. No way could he know, right? "Yeah, you know, just hanging out with Gems." That wasn't a lie.

"Right. Nothing special at all."

"No. But I'm glad you're here. I did want to talk to you about the plan. How long is this whole engagement thing? Adrianna suggested the wildest thing to me the other day when she came by to talk about this wedding. I know she's your sister and she's excited, but you haven't even spoken to me about any of this. So we should probably do that, shouldn't we?"

The muscle in his jaw ticked, and he gave me a terse nod. "Yeah, we will. Just not tonight. You should probably get some rest."

He turned and strutted away. And as I watched him stalk, all muscle and sinew and looking like a caged jungle animal, I admired the view. But I also had the sinking suspicion that he knew I was keeping secrets.

CHAPTER 25
SAINT

WE WERE PLAYING a game of pretend.

Kaya was busy pretending she hadn't just taken off over the weekend without telling me where she was going, and I was pretending I hadn't gone after her like a lovesick fool.

Just thinking about those harrowing hours made my stomach turn. Not knowing where she was had my mind hooked on a constant nightmare I couldn't shake. What if I had failed to protect her? What if something had happened to her? What if I never told her what I had started to feel?

Nope. That last one wasn't anything I was going to focus on.

After we got rid of her tail, we found her and Gemma at their hotel outside the Zagreb Airport. And wouldn't you know it, no sooner than dropping off the car at the adjacent rental company, they jumped on a fucking plane to go home.

For the last day, she'd been acting completely normal. As if she hadn't just left the country, scared me half to death, and gone on some goose chase for something she hadn't communicated with me. I'd ask if she'd had a good time, and she'd smiled at me glumly and nodded.

And now, she was at home pouring over those papers of her

mum's. She was wearing some kind of charm around her neck. It looked like it was a couple of inches long and wooden. She kept running her fingers along the edges as if chasing over something.

"Is that new?"

She frowned up at me. "I'm sorry, what?"

"That charm you're wearing, is it new?"

"Yeah, um, I just picked it up recently."

"Oh yeah? That's interesting. Where?"

She blinked at me once, then twice, then cocked her head. "Nowhere special. I'm sorry I've been distracted. I know that you wanted to meet and go over our contract again."

Her lips just mouthing the word *contract* had everything in my gut going tight like a stone just dropped in it. Oh yes, I wanted to talk about the contract. But she was keeping things from me, and there was no way I'd discuss that with her until she confessed. I was not about to have a relationship with a liar again.

But isn't that what you are doing to her?

With a shake of my head to clear out that lousy thought, I joined Kaya on the floor. "Yeah, I don't think we should talk about that right now."

She blinked at me owlishly. "What?"

"The contract is not important."

"Right. It's just my life."

"Well, there's no point in having a contract if you can't be honest with me."

She lifted her gaze. "What?"

"So from what store did you pick that charm up?"

With her tawny skin, it was hard to tell when she paled, but she got the general gist. Eyes going wide, jaw going slack, looking a little like she might faint. "You know?"

"Of course I know."

I leaned back, crossing my legs at the ankles. "As a matter of fact, I chased after you."

"Jasper, I should have told you. Please forgive me."

"You *should* have told me." I picked up one of the highlighters she'd been using and twirled it around my fingers, twisting around and around. "You lied to me. You're not a prisoner here, Kaya. I'm trying to help you. I'm trying to keep you safe."

"I know. Look, I should have said something. I just... We weren't going to be gone that long, and I just wanted to chase down a lead."

"By yourself?"

"No, Gemma was with me."

"So you lied to me like I'm your parent?" I scowled at her. "Do you understand something could have happened to you?"

"Nothing did, and we're fine. How did you know we were gone?"

"I went to see you. I wanted to take you to brunch, but guess who wasn't where she was supposed to be? Imagine how that made me feel." I let my rage simmer just under my skin.

"I'm sorry." She inched back.

I frowned at her movement. She looked frightened. I forced a more measured voice. "I am trying to keep you safe."

"I know. I will be more communicative, but you and I barely know each other, and it's tense. I don't know how to do this."

I leaned forward. I watched the base of her throat and the rise and fall of her chest. "I have an idea. Why don't we go to dinner tomorrow night?"

"Yeah, sure. Um, except, I can't do it tomorrow."

I frowned. As I leaned closer, her breathing became shallower. I could feel the puffs on my cheeks as I leaned forward with only a few inches separating us. "Why can't you go to dinner tomorrow?"

She swallowed hard. "I, um, I'm going out."

"Who with?"

"Westin. He asked me to dinner, and I said yes."

I was going to fucking kill him.

She had a bloody date. A goddamn date with fucking Rook. That piece of shit. He knew how important this was to make everything look real, but he was going to take her out? My fiancée. Just what the fuck was he playing at?

I was going to put a hole through his face.

Tuesday was a Rogues day for me. Standard training, ops review, and breakdown. As we suited up, Lachlan slid me a glance. "All right?"

"Yeah, I'm fine. I'm great."

He nodded. "Yeah, sure. Seems like you really mean that."

"Of course, I mean it. I'm fine."

He laughed. "Okay, this is the part where you're going to tell me how it's going with Kaya."

"Nope. This is the part where you mind your fucking business."

The problem with Lachlan King was not just his cockiness, but the fucker acted like he knew everything. And he just loved to nail me.

King just laughed again. "So, trouble in paradise already?"

"Nope, I'm fine."

Tabatha Smith joined the two of us. "Will you two stop chatting away like a couple of gossipmongers? There's work to be done. We've got to practice for this rescue mission. Do your bullshitting on your own time."

I frowned. "Who's the team?"

"It's the three of us, Saff, and Rook."

I scowled.

Lachlan lifted a brow at me. "Rook is solid. A little brash, but he follows orders in the field. You know that."

"It's fine."

Tabatha stared at me as if I'd sprouted two heads. When she wandered off to find Saff so we could get started, Lock nudged me. "What's the problem? You and Rook not getting along? Not one happy family?"

"I'm not playing happy family with him."

"Oh, you're sore, huh? How is that whole love situation going anyway? Kaya seems like a smart girl. She hasn't noticed anything untoward?"

I scowled at him. "I didn't give you any shit when you were pining away about Saff."

"Oh, lies. You almost had me believe that she was shagging her own brother. You're so full of shit."

I grinned. "Yeah, that's fair. It was so easy though. I could have mentioned that they were siblings. But the way you kept eyeballing Gabe every time he was in the vicinity was hilarious. And that was just because he had a real hard-on for her protection."

He rolled his eyes. "So what's the problem with Kaya? Or are she and Rook getting along a little too well for your liking?"

"That little twat. Every time I turn around, there he is offering to help her with her homework having taken that class at university recently. And the way he just talks to her..."

"And are you the old man in the room? Is that the problem?"

I just barely resisted the urge to hurt him, and he laughed nefariously. "Mate, you should see your face. So, it's not just for show then?"

I frowned at him. "What do you mean?"

"Your little suggestion that you should provide protection by offering to marry her, at least for the cameras."

"It's more complicated than that."

"What is it?"

I sighed. "We don't have time to get into it right now."

Lachlan eyed me suspiciously. "However complicated it is, it's probably because you didn't tell her the truth yet. You have that look on your face."

"I don't have a look."

"Oh, you have a look. It's the look of someone who's trapped. She likes Rook, and you think they have a thing going on."

"I know they don't have a fucking *thing*."

Lachlan just laughed. "Okay, if you say so."

We got our assignments for the training op. Lachlan was supposed to sneak around the back. Tabs was going in through the front door with Saffron. They were trying the good old Berlin tactic of two women in need of help. It was my job to get to the perpetrator, and then Lock would meet me and help me extract the hostages. Except, on our first round, as I approached Rook, doing his level best to play the baddie, when we engaged in hand-to-hand, I may or may not have pulled my punches, and landed him flat on his back.

From the ground, he smirked at me. "Lucky hit."

"No such thing as luck."

He jumped to his feet with his usual grin. "Next time, I won't take it so easy on you, old man."

I wanted to hit him all over again, but Lachlan pushed us apart and waved Rook away. "What the fuck is wrong with you?"

"Nothing."

But he didn't budge. Didn't move out of the way. "Tell me."

"He's going on a date with Kaya."

Lachlan's eyes went wide. Then he coughed a laugh. "Ooooooh, boy. Even with the ruse set up?"

"I just know what she told me."

"So, they're going out. You know, maybe you could just tell her how you feel? That would be noble."

I scowled at him. "I don't *feel* like anything."

"Except we've had this convo twice now. The first time, you damn near knocked Rook out, and the second time, you clothes-lined him."

"He walked into my arm."

Lock laughed. "If you say so. Maybe you'd be better off just talking to her. That might fix this."

"No, I have another solution in mind."

Lock lifted his brows. "Why do I have a feeling I'm not going to like this?"

"I'm going to ruin their date."

———

Kaya

It wasn't that Westin was bad company. He was funny. He'd taken many of the same classes I was currently in, and the conversation was light, easy. I just wasn't into it. Which was so surprising because he was lovely.

But he's not Saint.

And Saint... I hadn't seen hide nor hair of him since early that morning. He'd just sent me cryptic texts when I was in class earlier telling me he'd be home late.

I wasn't sure what that meant because he'd been coming home late some nights. When I'd tried to ask him about it, he wouldn't tell me anything.

Also, this isn't your home.

No, but it had started to feel that way a little bit. A home away from home. The opportunity to still resume some of my normal life. Whatever the hell that meant.

"Earth to Kaya. Well, how was it?"

I dragged myself out of my reverie. "It's really good. How did you learn to cook? Did your grandma sit you down and show you how to do everything?"

He laughed. "Nope. She's not really the type. She likes to gamble. Drink. But *her* Nana had these great handwritten recipe books, so we read them together and I tried the recipes out on her."

"Oh my God, how old were you?"

He laughed. "Let's just say I was a precocious one."

"One?" I was convinced he was full of shit.

"Like I said, I was precocious."

"Okay..."

That was the thing about Westin, you never quite knew when you were getting the truth.

But his sauce was to die for, so that much was true. He could really cook. He wasn't lying about that, but I could see it. That thin line of deception, that marker where people put their pasts and things they didn't want people to see.

"So, you and Saint," he said. "I get the feeling I'm stepping on his toes."

I hadn't expected him to be so direct. "No. Not at all. We're not... we're not real."

He gave me a soft smile. "Honestly, I would have been on shift tonight anyway, and figured I would make you a meal. But I wanted to test the waters when I asked you out."

"Oh, you could have just said so."

"Yeah, you're right. I could have. But it's more interesting watching your brain try and talk yourself out of being completely into Saint."

"I'm not completely into him. He is stubborn. Taciturn. What the hell is wrong with him? He never says anything. Keeps everything close to the vest. And he's bossy. Soooo bossy. What the fuck? I don't think I've ever met a man that bossy. And he's moody. I never know what I'm going to get."

Westin laughed. "He's also one of the best blokes I ever met."

"How long have you been working for him?"

"Not long. It was only in the last year that we've gotten to know each other better. He's actually not a bad mentor. And what he's like now, that's new. He's not usually like this. He smiles a lot more. Smiles easily. He'll be the first one with a joke. But he's got family stuff that has overloaded him recently."

"That doesn't even sound like the same man I know."

Westin shrugged. "If you do have some feelings for him, I'd say be a little patient. Your whole life is just getting back to even, and his isn't. He's been in turmoil for a long time. You guys would understand each other, and I think—"

The front door opened then, and Saint marched through. He

gave a nod to me and a scowl to Westin, but that was it. He didn't interrupt us, didn't say anything.

I frowned at Westin. "Are you trying to convince me that he's affable, funny, kind, warm?"

He nodded. "Yeah, under normal circumstances he is. Right now, his jealousy is eating at him. He's stressed out with whatever is going on at work and all that family drama with his old man."

We moved onto other topics, and conversation with Westin was easy. We had so much in common. It was like finding your long lost friend after years of separation.

After I helped him clean up the dinner dishes, we ended up back in the living room listening to some music and track combos a friend of his had made. "Oh wow, he's really good."

"Yeah. He DJ'd one summer in Ibiza. That kid is wild. He started at fifteen, and wowed the organizers when he was nineteen. They gave him anything he wanted.

"How the hell did a nineteen-year-old pull that off?"

"He's tall, looks the part, and he's one hell of a liar."

I shook my head laughing. "Oh my God. Did you go with him?"

Westin blushed then. "Um, you could say that."

"This I have to hear. How much trouble did you two get into?"

"You know, this is not the right course of conversation. Suffice it to say, we partied in Ibiza with a couple of impressionable young women."

"Oh please, do tell me everything."

For the first time since I'd known him, he looked embarrassed. It was fascinating. "I'll bet you—"

I had something very funny and fitting to say. Honestly, I did. The problem was, Saint had opened the door to his bedroom and sauntered out in nothing but the smallest towel I had ever seen. It was so small, it barely covered any of the goodies as he stalked out toward the foyer again.

My mouth went dry. Our gazes locked, and I could not tear my eyes away from him.

Broad shoulders, his body formed a perfect triangle. Narrow, tapered waist. Eight pack on display. And he was nicely muscled. Not too big, just fully developed. And then that happy trail vanished and disappeared behind the too small towel that Saint had tied at his left hip. And for the love of God, I would swear up and down I could fully see the imprint of his dick. Any second, I was expecting to see the engorged tip hanging below the towel.

Westin groaned. "Mate, what the fuck are you doing?"

Saint grinned at both of us. "Not interrupting, am I?"

I shouldn't stare.

I *knew* I shouldn't stare because that was ridiculous. He had rejected me. Basically told me I was too young and didn't know what I wanted. But still, I had eyeballs, and they were in perfect functional order. Jesus Lord, when he grabbed his phone, his gaze remained locked on mine as if taunting me. I could almost hear him speaking with his eyes saying, *Oh yeah, you want this.*

And then he casually strode back to the bedroom. The view from the back was so good. Not as great as the front, but geeze, what a spectacular arse. When he shut the door of his bedroom, I could feel the vice grip he had on my soul.

Suddenly, I couldn't breathe, couldn't think. When my gaze returned to Westin, he was sitting back staring at me with a lifted brow. "You haven't heard a word I said in the last thirty seconds."

"O-oh my God. W-what happened to cutting me some slack? You saw what he just did."

Under his breath, I could hear him mutter, "Dick."

Weren't they friends? Why was he calling him a dick?

Suddenly, Westin stood. "It's time for me to go."

"What? We were having fun."

"And I know when I'm beat."

"What's that supposed to mean?"

He gave me a sad smile and shook his head. "Ask him. I'll come back tomorrow and get all the kitchen equipment. Thanks for the help cleaning up."

"Of course. Thank you for dinner, and the chat, and the music."

At the door, he ruffled my hair and then gave me a big hug.

And as he held on to me, I could swear I felt a breath and heard a low growl just behind me.

Westin released me immediately. "I'm going. I'm going."

I whirled on Saint. "Just what the fuck is your goddamn problem?"

CHAPTER 27
KAYA

My breath caught. Saint looked furious, but so was I. "What are you doing here?"

"I wanted to see if he was going to give a good night kiss."

I lifted my chin. "I see you're making sure your clause is religiously followed."

"Yeah, I am. Are you going to be seeing him again?"

Now I was really pissed. "And what bloody business is it of yours? From the moment we decided to do this, you've held me at arm's length. All I've wanted to do is ask you some questions and sit down and talk to you. But then you kissed me and walked away and said we need to figure out a contract before you kissed me again. And then you barely speak to me for a week."

"And then you lied to me about going to fucking Croatia."

My eyes went wide. "How dare you? I'm not a prisoner. Look, you've done me a favor. You gave me a place to stay and you protected me, but this is bullshit. I didn't sign up for this. I'll just go stay with Gemma."

"The fuck you will." He started closing the gap between us and I backed up. For every step I took back, he stepped forward, crowding me.

Finally, I planted my feet and stared back at him.

"If you think you're going to run after Rourke, you have another think coming."

A shiver ran up my spine, but I held his gaze. "Oh yeah? How are you going to stop me?"

His gaze traveled from my eyes down to my lips and lingered there. The hum in my blood gave me several ideas on just how he planned to get there. He bit his bottom lip, and I had to visibly clamp my teeth to help me keep from moaning. Oh Jesus, Lord. Everything about Jasper Saint was a goddamn problem. "Why did you come out naked?"

"I didn't come out naked. I had a towel on."

I laughed. "The towel barely covered anything."

"It covered the important bits."

"You did it on purpose."

He cocked his head with a willful smile. "Prove it."

I shook my head and tried to squirm around him, but he barricaded his arm against the wall right next to my head to keep me from moving.

I tried the other side and he did the same thing with the other hand.

"Now, like I said, where the fuck do you think you're going?"

"Anywhere away from here. This is a mistake."

"The hell it is." And then he slammed his lips down on mine, wrapping his hands into my hair and around my body. He pulled me tight against him. All I could do was hold on for the ride.

Saint kissed like he was starving. Like this was the only opportunity he would ever get to eat again. It was a clash of teeth and tongues. And then I pulled him closer. I wanted more. I wanted to drink from him. I wanted everything he could give me. I was so desperate, needing him to do something about that ache between my thighs. That ache that had been there from the moment of that first kiss at the auction. The ache that had kept me from sleeping properly for weeks now. I just needed him to do something about it. He had what I needed. I would do anything to get it, and I was afraid he knew that.

He bent down and picked me up, and I had no choice but to wrap my legs around him like the last time. He backed me up against the wall again. This time his hands slid up my legs under my skirt, grasping my arse, kneading the muscle and hitching my hips just so I could feel the blazing-hot, rigid length of his erection against my pulsing heat. All he was doing was making me ache so much worse.

Oh, good God, I just needed him to give me everything.

His teeth scraped along my neck and his whisper was harsh. "You fucking smell delicious. Coconut and lime has been driving me bananas for fucking weeks. It permeates the whole goddamn house."

"I'm sorry."

"No you're not. You are a naughty little thing, and you are not sorry. You do it on purpose."

When he said *on purpose*, he deliberately ground his cock against me, and I whimpered. "Are you not doing this on purpose? You walked out here naked on purpose. I kept wondering if I was going to see your dick peek out beneath the towel."

"Yeah, I wondered if you could see it."

My eyes went wide. He lifted his head to meet my gaze, and his dirty little smirk made me want to hit him. But he caught my hand swiftly before I could even strike out and then caught the other one. Held both of them in one of his enormous hands before kissing me again. When he drew back, he whispered against my lips. "Ah, there's my little Sprite."

I struggled in his hold, knowing full well I wasn't going anywhere until he felt like releasing me. He carried me through the foyer. I thought he was taking me back to the living room, but no, we went further. Then he went left into the main bedroom. The enormous corner in the back hall where I never ventured. His room. All I could do was swallow hard. Did I want this?

Hell, yes you do. Just let him make the ache go away and then go worry about what everything means later. Don't overthink this.

He nipped my clavicle. "Are you still with me?"

I gave a little squeak of alarm. "Yes, I'm ready."

"You're not still thinking about him, are you?"

"Thinking about who?"

He grinned at that. "Right answer."

And then he tossed me on the bed.

I gave a very un-ladylike squeak as I bounced. "Oh, for fuck's sake, Jasper!"

He grinned then unsnapped the button of his jeans and eased down his zipper.

I licked my lips nervously as I watched him. All I could do was take in the show that was him. His skin was flushed, and his gaze was locked steady on mine as he pulled his jeans down. No boxers.

I was weak. I a hundred percent looked. And when I did, my mouth fell open in surprise and a little bit of determination.

"You keep looking at me like that, and I'm likely to think you want to put me in your mouth."

All I could do was swallow hard around the sawdust on my tongue. I *did* want to put him in my mouth. Jesus.

When he started crawling toward me on the bed, I was filled with an overwhelming sense of panic. I wanted to flee. But he caught my ankle too quickly and tugged me under him. "Oh no, I'm not going to hurt you. You can tell me to stop at any time. You're not going to just run, though. You're going to use your words and tell me what you want."

I blinked up owlishly at him. How the hell was I supposed to use my words? Jesus Christ. Did I have words? Between my thighs, I could feel the pressing length of him. He was huge. That was the only way to describe him. Fucking huge.

He brushed his lips over mine, and this time they were soft, pleading. The question was in the kiss. Is this okay? Do you want to go? And I knew he would let me go immediately. He didn't want to, but he would let me go.

I wrapped my legs around his waist, and he grunted softly as I deliberately brought him in closer contact with me.

"You are shockingly strong." He whispered against my skin, and I gave him a little squeeze with my thighs. He pulled back, choking out a laugh.

"Okay, you're impatient. Is that what you're telling me?"

"Yes, I'm impatient."

"Fair enough. Let's get rid of these clothes."

He pulled back, and I mourned the loss of his weight, the sweet, delicious pressure of it. The heat, the feeling of being cocooned and safe.

He started to tug my dress up and over my shoulders. His hands slid up my legs, pausing at the edge of my knickers. His gaze lifted to mine, and on his brow was a silent question. All I could do was bite my bottom lip, nod, and sputter out, "Yes. Oh God, please, yes, yes, yes."

He slid the fabric aside, sliding his fingers inside me. And then he cursed. He squeezed his eyes shut, leaning forward and dropping his forehead to mine. "You're so wet. Jesus Christ." I heard the hitch in his voice, begging for control. Then his thumb stroked over my clit. I bowed my back, reaching for him, pulling him down to kiss me, inviting his fingers. He added another one as his thumb slid in quick, rapid lashes over my clit, and I knew that this was going to be fast and rough and dirty, and I was going to go off like a rocket.

With a frustrated growl, he tore his lips from mine and pulled his fingers from me before yanking down my knickers and throwing them over his shoulder.

One hand slid behind my back, and with a quick snap of his fingers, my bra unlatched. My eyes went wide in surprise, and he just chuckled before kissing down my ribs and my belly, pausing just over my mound. His gaze drew up my body and met mine as he cocked his head. "God, just looking at you makes me weak."

Fucking hell, he was going to destroy me. I could feel it. I wanted him so badly I couldn't breathe. When he planted his mouth over my sex, I screamed, "Oh my God. Oh my Goooood!"

I could have sworn I heard him snarl, but he kept his mouth right where it was, his gaze not meeting mine, though it kept flickering to the bedside table.

"Do you need to get that?"

He scowled at me like I had asked him something wicked. The phone did a trilling sound again.

"You can get that if you—"

He kept his mouth planted on my clit and slid a finger deep inside me, finding that vulnerable nerve. Stroking me. Teasing me. Sucking hard on my clit, letting his tongue play.

His phone trilled again and his brow furrowed, but he kept doing what he was doing. He clamped one big palm on my knee to keep my legs open and then slid another finger inside me. This time, as he worked both fingers and sucked on my clit, only pausing to change up the strokes with his tongue, I dove my hands into his hair, pulling him into me, grinding against his face. I screamed again, breaking apart in tiny little pieces. Oh dear God.

He lifted his head, still stroking me with that slow glide and retreat, letting me ride out my orgasm, coaxing more heat from me.

His phone trilled again, and this time he reached blindly and pulled it up to his face. Whatever he saw had him muttering under his breath. "Fuck. Goddamn it."

"Do you have to... Is something wrong?"

"Yes, something is wrong. And yes, I have to go, but I need one more from you before I do."

My eyes widened in alarm. "I don't think I can..."

The smile he gave me was so dirty. "Don't say that. Just one more to tide me over."

Then he dove back in, holding me open and bare to him. All of me. Every part.

I couldn't have been happier that Gemma always insisted on dragging me with her to get waxed. He dove in, fucking me with his tongue, his thumb over my clit, and his fingers tracing that line between my pussy and arse, and then he did something no one had ever done to me before.

He stroked the tight pucker and teased that hint of something dirty. That hint of something new and forbidden. He kept fucking me with his tongue, shoving it inside me as deep as it could go. One thumb still playing with my clit, determined to pull another orgasm from me. And as his green gaze met mine with an intensity strong enough to make me shake, I broke apart again, unable to even grasp onto his hair because my arms were too weak. But still, another orgasm went up my spine, threatening to break me apart completely. Then he shoved back with a satisfied grunt. "Fucking hell. I've never wanted to disobey an order more in my fucking life. But I have to go, Sprite."

I struggled to sit up. "What? Where are you going?"

He glowered at his phone. "Duty calls. But you and I, we're not done."

CHAPTER 28
SAINT

I WAS ready the rip the head off a fucking wildebeest. I'd fucked up.

All I could do was smell her fucking coconut and lime shampoo, or body lotion, or whatever the fuck it was.

My cock was rock hard. The whole drive to Rogues Division, I'd been shaking. Shaking with need.

I could have sworn I had seen Rourke's car behind mine, but when I pulled into the parking lot, I didn't see him. I had maybe handled that whole thing poorly.

Oh, you think?

I shouldn't have gone anywhere near their fucking date, but just knowing Rook might have his hands on her, was going to try and get in her fucking knickers, I hadn't been able to think about anything else. I was just desperate to stop him from touching her, tasting her, from having his face between her fucking thighs and wearing her goddamn legs like earmuffs. I'd bloody lost it with Rook, but I couldn't let him touch what was mine.

Yours? Didn't you say that you couldn't go there with her? That you had to take care of the Elise thing first? That shit was too complicated. Weren't you the one who said that?

Yes, I said all those things. But fuck, Rook touching her? No. Just fucking no.

I sensed the shadow before I saw it. I was already shifting into a fight stance at the edge of the parking lot before the force of muscle hit me.

It didn't dislodge me much.

"Rook, if you're going to sneak up on someone, at least have a fucking weapon. Hand-to-hand, you can't win."

"Did you fucking hurt her?"

I frowned. "What?"

"Kaya, did you hurt her?" he growled.

I frowned. "Are you fucking serious right now? Of course, I didn't hurt her."

"If I get back and she's hurt, I will fuck you up."

I shoved him back. "I welcome you to test the validity of your threat. Let's do that."

"You bloody wanker. If you—"

"She doesn't want you, Rook. She's fucking mine."

"You don't think I fucking know that? She's sweet. And for some reason, she fucking wants you. I have no idea why, but there it is. I just don't want you to destroy her because you're in love with someone else."

He shoved me back, and again, I did not budge. I heard a sharp whistle and looked up to see Saffron Abott booking it toward us. Before I even knew what had happened, something hit my leg. I went down, and so did Rook.

Saff stood above us both. "Will you two idiots stop this bullshit? Please tell me you're not pissing at each other over a girl? Rook, you've been called onto the Macallan mission. We're going to run your part again. But you, *Romeo*, have been called into Gabe's office."

Rook rolled to his side, groaning. "Fucking hell, Saff, that hurt."

"Yeah, I'm glad it hurt. When you two idiots start fucking with the merchandise, it pisses me off."

From my position, I frowned up at her. "Merchandise?"

"Your pretty-boy billionaire faces. Rogues depends on you billionaire twats looking the part. If you're all roughed up because you can't keep your dicks in your trousers, then you're fucked. People start asking questions about why you look like a ruffian. You'll smear your billionaire cache. Enough."

Rook and I growled at each other, but I pushed to my feet and gave Saff a nod. "Fine, I'm going."

"Yeah, you do that." I could feel her glare as I marched off.

When I reached Gabe's office, he already had the scotch out. "And how is the engagement bliss going?"

"Fuck off."

Gabe gave me the widest grin I had probably ever seen on his bloody face.

"Was that a smile?"

Gabe laughed. "Oh, yes. That was actually amusing to watch. You think I didn't have you and Rook on camera since you left the penthouse?"

I groaned. "For fuck's sake."

"Is this jealousy display going to fuck with my missions or not? Rook is solid, but he tends to have a slight attachment issue. He thinks of people more like puzzles to solve. It's nice to see him personally engaging for once."

I frowned. "Oh, he personally engages all right. Can you tell him to stay the fuck away from my wife?"

Gabe cocked his head. "Well, she's not your wife, *yet*. And this is just a mission, right, Saint?"

I glowered at him as I stood with my back pressed against the door. "Yeah, just a mission."

Gabe nodded. "We have a problem."

A chill wound around my spine. "What?"

"Lohman's's done a runner. Had help obviously. It happened during medical transport."

Bullshit. "What the fuck? Why didn't you call me?"

"I did call you as soon as it happened. You took a moment to answer."

Shit. I'd been face deep in Kaya when he called. "I'm going after him."

Gabe simply nodded. "You will. When we're done here, I'm sending you after him. What he doesn't know is he's tagged. But there's something else. I called to give you information. I didn't want Kaya hearing any of it. I had to get approval to share this with you."

Fuck, what now? "Okay, what is it?"

"Kaya's mother was a Rogues agent. Code name Dove."

My gut knotted.

C'mon, like you didn't know? Like you didn't sense it?

"Are you fucking kidding me?" I shoved off the door. "The last time we discussed her, you didn't think it was important to tell me?"

Gabe crossed his arms. "Back to your position, soldier. It was need to know until I had approval from Oversight to tell you."

Fuck. "What happened to her?"

"That's the thing. In five years, we haven't seen hide nor hair of her. She just vanished off the grid. We knew about the girl. She was undercover when she had the baby. We kept tabs on her. She was part of my mother's class at Rogues. A class called Ravens. When my parents were gone and I took over as acting operations director, I was briefed on all past missions and agents.

"How long has Oversight known about Kaya?"

He sighed. "She popped on facial recognition the night of the charity auction. Oversight thought it was her mother at first which was why they wanted her protected."

"Don't bullshit me. They wanted her watched. A field agent in the wind for that long? Loyalty will be called into question."

"And you're right. The prints on your tuxedo buttons we dusted told us it wasn't her. But she still needed protection."

"Monitoring," I corrected. "Fuck. When I went into this marriage you should have told me."

"I asked if you were sure, Saint."

He had. And when I thought about it, I knew I wouldn't have done anything differently.

Gabe continued. "This past weekend, her mother's print showed up in a stash house in Zagreb. She took out a few men. She wiped the place down good, but we got a partial fingerprint off one of the men's glasses. It looked like she stabbed him in the eye."

I cursed under my breath. "*We* were in Zagreb."

"Yes, I read the report. My guess is the men were tailing Kaya and she took them out."

I whistled low. "Christ."

"From Rook's report, I see that you ran into them here outside the city." Gabe clicked something on his desk and a map of the city pulled up on a massive digital screen, highlighting where we'd been when we managed to cut off the men following Kaya.

"Do we have cameras on where they went after that?"

Gabe nodded and showed me the route. "This is where we tracked them. They must have tried to double-back to find Kaya and her friend again, but they couldn't so they just returned to their stash house. It appears Kaya's mother was following them and keeping an eye on Kaya."

I frowned. "But why wouldn't her mother just reach out to her?"

"My guess is she knows exactly how dangerous it is."

"Why didn't you call her in?"

Gabe sighed. "We haven't had contact with her in years. She's been dark. Croatia was the first time we've gotten a blip in five years."

"You could have gotten Kaya killed. You should have told me."

"I'm aware. Oversight would have absolutely loved bringing

her in and using Kaya to bargain, but I never told them. That was my call to keep her off their radar. But it's too late for that now."

I crossed my arms and cursed. Who the fuck were the people I was working for? "Why do you think she vanished?"

"Best guess, to keep her daughter safe. We've got no signs from the Dove for years. Until now. Which means she's alive and protecting her daughter. You've got to get Kaya to talk to you. If we can bring them both in safely and help them, we need to."

My stomach sank. "Do you want Kaya's help, or do you want to use her as bait?"

He gave me a nonchalant shrug. "I just want to bring home an agent. And Kaya just wants her mum. We can do that right now. Lohman was the last person to see the Dove. We need him alive. He can help us keep Kaya safe. Are you going to help us?"

———

SAINT

It seemed I wasn't making it home tonight after all. Goddamn it, I was so keyed up I couldn't even think. As I strapped up with weapons, I knew I had a feral energy about me, because everyone stayed the fuck away.

Only Lock dared to approach. "Mate, are you ready to do this?"

"Let's just get the asshole and get back. I have things to do."

He nodded. "You know we're not going to be back until morning, right?"

I ground my teeth at that, but Lock was likely right. I wasn't getting back to Kaya. Not today.

Lock and I strode out of the armory, and I ran straight into Rook. I scowled at him, and he lifted a brow. "What's wrong? Still mad I had a date with your bird?"

Someone, I'm not saying who, but *someone* growled. Lachlan stepped between us. And then like the mate that he was, he stood in front of me and crossed his arms, glowering at Rook.

Rook shrugged. "I'm doing my job. The fact that I get to needle him in the process, that's just extra pudding."

Lachlan's voice was low. "If you know what's good for you, stay the fuck out of his way. Get strapped for mission."

"That's what I'm here to do. You two gossips are the ones stopping me."

As he passed, Lock deliberately placed himself between me and Rook.

"So you broke up the date?"

"Yup," I grunted.

"Do you want to tell me how you did that?"

I shrugged. "How does one normally you break up a date?"

Lachlan narrowed his gaze. "What is with you?"

"Fucking nothing. Let's just do this."

"This isn't you. Remember that and get your head in the game."

He had a point. I had such a hard-on for Connor, but now that it was time to bring his sorry arse back here, I was focused on fucking Kaya. I muttered under my breath, "And if Rook is fucking here, who's with Kaya?"

Lock eyed me up and down. "Oh my God, you're shagging her."

I blinked in surprise. "What? No, I did not shag her."

He scoffed. "Maybe not, but you are fucking going ballistic over her. You have that feral look to you. Like you might just rip somebody's head off." He considered. "Actually, come to think of it, that's a good vibe to have. This is not going to be easy."

Once the team was in the helicopter, Saff pulled out a tablet. "According to intel, Connor has a hidden family. Girlfriend, kid, the whole thing."

I glanced up in surprise. "What?"

Saff nodded. "Yeah, in a small village near Edinburgh. He's had her tucked away for years off the radar. But if he's running scared, he's likely gone there."

I could feel my blood start to hum again. This was it. I was going to get to drag his sorry arse back and he was going to *have* to answer some questions. Like why the fuck was he after Kaya?

After Saff was done with the briefing, Lock leaned over to me. "You didn't know about his family?"

I shook my head. "No. And why is his family living like that if he is so rich?"

Rook shook his head. "I have no idea. But we're going to pick him up and find out. And we'll have someone new to interrogate."

"Mate, a woman and her kid?"

"If she's hiding him, that's aiding and abetting."

"You're going to interrogate a six-year-old? Do you hear yourself?" I asked. But I knew he had a point.

I sat back, closing my eyes. This was so fucked. But the need to protect Kaya was my only concern. Everyone else could fuck right off.

We landed in a field at the edge of the village in tall grass. Just beyond the tree line, we could see the twinkling lights of a high street. We moved with stealth down some alleyways to the cottage, staying out of sight.

If he was licking his wounds, it was here in this idyllic village. We all had our approach points. Rook and I were going straight and direct. Lock headed east. Saff headed west. Converging at all points toward the house.

And then Rook spoke in my comms. "If you fucking wanted her, why didn't you just protect her in the beginning?"

"Shut your mouth."

"It's a valid question. You fucked her yet?"

I glowered at him. "Would you mind your goddamn business?"

"Unfortunately, you have made this my business. She's my damned assignment too."

"An assignment you seem to quite enjoy."

He sighed next to me. "Is she fit? Yeah. Is she smart? Hell, yes. And she smells like fucking summer. Unfortunately, I can *also* see the way she looks at you."

I shook my head at him. "Eyes on the prize. We have a mission."

In our ears, Lock agreed. "Yeah, eyes on the prize. Besides, if you cunts are going to gossip at least wait for me."

Saffron laughed. "Oi, you lot shut the fuck up. Stay focused."

We crossed the street easily enough and approached the cottage.

Then we did a quick scan for explosives, booby traps, anything.

When we didn't find any, Rook and I advanced quietly. From the outside, the door looked like something out of *Snow White*. Arched doorway, painted red, set in the stone of the cottage. But it had a heavy-duty security lock on it. One with what was apparently a six-figure combination.

Rook bent down and took out a device. "I know you're not particularly thrilled about me being on this mission, but at least I have use."

I ignored him.

"Could you do this?"

Once again, I ignored him.

He sighed but then worked his magic. It took several seconds, but eventually the lock turned green. And then he scrambled back.

In my comms, Lock muttered. "King in position. Ready."

Saff responded. "Heir in position. Ready."

I responded. "Rook and Saint in position. Ready."

And then we breached. King used a loud flash bang in the back of the house to sow confusion. From her side, Saff threw out some smoke. Rook and I donned our gas masks and breached through the front door.

King shouted, "I have movement."

Saff rumbled, "Me too."

I heard a series of grunts and kicks.

Rook and I were in. No one was in the front room, but a little girl was in the kitchen, holding a glass of milk. Connor Lohman was standing behind her with his arm around her neck.

Our earlier discussion came back to haunt me. Could I allow Lohman's child to be collateral damage? I knew in that moment, seeing the wide-eyed surprise and fear on the little girl's face, my answer was no. It was not who I was. I wanted to make him pay for Elise, for putting Kaya in danger. But I wasn't willing to sacrifice someone else. Especially not the innocent.

"If you step any closer, I swear to God, she will die."

That was the thing with villains. Not only did they immediately know your moral failing, but they were more than happy to use it against you. The little girl stared at me, wide eyed with terror.

Meanwhile, in my comms I could hear Lock and Saff clearing their rooms. From what I could tell in Saff's room, there had been a bit of a scuffle, but she'd handled it easily.

The little girl's eyes were wide as she stared at me. I took off my night vision goggles and my gas mask. "Sweetheart, hi, look at me. My name is Saint. What's yours?"

Her lips quivered. "Cecile."

"Hi, Cecile. Okay, I know you're very scared right now, but we're not going to let anything happen to you, are we?" I pointedly glanced up at Lohman.

He tightened his grip. "Shut up, Saint. You don't know what I'm willing to sacrifice."

"For what? For your own life?"

He shook his head. "You don't understand. It doesn't matter what I do, or what you do. When he finds out, he'll come for them anyway. They might as well be dead."

"So you're going to hasten it? What's wrong with you?"

His arm tightened around the little girl's neck again, and she cried out. "Daddy, no."

He crooned something in her ear, and she stopped struggling. She still had that worried crease between her brow, but she didn't move. He probably told her it was just pretend and he wouldn't ever hurt her. The kind of thing all fathers said to their children.

Had mine ever reassured me like that, our relationship would have been a lot better. Connor started to pull her toward the back door, moving them backward. Rook had a bead on him and wasn't letting up.

I approached slowly with my hands up. "Lohman, let the kid go. We don't want to hurt her."

"I know you don't. And I don't want her hurt. But I'm between a rock and a hard place. I can't let you keep me. He's coming. I need my best chance at survival."

At that moment, Saff came through the door with Cecile's mother, I presumed. When she saw that Connor had her daughter by the throat, she screamed, which only made Connor tug harder.

My eyes went back and forth, and Rook inched forward with me. He growled out, "What's the play? What are we doing?"

Without answering him, I pulled the gun from my holster and fired.

CHAPTER 29
SAINT

I was antsy. All I wanted to do was interrogate this fucker then get back to Kaya. But it was already Wednesday, and I knew she'd be at school. I'd have to wait to see her.

Once again, I found myself pacing outside the door of the interrogation room. Finally, Gabe came out. "He's ready."

I gave him a nod and headed in, but he abruptly stopped me. "For what it's worth, I would have told you about Dove sooner if I could have."

I clamped my jaw tight. "That's the thing with you, Gabe, I'm never quite sure if I can trust you."

"You think that we operate in a vacuum. We don't."

I shook my head at him. "You're missing the point. As a team, we should always feel that you have our back. I don't always feel like that with you."

Gabe nodded. "I will always do what is in your best interest. It might not necessarily be what you want or what you think is right, but it *is* in your best interest, always."

I scowled at him. "Whatever. Can I go in? Or do you have some other pressing mission for me?"

Gabe sighed and stepped aside. "He's all yours."

Lohman scowled at me when he saw me walk through the door. "Oh, is that you gloating?"

I grinned. "A little bit, yeah."

"Fuck off, you tosser."

"What do you want with Kaya Reynolds?"

Even though he was handcuffed, he easily flipped me off.

"All right, maybe I'll make this question easier. Why are you trying to kill her?"

He laughed. "Kill her? We've been bloody trying to take her, mate. Do you understand how much she's worth?"

"What does Antonio want her for?"

He just laughed. "Oh, for fuck's sake, how are you lot so dumb? Don't you get it? I already tried to help you once. I told you, you didn't even know what you have. Think about it. How did someone like me get to be someone like this? And without the old man knowing. I was always smart, but I had real shit luck. Old man Igno liked to use me." He rolled his eyes. "But he never gave me my due. He never gave me a shot. So I found my own opportunities."

"What does that mean?"

Connor laughed. "My God, fucking hell. It's Dove. She took something from him. And well, I took it from her."

"How do you know Dove? What did she take from him?"

"Your Kaya, your special little love, the one you'll do anything to protect. She's the spitting image of her mother. There's no hiding her. Igno is coming for her. And he wants the same thing that he's always wanted."

"What's that?"

He laughed. "Revenge."

"Revenge for what?"

He sat back. "I get the impression I'm doing your job for you."

"Well, the thing is you weren't very good at staying captive, but Gabe's nice, you see. Offering you someplace to hide your family. I would never have done the same."

"Fine. Fuck. Whatever. The girl's mother. Antonio didn't know at first that she was a spy. And sure, he was into her. But what everyone seems to forget is that he isn't sentimental. She was more of a possession than anything else. She was his architect. He hired her for this fucking building in Italy that was supposed to be his crowning achievement.

"Anyway, he had a big deal going. A hundred million dollars' worth of arms. He had me cooking books. He knew I was smart. He also liked that I was good with my hands, but he was never going to let me get anywhere or advance in the organization."

"We know this. Get to the important part."

He sighed. "All right. About five years back, I was still working my way up. Igno could see I didn't want to be small time, but he kept telling me to wait my turn. To learn, to watch him. So I did. I listened. Then this bird shows up. Beautiful, the most stunning eyes you have ever seen. A mouth that looked like it was made for sucking cock. Igno was obsessed with her, but she was all business, which only made him want her more. The more she resisted the more he wanted her. Whatever she was doing worked, because he gave her unprecedented access.

"He took her at her every word. She started advising him more so than any of us. But Antonio was still Antonio, and he doesn't really trust anyone. He never let her have any kind of *full* access. She also knew that I was looking for a way to shake off the old man. I wanted my freedom, see? She came to me to make me a deal. Told me all the things she knew I would want to hear, and I believed her. And then one day she says that we're both getting out from under his thumb. She's got a great plan to take something very valuable from him."

I sat down on the table across from him and leaned in. "Go on. What the fuck were you taking Connor?"

Connor laughed. "Diamonds."

I blinked rapidly. "What?"

"Diamonds. Look, Igno had a big-time deal going. Arms. Supplies. He was empire building. And that was the price. So he was going to pay the arms dealer in diamonds, which was what the crazy fool wanted. Dove, that's what she called herself, she hijacked his deal. Antonio had the diamonds. But mid-transport, they had a car accident. She swapped his diamonds for fakes. Same pouch, same everything, because I told her ahead of time what it was going to look like."

"So you made a deal?"

"The old man would have fucking bled me dry. It didn't matter what I did for him. So yeah, I made the deal. Our deal was she'd give me a cut."

"And did she?"

Lohman nodded. "Yeah. She gave me three of the diamonds. I stashed them because obviously I knew what to expect. I slowly used them to buy more property abroad. International kind of shit. Everything was cool. Igno was pissed, obviously, when Dove vanished. Years later, I'd worked my way up in the organization. I was one of the advisers, and he was still bleeding me, man. Still squeezing. And then I see Dove. I've got a kid, a girlfriend, not that Antonio knows anything about them. Anyway, I'm at a fucking corner shop, and there she is, walking around as if she's not bloody hiding.

"We both knew what we'd done, but neither one of us wanted any trouble. But then she finds me at my house. I had to sneak out to talk to her. She wanted to know if I'm going to tell Igno I saw her because she knew I still worked for him. But I had no beef with her. And if he found out what I had done, he'd be after my head. I told her such. She threatened me. I told her to fuck off. And then she threatens my wife and kid if I ever told Igno that I had seen her.

Then she says she has some even better deal for me. Some kind of real estate deal. Something Igno wanted to buy, but the investors wouldn't let him have a cut. She said she'd give me a chance to get in on the deal. When I asked her how I was going to manage that because that takes big money, she said she'll give me more diamonds."

I pushed back and started to pace. "So she helped you find an investment. Why?"

"Mate, I don't know. I thought maybe it was payment to shut me up. I was supposed to meet her a few nights later. Except when I went to pick her up, she was twitchy in a bad way. Real tense. On edge. She shoved me back in the car, told me to drive, and told me she needed something from me before she'd give me the diamonds. She had a pouch of them. A good lot that I was supposed to use to buy into this investment."

"Okay, what did she need you to do?"

"She needed me to plug a flash drive into one of the mainline computers for five minutes and then unplug it."

"Okay, that was it?"

"Yeah, and then she wanted me to find her a solicitor. Someone hush-hush who wouldn't say a word. I gave her a name. She gave me the flash drive and told me once I'd done it, I'd find the diamonds."

"And?" I ran my hands through my hair. He was killing me.

"And what?"

"And did you fucking do it?"

He wiped at his nose with the back of his hand. "Next time I went to Edinburgh, a pouch of fucking diamonds was in my post box along with the name of some bloke from Croatia who could make my money look clean. I used that to buy into this investment company."

"And you did it with the diamonds that she stole from Igno?"

He nodded. "I never saw her again after that."

"So you didn't kill her?"

He coughed. "Are you fucking kidding me? The woman was a fucking ghost. Sure, in the early days Antonio liked to send me out like I was the hammer. You know, beat people up, dispose of the bodies and shit. But her? She was that kind of spooky shadow that you hear about in your nightmares. I couldn't touch her. Then she vanished and I never saw her again."

"Then what the fuck do you want with Kaya?"

"The woman I saw at the auction was the spitting image of Dove. Younger, yes, but she looks just like her mother. All that pretty brown skin. You know, I'd never fucked a bla—"

Before I knew what was happening, I lunged myself at him and grabbed him by the shirt. "What the fuck did you say?"

"Easy, mate, easy."

"I'm not your mate."

"Fine. Fuck, sorry. Anyway, she looks exactly like her mother. I didn't know she had a kid, but it didn't take me long to figure it out. She looks about twenty, which would explain a lot about why Dove took off and he's had a bounty out for Dove for twenty years. And there was a woman with her face. Right in front of me. I saw a chance to use her."

I cursed under my breath. "Fuck."

Lohman licked his lips. "And as for the other bird, Elise, Igno and her dad go way, way back. He owed Igno a lot of money, so he essentially sold her off to you to gain access to your company and pay the debt he owed. But she fucked up and didn't start paying off quickly enough, so Igno had her dealt with."

I scowled. "Was it you? Did you place the bomb?"

He shook his head. "No. It wasn't me."

"It's your calling card. Why should I believe you?"

"Because I can help you save the girl."

***

KAYA

All I'd heard from Saint was that he had to take care of something for work, but he'd been gone all night. I hadn't wanted to be needy, so I hadn't blown up his cellphone. But I checked in on him with Maureen to see if he had any meetings this morning. She'd said no, but he was still dealing with the issue from last night. All I could do was worry. And worry I did.

Even in class, I was distracted. And being distracted on critique day was a bad call. Even if Xander liked you, he was brutal. When he got to me, my palms were sweating, even though I thought my photos were serviceable this time.

I knew it was going to be a rough one. When my images came up, Xander frowned. I could see that he hated the first one. We were supposed to photograph power, and admittedly, like half my classmates, I'd taken a lot of industrial shots, but they were flat and dull. Except the last one.

I had surreptitiously taken a photo of Saint. He'd been at his desk, jacket off, cuffs rolled up, staring at some papers. His eyes were intense, and he had his hand on his chin, a finger slightly stroking his bottom lip. He hadn't even seen me take it.

Xander then placed thumbnails of all my images on the screen and then turned to the class. "So, what do you see?"

A girl named Nicola Hering sighed from the front row. "I'm sorry, Kaya, but they all suck except that last one. That last one is pure sex."

I flushed. Next to me, Gemma giggled, and I slid her a glance. "Really, Gemma?"

"Well, she's right about the last one. And I don't think the others suck. They just look like what everyone else has done."

I sighed. "Which means, they sucked."

The only one anyone liked was the one of Saint. Xander leaned back against the desk and crossed his arms. "All right, so where did we miss the mark? Because most of you have given me pictures like this. Construction. Industrial. Yes, that's power, but it's flat and boring. No subject that's alive. But this last photo... I agree with you, Nicola. It is powerful. There is strength in the lighting, in the composition. There is obviously strength in the subject."

Xander turned his attention to me. "But there is also strength in the photographer. I can feel your self-assurance that it was the shot of the day. The sheer knowledge, the confidence."

I nodded. "Yeah, I had my camera at the ready, I just... I don't know. I took two of the same shot and he didn't even notice me."

From behind me, someone said, "Now I'm paying more attention."

With a gasp, I turned around. And there he was in the back row. How the hell had I not seen him?

Next to me, Gemma whispered, "If that is not the sexiest thing I have ever heard in my life, I don't know what is."

My heart went into full gallop and my body... Well, I needed a change of panties, because after the way he'd left me last night, wet and wanting, I might never recover. I still ached just thinking about him, his lips, his caress. And that tingle started again under my skin as I pulsed deep in my core.

The rest of the critique was brutal but necessary. I knew I'd phoned that one in. But when class was over, I was on my feet. I noticed several girls stopping to whisper and point. One was even bold enough to walk up to Saint and ask if he was the subject. He shrugged, but his eyes never left mine. When the girls saw that I was the object of his attention, several of them rolled their eyes, but Nicola cocked her head. "Are you her boyfriend or something?"

I couldn't even explain the hot flush of excitement when Saint met her gaze straight on and said, "No, I'm her fiancé."

Under her breath, Gemma whispered. "Well damn, if that didn't shut her down, I don't know what would."

As I approached, he pushed out of his seat and stalked toward me. Just watching him take those four or five steps was a revelation, because suddenly, I couldn't hear Gemma, and I couldn't feel anything but him and his gaze and the desperate need pulsing through my veins.

"Um, I'll just leave you two lovebirds alone. Call me later, okay?"

I nodded absently. "Yeah. I think we have some more files to go through."

At the mention of files, Saint frowned. "If you're going through the files, I'll be with you."

"You can't keep Gemma out of this. She's been trying to help."

"I'm not saying I'm keeping her out. I'm just saying I want to help so I can also curtail her more harebrained ideas."

Gemma rolled her eyes. "I'll have you know sir, that I kept her out of trouble. Nothing happened on my watch, see? So you can release those reins of control just a bit."

"Not likely."

When Gemma was gone, I turned to him. "What's wrong? You wouldn't be here unless something was wrong."

His gaze searched mine and then he shook his head slowly. "Nothing. I just wanted to take you out."

I blinked. "Out?"

"Yes, out. I asked you once, but then you had plans. So now I'm hoping you don't have plans."

I nodded. "Out. That sounds good. Do you want to have lunch?"

He chuckled softly, and I could see it when he laughed. He looked my age. Carefree and happy. That's what he was missing. There was always that intensity about him. "Lunch. That's an excellent idea."

I laughed. "Do you want to take it back to your flat?"

"Stop calling it *my* flat. It's *our* penthouse."

"I'm sorry, I called it a flat."

"I'm more concerned that you still think of it as mine instead of ours."

He took my hand and slid my fingers through his. The crash of electricity and need hit me hard. But I cleared my throat and tried to smile at him like I wasn't completely deranged.

"Just go with it," he said. "If I take you back to the flat, as you say, I'm going to jump you, and I want to talk first because talking is probably a really good idea."

I frowned, disappointed in his way of talking. "Okay, we can talk, I guess."

"Excellent. Then come with me. I know just the place."

I followed him out, aware that there was more than one guard posted outside. I wondered just how I was going to keep my hands off him all the way to lunch.

CHAPTER 30
SAINT

I KNEW I should tell her about her mother because would it affect everything. But still, I couldn't tell her. She looked happy to see me for once, and she needed something happy.

"Where are we going?"

"Oh, you'll see."

"That's not helpful."

"I know. You just have to be patient."

I remembered something she'd said about her mother. That her mum had loved the fair. It had taken me, well me and Maureen, looking for something that would suffice, but we finally found a fair in Sheffield, and the weather was holding.

When we arrived at the helipad, her eyes went wide. "Where the fuck are we going?"

"Relax, this is a good thing."

I tucked her in the seat and gave her a headset, and she looked at me warily. Still, I could see it in her eyes, the delight, the excitement about something new, something different.

We didn't say much during the helicopter ride. When the pilot landed, there was a car waiting for us, and she kept pestering me with questions about where we were going until we arrived at the little fair. All I cared about was that there was a Ferris wheel. Because she'd said on her birthday, her mother had always taken her to ride the Ferris wheel and gotten her cotton candy and cake. I could do that at the very least. The cake might be from the best baker I could find in London, and I might have had Saff help me find a cotton candy maker. One that let you do your own flavors. And with Gemma's help, I was also redecorating her room.

That's not a gift. That's a punishment. You want her in your room.

I did. But I wanted to give her a place that seemed like hers.

When we finally pulled up to the fair, her lips broke out into the widest smile I'd seen from her yet. And then she started to clap and squeal and stomp her feet. "Oh my God, you did not."

"I did. I listen when you speak. When you told me about your birthday, I was paying attention. I can't believe you went to class on your birthday."

"Well, I thought... You had to work, and when I didn't hear from you this morning, I assumed you were still working, so I called the office. Maureen said you weren't there, but that you had worked last night. I don't know. I just figured you forgot."

My heart squeezed. How could she think I would forget? It had clearly been important to her. I wasn't going to forget something like that.

"And last night was..." Her voice trailed.

Just thinking about it made my dick twitch. I was still so on edge I felt like I could rip the head off a full grown grizzly bear. But I kept it together because today was about her.

"It's a birthday present and an apology. I was a dick and a complete twat last night."

Her face fell just for a moment before it quickly brightened again, but the second brightening was a false one. And then I realized what I'd said. "No. Not because of what happened after. But breaking up your dinner date, that was a prick move. I'm sorry."

"Then you're not sorry about what happened after?"

I gave a harsh and decisive, "No, I'm not. And for the record, just so we understand each other, it is one hundred percent on my mind right now. And it was on my mind when I came to fucking pick you up from school. But today is your birthday. It's not about me and how desperate I am for you. It is about doing something for you. So come on, let's go have fun. I believe we have a Ferris wheel to ride."

Kaya stared at me for a long moment and then sprang forth and wrapped her arms around me. "Thank you. Thank you. Thank you. Thank you."

"I wanted to give you something that was familiar. Of course, Harry and the boys need to follow us, and I did shut it down for the day."

"You what?"

"It's your birthday. What use is being a billionaire if I cannot shut down a Sheffield fair for you?"

"You're going to spoil me. Whatever will I do next year on my birthday?"

Next year. She assumed we wouldn't be together.

Well, you won't be.

That hurt. Despite everything I was feeling, I knew we had an expiration date. Which sucked. But everything in me screamed to show her that there didn't *have* to be one.

That terrified me. The idea that I could keep her and I could say something that might make her stay.

The fair, as it turned out, was surprisingly fun. Kaya was like a kid in a candy store giggling as she ran from ride to ride and even encouraged some of the other guys to get on rides with her. I never would have thought that some of the lads were complete wusses when it came to riding rides. Harry looked green around the gills when she insisted that he get on one of the whirling upside-down ones. I, on the other hand, a completely manly man, managed to pretend I loved every minute.

After several hours of riding the Ferris wheel and other rides, and after I'd banged a mallet until I finally managed to win her a giant stuffed panda, we went home. In the elevator, she yawned, and her smile was sleepy as she said, "This is by far one of the best birthdays I've ever had. Thank you."

"You're welcome. I'm glad I could give it to you."

She looked relaxed and sleepy. I was tense, because I had no idea how she was going to take the gift inside. My palms were sweating, and I could feel my heart rate pick up. I felt mildly out of breath because I was nervous.

When we arrived at the security panel, I swiped it open. I stepped back to let her in first. I knew security had already swept it so it would be safe. When she walked inside, she stopped short in the foyer. "Saint, what in the world?"

I stepped in behind her and found the main living area full of balloons. Mint green and white because she'd already told Maureen mint green was her favorite color. And on the table, I could see Maureen had gone a little overboard.

I had no idea where the hell we were even going to store all of these cakes. There were six of them with little labels in front identifying what flavor they were. And Maureen also had the cotton candy machine set up, and Kaya ran over to it. "Oh my God, we can make our own cotton candy?"

"Yes, we can."

Kaya ran straight for me, throwing her body against mine. I caught her easily, my hands on her arse and her legs wrapped around me. Her arms wrapped around my neck as she squeezed. Holy fuck me. The rush of endorphins bonded me even closer to this woman. My hands were on her arse already. All I needed to do was slide her down just a little and she'd be sliding over my dick. Yes, that was what I wanted. That was what I needed, but—

No, that's not what we're doing, you twat.

I eased her down gently off me and away from my dick before I could do something I was going to regret. "Before we have cake, you have a present that I want you to see.

"Before the cake? Oh my God, is that a strawberry cake?"

"Yes, it is."

"Can I have one piece first?"

I laughed. "Yes, it's your birthday. Go ahead."

She cut herself a slice and grabbed two forks, handing me one. Then she cut a bite, but instead of shoving it in her mouth she moved toward me.

"Oh God, what are you doing?"

"Well, I have been in danger. You should probably taste this for me."

"I'll taste anything you want. Is there somewhere in particular you want me to put that frosting?"

I could see her skin flush pink. "I might have a couple of ideas."

"Excellent. Hold that thought." I took the fork from her and gently shoved it in her direction. When she wrapped her mouth around the fork, I swear to God I could feel the pre cum leaking out of the tip of my dick. *Fuck. Fuck. Fuck.* I was never going to make it.

I took her hand and tugged her down toward the bedrooms.

"Oh God, okay. I didn't know we were already going to do this, but let's do it."

I turned to her. "That's not what I'm doing. I swear."

I walked down to her bedroom on the left side of the hall. I opened the door, hit the lights, and waited. Kaya frowned for a moment, but then her breath hitched. She stepped forward into the room and glanced around.

"What have you done?"

<hr>

Kaya

Saint shifted from foot to foot, and all I could do was glance around the room that was so familiar to me.

"What did you do, Saint?"

He shoved his hands into his pockets. "I wanted to give you something, a space that was yours. Maybe everything is not exactly perfect, but thanks to Gemma, I got most of the details right, and it'll give you someplace where you can take a breather. This whole situation is fucked up and weird, and I just wanted to give you some normalcy away from the chaos."

Watching him, I blinked rapidly. "Normalcy from the chaos." Tentatively, I stepped into the room. It was almost exactly like my bedroom in my old flat. The throw was a little different, but that one I had knitted myself. It was something I would do to keep my hands busy as I used audiobooks to study. "I cannot believe you did this."

When I slid him a glance, he was rubbing at the back of his neck, watching me warily, the moss green of his eyes appearing darker. "Do you like it?"

"Yes, I'm just a little overwhelmed."

"Is it too much? I'm sorry."

"No." I marched up to him and placed my hands on his chest, making sure to meet his gaze. "It's not too much. It's… perfect. I didn't even know that I needed this until I saw it. It makes me feel taken care of, which is not something I am used to. And I don't even know how to say the words because thank you is not enough. Thank you doesn't even begin to cover what you've done for me. A month ago, I didn't know you. I was living a completely different life, and then everything turned upside down. Some of that was my own doing, but every step of the way, you have been there. You took me in when you didn't have to. You suggested marrying me. God, that has got to be the strangest solution to a problem I've ever heard. You've done nothing but take care of me. And this is just… I do not have the words. Thank you isn't enough, but I will keep saying it until I either find better words or find a way to make them enough. Thank you for this. For everything. I don't know where I'd be right now without you."

The corners of his lips curved into a wry smile. "Well, I happen to know you very well. You are a survivor. You would have survived and come back swinging. I know it. Anyone who sees you knows how capable you are. Anyone decent would have tried to help you."

"Yes, but you've done it in your spectacular Jasper Saint way. And I suppose I haven't made it easy."

"Now that you mention it, you did get me shot at that one time."

I fought the smile trying to break free. "Oh my God, one time. One time I get you shot at, and you never let me forget it."

"Well, there's nothing like the ring of bullets to make you realize your own mortality. But hey, I'm always grateful, because I wonder if the two of us would have even connected."

"You know, not to be too fatalistic, but I believe we would have. Under different circumstances, maybe, but we absolutely would have met. And to be fair, I probably would have gotten you shot at again."

He laughed then. "You know, that's fair. And I'll take it."

"Excellent." We'd been interrupted the other night, so I wasn't quite sure what to do. If we were picking up where we left off, or what it all meant. But I did the thing that I wanted to do in the moment instead of holding myself back. Instead of trying to over-analyze the situation, I stood on tiptoes and kissed him on the cheek. Just when I thought I had a handle on everything that was going on, he had to go and build me a room. There was no way in hell I could keep my feelings in check after that. It didn't matter how hard I tried.

I was going to fall hard.

CHAPTER 31
KAYA

"You had better marry that man for real. He made you a room!"

"I know it's so sweet. I've never had anyone do anything like this for me, ever."

"But? I feel like there's a but in your voice," Gemma prompted.

How did I make her understand? "I've never been able to trust anything. I'm always holding back, waiting to see if it lasts. I need to process. And even after a while I worry that it will all vanish."

"Honey, these circumstances are unusual and would set anyone off kilter. But try to live in the moment, and when good things happen take them at face value. He gave you a gift. Accept it. And maybe you learn that not everything is chaos. Sometimes it's a little slice of peace. Like your new room."

"How did you get so wise?"

"It's all the wine I drink, darling. Don't over think it."

"I'll try."

The doorbell to the penthouse rang not thirty seconds after I said goodbye to Gemma. That meant someone had gotten past the armed doorman downstairs.

Okay, calm down.

I had never heard it ring. I knew it must just mean the visitor was obviously on the approved list or probably just Westin. I checked the panel and expected to see a smiling, somewhat goofy, handsome face. Instead, I saw a face that was all too familiar, and my stomach sank. But it was not the face of the man I spent so much time thinking about. This was a different, older, harsher version of Saint's face.

I opened the door with a knot in my gut, knowing this was not going to go well. "Mr. Saint, Jasper is not here."

"I know Jasper is not here. Jasper is where Jasper always is. Off playing soldier."

"Excuse me?"

He rolled his eyes. "Don't tell me you don't know. Just move out of the way girl. I'm coming in."

My attempts to stop him were futile as he pushed past me into the living room. I could have stopped him, but he was Saint's father. Besides, if there was a problem, I could just run screaming and Westin or one of his men would come running for me. They knew he was here, so it must be safe, right?

He glanced around the main room. "Well, I see you've made yourself at home. You know, this thing that you're doing," he clasped his hands together, "it's not going to work. You can't fool me. And I don't want you to be disappointed when you try to fool yourself."

I frowned at him. "I don't understand what you mean."

"You know, the thing with Jasper. I know you two getting together was rather hasty. And it's fine. I'm not judging. All I'm saying is, everyone knows it's not going to last."

I frowned at him. "Can I ask you a question?"

"Of course, dear."

"Why do you hate him?"

He frowned. "Who?"

"Your son. Why do you hate him? What's he done to you?"

"I don't hate either of my sons."

"Are you sure? Because here you are, trying to, I don't know... scare me or something? Why don't you cut to the chase and save both of us some time."

"I don't hate my son."

"Okay, sure, let's go with that. But you act like you're in competition with him. I don't understand it. I mean, why?"

His brow furrowed as if he wasn't quite sure what to do with me.

That's right, keep him on his toes.

"Where are you from?"

"Answering my question with a question," I said. "I've seen that before. Usually with therapists. Are you working with a therapist, or do you just need one? Maybe it should be family therapy. I feel like it would do you lot a world of good."

He glowered at me. "You want me to cut to the chase, fine. We all know my son asked you to marry him so he could get his inheritance. I'm here to encourage you to do otherwise."

I understood what was really happening. "Oh my God, you're about to do that clichéd old rich people thing. You're going to walk in here, tell me I'm beautiful and smart, and I could do better."

"What?"

"Oh, or are you going to do the thing where you tell me that I'm a street urchin and clearly a gold digger who is only after Saint's money?

"Or what about this one... Are you going to try and fuck me? I mean, I feel like in the movies, it's usually one of those three things. Knowing the likes of you, you've probably tried out all three. Which is it to be tonight? I've seen all the movies, and I know how to respond accordingly."

"You are clearly insane, girl. What is it you want? I know it's not my son. I know what he's like in relationships, and he will never be what you want him to be. Did you even know anything about him before your hasty engagement?"

I studied the older version of Jasper, wondering where in the

DNA they had diverged. I couldn't see any obvious signs of differences. Saint was his father's twin in looks except for the gray in his hair and his beard.

"Atticus. It is Atticus, right?"

Saint's father lifted a brow. "Oh, are we on a first name basis? So it'll be the latter of your three scenarios then?" His voice dropped an octave in his attempt to go seductive, and I held back a shudder of revulsion.

"Whoa boy! Don't get the wrong idea, Atticus. I want to be very clear. My name is not Elise, and you don't know your son at all. He's kind. He will literally lay down his life and give everything he has in him to protect the people he cares about. Hell, he'll do it for strangers. He doesn't believe in playing games. He's direct. He's honest. He's everything you wish you could be. Let's not pretend for a moment that *you* know anything about him. I'm just curious as to when you stopped giving a fuck about your children. Did it happen slowly over time, or were you just not ever that interested in kids? I mean, it's not my business, of course, except for the fact I will be your *daughter-in-law* in just a few short weeks."

He strode forward then, but I held my ground. I knew if I ran now, he would expect me to run forever. I lifted my chin, because at the end of the day, I could take care of myself if forced to act. If he put a hand on me, he was going to regret that.

When he saw that I wasn't budging, he scowled. "Listen here, you halfwit, you know nothing about Elise. Nothing about that relationship. You don't know my son."

"Yes, I do. It's you who doesn't know him. Now if you don't mind, can you please leave? I will tell Jasper that you were here, and that I just simply didn't feel safe alone here with you. In fact, I'd like your access to the penthouse revoked."

He sputtered and glowered. "You can't cut me out of my own home."

"Your home?"

"Jasper grew up here. Well, here and at our country house. It's the house that comes with the board seat. My father-in-law saw to that."

I laughed then. "How does it feel knowing that all of this was courtesy of your father-in-law? It really must eat at you to know that your children are the ones on the board and that you have been made obsolete. Shelved because of your own actions."

I could tell the moment he knew he'd underestimated me. He'd thought he could make me run, but I wasn't going anywhere.

But maybe you should. After all, what the hell do you know about these people? All you know is that Jasper saved your life. Is the drama really worth it?

The longer I stared at his father, the more I knew without a doubt that the drama was absolutely worth it. Jasper had protected me, and now I was going to protect him.

Saint

Even before Kaya caught my eye, I knew my father had been there. Security at the front desk had called immediately, so I expected trouble. But when I walked in, Kaya just smiled at me from the couch. "Hey, how are you?"

I glanced around, perhaps looking for a dead body. Was she okay? She seemed chipper. "Um, everything is good. I was thinking maybe we could go out and grab dinner."

"Sure. Good day at work?"

I blinked at her. "Okay, I know you've seen the old man."

"And?"

"You don't look upset."

"You two are really going to have to give me more credit. It takes a lot more than that man to upset me."

"He purposely tried to upset you?"

"Of course, he did. He didn't manage it though."

"Okay, you seem rather calm for someone who had to deal with that bastard. What happened?"

"I mean, the standard. He came here to test me and epically failed. I asked him to leave."

"Did he hurt you?"

Her eyes went wide. "No. I'm tougher than I look."

My father was my size. He could have hurt her. That was one of the things I used to tell myself about my father and Elise. That he had forced her somehow. That she hadn't wanted to be with him, but he was powerful and she had no other options. Even though my brain knew the truth, I let the lie prevail. "Okay, I was worried."

"You shouldn't be worried." She pushed up from the couch. "Where are we going? Is it fancy, or can I wear leggings?"

"Come as you are. I know this spot around the corner. Best burgers in the city."

Her stomach grumbled, and I smiled. I liked this. This ease with her. There was still an edge to our conversations though. So much I wasn't sure what to say and a lot of secrets.

"Before we go though, can you explain to me the whole *Jasper needs to get married in the next three months* thing?"

I froze. "What?"

"Yeah, your dad was talking about how you are using me to get your inheritance, blah, blah, blah. And you know, he let it out that you needed a wife. Which honestly, it would have been nice to know. But I understand, of course, that you would want something for saving my ass."

"Kaya, I already told you, I don't want—"

"No, it's fine. I just wish I'd known because I honestly felt like I'd been hit in the chest."

Fuck.

I reached for her, and she stepped just out of reach. "No, if we're going to have a conversation, we're going to have a real *conversation.* You're going to explain to me what the fuck we're doing here. Are you my fiancé for the sake of my safety or your money? Which is it?"

"I'm sorry. Fucking hell, I wanted to tell you. I did. But things were already complicated between us, and I didn't want to add to that."

"So you lied to me on purpose? Bloody brilliant. I hate being lied to. I mean, I knew why your father was here and what he was doing. I figured he was here to either offer me a check, use my past against me, or try and sleep with me."

I growled low at that. "Did he fucking touch you?"

She shook her head. "No, relax. He didn't scare me. Made me laugh, actually, because he was so very predictable."

Just the idea that he would try that stopped me from breathing.

Kaya stepped forward then. "What's wrong?"

"Nothing. Nothing is wrong."

"Don't lie to me. If you don't want me to walk out that door, which I should because you lied to me, although where would I be going, then talk to me, Jasper."

Her voice softened when she said my name.

I stepped around her and started to pace. "Fuck. I don't know where to start." It took me a minute of pacing before I got my thoughts under control. I didn't want to have to say all of this out loud. Especially to Kaya.

"Long story short, you've heard some of the details. Elise never actually wanted to be married to me. Her family sent her to find a rich husband to alleviate their financial losses. I was deployed and Elise liked the idea of me not being around. And then, well, she simply traded up."

Kaya winced at that. "Well, it's true she traded, but not up. That was her loss, not yours."

"Anyway, she was playing fast and loose with the commitments she'd made to get her family out of trouble. She crossed the wrong person, and it got her killed. My father-in-law went off the rails because he thought I did her wrong. And then I came back from deployment to find out what been going on between her and my father."

"I'm so sorry."

"But my father was right. It's part of my grandfather's clause in his will that to get full access to the board seats, I *do* have to be married. I have a one year grace period from the time I took over. Right after Elise's death, dad started to spiral and made some bad choices. The board unseated him, leaving me next in line. Since I took over nine months ago, the clock has been ticking.

Kaya stepped in front of me. "Then I fell in your lap. Convenient, wasn't I?"

"You did fall in my lap, but you needed help. I found a way to help you and myself at the same time."

"Why the fuck did you not tell me? I could have really laid it on. Really sold it."

"I needed you, and I took advantage."

"Right. Here's the thing... Obviously, I'm not leaving. You have done what you said you would do to protect me. You've been admirable doing it, too. But you want me to trust you, and I can't because you lied."

"I'm sorry. I needed you, and I'm trying to get off this carousel. There might be a way. I just didn't think there was a reason to tell you unless it was urgent."

She licked her lips. "I don't like surprises, especially not surprises like your father, okay? So no more."

"I promise. No more."

Except that secret government organization that you and her mother are a part of.

———

She was giving me a second chance.

One you don't deserve.

Because of my mission, I still couldn't tell her the whole truth, but I would tell her as much of it as I could. And I could only pray then when she found everything out, she didn't leave me.

Not that I was ever letting her go. Now that she was here, now that she was mine, I knew the only truths that mattered were that I was keeping her and I needed to find a way to tell her about Rogues and still keep her safe.

I took her hand and pulled her to her feet. Her gaze searched mine as I hooked my fingers into the belt loops of her jeans and tugged her close. The kiss I gave her was meant to be gentle, very sweet. It was meant to be an apology. It was meant to be me asking for her forgiveness. But one sweep of my tongue over hers, and the inferno took over. The climbing heat of it made my skin itchy and tight. And the only way to soothe the discomfort was having her touch me.

In seconds we were roaming hands and clashing teeth and sliding tongues. I tried backing her toward the hallway. If things were getting out of hand, I wanted to be near a bed. The couch wasn't nearly big enough for what I had planned.

My foot hit something, nearly tumbling us over, and I was forced to tear my lips from hers. Searching her gaze, I whispered, "Kaya, what are you doing to me?"

When she lifted her heavy-lidded gaze to meet my, her pupils were dilated. "I could ask you the same thing."

As it turned out, we hadn't made it anywhere near the hallway. But I was too impatient now. I just needed more of her. More of her taste on my tongue. More of her hands in my hair. More of her grinding her hips against my erection. Every cell in my body urged me to hurry, to bury myself inside her. But when I kissed her again, she slowly melted into me. Her tongue teased and drove me mad.

She had the power in her touch and in her kiss to burn me.

Without breaking our kiss, I slid my hands down her arms and brought them up to wrap around the back of my neck. I pulled back momentarily. "I can't stop touching you."

Kaya arched into me, the curves of her full breasts pressed into my chest. I slid my hands under the silk of her blouse. When my thumbs came into contact with the soft flesh of her belly, we both hissed.

I slid my hands up her satin skin, pausing when I encountered the silk of her bra. I watched her carefully as I lightly skimmed the soft flesh, but I let my hands continue to travel upward, pushing her T-shirt over her head.

The fabric fluttered to the ground without a sound, and I turned my full attention back to her exposed flesh. Shit. She was stacked. "God, you're so fucking perfect." Her full breasts pushed against the fabric of the satin, and I desperately tried to swallow around a mouthful of sawdust.

I reached behind her. I bent my knees and dipped my head, making sure our gazes met as I silently asked for permission. When she nodded, I exhaled the breath I'd been holding and released the clasp.

Kaya slid the straps off her slim shoulders then arched her back in silent offering. Shit. Perfection. So lush. So full. Taking advantage of her arched form, I hovered my mouth over a puckered bud for a moment. She shivered in my arms. Pressing my lips over the raised peak, I suckled her gently. Her answering moan was low and throaty, and I tugged harder, trying to taste every rich flavor of her skin.

"Jasper."

It was like I could feel what she was feeling. The desire now thundered like a crescendo in my skull, and so did the longing. I would be happy to hold her all night, doing nothing more interesting than playing with her curls.

Kaya reached for me, and her delicate fingers tugged at my T-shirt. As she leaned in close, her sweet, flowery scent commingled with mine.

She slid her hands under my shirt, and my muscles twitched as she worked them up over my pecs. Lightly, she skimmed my shoulders as she slipped it off over my head. At the contact of skin on skin, my cock jerked against the fly of my jeans, urging, begging me to bury myself in her and get lost.

Heat flared in her eyes as my cock nudged her belly. She reached for my jeans, and I bit back a curse. "God, Kaya, you're killing me." I had to get control and quick before I did something stupid. Gently, I eased her hands away from my belt.

I was far gentler with her jeans and that flimsy scrap of material she called a thong. I groaned as I cupped the generous curves of her ass. "Put your legs around my waist."

When she complied, I cursed as her wet heat slid against the thin material covering my straining cock. I braced her on the side table before kissing her slowly. Sliding my tongue against hers, teasing her until she mewled and writhed against me.

I let my hands freely roam from her ass, to her flat, firm waist, to the generous handful of her breasts. I only lightly circled the tip with my thumb, and Kaya clamped her thighs around me tighter, trying to draw me closer.

Dipping my head, I grazed first one nipple, then the other with my beard. I followed up with my tongue and with playful tugs with my teeth.

"I—Christ."

As I feasted on her chocolate-tipped nipples, I whispered, "You taste like heaven."

She answered with a rotation of her hips, and my cock jerked against my zipper, insistently desperate for her heat. I slid a hand between us, searching for her slippery heat. I growled her name as I dipped a finger into her slick channel. "So fucking wet."

She bucked as I withdrew my finger then slowly slid in again. I buried my lips in her neck. With each gentle slide and retreat of my finger, I whispered to her. How good she felt. How I couldn't wait to taste her. How much I wanted to slide into her slick heat.

Even though she dug her nails into my shoulders and softly whimpered, I took my time. Never mind that I was on the verge of spontaneously combusting. I kept up the slow, lazy retreat and entry.

She rocked her hips into my questing hand. Hell. She was so hot. "Saint, please stop teasing me."

I smiled against her flesh. "This is called seducing."

She gave a little frustrated growl, and I chuckled. Finally, I reached between us and snatched the condom from my pocket.

I dragged my head back to watch her. With trembling hands, she took the condom from me then tore the foil and discarded it. She met my gaze levelly and reached into my jeans.

Fuck. *Oh fuck.* Her sure fingers froze my brain synapses for several seconds. Not once did she take her eyes off me. She pumped me slowly, then again, and I bit back a strangled choke. "Fuck me," I ground out.

"Saint, please…"

As she moaned my name, I knew the danger. This would never be enough. I would need this like a drug. I would crave it. She was already under my skin.

"Saint, I—"

Reaching between us, I stroked her clit with my thumb in slow circles even as I picked up the pace. "Kaya, God, you feel so good."

Her body clamped down tighter around my fingers as I drove her higher and higher. With a shuddering breath, her legs tightened around my waist, pulling me close.

She whispered my name, and her body clamped tight around my hand just before breaking apart in my arms.

I ground my teeth together. The tingle in my spine morphed into molten fire. But I ground my teeth and held off. I felt like I might die from wanting her.

When she reached for my jeans again, and I swallowed hard and tucked her against me. "Shhh, that was for you."

"But—"

"But nothing. I would die a thousand deaths just to watch you come. We have time. I'm keeping you, remember."

"I think you have that wrong," she whispered. "I'm the one who's keeping you."

CHAPTER 32
KAYA

Things with Saint were somewhat back on an even keel. I didn't feel quite so bad that he was going out of his way to help me because I now knew he was getting something out of it too.

But more importantly, everything was out on the table.

He'd even stayed to make me tea before heading to work and leaving his security guys to take me to classes. It was Ryan and James today.

"You, my love, looked like you have been thoroughly fucked. And can I just say, it looks like it was some good fucking too? Look at you. You're glowing!"

I hissed at Gemma as I sat down and got ready for critique day. "Would you hush your mouth? Jesus, anyone can hear you."

"Oh please, the jealous hussies over there? They should hear it. That fine man is making you all tingly and pink in the face."

"You can't tell that I'm pink in the face."

"Well, I couldn't until now."

I groaned. "Honestly, how did you know?"

"It looked like you had bounce in your step. You also look like you can't walk."

I rolled my eyes and pulled out my laptop. "Shut up."

"So, let me guess, birthday celebrations were everything you wanted?"

"Yes, they were..." How did I even explain? The kind of gift he'd given me was something even my mother hadn't given me. He'd built me something so I would have somewhere to go. A refuge. A place that was my own and felt anything but temporary.

"Do you want to explain that sigh for me?"

Hell, I didn't know. These were questions I did not have answers to. Usually, I hated my birthday. Especially after my sixteenth one. But now? Now I loved my birthday again.

Xander came in then. "Everyone, you know the deal. Let's have our first victim down front and prepping."

Luckily, I was not presenting this week since I'd presented during the previous class. I'd be part of the rapid-fire critique, of course. But having to present, talk to everyone of your decisions, it was torture. Gemma rolled her eyes. "Ugh, Nicola really likes landscapes. If only I could buy her a personality, I really would. Do you think Saint has enough money to buy her a personality? I could ask."

"You're not asking Saint to buy her a personality. I don't even think he has that much money."

Gemma snorted. "Glad to see you're still in there. I thought he'd fucked all the clarity out of you."

I grinned. "It was everything you'd imagine it to be."

Gemma squeezed my knee. "Well, good for you. About time you got bloody shagged. Oh, Andrew has been asking about you."

"Oh God, why would you tell me that?"

"Because he has been asking. He called, said he saw a news article about you getting married to somebody. He doesn't believe it."

"Jesus, that's the last thing I fucking need."

"I can try and talk to him if you want."

"No, I will deal with him."

"Okay, because if you don't, I have the feeling your husband-to-be will because I know he talked to *The Sun*."

I turned to her, mouth agape. "He did what?"

"Yeah. They were asking questions of your friends, for commentary, and he was like, 'There's no way on earth she'll marry that guy.' So maybe we should do something about him."

Gemma, of course, knew about the whole fake situation. But now that was even murky waters because it didn't *feel* fake. I was marrying him, wasn't I? That felt real. "How much of a problem do you think he's going to be?"

"Honestly? You're going to have to deal with him promptly."

And that was why I loved Gemma. No matter what, she was going to tell me the truth. It looked like I was going to have to have a conversation with Andrew whether I wanted to or not.

After exchanging a few text messages, Andrew met me at the cafe an hour after class. Ryan and James were sitting at the table next to me, trying to look nonchalant and blend in. James managed it better than Ryan. At least they'd both ditched their suits and looked normal-ish except for the fact that they were enormous. Especially Ryan. He was a six-foot-five hulk of a guy, but I knew from experience that he was shockingly fast. When I went running, he kept up with ease, even when I tried to drop him.

He would never say anything, just school me with his eyes. His quiet reproach was the worst, like a parent's. I actually had started to like them all and didn't mind having them around.

"Who the fuck are the freaking dudes over there?"

I glanced up startled. "Oh, hi."

"Who are they?"

I frowned at him. "No one. Don't worry about them."

"I saw them following you around the other day too. Could they be courtesy of your new fiancé?

I sighed. "Andrew, let's not do this, okay? Can you and I just... I don't know, talk?"

"Were you ever going to tell me that you were getting married to somebody I don't even know?"

"First of all, it's none of your business who I'm marrying. Second of all, we've been seeing each other for a while, and I didn't know it was going to be serious at first, so I said nothing. That's why I really couldn't come to your department thing. I'm seeing someone."

"But you and I—"

I took a deep breath. "Are only friends. Have only *ever* been friends. I value your friendship, but that means that you can't talk about me to the press. That was really rude, Andrew."

He frowned over at my bodyguards and James scowled back. "I don't like it. He's controlling you. Look, he's got men following you around."

"Andrew, I need you to understand that you don't know everything about my life, okay? They're there for my safety because I nearly got mugged." That was sort of true. "Jasper was worried, so he hired bodyguards."

Andrew's gaze shifted. "Still, I don't like it."

"Well, the good news is you don't have to. Only I have to. And as my friend, I would hope that you would be happy for me."

"But I don't know anything about him. And he just came out of nowhere. Where was he all this time when I was putting in the work?"

"Putting in the work? Are you kidding me right now? Do we need to take you to the school nurse for your hearing problem? Let me repeat. We. Were. Never. Going. Out."

He sighed. "Fine." He got the attention of the barista and held up two fingers, meaning he was ordering us two Americanos. I didn't have the energy to tell him I really, really didn't like Americanos. I always told him not to get me one, but he got me one anyway. And if he was paying attention, he would have noticed I never drank them. But maybe Ryan or James wanted one.

"Listen, I guess maybe I should tell you that some other guys approached me after I talked to that reporter."

My heart fell into my stomach. "What?"

"Yeah, they were asking about you and stuff."

"Lord Jesus Christ, what the hell did you tell them?"

"Nothing. I didn't tell them anything."

"Are you sure?"

" After the gas leak at your place, I don't even know where you're staying."

"Yeah, well, I'm keeping that to myself for now."

"I get it. I fucked up. I'm sorry. I do want you to be happy. I just always thought you'd be happy with me."

"We're just friends."

"Yeah, I know. Gemma told me that. I just didn't listen."

"Please listen to her. Now, I've got to go." I stood to leave, but he grabbed my hand. James was right there, hand on his wrist, scowl in place.

"Aw, shit. Damn, Kaya, call him off."

I shook my head at James, but he still didn't let go until Andrew let go of me.

"Fuck. All I was going to say is that I told those guys to ask Gemma whatever they wanted to know."

My eyes went wide. "And when was this?"

"I don't know, about an hour ago?"

If he was telling the truth, then Gemma was in danger and I had to get to her, post haste.

———

Kaya

I tried to remember all the lessons my mother had given me.

I just couldn't believe Andrew. Why would he do something so stupid? Strange men were asking about me, so he just went ahead and told them that Gemma had been helping me? Jesus.

Who did that? We were friends. Why didn't he use his goddamn brain?

As I took the stairs two at a time, my hands sliding up the slightly rusted rail, Ryan jumped in front of me, stopped, and frowned.

He turned around and shook his head at James. Then James put his hands on his holster as both of them looked around.

"What's going on?"

My question was soft, hushed. I wasn't trying to draw anyone's attention.

They both stood still for a moment, and then just as James turned back around to face me, I heard a loud pop and he went down.

Years of living with my mother had taught me to not scream in situations like this, but do get down for cover. All of a sudden it was as if she was standing there giving me my instructions, reminding me of what to do, how to move. *Keep your mouth shut. Lay low. Get to cover.*

Even though James was down, I reached for him. Ryan shook his head, wrapped an arm around my waist, and tugged me up the stairs. We'd barely made it up two flights before mayhem broke loose.

There were three more men firing at us. Ryan didn't even hesitate. He fired back, but the gunshots didn't seem to make any noise.

I frowned at that. A silencer?

How many guns do these guys have? Let alone where did they get them from? And how the hell had they gotten permission for a silencer? I watched Ryan as he started to draw another gun out. He didn't even have to tell me what to do as he shoved me behind a massive donation box and leaped out to do the work.

Pffft. Pffft. Pffft. The sounds of bullets passing through a silencer. But there were too many of them. He was a sitting duck. They were going to kill him.

I could hear Saint in my head. *They're there to protect you. No other reason. They are there for you. You get out.*

But there was nowhere to go. Sure, I could attempt to go back to the staircase and either go down toward whoever the hell shot James, or go up to Gemma's and be a sitting duck at her flat.

I cowered, unsure of what to do. This was never supposed to be me. This kind of chaos wasn't supposed to be real.

For a long horrifying moment, I sat there frozen, terrified as James lay bleeding in the stairwell and God only knew what the fuck had happened to Ryan. If I stayed where I was, I was going to die.

It wasn't for me to try and analyze who these men were or what they wanted right now. It was time for survival. I reached for my hair, gathered my corkscrew curls with the elastic I wore around my wrist, piling them on top of my head. I was a lot of things, and maybe a coward was one of them, but there was no way in hell I'd let somebody else die for me.

With my hair secured, I reached my hands out and said, "Okay now, gentlemen, I'm pretty sure you have orders not to kill me. You've been very persistent. I'm also pretty sure maybe you got in trouble for the whole stunt with my flat, because that could have killed me."

Silence.

I placed my arms around the corner first then slowly poked my head around when I didn't hear shots. Three of them stood in a triangle pattern, and Ryan was down. Fuck. All three had their guns raised. One of them was down, so they'd added a fourth. Where had he come from?

"Okay, you've been told to bring me in. Can you at least tell me who you're working for?"

When they saw that I was alone, all three of them did the one thing that was going to be their demise. They put their guns away.

Typical.

But never ever underestimate a pissed off woman.

All those years of martial arts and self-defense classes. All those years of my mother teaching me what to do in case of an emergency. Those years where I didn't get to be a normal little girl. Instead, I was learning everything from Tai Chi, to Krav Maga, to Shudokan karate. A little Kenpo, a little Aikido. If this had been a movie, it was where they would have shown my fucking training montage.

'Gentlemen, let's not do this. You talk to me nicely, and I'll talk nicely back. If you don't talk nicely, someone is going to walk away crying. And I promise you, it's not going to be me."

All three of them laughed as one approached. "Come with us."

"First of all, you didn't say please, which we all know is the magic word. Second of all, you don't just reach for me. You don't get to touch me. You say please and thank you, and then we discuss our options. Did no one teach you proper respect and how to treat a lady? Boys, boys, boys," I tsked.

His eyes raked over me, making it very clear that he didn't think I was any kind of lady. He was within three feet now. Two. One. I snapped my leg out so fast, putting my whole body into it, leaning back with it and catching him directly in the groin. Then I launched myself at him. I looped my arm around his neck and turned us both so he was my human shield.

He was big. Heavy. But I leaned our weights back, forcing him to shuffle hard even as he was holding his groin and moaning. "Stay on your feet, mate. You don't want everyone laughing at you, do you?"

His friends paused now, too worried about shooting this guy, and I already had my hand at the small of his back, taking out his gun. Great news, they didn't see any of this with his body in the way. I reached around his large body, shot one of them, and as quick as the flick of my wrist, I shot the other.

My aim was shit. Mum and I hadn't really done much target practice. But I knew I'd at least I hit one of them because I heard a curse. And then they were the ones ducking for cover.

As the adrenaline poured through me, I adjusted my hold on the man in front of me, putting better leverage on his neck, bringing my hand up so it clutched his shoulder, and then bringing my left arm up to really brace my right one close to his face.

He started clawing at my arm. His fingers were meaty and big, but they were no match for my simple grip strength.

As a child, I loved to climb. Mum was always complaining that wherever we went I always found some place to climb. Whether it was trees, or boulders, it was the only thing I really liked to do outdoors. I'd developed my grip strength early on, and it was doing me good here because even though he was bigger, he was going to go to sleep in three, two, one. His body slumped as I double-checked to make sure he was still breathing. Because while they may be killers, I was not.

And then I grinned at the other two. "Aw, now, don't run. It's unbecoming of the stronger sex."

The one I hadn't shot approached, but he underestimated me again and didn't even pull out his gun.

He rushed me, and I held a fight stance. One foot back, hands up in Krav Maga position. Krav was my favorite as it was a much deadlier fighting style. When he was within a foot of me, trying to bum rush and grab me, I shifted my position a half inch to the left, snapped my foot up, and got him on the knee.

He howled in pain but managed to clip my ankle, taking me to the ground with him. I rolled and tussled in the worst position ever. He rolled with me, trying to grab me around the waist, but I fought like hell, throwing elbow after elbow, drawing my whole arm back across my face and delivering the blows up under his arm, just digging, digging, digging.

One.

Two.

Three.

Four.

Using my legs and knees I finally had the leverage to get on top for some good old ground and pound. I heard one of the doors open behind me, and with a slight turn of my head, I could see someone else coming out of one of the flats. Holy shit. Had they taken over someone's flat? There was still a whole floor between me and Gemma.

And then at the other end, someone was coming up the stairs.

Oh, hell, two I could take, but four? I'd need a miracle.

With my knuckles bloody after I delivered a proper hammer fist and the man in front of me groaned, I got to my feet, grabbing his gun, knowing I was going to have to do something to make all of this work. I saw a man at the end of the hallway. He was enormous, moving quickly. But I didn't have time to focus on him because I had to fight. I blocked a fist coming for me, diverting it, managing to hit someone. Someone else came from behind and delivered a sidekick, but I had to focus on the assailant in front of me.

I was in so much trouble. But then an all too familiar voice said, "Get your fucking hands off her."

CHAPTER 33
SAINT

I tapped Richard, my driver, and handed him my phone so he could set our new coordinates to follow her. He gave me a nod, and I rolled my window down to get more air because I felt like I was going to panic.

On my way to campus to meet Kaya, I had glanced at my phone and saw her tracker move. Where the fuck was she going? She was going in the complete opposite direction. The fuck? Then I texted her security team. My text looked a little something like this:

Saint: *Where the fuck is she going?*

Saint: *It's your job to protect her.*

Saint: *If something happens to her, I will have your heads.*

Saint: *Fuck it, I'm coming.*

There were no responses, which I hadn't really anticipated anyway. This was the problem when you had junior agents doing a standard security gig. They let the subject wander off and do whatever the fuck she liked.

All this after we just had a whole string of conversations about no more secrets and safety.

Except, you're still keeping a secret, aren't you?

She didn't know about Rogues. But then again, that was an order. She wasn't supposed to know. She was supposed to remain blissfully unaware. Gabe didn't want her in the loop, but he was willing to use her if he needed to.

His blurring of the lines made me very uncomfortable and made me wonder if eventually Saff would operate in that morally gray area too.

But I knew Saff. She couldn't operate in that area. It wasn't part of her makeup. When she was in command, she would do things differently. At least that's what I liked to tell myself.

Richard said, "It looks like she's at 4276 Illing Road."

I frowned at that. Why did I know that fucking address?

Wait. This was Gemma's address. She'd just gone to Gemma's, that was all. Suddenly that knot that had been forming in my chest eased, and I took my first deep breath of the last two minutes.

You've got it bad, man.

As we continued to speed down the street, I kept ignoring that voice and repeated *it's just Gemma's* multiple times to myself. Damn it, there wasn't danger lurking around every corner. Not everything was going to be a complete and utter cluster—

The scream I heard from the direction of the building sent me stumbling out of the car as Richard immediately hit the brakes.

I knew that scream. I'd heard it before. It was Kaya. I ran up the stairwell, not bothering with the elevators, taking the stairs two at a time instead. I could be faster than the fucking elevator.

But on the way up I saw one of her guards, James, his prone body on the sixth floor landing. There was blood coming from his shoulder. He wasn't moving, but he was breathing steadily. What the fuck? I called back to Richard, who had followed me from the car. "Take care of him."

I went after Kaya.

This was why we didn't go into scenarios without back up.

But God, what was happening to my Sprite right now? When I

reached the hall of the eighth floor, my eyes went wide. There was my future wife, kicking ass.

There were three men. One on the ground with a gunshot wound, and a second holding his groin and groaning.

I glanced around. "What the fuck is going on?"

The third man reached out and tried to grab her shoulder. She grabbed his hand and spun around, twisting his hand at the wrist until his arm twisted in an altogether wrong direction. Then Kaya adjusted her positioning and dropped her weight. The sickening crack reverberated off the walls. She didn't even seem to take in the carnage as she spun on her heel to catch the other perpetrator, who'd recovered from his groin injury, with a spin kick, hitting him in the gut. When he stumbled back, I roared as he approached her again. "Get your fucking hands off her!"

Kaya's eyes went wide, but when she saw who I was aiming for, she spun to deal with the other one. Kaya ran straight for him, did a little hopping skip thing, and lunged herself forward with her knee to his face.

Oh, fucking hell, she's hot like this.

I didn't have much time to admire her handiwork as I grabbed the other perpetrator from behind, hooking an arm around his neck. He quickly spun out of that hold, leveraging a jack hammer punch. I caught his wrist though, sliding up under it, pushing it away from me and holding it in position with my left hand while delivering straight punches to his face.

One.

Two.

Three.

Then I reached my hand to his right shoulder and pulled him in for a knee strike. Two of those and he went down groaning, but he still grabbed at my ankles. I sidestepped him. I didn't even consider shooting him until he tried to get back to his feet again. With a groan, I pulled out my tranq gun and finally just fucking shot him.

I whipped around in alarm and found one of the men had his arm around Kaya's throat, pulling her backward. She was clawing at him and trying to make space to breath, but he wouldn't allow it. He just tried to drag her back toward the stairwell.

His friend was on his feet, fist coiled and ready to hurt her. Ready to put his hands on my Kaya.

All I did was kick out, sweep his legs up around and he went down. As he tried to stand, I backhanded him, but he was on his feet, snapping a punch quickly, which I blocked. I aimed to grab his foot, but I missed.

His next attack was fast and furious. I blocked two and got hit with one that rang the hell out of my jaw, and then his foot connected to my gut again. I groaned, but I didn't go down. I just went after him. My fist at the ready, he managed to block almost all of my counter attacks, except for the most important one.

A throat punch followed by a sweep of his legs again and another tranq dart to the heart. As he sagged, his eyes were wide and unblinking.

I could tell he was still breathing by the way his chest rose and fell. I quickly turned back to Kaya, who was now standing, gawking at me and staring at the men who were down. "Who the fuck are you?"

"Kaya, relax. You're okay. I've got you. No one is going to hurt you while I'm here, okay?"

Instead of running toward me and jumping into my arms, she was backing away from me, about to run off.

"I asked you a question, Jasper! Who are you?"

And I knew there was no more holding onto my cover. "Listen, you can trust me. Just let me bring you in."

"Bring me in where?"

"To Rogues Division. You're a sitting duck out here."

"What the hell is Rogues Division?"

"It's a place where I work. And they can help you."

She shook her head. "You promised me no more secrets. I think I just found your last one."

She was backing away, likely going to attempt to run on her own. She was not ready for that. I had no choice. As much as it pained me, I had to do it.

One shot from the tranq gun.

Down she went.

CHAPTER 34
KAYA

MY MOUTH TASTED LIKE SAWDUST. My tongue stuck to the roof of my mouth. What the fuck happened? I lifted my head, and somebody with a rich, deep baritone stopped me. "Easy does it, Sprite. Try and relax."

The hell I would relax. I tried opening my eyes and found myself surrounded by bright white light. Everything was white. I shut my eyes immediately and tried again more slowly. As my eyes adjusted, I saw that I was in some kind of a hospital room. Slowly, realization dawned. I'd been fighting. Was I hurt?

I frowned again as I remembered. Saint had come for me. He'd come to help. I'd been on my way to warn Gemma that Andrew had opened his goddamn big mouth, and then, James... Oh God, James and Ryan... and Saint.

Something else pricked at my memory, but I couldn't put my finger on it. It was evading me now as I worried about Saint. Was he here too?

I glanced around and saw I was in possibly the most pristine hospital I'd ever seen. All white everywhere. The beds were lower and... What the hell was that?

A man turned around. He was familiar. Good-looking. Dark

hair. Jawline that might have belonged on a male model. Who was he? Why did I know his face?

When he saw that my eyes were open, he smiled. "Hey, there you are. How are you feeling?"

I opened my mouth to talk, to ask him all the questions I had, but nothing came out. Goddamn, I felt like dirt. Like prime, grade A dirt. Why did I feel so bad? I opened my mouth again, my tongue sticking to the roof of my mouth, and he immediately came over with water. "I'm sorry about that, I was just filling the pitcher when you started to stir."

He handed me a glass, and I glanced at it dubiously, but I needed it.

I took several long gulps, the cool water quenching the fire in my throat. "James, Ryan, Saint... Are they okay?"

He blinked at me rapidly. "Um, yes. James is just fast asleep now in surgery, but he will be fine. Ryan just got a slight concussion. He'll be good too. And Saint, well... Saint is very hard to kill."

He said that with a smirk. As if it was funny. Why was it funny? Why was he joking about people dying? Again, something pulled in my memory banks and I couldn't quite remember what it was?

"Where is Saint?"

"Um, he had to do something. Brief someone. He'll be back though. I'm his best mate. He asked me to look out for you. We've met once. You probably don't remember."

"Where did we meet?"

He laughed. "I see I need to make a better impression."

Then I remembered where I met him. At the auction, when I'd been running, he'd been right there like a brick wall.

"The auction."

"Ah, your memory is returning."

That it was, because in the same second I remember him, I remembered something else. Saint had come for me, but then what had happened?

"Listen, take it easy. I know you want to get up and run around, but you took a couple of hits. You've got some bruising. Certainly a bruised rib."

I frowned at that and groaned when I tried to sit up. "Ow."

"Didn't I just say you had a bruised rib?"

I scowled at him. "You have a shitty bedside manner."

"Yeah, that's what my wife says too."

I realized I knew him from somewhere else too. The engagement party. He'd been on the fringes of the party. But I remembered something else. His wife-to-be, Saffron. "Your fiancée, I know her."

He smiled then. "She attended your engagement announcement."

"Right, and you are Lachlan."

He grinned. "Yes, Lachlan King."

My brow furrowed. "The billionaire?"

He laughed. "Yeah. Honestly, I think people throw the word around too easily these days."

"Right. Can I see James and Ryan? They saved my life."

He nodded. "As soon as James is out of surgery, sure. And Ryan, I think the doc has him resting, but when he gets up, I'm sure he'd like to see you and know that you're okay."

"And Saint. You said Saint had to talk to someone. Who is he talking to?"

Lachlan's wide-open smile shuttered. He was still smiling, but now there was a mask. "Don't worry about that right now. You just worry about feeling better. And don't worry about your friend, Gemma. We sent some people to watch her. She was brought here from class and was already here when you got here."

"Where is here?"

Again, the masked look. "I'm going to let Saint and Gabe explain that to you."

"Who the fuck is Gabe, and why should I care?"

He guffawed. "I knew I liked you."

"What's that supposed to mean?"

"As Saint's best mate and someone who told him to tell you everything, I want to see the look on your face when he explains it all."

My brow furrowed as Lachlan King scooted out of the room. Then the door swung open again, and another man walked through. He was slightly older. Late twenties, maybe early thirties. Also stupidly handsome. Like honestly, it was ridiculous. He had a sharper nose though, and deep set eyes. Dark hair, and his eyes were a startling, piercing green. Like the kind of electric green you saw in anime drawings of heroes.

"Miss Reynolds."

"You can call me Kaya."

"I'm Gabe Webb. You're in Abott manor."

"A manor? That's fancy."

He surprised me with a chuckle, as if it didn't happen often, but it made him look younger. Like a perfectly normal handsome man that you would meet out and about, and you would be flustered when he spoke to you. "Abott. Abott?" My brain started to go through a string of people. "Saff Abott. Are you married to her? I thought she was engaged to Lachlan King?"

He laughed then, and he looked really young. The quick flash of dimple was startling. Good lord, the man was handsome. It didn't do much for me, but I could see Gemma legitimately drooling. "She's my sister."

My brows lifted. "Adopted, right?"

He laughed. "Yeah, I think that's pretty obvious."

With her onyx skin and his missing melanin, it was the only assumption I could make. "Where is Abott manor, and what am I doing here?"

It was then that Saint walked in. "I've got it, Gabe. I should do it."

I tried to prop myself up, but my shoulder screamed in agony.

I glanced down at it and frowned when I noticed the sling. "What the fuck?"

Saint came over. "Hey, relax. Just lay back. You dislocated your shoulder."

How had that happened? I'd been fighting, and then, ugh... Someone got a hold of me. And then Saint was there, and he was... I had missed something.

What was I missing?

Saint sighed. "Your shoulder has been aggravated. We've reset it, but it's going to hurt for a few days."

"What is going on?"

Gabe's grim expression was back, and he looked like a recalcitrant father. Like he was about to deliver some bad news I did not want to hear.

It was like someone unlocked the barriers of my brain and I remembered. With a glare toward Saint, I tried to scoot away from him. "You shot me."

Saint winced. "Yeah, I did."

"Who the hell are you? Where the hell am I?"

Saint sighed. "I'm exactly who I said I was. I'm Jasper Saint, and you are at Abott Manor."

Gabe rolled his eyes. "Abott Manor is also the home of Rogues Division. We're a secret government facility. Saint is one of our operatives."

I turned to him, finally understanding. All the half-truths, the hours he kept, the things I couldn't add up in my head. The outright lies. "You're a fucking liar."

CHAPTER 35
KAYA

"I have to tell you, I'm getting pretty tired of you people tranquilizing me."

Gabe Webb gave me a wide grin. "Well, if I hadn't done something, you were likely to kill Saint."

"I feel like that would be an improved status for him."

He smirked. "Sometimes I might agree with you."

"You should have let me kill him."

"Well, in this instance, I still need him. Thank you for agreeing to meet with me."

"Did I have a choice? I woke up to some very large men standing over me, telling me I had a meeting with you. So, here I am."

"I know this is disorienting."

"Well, generally when you tranquilize someone and they wake up in a different place, it's disorienting. I've been B.A. Baracus'd."

His brows lifted. "An *A-Team* reference?"

"I loved *A-Team*. I used to watch reruns all the time."

"Fair enough."

"My foster dad is American. He got us all into watching the DVDs. Can you imagine?"

"I can imagine." He sighed and stapled his fingers as he sat back. "Listen, Kaya, I know none of this has been easy, and well, you have a right to be angry with Saint. But you should know that he was following my orders."

"Orders, is that what those were?" Every time he kissed me? Every time he touched me? Every time he made me feel seen? My birthday, were those orders too? "You have a funny way of doling out orders."

"You're angry, and you have every right to be. But we're in a delicate situation here."

"Look, I don't know anything about anyone. I'm a college student. That's it. All I want is to just go back to my life where there is no chaos. Since I met him and all of you people, there's been nothing but chaos in my life."

Gabe cocked his head. "Is that true?"

"Of course, it's true. My flat got blown up. Gas leak, my ass. I've had men chasing me. I've gone on television and told the world that I'm marrying that arsehole."

Gabe just crossed his arms then sat back and watched me. I scowled at his apparent nonchalance. "What's that look for?"

"I don't have a look."

"Yes, you do. I don't even know you, and I know that's a look."

"All right, fine. Would you argue that all of that is our fault?"

The hell? "Of course, it's your fault. If I had never met Saint, I would have been able to ask Connor Lohman my questions, and then gone on my way and found out about what happened to my mother. Come back to my life. But no, there you were."

He grinned. "I would actually argue that you were born for this. From what Saint tells me and what was on Ryan's and James's body cams, you're a hell of a fighter. You didn't get that way by accident."

"They had body cams?"

He nodded slowly. "They did. The way Saint tells it, you're nearly as good as my sister."

"I'm not a fighter. I'm a woman who wants to go back to her life."

"Okay. What does that look like? Because you had a choice, you know. Your normal life was still normal, but you chose to be at that auction. You chose to get answers from Connor Lohman. That was a choice *you* made. That was you choosing chaos, because you could have done nothing. You could have told the police and hoped for the best. Instead, you went after him. And from what Saff and Saint told me, you were quite insistent that Connor Lohman had the answers you needed."

"This has to do with Connor? Are you working with him?"

Gabe scoffed. "Pay attention, Kaya. We're not working with Connor Lohman. You are at a secret government facility. Her Majesty knows we are here and how we operate. We take on missions that the Crown can't take on publicly. We are Rogues Division. Jasper Saint is one of mine. He's a billionaire Rogue. A man who walks that fine line between military and society. A man who can get close with his money and access and power. The Rogues make sure the boogeymen don't bother the good normal people. You activated the boogeyman by going to that auction."

I shook my head. "All I wanted was Lohman, and he vanished into thin air."

"He didn't vanish. My men took him."

My eyes went wide. "I knew it. I *knew* it."

"That was the mission. One you interrupted."

"I did no such thing. You didn't have to involve me."

"But I did. You see, when you met Lohman at the bar and touched his phone, you set off a chain reaction you weren't even aware of."

"I don't know what you're talking about."

Gabe sighed. "Okay, let me break it down. You've been looking for your mother, wanting answers about her disappearance, right?"

I swallowed, my stomach falling out, because I knew he was

going to tell me something I wasn't ready to hear. At the same time, I was so desperate for information, desperate for any knowledge, that I subconsciously leaned toward.

"Your mother, Keilani Cassandra Reynolds, she was a Rogues agent. Her call sign was Dove."

I shook my head. "No, she wasn't. I would have known. She wasn't sneaking off on missions. She was with me."

Gabe nodded. "Yes, she was. Twenty years ago, she was undercover on an assignment. Antonio Igno had started to make a name for himself in the underworld. Guns, trafficking, drugs, you name it, he had a finger in it. She went undercover as his girlfriend until suddenly, one day she called in asking to come in from the cold. Then she vanished into thin air. Our agents looked for her, worried that Igno had discovered who she was and done something to hurt her. We only found her because of a fingerprint at the hospital where she gave birth to you. It was completely by accident. They were checking in on another patient. Someone who'd been brought in on a stabbing, and she touched something of his. When it got processed, her fingerprint was picked up by the system. And that's how we knew where she was. And how we knew she'd delivered a baby girl."

I swallowed hard. Sweat started to roll down my back and into that little dip behind my bra. I could feel it gathering steam as it rolled down my lower back.

"She'd gone to great lengths to conceal her pregnancy. We'd already gotten approval to bluff the assignment and pull her out. She went to great lengths to conceal you. Oversight didn't want anyone discovering that you existed because she clearly didn't want that."

"You just left her on her own?"

"I wasn't in charge at that time, I was just a teenager. My father was the one who made the call. Rogues was under his direction then and he was her handler. I don't know how much communication they had before or even after she was in the wind. He left her fresh IDs and money at a safe house. We have confirmation that she picked it up. Whether she knew that my father had given her support or not, I don't know. Either way, she was in the wind for fifteen years. She was very good at hiding. And then suddenly, you turned up.

"What you're saying is it's been you and your men chasing me?"

"No. I wanted to leave your life intact. I think it's what my father would have wanted. It's certainly what your mother wanted. Your problem is that there was never any hiding for you once you came out into the light."

"I don't understand what that means."

"It means Kaya, that you are the spitting image of your mother. You must know that."

"I look a little like her, I think."

He shook his head. "No, you're essentially her identical twin." He turned his monitor around and showed me a photo of my mother. She was in workout gear, her hair natural, long, springing curls that flowed down to the middle of her back. Her dark skin, luminous. She was laughing with someone. She'd never looked like that with me. Never once carefree. But I could see now that Gabe was right. It wasn't just mere resemblance. I looked exactly like her.

"Okay, I look like her. So what?"

"You look exactly like your mother, and you walked up to the last man to see her alive. Did you think he wasn't going to recognize you and know who you must be? He alerted people. Antonio Igno had been looking for her for years. I thought he was looking for you, but I think now, he might have been looking for her instead. I'm not sure."

"Well, I don't have anything of hers except some papers and apparently a property she left for me in Croatia. But nothing else. I don't know anything."

"Well, I'm sure you know more than you think you know."

"I don't. I just want to go back to my life."

He leaned forward then. "You and I know there is no going back to your life. No returning to before times. There is only forward. The choices you make now determine where you get to go from here. Your mother was a good agent. Respected. If my father helped her, it's because he cared about her deeply. From what I hear, she was one of the best, and she obviously taught you a lot of what she knew."

"So what? You want to use me?"

"No. But Oversight might want to, so I want to keep your being here as quiet as humanly possible. In the meantime, we find out what Igno wants with you, and what Lohman wants with you."

"I did this? I started this whole hunt-me-down thing? Who or what the hell is Oversight?"

Gabe shrugged. "Oversight is who I report to, but there are no names, just a department."

"My chatting up Connor Lohman started all this?"

He nodded. "But I have to think Saint is right. Lohman's men, Igno's men, they're not trying to kill you. They're trying to take you as far as we can tell. So right now, our entire job is to keep that from happening."

"I don't want any of this."

"Well, tough shit. It's happening."

"I just want to go back to the day before the auction."

His face was grim. "One more time from the top. There. Is. No. Going. Back. You have a choice to make. Are you going to run, or are you going to fight? I didn't know your mother, but I know what she would want you to do."

CHAPTER 36
SAINT

I PAUSED OUTSIDE of Gabe's office, my arms resting on the door frame. I had cocked this up completely. Absolute fucking mess. Now I had to walk in there, look her in the eye, and say that I knew I had fucked the whole thing up. She was pissed and rightfully so.

Fucking hell. What was there to say? 'Hey Kaya, while I was busy falling for you, I may have lied about everything. Sorry, mate.' I was so fucked. So I just opened the door, ready and willing to take whatever bullshit was coming my way.

When I opened the door, she was sitting on the couch, leaning forward.

"Hey, Sprite, are you okay?"

She was rocking back and forth. "I don't know. I suppose so. How do you want me to answer that?"

Fuuuuuck. This was bad.

"You are a liar."

"I am. I wish I could say I'm sorry, but I can't."

"So you just lied and that's okay?"

"No. It's not okay. I just want you to know I didn't mean to hurt you."

"But you did. You, not the guys chasing me and shooting at me.

You, Jasper Saint hurt me."

I stepped forward, closing the door and pressing the lock behind me. God help me if anyone of them came running through looking for Gabe. Gabe had already told me to come talk to her and that he'd leave us alone for a chat. "I couldn't tell you. Those were my orders."

"Right, those infamous orders." Kaya pushed to her feet and strolled over to me, jamming a finger in my chest. "Tell me, was it part of your orders to kiss me? To slide those big fingers of yours inside me and make me come, were those part of your orders too?"

My cock pulsed. Fucking hell. Her scent wafted around me, and I had to swallow hard and clench my teeth. "Kaya."

"No." She jabbed me on the chest again. "Don't you dare Kaya me. The whole time, you looked at me like you cared about me. But the whole time, you were lying. You just lied, and God, I believed you."

"I didn't lie. I just didn't tell you who I was."

"Oh my God. Are we doing semantics?"

"If I have to."

"Fuck you, Saint."

I winced when she didn't use my first name. "You're angry. You should be. This whole thing is fucked up, I know."

"God, was any of it real? Because I thought that you and I... that something was happening. Was I wrong?"

I swallowed hard. "You weren't wrong."

"Then what the hell happened? How did I miss this?"

"You didn't miss anything. I just wanted you, and I couldn't give you up."

"And so you didn't tell me? What the fuck, Saint? Honestly, what the fuck?"

"I'm a twat, what can I say? I know I fucked up royally, Kaya. I hurt you, and I was a twat. But you have to understand, you were never supposed to get hurt. None of this was ever supposed to happen. I wasn't supposed to fall for you. You weren't supposed to show up at that fucking auction. But when we danced, I could feel you under my skin. You were already rooted there, and I couldn't stop wanting you. And then you needed my help and I needed yours."

"Right. I do have one question about that, the whole get married thing. Was that part of your orders too?"

I swallowed hard. "No. Those weren't the orders. Once I told Gabe my idea, everyone was on board, but Gabe was pretty clear I was to be hands off."

She nodded slowly. "So, all those times you kissed me, you were breaking your orders?"

I swallowed hard, and she stepped closer. "Yes."

"Every time you touched me, you were breaking orders?"

I dragged in a deep breath and shuddered. "Yes."

"So I was just an assignment? None of it was real?"

"Kaya..." I could hear the warning growl in my voice. I could feel my control slipping. I'd never felt like this before.

There was a dangerous glint in her eyes. Something desperate and angry. But then there was also her. It was like she had the answer to a question that I didn't know how to ask yet. Together it made a cocktail that I couldn't stay away from. "Kaya, this is not a good idea."

"Why? Why is this not a good idea?"

"Because I want you too much, and this isn't a good idea. Not for you. Not for me. Not for either of us."

"You're telling me you want me?"

I swallowed hard. "Yes, you have no idea."

"How am I supposed to know that?"

I stopped looking over her shoulder and met her gaze then, letting her feel every crackle of electricity between us, and she stopped poking me on the chest, her eyes flaring, just a little. And then I backed her up. She only took one step though before tilting her chin up. "None of it was real."

"I'll fucking show you what's real."

Saint

Fuck the rules. I forgot about everything I'd ever said up until this point. We were inevitable. From the moment I'd seen her on that auction block, I knew exactly where this was going. And tonight, she was mine. I stepped toward her, and she took a step back, eyes locked on mine, a smile playing on her lips.

"What are you doing, Jasper?"

"I think you know."

"Oh, you know, I like to be sure. You've left me hanging more than once."

I smirked then. "I have never, not once, left you hanging."

I couldn't be sure if she was blushing, but the way she chewed on the corner of her lip told me she remembered exactly how many times I'd never left her hanging. "Is this what you want, Kaya?"

She stopped, stepping back then, her gaze level and her voice firm. "From the moment you kissed me and kept me hidden, this is what I've wanted."

"Thank fuck." I couldn't exactly tell you how I traversed the space between us. I couldn't tell you how many steps it took to get there. All I could think about was sinking my hands into her hair, angling her head just the way that I needed it, and delving in, stroking into her mouth, coaxing out that shudder and that low moan at the back of her throat.

With a clash of tongues, teeth, and hands, fabric ripped, moans escaped and she was in my arms, struggling to wrap her legs around my waist. I bent down and smoothed my hand over her ass and picked her up, backing her up toward the nearest flat surface.

We hit the wall with a thud, and her groan muffled against my mouth. I rocked my hips into her, and she rocked back, the friction making me shake. With every rock of my hips against her, her fingers tightened in my hair, tugging just a little. I tore my lips from hers. "Fuck, you feel so good."

"Saint, please don't stop."

"Never."

It was all I could mutter as I leaned into that soft spot behind her ear and inhaled. There was no thinking, no putting sentences together. It was all feeling, need, and desire thrumming through my veins, my heart threatening to explode outside the cage of my ribs. She was mine.

With a rough tug, I yanked up the fabric of the skirt she wore, my greedy hands seeking heaven. When I met the edge of her knickers, my fingertips seized her, and then I slid a finger past the elastic, and she hitched her breath.

"Saint..."

"Yes, Sprite?"

I teased her slick entrance with the blunt tip of my finger, and her hands clawed into my shoulders. I had her braced against the wall and I wanted to tease her. Get her to the point that she was clawing, begging, and screaming from need.

You'll be the one who's begging and clawing if you don't fucking hurry.

It was true. I could feel it at the base of my cock. With every hitch of her hips as she ran along the length of my cock, I had to grind my teeth against the desperate call to fuck her. Fuck her now.

But despite all my attempts at teasing, all my attempts to keep my control, Kaya was done fucking about. She let go of my shoulders, and I lifted my head, worried I'd nipped too hard and done something she didn't like. But oh no, Kaya wasn't even looking at my face. She was looking between us, fumbling with the buckle of my belt. I swallowed hard. "Sprite?"

"I'm done with you teasing me."

I was helpless to stop her. Just watching her delicate fingers undo my buckle, and then the button, and then the top of the zipper, I was mesmerized. Frozen. Completely unable to think or move. When she reached inside my trousers and boxers and found the smooth tip of my cock, I bit back a curse.

"Fuck, Kaya..."

"We can go slow next time. Just fucking hurry."

With a series of contortions, I let my trousers fall, the belt clanging as it hit the hardwood. I tugged her knickers aside as my hips notched between hers even tighter. I lifted her higher to make room and accommodate her slide down over me. The moment my cock made contact with her slickness, I hissed. Fucking hell. I was supposed to be in control here, but I was completely out of control.

Kaya's voice was soft. "Look at me."

I lifted my gaze, knowing what she would see there, knowing that I was completely laid bare. Right now, she owned me and not the other way around. I was putty in her hands. Anything she wanted, I would fight a thousand armies to give it to her.

Slowly, I rocked my hips forward. Her eyes went wide and her lips parted as she panted shallowly. I held her steady. "Easy. You're okay. It's just us."

She nodded. And I rocked back, trying to remind myself to breathe before I rocked forward again, notching myself inside her once more just a little deeper. The little fluttering sensations her pussy made around me had me holding my breath, trying to lock everything down. But there was no way she was letting me get away with that. Because the moment I broke eye contact with her to watch where I was joining her, she increased the pulsations, physically trying to pull me in. My gaze snapped back to hers. "Kaya, I'm trying to exercise some control here."

"Why?"

I drew back, and slid forward again, giving her another inch.

She whimpered. "Faster, Saint."

And then I realized what was wrong. She kept calling me Saint.

"It's Jasper. When my dick is inside you, it's Jasper. Not Saint. Do you understand me, Kaya?"

"Jasper, please."

With all the strength I could muster, I pulled back once more. I only meant to ease into her another inch, but fucking hell, she pulled me all the way in. As I sank into her, all I could do was drop my forehead to hers. "Fuck, you're tight."

"Well, you're big."

Despite myself, I chuckled. Which made her chuckle, and her laughter made her squeeze around me, making me rock forward once again. Oh God, that tingle at the base of my spine increased, aided along by a jolt of electricity, and I slammed a hand against the wall. "Fuck, Kaya, stop. You have to stop. I need control."

"What if I don't want you to have any?"

"We're already there, love. I'm too close to coming. And I haven't given you the requisite three yet."

"I can have two more later. I want one now."

I dropped a quick kiss on her lips. At least what was intended to be a quick kiss. But her tongue slipped out to meet mine, and because I was useless to deny her anything, I slid mine against hers, deepening the kiss, rocking back and forth, giving her all of me. Despite the sweat popping on my brow with my attempt to keep control, despite my need to hold tight, despite needing her to come before I did, she was making me lose control.

"Oh God, Jasper."

I picked up my pace, making a point to grind my hips against hers, to hit her clit just right. But we were in the wrong position. Seated deep inside her, I backed her off the wall, and she gasped when she no longer had her automatic brace. Her hands clutched my shoulders, her nails digging in deep as I turned her around, bent down, and sat her on the edge of the couch.

When I laid her back, changing my position to lean over her, she sighed in contentment. And then I started to move.

That contented look on her face suddenly became one of surprise. When I added my thumb to stroke over her clit, her eyes crossed before rolling back in her head. "Oh my God, so deep. You're so deep."

I had no words. Just the driving need to have her cum around my cock. The friction was so good, sending me in a spiral. No thinking. I just wanted the feeling to continue. I wanted that pulsing feeling around my cock. I needed it from her. When the telltale twitch started, I leaned forward again and kissed her deep, irritated that I hadn't even bothered to undo her blouse. Keeping up my pace, I started to unfasten the buttons. But fuck that, it was easier to just rip it off her. She had other clothes, and I could buy her closets full. Right now, I needed to see her tits. And my fucking gorgeous Sprite had worn a front clasp. "Oh, you beauty. You knew what I was going to need, didn't you? You naughty little thing."

Kaya's lilting laugh choked out as I dug deeper on a hard thrust. "Somehow I knew you'd like that."

I gave her another digging slide that made her groan low. "You've been seducing me from the moment you smiled at me on that stage. I wasn't kidding, Kaya. I was a goner from that moment, and I knew it."

With her tits free, I palmed her right one. I pinched her nipple using my thumb and forefinger, plucking the peak until it went stiff. Kaya was thrashing now, her head rolling back and forth. With my free hand, I went back to her clit, changing up my rhythm, giving her two fast strokes and then one slow, measured one with a press on her clit. I could feel it. The pulsing. The shaking. Her legs quivered around my hips, and I gritted down on my molars, trying to fight off my orgasm. At least one. Fucking Christ, I wanted to give her at least one.

Her back arched with my name a scream on her lips. And Christ Almighty, her pussy gripped me like she was a Venus Fly Trap and she was never letting her prey go. With another cry of my name, she broke apart, her body quivering, arms that had been reaching for me going limp, her head still thrashing, her pussy milking me. And then I let go of my control and gave it all to her as I came, seated deep inside her. I let her have everything I had to give as I fell over the cliff with her.

CHAPTER 37
KAYA

I couldn't believe I had agreed to this, but Gabe had called it my legacy.

What the fuck did that even mean? All I wanted was my mother here so I could ask her all the questions. Who are these people? Who are you? Because as it turned out, I knew nothing about her at all. The woman I thought she was didn't exist.

Or maybe she did. And you just knew her as someone else.

Next to me, I could feel Saint's tenseness.

The tension that swirled around us was more than palpable. I couldn't stay away from him, and it was likely very detrimental to my health. I was going to get hurt. But right now, staying away from him wasn't an option. It just wasn't.

So you're going to have to figure out what to do about that.

Just as soon as I figured out what the hell to do about Gabe's proposal. He wanted to try and use me to figure out who the hell the men chasing me were and what they wanted.

When Westin led us into the room, I checked all of the familiar faces. I had met half of these people at my supposed engagement party. Had they all been mocking me? Laughing at how naive I was? It didn't seem that way. But still, what if I had made a fool of myself by believing?

Can you let that go and just enjoy him?

That was the real question. But it wasn't one that was getting answered now.

Saint pulled out my seat for me. I smirked as Westin had already reached for my chair when Saint growled low at him, and Westin just sat on my other side, smirking at Saint. I was going to need to talk to him about that. Whatever the hell that was, it couldn't be healthy. I didn't want to be a thing that could be won. A possession, a prize. Gabe stood at the center of the room with some state of the art clicker and several images came up on the screen in front of us. I recognized one of those men. They had all been part of the gang that had tried to grab me earlier today. Or was that yesterday? I wasn't really conscious of time at the moment.

"In front of you are the capture squad that tried to pick Kaya up off the street yesterday."

So it had been twenty-four hours.

"We know their names, Ivan Maslov, Trent Jacobs, Ethan Maslovovich, and Ricardo Lucci. They're all lieutenants of Antonio Igno. Interrogations started with them today, but we'll take another shot at them later tonight. Lucci already cracked. We're of course verifying all information he gives us. All we know is that Kaya Reynolds," he indicated me with a nod of his chin, "was spotted at the auction gala several weeks ago. Once she was flagged, Igno put out the request for a capture squad."

Capture Squad? Who were these people?

My skin started to prickle as several eyes started to dart toward me. The ones I recognized didn't look at me, but the others, all agents in this clandestine organization that my mother had been part of, stared openly. Maybe that was the most difficult part, knowing she had this secret life the whole time.

Was it really that secret though? She had trained me. Wherever we moved, she immediately enrolled me in martial arts. I had been instructed in all disciplines. Once when we were in France, I even learned some savate. I just assumed she thought it was important that I learn how to defend myself. But when she was gone, I shoved down those skills. It was like I had locked away every feeling I had about my mother.

Well, they came back with a vengeance, didn't they?

I didn't even want to think about it. The blood and the bruises and the breaks. I just wanted to close that all off and shove it away.

"Three times now, the squad has gotten close. The first was not when they were chasing after Kaya and Saint near the All Saints Tech building. The first began at the auction. They recognized you there, correct?"

He was addressing me. All eyes turned to me, and the prickly heat of all that attention was unnerving. "I assume so. I made eye contact with one of them and he seemed to be in pursuit, so I ran. We saw them again at the All Saints offices. They tried to take out Saint, but I didn't get an impression other than I was to be captured. I guess. I don't know."

Gabe nodded. "Then they did this to her flat." He pulled up the photo of my burned out flat, and my heart squeezed. The pain of knowing I lost everything was fierce. But it eased just a little thinking about the room Saint had created for me. The refuge he'd made me inside an unfamiliar space. The way he'd made me feel at home.

Westin spoke up. "Do we know the exact target? Is it capture or kill? Because that looks like a kill attempt."

Gabe nodded. "Our best guess is they were trying to flush her out. Especially if they've been watching her place and it seemed like she wasn't there. Matter of fact, they timed it so that not many students were at home. There were no casualties. The blast was mostly concentrated to her flat. It did reach into her neighbor's flat as well, but her neighbor was not there. Injuries listed were mostly smoke inhalation. It was a controlled blast. Too controlled to be a gas explosion."

The side door eventually opened and everybody tensed. I could feel it. It was like a heavy weighted blanket fell over the entire room, but not in a comfortable, cozy kind of way, but in a way that was restrictive. The man that walked in held his jacket in front of him and he was being escorted by Ryan who was now on his feet. Ryan met my gaze and gave me a nod and a wink. It was his way of letting me know he was okay. I'd only managed to visit him for a few minutes last night, but he hadn't been awake. The entire room just scowled at the man he accompanied, who grinned unabashedly at everyone else.

"Kaya, this is Drake Webster. He's a consultant we use from time to time. He has inside knowledge of the Igno empire."

I nodded at him and he grinned at me. Okay, had I been transported to some special island where they train models to be spies? I certainly hoped Gemma was still hanging around because she would have a field day. Although, as I glanced around the room, some of the men, while good-looking, were more on the average good-looking scale. But this one, like Gabe, Saint, Lachlan, and Westin, though older in his thirties maybe, was next level handsome. Almost like they were an elite team of pussy bait. Honestly, it was distracting. Webster looked at the screen in front of him and smiled.

"Oh, all the familiar faces. What did they do now?"

"They tried to grab her," Saint said gruffly as he nodded at me.

Webster leaned forward, his gaze on me now sharp and shrewd, and then something cold crawled up my spine. The previously dancing, glittery eyes were dead. Cold. When he turned his gaze away, I was relieved. Tension ebbed out of my body, but now into Saint's then Westin's. I glanced across the table at Saffron, and her jaw was tight. Her whole body was tense. I could see the muscle in her neck, and it looked as if Lachlan was holding her hand under the table. To contain her?

She hated this Webster guy. I could tell. It was in her body language.

Gabe was the only one in the room who was neutral to him. And why was that? Who was he?

Webster spoke again. "You look like your mother."

Gabe nodded. "Yes. We're pretty sure that's how they spotted her. Igno has had a standard trace and trap flag on her mother for twenty years. When Kaya turned up a spitting image, his memory activated. The only problem is, they have the wrong woman."

Lock whistled low. "Jesus Christ. So now they're chasing her thinking she's her mother?"

Gabe nodded and Drake sat back and laughed. "Oh, this is a trip. All right, do you know what they want with her?"

Gabe shook his head. "That's why you're here. Insight."

His gaze slid over me again. His perusal was less cold than before, more assessing. "I can only guess. The Dove was before my time. But even when I was put undercover, Igno was still obsessed with her. Decades later, she still had an effect on him and his operations. Her photo was ever present and every new recruit was put on the lookout. She was the only person to ever double-cross him and live. That's if she's alive, of course."

His gaze met mine again. While his words were glib, his eyes were soft somehow. As if he knew what he was saying was hurtful and he was sorry about it but needed to say it.

Or you're reading too much into it.

"I'm not sure how much you've heard, but about twenty years ago, Igno had arms deals with Red Legion. Standard shit. It was millions of dollars' worth of arms he was buying. Igno, at that time, was more a middle man. A common broker before he became a power player. He had a buyer, he had a seller. He was going to keep a cut on the arms from the south and give the rest to the other buyer. Together, they had amassed a hundred million dollars in diamonds."

Everyone around the room whistled low. "The buyer gave the

diamonds to Igno. Igno held on to them until the buy. This was an industry built on trust, and everyone trusted Igno. He delivered. And he was ruthless with those who tried to double-cross him. He was like an insurance policy. Until he went to make the buy. He had the diamonds, or what he thought were the diamonds. And it went to hell from there. The seller checked the authenticity, found out they were fake, and it became a gun fight. Igno walked away clean, but when he went to his buyer with accusations, there was another fight. Again, Igno walked away. But he understood. Someone who had access had taken his diamonds. And he'd always assumed it was, what did you call her? Dove? So he put a hit out on her, but she slipped the net and he never caught her. Which is why I think his men are so interested in her."

I sat up straighter. "But surely by now, she has done whatever she was going to do with those diamonds. He's not going to get them back."

Webster shook his head. "No, she wouldn't have kept them. She would have hidden them. Rumor was, she shared his love of puzzles. The two of them used to love to work puzzle games together. There was this puzzle maker in Edinburgh, Martin Altair. He was obsessed with Lucas prime numbers. He apparently made an un-openable puzzle box once. Dove and Igno would mess with that thing a lot. She took it with her when she left. I assumed she found a way to open it and put the diamonds in there and stashed it. I think that's what he's really looking for, and he thinks you know where it is."

"I haven't seen my mother since I was fifteen. How the hell would I know where something like that is?"

Gabe's stare back was harsh. "It doesn't matter if you know or not. He believes that you do. Which means we are on a race against the clock."

———

Kaya

Saint turned to me. "Do you know what this thing is? Do you know what we're looking for?"

I frowned. "Mum was always fiddling with things like that. I don't know if I've seen it. I need to finish going through her papers."

Gabe nodded. "We'll have a team go through them with you."

I don't know why, but that irritated me. "No. I will go through them and bring you anything I find."

A hush fell over the room, and I could tell Gabe was a hair's breadth away from trying to order me to. But I didn't work for him, and I didn't know him. Hell, I didn't know any of these people. I'd met Saffron and Tabatha, and they seemed nice. Lovely. But again, I didn't really *know* them. I didn't want them going through the last things I had that belonged to my mother. Which was not much.

"Like I said, I'll go through it. I'll give Saint the information and he can bring it to you."

Saint met my gaze and frowned. He opened his mouth to say something, but Gabe interrupted him.

"I'm sorry, you misunderstand, Miss Reynolds. You're not leaving the Rogues campus."

I opened my mouth to argue and tell him to fuck right off. He must have read it on my face because Saint clasped a hand on my knee and squeezed hard, warning me. But I grinned up at Gabe. "Excuse me?"

Gabe sighed and then glanced around the room. "Dismissed for the time being. We'll regroup when we have more information."

Saffron gave me a soft smile and then leaned down to whisper in my ear. "My brother is a dick. Hold your ground."

And then they were gone, everyone but Gabe and Saint and me.

"Miss Reynolds, I can see how—"

"First of all, call me Kaya. Second of all, I don't work for you, so you can't control me. And third of all, I said what I said. Those are my files. You can't have them."

Gabe blinked once, and then twice, and then glanced at Saint as if Saint was going to turn around and be like 'Oh, it's for your own good. Do what you're told.'

But I could tell by his posture that was not what was going to happen. "You heard her, Gabe. After the last couple of days she's had, she needs to see her friend. She wants to check on Ryan, all things you haven't let her do. She probably also wants to sleep in her own bed. My bed... a bed."

I smirked at that flub. "Not to mention, the files are back at Saint's."

Gabe grinned. "I'll send a retrieval team."

"You won't find them. My mother taught me a thing or two about hiding things. And I don't think Saint is giving you permission to tear up his house right now. So you can let me go home, retrieve them, and give you the information you need."

Gabe crossed his arms. "I'm sorry, but you do understand the gravity of what's going on, the kind of people that are after you, right?"

"I thought you were the best in the business. Didn't you just give me a whole lecture about how my mother had been trained for this? What a great agent she was? Didn't you just feed me a whole line of bullshit about how this was my legacy, blah, blah, blah. And now, when I want to honor that and tell you that I don't trust you, I don't know you, you try and be bold with me? I'm not having it. You can't force me, so you might as well get used to the idea. I'm going back to the penthouse. You can send as much security as you want with me. Saint, Westin, whoever. But I'm going back. I'm going to get some rest. I want to go through her papers on my own. You'll get photocopies. I'll give you any information I find out. But I'm not staying here. This isn't my home."

I licked my lips and swallowed hard. "I don't really have one anymore, but this place is chaos. This is where my mother came from. I can't do this. So that's what's going to happen if you want my cooperation. You can hold me against my will, but then I'll give you nothing. What's it going to be?"

Gabe lifted a brow and met my gaze directly. I think he could see that there was no way in hell I was backing down. Then he sighed and turned his attention to Saint. "You stay on her like glue. Right now, she's our only lead. If something happens to her, it's your head."

Saint glowered at him. "If something happens to her, that's my heart." He pushed to his feet. "Come on."

My skin flushed as heat suffused my body. As we marched out together, I whispered to him. "Did you mean that?"

"You mean the part about you being my heart? Of course I meant it. My heart would shatter if something happened to you."

I didn't know what to say about that. I wanted him. I felt safe with him. He wasn't something I was used to.

"Did you mean what *you* said?" he asked.

I paused and glanced up at him. "About what?"

"About him never finding the files that your mother left for you."

I smirked. "No. The files are on the dining room table. Anyone looking could go grab them right now."

He laughed. "Fine, let's go. But first, I think there's someone you should see."

We took a left toward what I remembered as the infirmary. When he pushed open the door, I expected a doctor waiting to examine me again. Instead, I found Gemma in bed arguing with a nurse.

"I am fine. There's nothing wrong with me. I don't have a concussion. I just feel slightly groggy because you motherfuckers tranq-darted me. Who does that? If you think for one minute—"

Her gaze skittered and fell on me. "Oh my God, you're okay." She hopped off the exam table, batting away the nurse's anxious hands. She ran and hugged me, squeezing tight. "Jesus fucking

Christ, I have been so worried. I saw you when you were knocked out. I mean, who the hell uses tranq darts anyway? Then this bozo over here told me it was your second dose and they didn't know when you were going to wake up. I was livid."

"I missed you. Are you okay?"

"I'm fine. I was in class, and that guy—" She turned and pointed at a guy dressed in black ops security gear. Tall, good-looking, silent, and stoic. Great body. His gaze flickered over Gemma, and then his lips twisted into a smirk. "He said that one," she pointed at Saint, "needed me for something to do with you and I was to go with him. And I said, sure, I'll come along. Just show me a text from him, because you know, you never can be too careful." Gemma was pacing around, waving her hands and gesticulating wildly as she acted it all out. "And then, when I insisted I needed to see a text from Saint saying that he had given instructions, that motherfucker over there pulled out a tranq gun and darted me. I woke up here. And then these nurses won't leave me the fuck alone. They kept checking me for a concussion in case I fell and hit my head. They kept asking me memory questions, but they wouldn't let me see you. Are you okay?"

I hugged her tight again, letting the familiarity of her scent wash over me. I was holding her too tight, I knew that, but I was so relieved I couldn't let go of her.

"I'm fine. I'm just worried about you. Andrew fucked up. He talked to the wrong people. They might have been looking for me at your place."

I couldn't tell her I had plans on murdering him with my bare hands and a rusty spoon. So instead, I said, "I will deal with him. I don't want you to worry."

"I don't even know what to say about him, but that's a whole other problem for another day."

"There were guys who tried to get in your flat."

"Duh, I wasn't even there. I was in class. Well, on campus, prepping for my critique."

Xander's fucking critique. I'd forgotten. "I haven't even had a chance to shoot this week."

Saint's voice was low. "I already informed him. He understands. He sent your assignments. You can do them remotely and send them in."

I blinked at him. Should I be angry that he'd summarily taken over my life, or should I be relieved that he'd taken that off my plate? I wasn't sure. Either way, I didn't have to worry about it for the time being, which was a relief.

"Actually Gems, I think we need to find you someplace safe to stay for a while."

"Oh my God, am I coming to live in the penthouse too? Because I'm a fan."

Saint laughed. "Well, there's more than enough room if that's what you want to do. We'll get security to watch you there."

I turned to him. "We'll be there too, right?"

Saint winced. "We put off Gabe for now. But you will be in protective custody if you need to be."

My eyes went wide. "Son of a bitch."

"Yeah. But you got a temporary reprieve, so let's enjoy it. We should get back. Let the nurse poke Gemma some more and then we can all make some decisions about what we're going to do."

Gemma gave me another squeeze. "All right, go. Come back and then tell me what the fuck is going on, yeah?"

"Apparently, my mother took something important from someone and hid it somewhere only I could possibly know about. I have to go through her papers to see if I can determine where that is."

"Oh, I'm your partner in crime in this. I should be coming with you."

"I know. But I think I narrowly escaped this place myself. You might have to stay until you're fully checked out. And then until you agree to some kind of protective security detail."

Gemma smirked at the man in the corner. "Yeah, I'm not entirely opposed to my current security detail."

I laughed with a snort. "Oh God, same old Gemma. I love you. I'll see you later, okay?"

She kept checking out her guard, who wasn't quite sure what to do with that. He just stared at her bemusedly.

It took another thirty minutes to leave the freaking compound, security checkpoints, eye scanners, face scanners, they had all my information. I couldn't even argue with them because they'd taken half of it while I was knocked the fuck out. By the time we returned back to the penthouse, I was completely knackered. I knew it was important to look for information, but all I wanted to do was crawl into bed.

With Saint.

Hell, I didn't even know if that was on the table right now. I'd negotiated to come and get the papers, but we needed to go through them and we had no time.

Saint didn't even break his stride, just marched toward the kitchen. "I'll put coffee on."

"Oh my God, you're a life saver."

"I like to pride myself in knowing what you need."

My thighs clenched together as my core pulsed.

Oh, he knows what you need.

Going through the papers was tedious. There were all these little notes and tags in the margins, but I didn't understand what any of them meant. And for that matter, neither did Saint. It wasn't some kind of like encryption code or something that was central to Rogues. It was something else.

Finally, in the corner of one of the pages, there was a photo I didn't recognize. This was something we'd done when I was a kid. Cut out photos of all the places in the world we wanted to visit. Some places we had, and some places we didn't make it to before she disappeared.

There were all kinds of places that had been highlighted for her. One was Jamaica. That's where her dad was from. The other had been Ghana, where her mother was from. We'd gone to both when I was very young, but she wanted to take me back to those places so badly. I frowned when I noticed there was a photo of Zagreb, photos of Scotland, Toronto, and Cape Town. Some of these places we'd been to, but as I examined the photo from Ghana, I noticed in the corner of the paper there was a set of numbers.

"Hey, do you know what these numbers mean?"

Saint leaned over my shoulder, and the scent of sandalwood cocooned me, tempting me, drawing me in, and I just wanted to nuzzle. But now was not the time for nuzzling. "I don't know for sure, but they look like coordinates. Hold on, let's put them in."

Saint pulled out his phone and typed in them quickly. Thanks to Google Maps, we got the exact location. A house in the core of Ghana. In the Countenance neighborhood. I'd seen photos of that place before. Where had I seen those photos? "I haven't been there, but I've seen pictures of that place. What is it?"

Saint peered at his phone. "From the looks of it, it's just a house. It's in a residential area from what I can tell. This doesn't look like a business."

The lullaby Magda sang pricked in the back of my mind.

For the girl to shine, even she must be pruned. For even a diamond began as coal.

When it's time to go home, you will know. When it's time to go home, you will know. And then you will be returned home with open arms.

I thought it meant the house in Zagreb where she'd clearly wanted me to go. She'd bought the house for me. But what if she meant this place? I checked the photo of Jamaica to see if there were any coordinates on the back. Then I checked the one from Zagreb. No. Just the one of Ghana. "I think I might know where that puzzle box is."

CHAPTER 38
KAYA

I'D BEEN to Ghana before when I was six or seven and loved it. The sights, smells, and sounds held such familiarity for me. Mum had always talked about going back and I'd loved the idea of it, but we never made it.

Mum had always said she had things that needed doing. But as far as I could tell, she was always working survival jobs. So I'd wondered what was so damn important that she couldn't go home. Now I knew.

My mother had been part of this whole world I didn't understand. All these people had an interest in her survival. But nobody, not one person seemed like they were trying to help her. I'd compartmentalized everything Gabe had said until I'd gotten on the plane. And I'd had seven hours from London to Accra to really mull it over.

When we stepped onto the tarmac, a man was waiting for us in a soldier's uniform. His skin was onyx, his brows full. And then he beamed a welcoming smile to me. "Welcome home."

I blinked up at him in surprise. "Um, thank you."

"We like to say, Akwaaba." He shook hands with Saint. "Follow me. I'll walk you through customs. It'll be faster." His voice was deep and booming and heavily accented, but there was something so soothing about it. He was also enormous. Even taller than Saint. Broader, too.

Customs was fairly easy. Standard. We had to get emergency visas. That was also taken care of. And then we grabbed our overnight bags and walked out of the airport. That was when the chaos began. Chaos. It was a funny word. I'd spent years trying to avoid it, trying to avoid complications. But my whole life had become one giant complication, and there was no going back.

There was a sea of people. They were shouting behind the barricade, trying to get our attention. Lots of hackers selling mosquito netting and repellant, selling some chips, and then there were taxi drivers. Very insistent with their shouts of, "Madam, madam. Sir, sir."

I didn't know which way to look, and I was completely over-whelmed.

It wasn't until we were escorted to a waiting car that I breathed a sigh of relief.

Ah, dear God, there were so many people, all in bright colors, just out here working. On their hustle. It was intriguing but exhausting.

The driver we'd been assigned took us out of the airport, and fascinated, I stared out of the window like a tourist. My eyes were wide, trying to drink it all in. The smell was familiar. If heat had an aroma, this would be it. It smelled like warmth and dust and distant cooking food. Something delicious was in the air, and my mouth watered. In the distance, I could hear drums and music and the constant honking of horns. I relaxed just a little. This was familiar.

Within twenty minutes we were at our hotel, and I frowned at Saint. "We're not going to the house?"

"It would probably be better if we do that tomorrow. We've had a long trip. Besides, we want time to look around. If it gets dark and there's no electricity on, it's going to be a problem."

"Oh, right. Good point."

In the morning, Saint rented a car from a rental place right next to the hotel, and we drove out in the middle of Accra traffic, which was an adventure all in itself. When we approached the house, we saw the keypad and I frowned. There was no climbing over the walls because there was razor wire surrounding the property. Saint had a decryption device, and he was quick to put it up to the lock, but I shooed him away and typed in my birthday. Sure enough, the gate opened.

He frowned at me. "I thought you said you'd never been here before."

"I haven't. But I don't know. I just figured I'd try, I guess."

"Okay."

How was I supposed to explain to him that I just *knew*. Inside the walls, there was a wide-open courtyard. To the right was the larger gate opening for the car and a roundabout where the cars could park. Nobody came out to greet us, but it was clear that somebody took care of the property. Plants were in full bloom, and none of them were dead. The grass was cut low, and it was very, very green. Which meant it was watered frequently. Somebody had been taking care of this place. But who?

I called out. "Hello, is anyone here?"

No one answered. We walked across the courtyard, our shoes making a shuffling sound over the pavers. Again, another code at the door. This time, I used my mother's birthday. I wasn't sure how I knew to do that, but I just did.

Saint just observed me and said, "Looks like she expected you to remember something."

"And I do, I guess."

He stepped aside, letting me walk in the house first. And there was a familiar scent in the air. Jasmine and vanilla and hibiscus. I wanted to lean into that scent. I wanted to let it waft around me. It was so familiar. It was the smell of my mother. Had she been here? Was this like Zagreb were she'd anticipated me returning?

A search of the house yielded nothing until I got to the main bedroom.

In the bottom drawer of the night stand, I found a photo of me as a kid with my mum in the garden we'd had at a house in Calet. I must have been about five or so. We were sitting on the ground trying to build a treasure box for my most precious items.

I was young, but I remembered that day with a startlingly sharp clarity. We'd moved again the next day. The swell of emotions came on hard and fast, and I was unprepared for the pang of loss. I missed her. Fiercely.

Beneath the framed photo was a metal case. I pulled it out, and inside I found an intricately carved wooden box. It was about the size of a loaf of bread and cut into a funky geometric pattern. It looked like Lego blocks that had been stacked together trying to build something. Saint found me sitting on the bed and staring at the box.

"You found it?"

"Yeah, I did. Just one problem. I can't for the life of me figure out how to open the damn thing."

———

Kaya

The tears pricked my eyes. Hearing people tell me I was the chosen one, the one to do the thing that they needed, I knew people were counting on me and I couldn't even open the box. I grabbed it with both of my hands and shook it hard. I'd known how to get into the house. I'd known the code for the key pads. So why didn't I know this?

Why hadn't my mother told me anything, like why I needed to be so cautious? Why hadn't she told me who she was and given me a reason not to be afraid? Why?

My frustration must have been clear on my face because Saint tried to comfort me. "Sweetheart—"

I shook my head. "Don't you sweetheart me. I don't want to hear it. I don't belong here. I don't know what this is. I just want my life back."

I could feel the weight of him as the bed dipped. "I know, love. I know." He wrapped his arms around me, and for the first time since this had all started, I let myself cry. The tears poured down my face and I just let them fall, because what else was I going to do? How was I going to make this work? After everything we'd done to get here, I had failed. I had failed my mother again. I had failed myself. I was failing a whole team of people who were trying to help me.

But I let the tears fall, nonetheless, because I had no plan. I was in a sea of chaos and this was of my own doing. How could she leave me a legacy I didn't understand?

I'd come all the way here, all the way to her home, and I still had no idea what to do or how to make this work. How to bring her back.

Saint's arms were tight around me, and we laid back. He tucked me into his side, letting me sob. He didn't try to stop me, he didn't tell me to hush. He just rubbed slow circles on my back and let me weep.

I wasn't sure how long we laid there, his arms around me like a vice grip, my head tucked into the crook of his shoulder. When I finally pulled back, I scrubbed a hand down my face. "I'm going to go wash my face. I also want to see if there's a bath here."

He laughed. "You want to take a bath in a house that isn't ours?"

I turned slowly. "You just said *ours*."

He massaged the back of his neck. "Kaya, I'm supposed to be keeping you safe. I've already taken things too far with you."

I stopped and stared at him. "Do you want me?"

He sat on the bed, gaze pinned on me, Adam's apple bobbing up and down. "You have no idea how much. But I'm your bodyguard. My job is to protect you. Nothing else."

"So are you going to tell me that this is all about the job? Or is this a little bit about us?"

I didn't wait for an answer because I was afraid of what the answer was going to be. In the bathroom, there were fresh towels, sparkly white and soft. This place had a caretaker. Someone who looked after it. Was it an Air BnB? For the love of Christ, I needed some answers.

As I washed my face, I took it all in. My mother had kept a wealth of secrets. I hadn't even known who she really was. I had to come to terms with that and live in this reality. My whole life, all I'd said was that I wanted calm, a chance to live a quiet life. But did I really want that? Because as dangerous as this was, for the first time in a long time, I felt alive. Granted, it wasn't ideal to have people shooting at me, but it did feel incredible to use the skills I had, to be strong, to be able to fight for something that was important. I hadn't even known that my mother had left me a legacy, and I wanted to fight for it. But if I fought for this, then that meant I couldn't go back. Going back also meant I couldn't have Saint. Hell, given that look on his face a few minutes ago, I might not have him now.

There was a soft knock at the door, and I knew who it was. But still, I hesitated before opening it.

For the sake of the mission, we shouldn't act on this thing between us.

He was going to tell me that because he was meant to protect me, he couldn't go there with me. He was going to say all these things that were sane and rational and made sense, but I didn't want to hear it. Because I wanted him. But I wasn't a coward. If he didn't want to be with me, I could face that. After all, I had a whole future ahead of me that I hadn't planned for. I dried my face and then opened the door.

"What?"

He braced himself in the door jam, the muscles in his forearms and his biceps tensing. "I can't do this with you."

"Yes, I understand. Orders and the whole thing." I drew in a deep breath. "You don't have to explain to me. I get it. I just—"

He lifted his gaze, and I saw the fire burning there, the hunger, the desperation. "If we do this, there's absolutely no going back. I'm making the choice."

"What choice?"

"I want you. Fuck everything else."

That was when Jasper Saint backed me up.

If I was smart, I would have taken several steps away and fought the pull between us. But I wasn't smart. When his lips descended on mine, I could hear the growl he made at the back of his throat, and I relished it. He was mine.

Saint

I might not always have the right words for her, but I had this. As I used my thumbs to tilt her head back at just the right angle, I kissed her deep, pouring everything I had into the kiss, letting her know how much I could feel her pain, how much I was attuned to her.

When she pulled back, she tugged me with her. "I don't want to think about this. Make me forget all about it?"

I nodded as we tumbled into the bedroom. I knew exactly what she wanted. She wanted a fast and dirty fuck, which I would almost always oblige her, but I could feel it. She needed more than that now and I intentionally slowed things down. She frowned, almost as if she was asking why I wasn't giving her the quick and dirty version.

I lifted a brow. "I can give you more than that right now."

She opened her mouth to argue with me, but when I nipped at her bottom lip and gave her a gentle kiss instead of the rough one she expected, she sobbed into my mouth.

We were always in a goddamn hurry. Always desperate. But this time, I took my time. There was no rushing, no clawing of hands. I managed not to tear her clothes. Almost. She did lose one bloody button.

When I laid her out on the bed in front of me, trying to decide what part of her to devour first, she reached for me. Again, the question was in her eyes. She was asking me to tell her with words, but I couldn't quite figure out how to say it. All I could do was show her with every kiss from her painted fuchsia pink toes to the ankles she'd scraped in the fight at Gemma's. The tiny scar was healing already. I moved to the slim muscle of her calves as I worked my way up and told her what I felt without words. When I kissed the inside of her knee, she obligingly relaxed her legs, leaving them open for me.

I told myself not to look because once the Promised Land was in view, there was no fucking turning back, and that control I was working on would be shredded.

The plan almost worked, until I was kissing her inner thighs and allowed myself a little peek. The view of her plump pussy, slick and wet for me, had me salivating. And Kaya, the little Sprite, was sliding her fingers through her folds.

So much for taking it slow.

My mouth joined her fingers while those pretty pink tips slid over her clit, and I dove in, enjoying my feast, spreading her thighs wide with my hands, fully savoring the meal she'd laid out for me. And then she called my name in that begging, desperate plea I loved to hear. "Jasper, please. I'm begging you. Just let me come."

I eased back off her clit just a little. Just enough to bring her back before she could crash over the edge.

She screamed in frustration and tried to slide her hands in my hair to drive me back up. But all I did was go right back to my previous task, enjoying my fucking meal. Against her pretty brown flesh, I murmured, "You're not in charge here Sprite. I am."

All I got was a whimper and a futile grasping of my hair. It was only when I could feel her legs quaking that I eased up again, kissing her thighs before I headed up for her belly, nipping at the gentle curve of her hips, and then soft stopping for my second meal. Her nipples called to me, begging for attention. The peaks were taut and rigid, calling my name.

Who was I kidding? I had no control over this one. It didn't matter what she needed from me. I would always fucking lose control with her.

Fucking get it together, mate. She wants to forget.

And I'd let her. But first, I wanted to remind her that she was loved.

I drew the tip of her breast into my mouth, sucking deep. She arched under my onslaught, and I moved over to the next one, the abandoned one, now a plaything for my thumb. Her hips rolled under me, and I wrapped my hand around her waist, holding her still. Keeping her in position. And when I finally released the other tip with a pop, leaning up to kiss her clavicle, Kaya was writhing.

"Jasper, I'll do anything for you. Just... could you let me come, please?"

"I'm delighted you asked so nicely, Sprite, but the answer is no."

She groaned and tried to toss me on my back, but I easily restrained her, smoothing my hands up over her arms and pinning them both with one of my hands.

"I'm going to make love to you now."

"Isn't that what we've been doing?"

"No. You've been trying to fuck me. You want to forget, I get it. And I'll help you. I can make it so that I'm all you see. But I want you focused here. Do you hear me? I want your mind right where it should be."

And as I dipped my head to slide my lips over hers, I slid my cock all the way home. I held her hands as I loved her. I kissed and licked and caressed, pumping deep, showing her just how good we were together, letting her know she was safe with me and I wasn't letting her go.

When her first orgasm crashed into her, she screamed my name and snapped her gaze open, eyes locked on mine. She was a fucking beauty. Spectacular. Squeezing me. Daring me to let go. But there was so much more I wanted from her. So much more I was going to take. So much more that I needed.

When I pulled out, she gasped. "Where the fuck are you going?"

With a chuckle, I released her hands and rolled her onto her stomach. I splayed her legs slightly, tucking her back against me. "Nowhere."

With a hand under her, I lifted her belly and her hips, putting her at just the right angle for...

Fucking bliss.

In this position, I wasn't going to last long. I knew and she knew it, because goddamn it, she was still pulsing around me. When her fingers joined mine on her clit, I lost my goddamn mind. I dropped my hand to her ass in a sharp crack. That earned me another internal squeeze, and I grated out a curse. "Fuck me."

"I'm trying to."

Of course, I couldn't help but chuckle, and I leaned forward and bit her shoulder. "You are naughty."

As I drove forward, I gave her another heavy smack, and she keened in my arms. And oh fuck me, was she coming again?

There was no holding onto control anymore. She was coming for me in another blinding roar. My hands slid down her back, and mindlessly, I fucking let go, telling her with every fiber of my body that she was loved. That regardless of what the hell else was going on with us, I had her and she had me. And I was hers to do with as she pleased.

CHAPTER 39
SAINT

IT WASN'T EXACTLY like I couldn't keep my hands off her. Okay, it was a *little bit* like I couldn't keep my hands off her.

The whole flight back, I needed to be touching her, to have some connection point. I had it really, really bad. But this wasn't terrifying. This was Kaya. I could see her. She wasn't going to hurt me. Everything she thought was written right on her face. There was nothing hidden. No lies, no secrets. It wasn't going to come back and hurt me. Not like before.

She lifted her gaze and smiled at me. "You're staring at me again."

"I'm wondering if I can magic off your clothes."

"Would you stop it? We are on a plane."

"We should have gone private, I told you."

"Think about the environment. We fly commercial."

I rolled my eyes. "Yes, but on the private plane, I could have you naked in front of me right now, and you would be screaming my name."

She lifted a brow. "Are you sure about that?"

I nodded my head. "I am. A hundred percent sure. It would be just like last night."

I watched as a soft flush crept up her neck. "You're incorrigible."

"Well, the thing is, I tried to stay away from you at first. That was clearly a disaster. Because once I touched you, I couldn't stop. Didn't want to stop."

She frowned at that. "Is Gabe going to make you stop?"

"Fuck, Gabe."

"Well, I'd rather not. But if you insist..."

I growled at her and leaned forward to nip at her shoulder. She giggled and slid her hands into my hair, lightly scratching with her nails and sending bolts of electricity to my cock. "Fucking hell. Maybe we can make it to the loo."

"No. We can wait until we get back. We can go home."

I loved the way she said *home*. She'd been with me for almost a month now. It felt like a home having her there. It one hundred percent felt like she belonged there. The problem was that it wasn't safe. Until we had a better understanding of why Igno was after her, she was better off at the compound.

"Yeah, but we'll have to go into Rogues first."

You're lying to her again.

I wasn't lying. I was delaying the conversation. And maybe she just needed to see that Abott Manor could also feel like home.

"Fine. I understand your concern, but honestly, I want this all to stop. What if I use this," she used her toe to point at the wooden box in front of her, "to draw out whoever's after me? Antonio Igno is after my mother. She stole from him, right? What if we make it known that I have what he wants? Draw him out, apprehend him, and then it's over."

I stared at her. "Are you fucking kidding me?"

"No, I'm not kidding. What's the problem?"

"Kaya, you're asking me to use you as bait? Surely you know I would have an issue with this."

"But why? It's clear that's what Gabe wants. Igno wants me.

We can end this right now if I make myself available. If he tries to get me, you get him. What's the problem?"

"I don't want to risk something happening to you. Why don't you get that?"

"I get it. I do. Honestly. But this is the easy fix. The way in we've been looking for. I'm willing to do it because I want my life back."

"Your calm safe life before *I* walked into it?"

Her gaze searched mine. "No, actually. I had a revelation about that. It's like I've been hiding from myself all this time. Hiding from what I'm good at and what I'm capable of. And I don't want to do that anymore. I want to embrace all the parts of me. Even the parts that I don't know that well yet. And to be able to live that life, I can't have an albatross around my neck."

"Absolutely not."

"What did you say?"

"You heard me. I'm not letting you do it."

"I don't think you have a choice unless you have a better idea, because as of right now, I cannot open this thing. But at least I have it. If you can think of a way to get Igno off my tail, I'd love to hear it."

"We're already getting married. He wouldn't dare touch you."

"You keep saying that, but I'm not entirely sure. And here's the thing... You can't actually *stop* me from doing this."

"The fuck I can't. You are mine to protect, damn it." She was also mine to love.

Oh, easy there, mate. Who said anything about falling in love?

My heart frantically skipped inside of my chest, traitor that it was. Kaya wasn't going to back down though. Ever.

"I'm sorry, Saint, but that's not your call to make."

———

Kaya

"This is ridiculous. I'm not letting her do it." Saint sat back, arms crossed with a determined look on his face.

But it was Gabe, hands planted on the table, that I really took note of. His gaze was level. "It's not your choice to make, Saint."

"You're trying to put the woman I care about in harm's way just to see what pops? I refuse to let that happen."

"These are your orders. And you'll be happier getting these orders from me than from Oversight. If they start meddling, there's nothing we can do to protect her or anyone involved."

I sat back just watching the room.

Saff was pacing. "Gabe, stop being ops command for once. Think about how Saint feels. Just put yourself in his shoes. Would you let me do it?"

Gabe growled at her. "Over my dead body."

"Well, now you see."

Gabe shook his head. "I wouldn't let you because you have Rogues secrets. She'll be safe. We'll have someone on her at all times. I give you my word."

Lachlan just rubbed his jaw. "Look, on the one hand, I hear what you're saying, Saint. I hear why you don't want Kaya involved in anything like that. On the other hand, if it means long-term peace for her, I'd let her do it."

Saint scowled at him. "Are you fucking serious? After every-thing, you would let her do this?"

Lachlan sighed and leaned forward. "What I'm saying is that if it's a way to keep her from having to run, then I think we should at least hear the plan. And then we get the final veto power. There's nothing wrong with having a plan. But this she's-not-doing-it thing doesn't help. If it's a good enough plan, one that even you think will work, don't we owe her peace?"

Everywhere around me, people were having conversations about me like I wasn't there. Gemma, who had been in the corner just listening, sat up. "Um, hi, I've met all of you by now, but for anyone who's forgotten, I'm Gemma, the bestie. My real question is, will he keep coming after her to the point that she has to hide every day of her life?"

Gabe nodded. "Igno will stop at nothing. Absolutely nothing. She can get him to his goal, to what he really wants. She's never going to stop looking over her shoulder. She'll run forever."

His gaze skittered to Saff, who patently ignored him.

Finally, I stood up. "Well, I'm glad that all of you have decided these things for me. You all have your opinions, and you want to carry them out. I understand. But not a single one of you has asked me what *I* want. And I recognize that you're used to that. Making decisions where the fate of the world is at stake. Look, I hear you Saint, I do. I don't want to be bait for this guy. I don't want to invite that kind of chaos into my life. And let's be frank, he managed to get one over on several undercover agents."

Gemma, ever the peanut gallery, called from the corner. "Actually, that was Andrew's fault."

She wasn't wrong. It was Andrew's fault. But the point was, Igno was good. His men were good. And they would keep coming for me. "I don't want to just sit here waiting for something bad to happen. That doesn't work for me. I can't do this. So maybe someone should ask me what I want and what this looks like for me at the end?"

Saint's gaze landed on me. I could tell that he wasn't thrilled. His jaw ticked. "Okay, what do you want?"

"I want a life where I'm not going to have to hide all the time. I'm exhausted. The constant running around and looking over my shoulder. I'm tired. I want this to be over. I'm a person, a whole-ass human being with a whole-ass opinion, and I want my life back. I want to be able to go to school and know my friends and family are safe. I don't want to worry that someone's flat is going to get blown up or that someone's going to get kidnapped. And if I can do something about that, if I can make a change so that no one has to worry or be afraid, I will. I'm a grown-up, Saint. I didn't ask for any of this, but I'm here now. You can't just tuck me in the corner and hope and pray that you've given me enough protection, because there will never be enough protection. And meanwhile, Igno gets to live a free life, walking around, enjoying his wealth. I want to enjoy my free life too. So whatever it takes, I'm ready to fight back whether you want me to or not."

CHAPTER 40
SAINT

I reached over and took Kaya's hand as I opened the car door for her. We were on the way to Edinburgh to follow a lead left by her mother. "Thank you for letting me come with you."

"Would you really have let me come on my own?"

I shook my head. "Of course not."

"Then don't sit there and thank me as if I had a choice."

I laughed at that. "Touché. But I'm glad I'm doing it with you."

Kaya gave me a soft smile. "As annoyed as I am to have a constant babysitter, I'm glad you're here too."

We'd started the drive up to Edinburgh early in the morning before the sun rose. We could have flown or taken the helicopter like last time, but it gave us some time together, and some time for Kaya to go through more of the paperwork while I drove. The more we tried to apply logic to the choices her mother had made, the more the answers to her clues eluded us. But what was really fascinating for me was the years that she'd spent on the run with no support from Rogues. Completely on her own, out in the cold, with a daughter to protect. I had no idea how she'd done that.

Kaya didn't know, but I'd pulled her mother's file and reviewed it. I was curious to know what had brought her into the group originally and what insights could be gained from her case files. Unfortunately there wasn't anything useful there. She was a really good agent. Decorated. But she was steadier than she was outstanding. From what the paperwork said, she was quiet, steadfast, and did her job. She understood the assignments, was good in the field and had everyone's back. So why had Rogues hung her out to dry when she left Igno? Why had she been forced to make that choice? I intended to find out. That wasn't what Rogues was about. We didn't leave our agents under fire. We got them out. But I decided that was a problem for another day because we were driving into the city.

Kaya glanced around. "I really hope we find some answers here."

"But if we don't, your mother will have left a trail. She knew what she was doing. She knew that she had to protect you."

She slid me a gaze that made my heart melt. I could see she was grateful to me for saying that. I could see how isolated she must feel in trying to understand what her mother had wanted from her.

Kaya pulled out the sheet with the address on it. "I hope he can help."

"Me too."

More importantly, I hoped we were going to find a friend, not a foe, but I wasn't telling Kaya that. When we arrived at the address in question, Kaya lifted the gate release and took a deep breath. "Well, here goes nothing."

As we approached the door, she hesitated for a moment. "I'm not sure about this."

"Sure you are. You've got this. Besides, I'm with you. Anytime you want to leave, we can go, okay?

She slid her tiny hand into mine, and I gave her the strength I could. With another deep breath, she opened the gate as the rain started to pelt us as if we'd angered the gods by daring to come this far.

Kaya rang the doorbell, and I could tell she was holding her breath by the set of her shoulders. When footsteps approached, her shoulders started to relax a little. The door opened, and presumably, Martin Altair stood on the other side. I had been tuned in to Kaya's response, but I hadn't been ready for his. His eyes went wide in shock and surprise. And then he staggered backward, clutching his hand to his chest and murmuring, "Holy shit, Dove."

Kaya frowned. We stood like that for several moments, him aghast, Kaya confused, and me watching for possible danger.

The shaken man finally stepped back. "Forgive me, sorry. We have to get you off the street." He waved us both in and directed us into his sunroom. "Um, please have a seat. Would you like tea?"

I declined, but Kaya just kept staring at him as if waiting for him to grow horns. "You called me Dove. Why?"

He looked like he wanted to flee, but forced himself to say, "Dove was your mother's designation."

Kaya frowned. "So you knew her?"

Altair nodded. "Yes. She was my friend. But I haven't seen her in over twenty years. Likely there's a good reason for that."

I sat forward even as Kaya stared at him, studying his face. "You knew her. She needed help."

"I know. L-let me get tea."

He returned with tea and biscuits, and it didn't seem to improve Kaya's disbelief anymore as she sat staring at him.

I tried to get the conversation moving as that feeling of unease from outside still plagued me. "Mr. Altair..."

"Oh please, call me Martin. After all, we are family."

Kaya frowned. "Are we?"

"Your mother was very dear to me. Like the daughter I never had. She saved my life."

"How so?"

"It was decades ago now, but I had been commissioned to make something. I consider myself an artisan. Some people like to call me a lock picker, but I solve and create puzzles. If you're here, you know that I did work for Antonio Igno. He was obsessed with puzzles. The unsolvable ones, the unbreakable ones. During a party he had at the Casino de Monte Carlo in Monaco, he requested that I make him a box. Something that couldn't be opened. And then when *he* couldn't open it, he tried to kill me."

Kaya sat on the edge of the soft velvet couch, leaning forward to hear more of the story. Eager for every snippet of her mother.

"Your mother stepped between the two of us and made him swear that if she could open it he would have to let me go. Much to my surprise, she did. I'm not sure how. It would require extreme mathematical talents and an excellent understanding of physics. Igno was so fascinated with her that he did let me go, but I'm aware he and his men have probably been watching me ever since she disappeared."

Kaya swallowed hard. "Can you tell me anything about her? I just... I have been looking for her since then."

Martin smiled. "Your mother loved you. And I know you don't remember, but I used to teach you about solving puzzles when you were small. You could do a standard Rubik's Cube in less than a minute. It was astonishing really."

Kaya frowned. "I don't remember that."

"Ah, but you wouldn't. You were only a wee thing. As you got older, your mother couldn't come and visit me anymore. She was afraid he would remember our connection, and that would put me, you, and her in grave danger. If you're here looking for me, I assume that means she didn't survive over the years, which is a real shame."

I leaned forward, squeezing Kaya's knee to provide some kind of support. "We have a question, in some of the papers her mother left behind, we found some clues that led us to find a puzzle box." I showed him a photo. "The design is yours, yes?"

Martin pulled spectacles out of the pocket of his cardigan and perched them on the edge of his nose. "Ah, yes. That's Dove's. I made that box for her."

"Then you know how to open it?" Kaya asked.

Martin's eyes went wide. "No, my dear. But I'd venture a guess that you do."

She frowned. "What do you mean?"

"Your mother helped me design that. She had exacting specifications, but I didn't build the locking mechanism. She wanted to add that herself. I built the frame, the logistics, the slide mechanisms to open it when it did finally unlatch, but I didn't build the lock or the key."

Kaya's shoulders sagged and she leaned back further on the couch. "So you don't know how to open it?"

"No, unfortunately, I don't. Where did you find it?"

"She hid it in a desk drawer in a home I'd never been to. But all the information to get where I was supposed to go was in her papers."

"Then she meant for you to have it. And if you think hard and long enough, I'm sure you'll know how to open it."

I sighed, frustrated, and glanced at Kaya. "Are you okay?"

"No, I'm not. It's just another dead end."

Altair stood. "Wait, I do have something of hers. She once wrote down the song she always sang. I didn't understand it. I thought maybe it was something her mother sang to her when she was little. Her mother was Ghanaian. Maybe you'll understand what it means."

He handed Kaya a slip of paper that he pulled from a book, and she sighed. She glanced up at me. "It's the words from my lullaby."

"Your lullaby?"

"She used to sing me this all the time. I didn't know all the words until now."

Altair nodded. "Well, I'm glad that I was somewhat helpful."

The old man showed us out, but before we left, he leaned in and whispered something to Kaya, and then she gave him a tight hug. The old man looked like she made his whole day as he rapidly blinked away tears and patted her back softly like a doting old grandpa.

When Kaya met my gaze, her eyes were filled with tears. "He loved my mother. I'm glad she had people she could count on."

"Me too."

I took her hand in mine as we exited the wrought iron gate, and suddenly, something made the hairs at my neck stand up, and I glanced around. Someone was watching us. "Kaya, I need you to walk very slowly to the car. And then I need you to follow directions exactly as I tell you."

She frowned over at me but nodded that she would do exactly as I told her.

"Okay, you're going to open the car door. Do you see that metal postal box? When I say, you're going to duck back out of the car and stay crouched down behind the postal box. Do you understand me?"

She frowned and nodded again. "What is happening?"

"You see the stairs leading down there to the garden?"

She nodded.

"When I give you the signal, run for that garden and duck down. Do you hear me?"

She nodded.

"Now, here we go."

Kaya glanced up at me as she followed my directions and sat down in the car. I closed the door, walking around to the back side of the car. When I did that, she opened the door again, sliding down low in the seat, and then climbed out and closed the door behind her before hiding behind the postal box. When I gave her the signal, she dove for the stairs.

Shots rang out, and I launched myself out of the car and over the retaining wall of the cottage style house. Leaping, I pressed the button and the explosion ensued.

A wall of heated rocks and shrapnel skyrocketed over our heads.

CHAPTER 41
KAYA

I couldn't hear a single thing. All around me dust, shrapnel and toxic particles floated around. Silence was pressing down on me with the weight of an elephant. We'd been shot at again. Our bloody car had blown up. How the hell were we supposed to get back?

And Saint.

Oh Jesus!

Jasper.

I pushed some of the rocks off me and tried to stand. Everything seemed in working order. Head was still on straight. I could move my hands, and I could feel my toes, sort of. Unfortunately, after checking my extremities, I noticed how quickly my heart was beating and how hard it was to get any air. I tried to calm my breathing. I tried to focus.

Saint.

Get to Saint.

As I moved, larger rocks fell off me, and I kept inhaling dust, making me cough.

There was a shadow above me, and when I squinted up toward the gray sky, a hand was reaching for me. I had no other option, so

I reached up and grabbed it. The strength in it, the warmth, the heat, the safety of it.

Jasper.

He was okay.

When he pulled me up, I climbed over the last two stairs that had seemed to survive the blast, and Saint quickly began dusting debris out of my hair.

Oh, wash day was going to be a bitch. Especially if I washed it now. I had none of my products. My afro was going to be dry and frizzy and not cute. Damn it, no cute curls for me.

"Let's go," Jasper said.

"Are you okay?"

"I'm fine."

"Jesus Christ, you really blew up the car."

"Yeah, good distraction, don't you think? Now we need to get out of here. We have a safe house in Edinburgh proper. Follow me."

We made it to the end of the street before he tugged me into an alcove and went to work really dusting me off.

Reaching into his pocket, he pulled out a handkerchief and then wiped it along my face. "You're a mess. Sorry. Are you okay?"

"What the hell is going on, Saint?"

"I'm not sure. I'm sorry. I should have insisted we stay at Rogues."

"No. We can't live like this. I can't hide my whole damn life, you know?"

"I know, but—" His gaze searched mine, and I could see how worried he was. Being a Rogue, he probably thought that he could protect practically anything. He was probably just now realizing what I had realized weeks ago. These people were going to keep coming for me unless I did something about it. Whoever wanted me dead because of whatever the hell my mother did, they would stop at nothing.

Saint led me down several side streets, until finally, we were walking the Royal Mile along with all the other tourists.

"Is it wise to be out in the open?" I asked.

"For now, yes. Whoever is after you is still trying to remain in the shadows. Trained assassins like them looking for a capture aren't going to risk lots of casualties in a public venue. That would leave too many tracks to follow."

I frowned at him. "I don't like the look on your face. You're worried."

"Yes. I gave you my word that I would protect you, and these people are making it very hard for me to keep my promise. So, of course, I'm worried. You are alive right now, I'm alive, and I damn well plan on both of us staying that way. "

Up ahead, there was a sign for something called the Witchery. Saint took a quick hard left.

"What is this place?"

"The Witchery is a restaurant. Two, actually. But we're not going there."

In the dark confined alley where the restaurant was decorated with some kind of fairy entrance, there was another door to the right. He typed something on the security keypad and the massive door creaked open. He used his body to shove it open further.

"Where are we?"

"Safe house. Up the stairs."

It was dark, and I had to feel my way around. When I finally hit the landing, I could see light from the window above, which guided me the rest of the way to the door at the top of the stairs.

He tapped in another code, and the door pushed into a tidy but comfortable-looking studio. A small kitchenette, wide-open living area, and what looked to be a small bathroom to the right. "Are we safe here?" I asked.

"Yeah. I'll call for Ryan in the morning. Come have a seat on the couch. I'll grab the first aid kit."

I shook my head. "I don't need first aid. I'm fine."

"You're not fine. You've got bruises and cuts. At least let me get you cleaned off."

"A shower is going to do the majority of that. Leave it."

But he ignored me. Instead, he came back with the first aid kit and a white washcloth, gently cleaning my face. His voice shook, and his hands trembled. "I'm so fucking sorry."

'Saint, you saved my life. If we'd gotten in the car, they would have shot us. If we stayed on the street, they would have shot us. You did what you could, and I'm still here."

'I just... I don't fucking know what's going on. I swore to myself I wasn't going to put another woman in danger."

His hands continued to shake, and I clasped them in mine, bringing them down into my lap. "Hey, look at me. This, this is not your fault. You didn't do this. Lay the responsibility at the feet of the real perpetrator. Don't go taking on any shit that's not yours. I'm not Elise. She made her own decisions, and there were consequences to her decisions. Those don't fall on you."

"But I-I promised I would keep her safe too. I believed everything she told me about her life, and I promised I'd keep her safe."

"It's not on you. Her decisions made her culpable. You can't take that on, and you can't keep looking at me like I'm her. I'm just a girl who's not quite sure what she did wrong."

His arms wrapped around me then, and he tugged me up from the couch onto his lap. He held me close and quietly murmured, "I promise, I will keep you safe. I promise."

But even with his whispered words, I knew the truth. He couldn't keep me safe. This was going to get so much worse before Antonio Igno caught up with me and mum's past mistakes that haunted me.

Kaya

Saint had been holding me for a long time. I had no idea if it was several minutes or hours, but I stayed tucked on his lap, letting him hold me and holding on to him as well. We were going to make it out of here, one way or another. We were supposed to survive. We were.

She taught you to be a survivor.

"I remember this one time when I was six," I said. "I wanted to know what I would do if I was ever separated from her."

Saint wrapped his finger around one of my curls. They were still damp, and there was hardly enough conditioner. But there wasn't much I could do. My hair would be a little dry, but I would deep condition it when we got home. In the big scheme of things, un-moisturized hair was not my biggest problem.

"We got on the Tube during the crowded rush hour, and she left me. I was distracted, playing with my doll or something, and she just vanished in the crowd and I couldn't find her. I was so scared."

"She did what?"

"Oh yeah, my mother was always testing me. It was no wonder that as a teenager I just thought she was simply crazy. Which isn't something you're supposed to say, but I just assumed she was mentally ill. She had to be, because who would do that to a child, right?"

He resumed stroking and playing with my hair, and I kept talking. "I was frozen for a moment. Utterly frozen. And then I remembered all the drills, all the things she'd said to do if I ever got lost. At the next station stop. Get off. So I did. It was so packed. A sea of people and none of them looking down. And if anyone did look down, I'm sure they assumed that I was with a parent. But there was a map to the subway posted, and I checked where I was. I had to navigate my way back, and I did. I got right back on the train going in the other direction."

"Not a single person stopped you?"

"No. You know what it's like during rush hour. No one's paying attention to a kid."

"That's fucked up."

"I saw a woman with a stroller. She was white, but I figured nobody would notice if I just tagged along with her and her kids, and then I just walked out of the same station where we'd gotten on. I turned left. I was on my way home. "

"Fucking hell. Even outside the station, no one stopped you?"

I shook my head. "No. I didn't realize I'd gotten turned around until I was a quarter of a mile down the way at this park we used to play at, and I realized I'd gone the wrong way. That really scared me. But I just kept hearing her voice in my head. 'Be brave, be strong, make it happen. You can do anything to survive.' So after a turn on the swing and one on the slide, I headed home."

Saint chuckled, and I could feel it through his chest. "Of course. You just needed a little fortification, a little dopamine hit before you had to do something hard."

"Exactly. Anyway, I did make it home. But I didn't have a key, so I had to sit outside. And by then, it had started raining, so I just pulled up my little hood on my little rain coat, and I sat there waiting for her."

"I'm not sure I like your mother."

"Yeah, the feeling was mutual. Especially during my teens. I sat there for five whole minutes before she came out from the back garden. She'd been following me the whole way."

Saint pulled back and stared down at me. "Excuse me?"

"Yeah, making sure I was safe. She had an eye on me the whole time, ready to jump out and claim me if anyone asked me anything untoward. I was so relieved I cried."

"Of course, you did. I would have cried, too, even though my father was all about the boys-don't-cry mentality. Idiot."

"And as I cried, she held me and told me how brave I was, and how she was delighted that I even took a moment for myself and my sanity to ride the swing. And how even when I was scared, I still managed to do what I needed to do, and that was what I needed to remember. In that moment, it was funny, because I loved her so much. I loved her for not leaving me. I loved her because she was my mum. But as a teenager, when I thought back to that day, I hated her. I hated her so much that it consumed me. It was all I could think about, how she'd abandoned me. I can see now that she was making me strong, building me a suit of armor, test by test, tower by tower." I shook my head. "Now I see it's more complicated than that."

"It's always more complicated than that."

"And you and your dad?"

"Unfortunately, Dad and I are not more complicated. He hates me because my grandfather hated him and put me in charge of the company. I think Granddad could see that Adrianna wasn't interested, and I think he could see that while Trevor was interested, he was trying to prove something. But sometimes I wish he'd chosen Trevor. It would have made Trevor happier. At least, I think it would. I always wonder if he thinks of it as a slight and that Granddad didn't trust him, didn't believe in him or something."

"Do you think it was a slight?"

"I don't know, but the guilt I carry might as well be mine, right?"

"No. Even the guilt I have for not looking hard enough for mum, I recognize that that's not on me. I was fifteen. You had nothing to do with your grandfather making his choices in this world. You were a kid. It's what you do with it and how you handle it when you know better or learn more, I think."

"You're right."

"Your mum's silence, you have mixed feelings about it?"

"Yeah. Badass agent on one end, complicated mother on another. But through all of this, part of me is wondering if she actually is there. If she's still alive, is she around? Is she watching me?"

CHAPTER 42
SAINT

Our ride back to London was certainly tense and fraught with anxiety. I could tell that Kaya had a lot on her mind. We'd come all that way and still gotten no definitive answers. Not to mention someone had tried to kill us, which was par for the course these days.

If Gabe knew how dangerous this was going to be, then what the fuck was he doing? This whole time, I felt like I was fighting with a hand tied behind my back and that there was always something that I couldn't see. Some aspect that I couldn't touch.

What was he hiding? What was he keeping us from?

Oversight had a way of slipping in personal agendas. We'd certainly seen it with Saff and Gabe. Oversight had been eager to get Saff in the field. Gabe not so much. The missions we took on, the prioritizations. Who was pulling our strings now?

We arrived back on Rogues campus later that afternoon. Gemma was the first one to reach the parking lot, and she threw herself at Kaya. "Oh my God, I thought you went and died on me. What the fuck?" She turned to me then. "You, you're in trouble." She whacked me on the arm. "You took my best friend into danger." And then in the same breath, she hugged me. "But then you saved her life. So, yay."

I rubbed my arm. "You're surprisingly strong."

"I get that a lot." She turned her attention back to Kaya. "Are you sure you're okay?"

"Yeah. Except for dry hair, I'm fine. Saint saved me. Honestly, without him, I don't know what would have happened."

"So what happens now?"

Gabe was hanging on the periphery. "What happens now is you debrief." When he turned his back to stalk back to the building, Kaya frowned at him.

"Well, he certainly does give off a welcoming aura, doesn't he?"

I chuckled low. "Yeah, that's Gabe for you."

When we reached the manor house, I watched Kaya's eyes go wide. "What in the Downton Abbey is happening right now?"

I frowned at her. "You've been to Gabe's office before."

"We left through the back and I was tranquilized by an asshole on the way into the place. I didn't realize what I was dealing with."

"Then welcome to Abott Manor."

"Abott? Is this Saff's house?"

"Yes and no. But mostly yes. Her grandfather was one of the Rogues founding fathers."

"Jesus."

"Yeah, exactly. Jesus himself."

At the front door, I wondered why Gabe didn't just take us through the back. It was almost as if he wanted her to see the normalcy before dropping her into the chaos of our world.

"Wait, so where are all the other offices?" she asked. "I'm sure you have interrogation rooms and all that stuff, right?"

Gabe angled his head. "We're headed there. The front of the house and upstairs, that's for me and Saff. In the back and down here are the Rogues offices. The subterranean level houses training rooms and a full gym and pool. Out beyond the house are the bungalows where many of our agents and trainees stay."

"Oh, so this is some acres and acres of land shit?"

Gabe turned to her with a grin. "Most of it we use for training."

"So at any point I should expect a magical royal stag or something to come running out of those woods?"

He shrugged and smiled. "I've never seen a stag, but a deer, and a fox, those are frequent companions."

"Ugh, fantastic. I'm partnered up with Snow White."

Gabe opened the door to his office and then stepped aside to allow Kaya in. I was right on her heels. There was no way he was keeping me out of this. When we were all seated, he leveled his gaze on Kaya. "Are you okay?"

"Yeah, at least, externally. I feel fine, thanks to Saint's quick thinking. I avoided a big hole in my head."

He sighed and sat back, his gaze flickering over me and then back to Kaya. "I'm about to give you some information I wasn't authorized to give to you before, but now that the efforts are escalating, I don't have a choice."

He pulled up a picture of Kaya's mum then another photo of Antonio Igno, and my stomach turned. He sighed. "Kaya, these are your parent's."

Kaya's furrowed brow only sloped lower. "No, that's my mum and that terrorist guy you were talking about. The guy she used to work with."

"Antonio Igno is your biological father. On your birth certificate, she named him as Daniel Jones. We couldn't find anything supporting that until a fake passport by the name of Daniel Jones was activated. Igno has been traveling on a variety of fake IDs. Daniel Jones was one of his aliases."

"You're wrong." While quiet, Kaya's voice held a core of steel.

Meanwhile, the internal pillars I'd propped my shattered heart up with started to crumble. *No. No. No. No. No.* After everything we've been through, there was no way Kaya was tied to him.

Gabe's voice was grave but steady.

I swallowed hard, trying to keep the bile down. Next to me, Kaya looked perturbed. Worried. "That man is my father? You're telling me that's what I have inside me?"

"His sins are not your sins. Try and remember that."

"Oh sure, that's easy. Not a problem at all." She frowned and turned to me. "Did you know?"

I blinked at her in surprise. "No, I didn't fucking know. You think if I knew I—"

Kaya blinked, her brows lifting.

I swallowed hard. "I would have told you."

Her gaze searched mine, and I could see the hurt in them. But she turned away from me and back to Gabe. "So does he know I'm his daughter?"

Gabe sighed. "All signs seem to point to yes. Especially after Connor slipped our nets. He might have gotten word to him at least that Dove had a kid. We had Rook put a couple of traps on for anyone who went looking for information about your birth certificate and discovered the record had been accessed. If he doesn't know yet, he will soon."

"Oh, fucking fantastic. It just keeps getting worse. He's been trying to catch me, but what's he going to do once he finds that I am his daughter?"

"That's what we don't know." He slid his glance to me and I could tell what he was going to suggest. I shook my head, but he ignored me. "You offered to be bait before. Maybe now is your chance. It's a big decision you need to make and one that you should make on your own." That last bit was clearly for me as he gave me a pointed look.

"We can get you inside his organization. We can put an end to this, find out what he wants, and act like we're going to give it to him. And then we capture him."

"You said it was dangerous."

"It is. I'm not pretending like it's not."

"You said that I could get hurt."

Gabe nodded. "We believed it was a high probability, but if he knows that you're his daughter, he's not likely to harm you."

"You don't know that."

"We don't. But it's either this or keep dodging bullets. Your call."

CHAPTER 43
KAYA

Something was wrong with Jasper. I saw it on his face back in Gabe's office. I just wasn't exactly sure what it was he was thinking.

He didn't want me to be bait for Antonio Igno. Hell, I didn't want to walk into the lion's den of a known terrorist. I didn't ask to be any part of this convoluted situation. But if we could end this now, end it for everyone safely, wouldn't that be better?

The look on his face told me he wanted to say something. His brows furrowed and suddenly he had lines around his mouth as if he was holding something in. Something big that he had to say or do. What was going on with him?

"Jasper, what's wrong?"

His gaze met mine then. I could see it all right there in his eyes. My world was about to come crashing down.

"Kaya, I'm sorry."

"Sorry for what?"

He shook his head. "I didn't know about your father. I didn't know any of that."

I relaxed marginally. "Oh, I know. You're just as surprised as I was. It's okay, we'll figure it out. I don't know what Gabe is thinking. I can't walk in there. I can't pretend that I'm excited to meet him and want to know all about him. That requires a level of acting I am not sure I have."

I was prattling on, but he continued to say nothing, and I frowned because I was worried. Something wasn't right, and this whole conversation was going very, very wrong. Why was he giving me that look?

"Jasper, what is it?"

"Kaya, you should do it. Gabe will have someone on you. This is something you should do."

I frowned. "What? You want me to walk into Igno's? Haven't you spent weeks telling me how dangerous he is? How I had to be careful? That was you, right?"

"I know. I know, but there will be Rogues all over you. You don't have to think you are going it alone."

"Are you one of the ones who'll be with me? Will you be watching out for me?"

I saw it then. It wasn't worry I saw in those moss green eyes. He was cooling off toward me. Toward us. He was shutting me out.

"What's going on, Jasper? Please talk to me."

"I-I'm sorry, Kaya. But you and I, it's not going to work now. And maybe it never was."

I staggered backward. Suddenly, I felt like the room was going to collapse in and around me. "What?"

"I shouldn't have taken us on this path. That was my fault. I just couldn't stay away. I wanted you too much, and now I've hurt you. With all of this going on, I have to stay away."

"What? You can't—"

He inhaled sharply. "This isn't a good idea. I have to make choices. I'm choosing my family."

I blinked at him. No, no, no. This could not be happening. "You're simply going to leave me?"

"Yes, Kaya. I should have stayed away. I wish I'd been strong enough, but I wasn't. And now look at this mess we are in because of it. You'll be safe with the Rogues. They will treat you right and you won't have anything to worry about. No distractions. I won't be on the team assigned to watch you."

"I can't believe you are pulling this shit after everything we've been through. You said you loved me."

"I said I care about you. That's different."

I searched his face, trying to determine whether this was some kind of cruel joke, but there was nothing to indicate he didn't mean every word. But damn it, I wasn't going down without saying my peace.

"I mean, how on earth could this even be a reality? Forty-eight hours ago, we were tucked into the safe house in Scotland. We made love. And now, I was about to walk in and give myself up to a terrorist, really told I had no choice, and the one person who could say something rational was abandoning me? This is fucking bullshit. What did I do to deserve this? Explain to me."

"I have to choose my family, Kaya. They've already been through too much, and with Igno being your father, I just... I can't."

"What? That's what this is about? You're walking away because of who my father is? I didn't fucking choose him."

"Don't you think I know that? Of course, I know that. You haven't done anything wrong. Every time I look at you, my soul aches because I am bonded to you. You think I don't feel this? Bullshit, I feel this. I'm just choosing to ignore it for my family's sake. They are the ones counting on me to do the right thing here, not go chasing after my heart. Trevor and Adrianna have been through too much already, and I cannot let my father win the company back. I'm not going to stand by on the sidelines and let him tear apart the company my grandfather built. I can't and I won't. But if the board finds out I'm engaged to Antonio Igno's daughter, they'll unseat me. Then this is all going to get dumped on Trevor, and that's too much pressure for him. He'd never make it. You know my father and his supporters will throw Trevor to the wolves and then find a way to cripple Adrianna. Do you understand? I have to choose them because my father never did. So I'm trapped in this position, even though I desperately don't want to do this."

"Bullshit. You know, I thought I could read people and you blew that to bits. Kudos. You put me in this impossible position. You got me to Rogues where my mother and the team obviously wanted me to be all along, so good on you."

"That's not what I was doing, and you know that Kaya. The last thing I wanted to do is go anywhere near you. But there you were with your eyes and your mouth and your determination, and fucking hell, you think I wanted that? I didn't. I don't. But I fell for you anyway."

"You didn't *fall* for me. That is such a load of shit. You swept in, gave me everything, protected me, and made me love you. But I was just an op to you. An assignment. I was a blind fool who bought all your lies. That's on me. I should have known better. But really, I didn't have all the information until now. So, you can absolve yourself from all this bullshit. I'll go and see Igno. I want this done. I want my life back. And I never want to see you again, Jasper Saint. Go back to your family. Go do whatever fucking business thing you have to do. I will go on this mission without you and live every day in a way that doesn't involve your sorry arse."

CHAPTER 44
SAINT

"Mate, this isn't exactly the healthiest hobby you've had of late."

Glowering at Lachlan over the rim of my scotch glass I shot back. "I feel like maybe you're not the best one to give advice when it comes to women."

When I left the Rogues campus, I headed straight to Notting Hill, knowing Lachlan would be at his and Saffron's house on Lancaster Road. Something told me I shouldn't be alone in my mourning, but fuck if I didn't hate hearing his advice. I was just lucky Saff wasn't around to bust my balls, too. She was on duty tonight, which was one of the reasons I knew to come here. That and Lachlan's selection of good scotch to drown my sorrows in.

Lachlan winced. "Well actually, I feel like I'm a hundred percent more qualified than you."

He reclined in his gravity chair, modern like the rest of the house, done by some Swedish designer. Soft gray, elegant, and clearly an item Saff had picked out. Lachlan had bought the place for her a few months ago as a spot for her to rest whenever she needed. Before he'd turned up, she hadn't really had much choice or say in what she wanted to do. So he saw it as his right and joy to give her the house she wanted, and I always admired him for that.

Then maybe you should follow his lead.

Impossible. I couldn't do that to my siblings. And even if I did stay with Kaya, she would get hurt. Knowing she was Igno's daughter meant my name wouldn't be enough protection. My siblings would suffer, and I couldn't do that to them after everything my father had done to us. I had to be the one to be there for them. The past is such a bitch. Trevor needed me. Adrianna definitely needed me. I had to be the fucking adult, and I shoved that dose of responsibility down with a fucking smile. But none of this shit was easy.

"Mate, do you think this is healthy? Watching her on security cams? Even if you're standing by this decision, you are only torturing yourself. And it's fucking sad watching you like this."

"Fuck off, Lock." I kept my eyes glued to the security monitor. Willing her to find Saff and Tabatha and just get the fuck off campus. Board a plane and just leave. Run. Go somewhere. Anywhere.

Where is she going to go that Antonio Igno won't find her?

She was good at hiding. She could lay low, right? At least that's what I kept telling myself so I didn't have to think about the fact that I had walked away from her. That I was leaving her alone to make this awful decision.

I shifted uncomfortably in my seat and stared back at Lachlan.

"Look, Saint. Gabe assured her she'd be fine. Gabe will always do what's best for Rogues, regardless of what's best for the agents. But you know he keeps us safe and will do everything to make sure he gets her out safely, too. But you don't have to make this choice. You can have the company *and* Kaya. There is a loophole somewhere in the old man's documents and you know it. Just fucking marry her. Then we'll fight like hell to hold on to your seat. Just be with her. You love her. You cannot just walk away from her and leave her in the middle of this shit."

I blinked my eyes as I tried to will away the tears, the sting in my nose refusing to give up. "No, it's done now, and she can make her choice without my interference. Maybe she won't do it."

That was bullshit because of course she was going to do it. She needed her freedom.

The guilt gnawed at me. But if I chose her, what would happen to Trevor and Adrianna?

Fuck. Fuck. Fuck.

"Call her right now, mate. You cannot let this go. You will regret it."

I just kept my eyes on the monitor. I'd broken her heart, and there was no going back. I could feel it even as I was saying the words to her beautiful face. I could feel her falling apart.

I knew the sting of falling for her would not be forgotten. But the stain of Igno was not something that I could easily overcome. It wasn't something the board would let go. I just couldn't fucking do that to my family. I needed to stop watching her, walk away, and let her go.

And then my world fell apart completely. On the security feed, I watched the back gate of Rogues, the door that led to the residence and Gabe's office, and I silently prayed, begged, and pleaded, that she wouldn't go back there. But when I saw her long strides headed that way, despite her small stature, I knew I was well and truly fucked.

Please God, don't do it.

Turn around and go back.

If she walked away, I could find another way to hide her. Maybe there was another way to keep her safe. But if she walked in to Igno's lair, there was nothing I could do. She'd be at the mercy of the Rogues agents, and none of them, *none* of them...

None of them loved her like I did.

But she doesn't think you love her.

Oh fuck. She was going to tell Gabe yes.

I watched with a sinking feeling in the pit of my stomach as she walked in and made a left toward Gabe's office. Kaya didn't know it, but with every step she took, I was with her. Mentally trying to hold her back, spiritually standing in her way, begging her to not risk her life.

What the fuck? I couldn't do this. I couldn't watch.

"Mate, just call her," Lock said. "Call her and ask her not to do it."

I shook my head.

She knocked on the door. Gabe must have told her to enter, because she walked in, and that was the end of my viewing. The dam finally broke, and the sting in my eyes gave way to tears. I roughly swiped them away with the back of my hand, but they kept pouring out of the fissure in my heart.

You forced her hand, and now you will live with the consequences. No one else is going to protect her like you would have. Not Gabe, Saff, none of them can keep her safe like you.

You did this.

This is your fault.

The chances are high that she will die.

CHAPTER 45
SAINT

T HAT THROBBING, pounding headache right between my eyeballs wasn't easy. Exhaustion didn't even begin to cover how I felt. There was no rest for the wicked because that was my penance. All over body pain from walking away from the woman I truly loved.

Elise had only been a facsimile of that. I felt responsibility for her, yes. Care, maybe, but I'd never really loved her.

As much as I'd told myself that Kaya needed me, she really hadn't. She was stubborn, mule-headed really, beautiful, and smart as a whip. I had walked away from that complete package of a woman, and I knew there would be no healing from that disastrous choice.

At the office, I found Trevor and Adrianna huddled over some papers. "What are you lot doing here?"

Adrianna wrinkled her nose. "Jesus Christ, I can smell the... What is that, bourbon? You reek of it."

"It's scotch actually. Top shelf. I don't drink bourbon. It's too uninspiring. No one wrote tales of heartbreak while drinking bourbon."

"Either way, you smell like a distillery. What the fuck is wrong with you? Did you do something stupid?"

"Matter of fact, I did. All for this." I stretched my arms around and did a little twirl, nearly upending myself.

Oh, you're fucking blasted, mate.

Last night without Kaya was a blur. I woke up at Saff's when she hit me in the face with a couch pillow. After she yelled for a while, I got a ride from Lachlan to the office.

Trevor wheeled over and did a turn around me. "Oh God, your clothes are wrinkled, and Adrianna's right, you smell like a distillery, your hair is disheveled, and let me guess, the headache is phenomenal."

"Why yes, it is. If you could close the fucking blinds, that would help immensely. Not that there's any sunshine anywhere. It's all gone now. But still the light in the sky is not helping."

Trevor laughed. "Oh, fucking hell, big brother has just realized that he's in love."

"Yes sir, I'm in love. And your dear brother walked away like an idiot."

My sister sat there with her arms crossed. "You fucked up, Jasper."

"I don't need you telling me that. You think I don't fucking know it? And just what the fuck do you know about love, Trevor? You'd shag any supermodel in a skirt."

"Not true. And I'll have you know that you can shag a super-model in trousers, too. Or my personal favorite, a pair of joggers."

I scoffed. "For all the pussy you get, why are you riding me about Kaya? Why do you care if I have a relationship? You don't believe in love anyway, so what's it to you? Besides, if you knew what I knew, you'd stop pushing."

Trevor's usually juvenile nature slipped, and he frowned at me. "I never want to make anyone as unhappy as Dad did mum, so yeah, I'll keep my supermodels. But you? I was waiting for you to show me it was possible. And you were this fucking close. It's a goddamn shame. How did you go about fucking this up?"

"Shut up. You don't know anything. I did what I had to do. You don't know who her bloody father is. But it's done. And now I will be miserable the rest of my life. But you two are safe, and that's all that matters."

Trevor laughed and then rolled back to the desk. "If you're done feeling sorry for yourself and being the hero we didn't ask for, Adrianna and I think we have a way out of this mess. So bring your sorry, hungover, probably still drunk arse over here, and we can get started on fixing this."

"There's nothing to fix. I'm not going to marry some random woman, and the woman I love will never speak to me, rightfully so, because I chose my company. But the hilarious thing is, I still need to get married to save my company. So I can't fix a fucking thing. It's like "The gift of the Magi" or something."

Adrianna shook her head. "That's what we're telling you. We found a loophole."

I lurched forward. The contents of my stomach, which was mostly scotch, lurched with me, and I had to fight to keep the bile down. I gripped the edge of my desk for purchase. "What loophole?"

"A loophole Grandfather designed to save your pompous arse. Yup, right here." Adrianna pointed at the provision in the incorporation documents. "When the lawyers first pointed it out, we all just assumed you had to get married, but if you look closer, there's a way out."

I frowned and my brain felt sluggish, booze soaked. "I have a way out? How did I not know this?"

"Yeah, mate." Adrianna slapped the papers on the table rather loudly. "Pay attention, little brother. The equity share capital provisions were set up in the incorporation documents when the company went public. Grandad stated that in order to takeover full voting rights and be CEO, you have to be married."

"Yeah, I know. That's what got me in this mess in the first place."

"Well, this little line here says that should you not meet the terms, the board takes over the voting shares. But this hidden line right after that paragraph says that if the primary heir chooses to *share* voting rights, all rights will be split equally among siblings without the need of the primary heir to be married."

I blinked slowly at my sister. "What did you just say?"

"Primary heirs don't need to be married to share their rights. Secondary conditions state that if all heirs share voting rights, the board cannot vote off the primary heir."

I couldn't put two and two together. What was going on? "Wait, I don't have to be married if I share the voting rights?"

"No, you drunken fool, you still need to get married eventually, but now we can buy some time and the board can't oust you. All you have to do at the next meeting is announce that you will be splitting the voting shares with me and Trevor. Then run off and marry Kaya. Even with her dubious paternal history, they cannot remove you from your seat."

"Are you fucking serious?"

"As a heart attack. You can have Kaya if you still want her. But you'll need to be married to someone sooner or later."

"Fucking hell, of course I only want Kaya, but she won't have me now."

"You don't know that, and most importantly, the board has no clue you are an absolute wankstain who dumped the love of his life."

"Did you find another way if I never get married? What happens then?"

Adrianna winced. "Well, then we could have a brawl. Because a Saint still needs to sit on the board, and dear old dad is trying to claw his way back. It's doubtful he'll get the votes, but Trevor and I don't have them either. The board would prefer you, but it's tricky."

"So, what you're saying is if I can still convince Kaya to get married, I'd split the shares with you and I could retain my seat on the board?"

Adrianna grinned. "Exactly. You just have to convince Kaya."

I laughed. "I love you. And I love that you found a way out. There's just one little problem with this perfect plan."

"Okay, what's the problem?"

"I hurt her in a way that I cannot take back. I let her go, and now she's gone forever."

My sister did something she had never done a day in her life. She hit me. Hard. On the arm. And then she proceeded to throw pens at me. Several of them. When she went for the stapler, Trevor waved his hand haphazardly as if he was going to stop her, and I had to duck out of the way.

Adrianna yelled, "Jasper Saint, if you fucking give up on getting Kaya back, I will kill you myself. You don't deserve her. Dad might as well take over the company because you're an absolute fool."

"We can't let him win," I growled.

"What's that now? Let me win what?"

My fucking father, always lurking around like the leech that he was. He was hard to shake.

"What do you want, Dad?"

"I'm just checking in with my offspring. How is that delightful wife-to-be of yours?"

"Fuck off, Dad."

"Oh, trouble in paradise? Let me guess, she realized you're a complete tosser?"

I scowled at him. He wasn't wrong though. I was a tosser. I had fucked up royally. I had no idea how to get her back or if I even could have her back. But looking at my father's smug face, and knowing my siblings were counting on me, I lifted my chin. "Is there something you want?"

"Oh yes, I'm just letting you know I'm meeting with the board members. You know, dinner with old friends."

"You're not going to win this time. You are off the board, and you aren't coming back."

I could have everything that I wanted. Most of all I could have Kaya. I just had to find a way to get her back. I had to fight for her and our future. The problem was I had let her walk into danger. So now it was up to me to get her back safely.

CHAPTER 46
KAYA

I STILL COULDN'T BELIEVE it. Was I really going to do this?

Gabe's contact was getting me in to see the boogeyman, the person I had been avoiding my whole life. And now I was supposed to walk in there and act like I *wanted* to be there? Bullshit.

No, not bullshit. Your life depends on it.

I waited at the cafe like I'd been told. All around me. I watched as pedestrians milled about Covent Garden, going about their shopping, completely oblivious that something else was going on in the world around them. Had I ever been oblivious? Had I ever had that opportunity?

A woman dressed in black leggings, a black tight fit knit top, and black trench approached. Her long coat was sleek, fitted. It had a fur lining. Her blond hair was pulled back in a severe ponytail. Her boots made a clipping sound as she approached. She looked like she belonged on a runway, not taking me to the firing squad.

"Miss Kaya Reynolds, I think I'm supposed to pick you up."

"Okay, who the hell are you?"

"Let's say that I am your father's concierge."

"Why does a grown man need a concierge?"

"Ah, you're a cheeky one. Of course, he anticipates that. And he's looking forward to it. But I'm afraid we have a schedule to keep, so if you'll follow me."

"I don't want to follow you. Where are we going?"

"You know, that's really not a good question to ask. And I can't tell you anyway, so please just come with me."

I hesitated, and she frowned. "You reached out to us. I mean, it was inevitable, after all. But I just wanted to make it clear that if you're not sure, it's too late for that."

I frowned back at her. "Fine, let's get this over with. Take me to the boogeyman. What does dear old Dad prefer to be called?"

Her ruby red lips parted into a sardonic smile. "You can call him Antonio. And I would tell you not to be afraid, but that would be foolish."

"Of course, it would be. "

"But I will assure you that your father doesn't want to hurt you. That's not what he has in mind. He needs you for other things."

"Oh, you mean the fact that I'm his daughter?"

She cocked her head. "Sure, let's start with that."

"Where are we going?"

"I'm taking you home."

I bit my bottom lip. "Just like that?"

"Come with me."

Did I really have a choice? "Fine. Let's go."

The ride through London was familiar and at the same time foreign. It wasn't something I'd anticipated. I didn't know where we'd go or what it would entail. I did think that I would be blind-folded at some point. Which worried me.

We stopped at Mayfair, and I glanced around. "Where are we?"

"Mayfair, love. We'll just be switching over to another car."

I frowned. "Switching cars?"

"I have already scanned you. I can see you don't have a device on you. But we'll just make sure no one's tailing us via drone or anything. We can never be too careful."

In the garage she entered, I climbed out and then she led me to a sleek Aston Martin. "I suppose this is one of my father's cars?"

She nodded. "Now, I do have to apologize."

"For what?" I asked warily.

"For this. It can't be helped."

Suddenly, I could feel a shadow behind me, and then a black bag was just yanked over my head, and I was summarily shoved inside the back seat of the car.

I kicked as hard as I could, trying to pull off the suffocating material. It was like a burlap, and I could barely breathe.

Oh God, why? Why was he doing this?

"Listen, if you just relax, it'll be easier. It won't be long now."

That was a lie. It felt like a lifetime. In reality, it was probably only thirty minutes to an hour. The roads felt less busy. Less stop and go. I didn't hear as many honking horns. Less jerking through traffic. We'd left the city.

Gabe had prepared me for this. So did Saff. When she dressed me, she'd been very particular about my clothing. Something that would be warm enough but wouldn't make me sweat. And they were determined not to put a bug on me. But when I was inside, I was to activate the tracking chip in my boot so they could come for me. And they had a maid on the inside. One who would make sure that there would be com devices left in my room. All that was very high tech. Saff had walked me through it again and again to make sure I understood what was needed.

She had tried to make me feel as if I wasn't going to be entirely alone. Except as hard as she tried to comfort me, I *was* alone. I one hundred percent was. Nobody was coming for me. Nobody was going to save me. I was going to have to save myself.

Saint will come for you.

I squashed that errant thought as soon as it bubbled up.

He'd made it clear his choice was his family. I couldn't even fault him for it. I had been the one that had fallen for all of it. The looks, the lovemaking, the way I thought he saw me. But if I had an opportunity to save my family, I would choose it too. All over again. If I could save my mother, make a choice that would help her by giving him up, I would.

Finally, the car stopped, and I waited for what seemed like forever before someone opened the door. And then someone stepped near me. His voice low, his tone educated, he said, "Tsk, tsk, Vatya. I told you, I didn't want her restrained."

"The black bag was a security measure. She can breathe just fine."

Someone untied my hands and then removed the black bag. I blinked rapidly, allowing my eyes to adjust. I stepped back when I recognized the man from the photos. But unlike the photos, the man standing in front of me was... handsome? His eyes were kind and his smile genuine.

"My dear, I am very, very happy to meet you."

I stared. This was him. The boogeyman. I knew what I'd been told. I'd seen the photos. I'd seen the carnage. Saff had told me what had happened to her parents. I knew what had happened to Saint's fiancée, but in this man's presence, all I got was charm. He looked like a younger taller De Niro. I knew better than to trust my eyes, because my mother had been afraid of this man. But what if I was different? That little voice tried to pipe up.

What if something about you is special? What if you could get him to pay attention, to stop hurting people?

Even I wasn't that tough. This man's charm was a facade. That was the mask. I wasn't seeing the real him. He wanted something, and it was my job to figure it out fast and then signal for my team.

The trick was not to fall for any more lies.

Kaya

Whatever I expected walking into Antonio Igno's home, it sure as hell wasn't this. Instead of the dungeon I expected him to toss me into when I arrived, I was given a beautiful room decorated in soft pinks and florals. Not really my style, but still, it was nice. And Igno had shown me to my room himself.

"I'm sorry, but I'm confused. You've been looking for me for years. You sent scary men to find me, and now I'm welcomed with open arms. I wasn't expecting this whole *I'm just looking for my dear daughter* routine."

At the door to my room, he smiled. "I'm sorry. My men have been known to be overzealous at times. I didn't mean to alarm you."

"Well, alarm me, they did."

"I understand. And you should be cautious. After all, you are my daughter."

I glowered at him. "First of all, can you stop saying that? I don't know you from Adam yet. My mother was terrified of you, and I don't have any evidence to act differently."

He pursed his lips as if hearing that irritated him. Well, it was the truth.

"Your mother and I had a... misunderstanding. I thought our relationship was based on love and trust, but she took off. Then I found out she'd been hiding with my only daughter."

"I'm not your only child though. I understand I have a brother."

"Yes, Massimo. He's excited to meet you."

Right, excited. Somehow, I'm not sure that's the right word.

"I know what you've been told," he continued. "And it's going to take a few days to get to know each other. That's all I want. I didn't know you existed until recently. I've been looking for your mother for a very long time."

"I don't want any of this. I just want a normal life." I reached for my backpack. "And I have the box you've been looking for."

He tutted. "That can all wait. I know you've been told many things about me. Some of them are true. Many of them are not. I think I deserve a chance to show you who I am."

"And if I don't like what you show me?"

He shrugged. "I give you my word that you can leave this house. You can go and live your life. I only want an opportunity to get to know you better."

My instincts screamed out, *No. Hell, no. Trust no one.* He was saying the right things, using all the right words, but God, could he be trusted?

Like you trusted Saint?

I swallowed and nodded.

"I'll leave you to it. You can get freshened up, and later we'll have dinner together."

"I don't have anything to freshen up with."

"Sure, you do. The lavatories are well stocked, and I think I have your size in the closet."

I lifted my brow. "How did you get my size?"

"Let's just say that I'm an enterprising gentleman. Everything should fit. If it doesn't, please let me know and I will take care of it."

"And the poor woman who went shopping for me... What happens to her if things don't fit?" I couldn't help the snark.

His gaze narrowed at my mouthy response. "I'm a man who is just trying to get to know his daughter. And if you give me the opportunity, that's all I want to do. Can you give me that? Three days, that's all I ask for right now."

I nodded. "Will you give me your word that you will let me go at the end of those three days?"

His brow furrowed. "You already intend to leave? Yes, I give you my word that you may go unharmed. However, I want you to know that I hope you won't go. I want you to stay because you are family. Of course, that choice will be entirely up to you."

I nodded. "Thank you."

He turned to walk away from me but spun back to ask, "How did you find me Kaya?"

This was the part where I had to lie my face off. He didn't know that Rogues had Lohman. "Connor Phelps. I met him at the charity auction a few weeks back. He and his men were quite... persistent. He said all you wanted to do was talk and gave me the instructions to meet you at the cafe." Mostly the truth.

He stroked his chin as he watched me. "And where is Connor now?"

"I have no idea. I haven't seen him since then."

Igno watched me warily as if trying to poke holes in my story. "We have a lot to catch up on. I just wish I'd known you before. We lost so much time. I have a whole legacy to share."

I deliberately hardened my face, giving him nothing. "Well, my mother certainly left a legacy too, didn't she?"

"How did she tell you that I was your father?"

"The papers she left me. Your name was in there, and I put two and two together."

He put a hand over his heart. "Maybe she meant for us to meet all along. But still, it's lucky you found me. I'll leave you to it."

When he closed the door behind him, I breathed a sigh of relief. I wasn't so stupid as to think that maybe he wasn't watching me. He'd given back my phone, my wallet, and all my personal items, but I'd been warned that I'd have no cell service here. But if I wanted to listen to music or something, I could do that directly from my phone downloads.

And I did just that, playing something loud as I pulled out my wallet and laid back on the bed. What Igno didn't know was that one of my so-called credit cards was a signal booster. It could get me through the jammed signal to send an encrypted message. I tapped one app quickly to signal the team and let them know I was in the house. I sat up and slid off my boots, massaging my heels with one hand while activating the tracker in the heel of my boot with the other. Anyone watching would just think that I was massaging my poor aching feet.

Then I went on acting as normal as I could and headed to the bathroom for a shower. I really hoped that they weren't so disgusting as to put a camera in the bathroom.

If I said that I wasn't drained by all of this, I would be lying. Even though I was my mother's daughter, this still took a lot out of me. After all, I had just walked into the lion's den to bring down the biggest beast I could imagine.

CHAPTER 47
SAINT

That night I had my game face on when I returned to Rogues. Unfortunately for Rook, he was the first to see it.

"Saint..."

"Fuck off."

He sighed. "Mate, I was never competition. From the moment she signed on to be your fiancée, she was yours. I thought we agreed to bury the hatchet."

I frowned at him. "You wanted her."

"Hell yes, I did. Still do. But she made her choice. Well, made it until you fucked up. Not smart of you to leave me an opening like that, Now I guess I have to be there to pick up the pieces you left behind. Best news is I'm great at cuddles."

The fucker winked at me, and I lunged for him.

Deftly he stepped out of the way. "Uh-uh, save it for the mission. Either you're going to go save her or I am. If I go and get her, I might get the invitation to stay."

"Go the fuck away." I shook my head. "I'm not here for you. I'm here for Kaya."

"Mate, am I glad to hear it. Now why don't you fucking tell

Gabe and the team that you're here so you can go get her instead of fucking about, yeah?"

"This doesn't mean we're friends or mates. I still don't like you."

Rook grinned at me. "That's all right. I'm growing on you."

"Like a fungus!" I called over my shoulder, and I could have sworn I heard him chuckle. I jogged into the residence and then down to Gabe's office. I still had fifteen minutes before time for the mission brief. The door was open, and he was dressed for an op.

"I'm here, Gabe."

He looked up. "Saint, glad to have you back."

"Don't get this wrong. I'm not back for you."

"Of course, not."

"Why are you dressed for an op?"

Gabe's gaze was steady and level on mine. "Do you really think that I would send any of my team in after her without going in myself? I made her a promise that I was going to take care of her. I wasn't lying. Besides, from the bugs she set once she was on the compound, we had some decent information come in on a couple of Igno's brokerage deals. She's done well, and it's time to get her out."

I could see it then, the strain around his lips. He was just as worried as I was. He didn't want to leave her in any longer than she needed to be.

'I thought you would send them in and watch from the comms unit."

"I gave her my word, so I'm going in too."

Keeping his word that he would personally see to her protection thawed my feelings toward him... but only a little. "Just stay out of my way when the shit hits the fan. My only mission is *her*."

He narrowed his gaze as if he wanted to argue with me, but then he nodded. "Roger. Let's go get our girl."

"*My* girl."

"Right. But Saint, no heroics in there, okay? Getting Kaya safely is your mission, and Igno is for the rest of the team, do you understand me?"

I nodded. "Yes, I'm bringing her out."

"Glad to hear it. I'm going to make sure she stays safely away, but then Igno is coming with us or he's not coming out at all."

"Roger."

As we marched out of his office together, we ran into Lachlan and Saff on the way, also heading to the training facilities downstairs for the mission brief. Lachlan gave me a head nod. We let Saff and Gabe go down together, and I hung back with him. Grabbing his shoulder, I asked "Are you sure about this?"

"Don't you trust Gabe?"

"I guess, but why is he coming with us on the op?"

Lachlan's eyes went wide. "What? He's on comms, right?"

"No, not comms. You saw how he's dressed. He has on tech gear. He's going in on the ground."

Lachlan whistled. "What? It's been like two years since he's been in the field. Three probably."

"Yes, but he's still better trained than any of us."

Lachlan kept pace with me. "Mate, are you sure you want to do this?"

"Are you fucking serious right now? If this was Saff, wouldn't you go in and get her?"

"Of course. And just like you covered me in the Winston Isles, I'm covering you on this one. We're going to bring her home. She just has to hang tight a little bit longer. I promise, she's coming home."

"Of course, she's coming home, I'm not leaving without her."

As we waited for the elevator, Lock slid me a glance. "And after we bring her home, are you going to tell her that you love her?"

"Let me just focus on getting her home first. I'm pretty sure she's going to be pissed off at seeing me again." I winked at Lock.

"But I find that my deep, growly voice usually works wonders to soothe the ladies."

"Good man. Now, let's go get your girl and give Antonio Igno a little pay back from the two of us."

CHAPTER 48
KAYA

THE PROBLEM with bad guys was that they never believed they were the bad guys.

Every cartel owner, mafia don, and head of a terrorist group believed that he was, in fact, the hero of his own story. Fighting the good fight by whatever means necessary.

Antonio Igno was the same as every other baddie.

As we walked around the compound, he regaled me with stories of his mother, my supposed grandmother, and how tough she'd been. His father was not a ruthless man, but quiet and with a steel core. To hear him tell it, his father, my grandfather, wasn't ambitious at all. He'd been a man trying to take care of his family, but it wasn't his goal to be any kind of don or master criminal. It just worked out that way, and his father reluctantly brought Antonio into the business when he was sixteen.

"That's where we were different. I wanted more than my father. I wanted to be important, to have my decisions matter. And look at me now."

I hardly had the heart, or the nerve, to tell him that it was bullshit and not something to be proud of because I was certain he wouldn't appreciate my commentary.

"Why don't you tell me about your mother?" he asked.

"There's not much to tell. You know most of it already. She kept us on the run. We moved constantly, running from the threat of you."

He had the decency to wince at that.

As we strolled along the gardens, my fingertips traced some of the hydrangeas, and I met his gaze. "You've been chasing her. She was afraid of you."

"She didn't need to be. All I wanted was her, but . Well, then I found out she'd stolen the box, I just wanted it back. I would have let her go if she had wanted to leave because deep down I loved her."

" I feel like I never knew my mother at all. Going through her papers now, it feels like I'm reading about a stranger. Tell me about her."

"Oh, your mother was beautiful. Flirty. Quick-witted and charming, but there was also something very serious about her. If you looked beyond the charm, the playfulness, she had solid strength at her core. She was intriguing. I wanted to know more about her."

"Were you two in love?"

"I certainly was, and your mother was always a romantic. I think she saw some grand romance in her life. And I don't know about her, but for me, she was it."

Something about that romance part ate and nibbled at the back of my mind.

I knew the mother that I had grown up with was different than the woman that Antonio had met. But I remembered something she'd said when I had my first crush and she knew it was destined for heartbreak.

Kaya, love isn't about a grand romance. Love is about little everyday choices to make someone happy. The choice to pick up the groceries, to clean up after yourself, to put someone else's needs ahead of your own. That is love. Romance is great. It can be fun, but it's fleeting. But a partner is the person you can truly love.

I watched the man who was telling me these things about my mother. Things I didn't know but could possibly be true. Or maybe they weren't and this was all some big lie.

"And she was always like that? Dreaming of a romance?"

"Yeah, you know, always looking at magazines. I should have married her. Honestly, I don't know what I was waiting for. I was a fool. I should have just done it. Didn't she tell you anything about me, growing up?"

"No. We were hiding and didn't ever discuss you. As I said, I didn't know your name until I found her files. She never made much time for romance with a life on the run."

"That must have really tarnished her passions. Your mother wasn't one for practicality. She depended on me for so much, and I'm quite saddened that you were deprived of so many things growing up. I should have been there for you, and your life could have been much different. She shouldn't have kept us apart."

I looked at him, observing his reactions to what I said. "Maybe she did change. I remember there were times that she would watch this old movie over and over again. God, what was the name of it? I can't remember."

"Ah yes, *Casablanca*. She loved that one, even though they didn't end up together. I always wondered how she could watch that. Like I said, she was a romantic."

I understood her well enough to know she would have told any lie to survive and complete her mission. At the core of it, she was a survivor.

He didn't have some grand love affair with my mother. He didn't know her at all. The movie she'd watched over and over again on repeat was *Carmen Jones* with Dorothy Dandridge.

"Really? *Casablanca*? I didn't know that about her."

"Oh yes, she loved it. She loved all those old movies."

"I do know that. But *Casablanca*. That just seems like a different person."

"You know, time can change things. But she was such a romantic when we were together. She believed love was the core of everything. We used to do these puzzles, you know. She loved them. Like the one that you brought me. The box she had constructed. Do you think you can open it? She must have shown you."

I shook my head. "No, I don't know how to open it."

"Oh, I'm sure you could if you thought it through. She must have given you some hint, some clue."

I watched him. His eyes scrutinized my face.

"I don't know what to tell you. I wish I had a different answer, but I don't know how to open that box. I'd never seen it until recently, so I don't know the first thing about it."

His gaze became intense then. "Now would not be the time to lie to me, sweet Kaya. Lying to your father would be a mistake. The kind of mistake that your mother made. I want you to take some time to really think this through, because you are going to get me into that box, or you won't be making it home to see your friends and loved ones."

I smiled up at him beatifically. "Aw, Dad! Here I thought we were bonding. In this moment I can tell you that one thing has become be very, very clear to me. Even if I did know how to open the box, the last person I would open it for is you."

Kaya

I stood in front of the man who was my biological father, staring into his cold, calculating eyes. How could I be this man's daughter, and yet he didn't feel anything for me at all? Whatever connection I thought I would find, the answers I'd been looking for, nothing was here.

I'd been left behind or lied to by so many people in my life. My mother had abandoned me. Probably, for a good reason, but still, she never came back. Never once checked on me. And maybe she couldn't at first. Maybe she was hurt or something, but in Croatia, Magda had said that she'd seen her six months ago. So she was lying to me by not showing up.

And you weren't lying to yourself?

The life I'd carved out for myself was a half-life. One where I was so careful of my emotions and never getting too close to anyone. Then Jasper Saint came along and made me feel safe. Made me feel like someone gave a fuck about me and what I wanted.

And then he left.

My mother and Saint had both left me all because of this man standing face to face with me.

And he was just that... a man, not the boogeyman. Sure he was dangerous, but he could bleed.

Best of all, I could fight like hell when necessary.

"I'm not opening that box for you. I don't know how or where to begin. I guess that makes me useless to you if I won't open it, so are you going to kill me? But then it'll never open, will it?"

He stepped toward me, clutching the box. "You will bloody well open—"

There was a light shaking under my feet like an earthquake, but the booming sound told me that it wasn't an earthquake. It was an explosion.

The Rogues had come. They hadn't abandoned me.

Igno turned his attention on me. "Was that your doing? We checked you for trackers, so how did anyone find you? Do I have to fire someone for their incompetence? And by fire, I mean kill."

"You can kill whoever you like. It's not my business what you do. But maybe you should skedaddle because someone clearly wants to find you."

"You're coming with me." He tugged me toward a side door, his fingertips digging into my flesh.

"The hell I am," I muttered as I fought the hold. In the doorway, he stopped by one of the potted plants and reached inside pulling something out with his free hand, then tucking it in his jacket lapel.

Christ, was that a weapon? He grabbed me, but I rotated my arm out of his hold and delivered him an elbow before bolting for the door. There had been one armed man outside. I just needed to disarm him.

I'm not an expert marksman by any stretch. I fared much better in hand-to-hand combat. Yeah, okay. I needed a better plan, because I would be more likely to shoot myself in the foot than anything else.

I bolted for the doorway, but then pain ricocheted in my skull. Igno was faster than he looked. For an older man, he could certainly move. His hands gripped tight in my curls. "You little bitch, you're just like your mother. I will show you what will happen to her if I ever see her again."

I struggled in his hold. "Sorry, old man, but respectfully, go fuck yourself." Then I delivered another elbow, wincing as I could feel strands of my hair being yanked out at the root.

Bile turned in my stomach as he leaned forward. "I lowered myself to fuck your mother. Do you really think I'd ever be interested in that n—"

"I'm going to stop you right there." His stance was open, and I delivered a back hammer fist straight to his groin, which made him gag and release me. As he dropped to his knees, I delivered a knee straight to his face. "What were you going to say about my mother? Yeah, I thought not."

As he was rolling on the floor, I searched for a weapon. When I didn't find one, I ran to the desk and grabbed a paperweight. Then I scooted around him and opened the door. Lucky for me, there was no guard, but where the fuck had he gone? All the security team probably had their hands full with the Rogues at the moment.

I saw no one in the hallway. Then I realized I'd only been shown a very small part of the estate. I ran blindly into what looked like a major corridor, but I was completely turned around.

Lost.

I had no concept of where to go, where to turn, or which way led out. I just hoped my fucking team was tracking me. When I heard footsteps, I ducked in an alcove, hoping the shadows would conceal me. I could hear my father's voice.

"Where are you going, little Raven? Did you know that's what they called your mother's division? Little spies that they sent out into the world. All of them Black. All of them beautiful. All of them deadly. I didn't find out about the Rogues until after she'd come and gone, taking my diamonds with her. My little Dove took off with a hundred and fifty million dollars' worth of my fucking diamonds. I'm getting my money, you bitch. So get your ass out of hiding and open the damn box. Do you understand me? And while you open it, we're going to have a little chat about how to treat your father."

If I ran, he would see me. I had no choice but to stay, hoping that he would go down a different hallway.

His footsteps drew nearer, and my heart thundered. I willed it to slow down, to not make so much noise, because fucking hell, dying today was not part of the goddamn plan.

"Come out, come out, wherever you are."

His feet went in a different direction, and I breathed a sigh of relief. As I listened, I held my breath and waited. When no more footsteps came, I darted out, only to squeak as a hand clamped around my throat. I struggled in his hold, but he just squeezed tighter, choking me, stealing all of my breath as I clawed at his face. A couple of wild swings barely landed because I had no air.

"No, no, I'm not going to let that happen again. Come with me, my darling girl. I do have to wonder how you believed any of that bullshit I said. You really must be desperate to believe that someone wants you. Your own mother abandoned you. Please, as if I would want a pathetic piece of shit like you for a daughter."

His words stung worse than the chokehold he had on me. And honestly, I was too pissed off to fucking die. How dare he say those things to me? How dare he act like my mother was no one and like I didn't matter?

Holding me by the throat, he pushed me down the hall into a much larger room and slammed me against the wall. "Now, like I was saying, open the damn box."

"And I keep telling you, you dumb fuck, I don't know how."

"Yes, you do. Your cunt of a mother and her puzzles. She thought I had real interest in her. Fuck no. I only needed her because I had a particularly sadistic business partner who liked to pay me with brain teasers. Fucking diamonds in a puzzle box. Now open that damn thang."

"My God, you are dumb. I told you I don't know how."

"I promise you I'll go easy on you if you do. I promise not to let any of my men fuck you raw. I promise to make it not hurt for too long. Just open the damn box."

"And I promise to make your life hell. I hate you. And I can't open your fucking box. Also, you're going to die."

He whirled around as a shot rang out.

CHAPTER 49
SAINT

I FIRED MY GUN, but when I blinked, Igno was still standing. Thankfully, so was Kaya, but there was pain in my shoulder. Fucking hell. I frowned when I touched it. The sticky wetness greeted me and I cursed. "The fuck?"

It must have been a random shot that got me when I stood to take out Igno. I didn't have any choice in the middle of this fire fight. "Kaya, run," I yelled as I went back down behind the table.

She made it only three steps, and Igno went after her. Crouching over, I fired in his direction and he stopped and yelled, "I swear before God, I will shoot her. I will shoot my daughter if you don't call your men off."

I shouted over the table. "Sorry man, I'm not in charge. They are not my men. I'm only here for her."

"Call them off."

"I'd love to, but no chance, Igno."

A barrage of bullets flew my way, and I ducked down. I wanted to lay down some fire, but I was too afraid of hitting Kaya.

Suddenly, it was silent. That sort of deadly silence where the air was filled with the smell of death and gunpowder.

Fuck. Fuck. Fuck.

Kaya. Where was Kaya?

I ran toward the door that she and Igno had come through before. As I slipped through the door, I hit my com unit. "I think Igno is headed toward the South tower. Someone give me assistance covering the guards."

All I heard in return was a gurgled reply. I didn't know who it was or if anyone was coming to help me. I didn't care. All I wanted was Kaya safe. All I wanted was her to know that I'd come for her.

She knows you are here. She knows you didn't abandon her.

Up ahead, I heard Kaya yelling, "I'm not coming with you."

I just had to get her away from him and everything would be okay. Despite the searing pain in my shoulder, I ran after her.

In the distance, I could hear gunfire and more explosions. For once, Drake Webster had provided decent intel. I was just as angry as Saff and Lachlan were when Gabe spared his life. We weren't in the business of killing people, but someone like that... The man murdered Saff's parents, and the fact that he was allowed to walk around was an insult. But sure enough, he was free. Well, in a sense. The deal was he got to breathe air while he turned on his former employer. And so far, he'd lived up to his end of the bargain.

I saw their shadows heading into the gardens, and I ran faster. The pain in my shoulder was only a distant ache, but still, I was moving sluggishly. Not nearly as fast as I needed to be to get to her.

Even as he tried to drag her into a tunnel, Kaya broke away, elbowing him hard and then punching him in the face before darting out.

That's a good girl.

Raising my weapon, I was close enough to shout, "Igno, stop. You don't want to do this. You don't want to hurt her. She is your daughter."

"Let me be fucking clear with you, she's no daughter of mine. She can't open the box for me. She has outlived her usefulness."

"Here's the thing, maybe she doesn't know right now, but

maybe in the future she'll remember. Killing her seems a little short-sighted."

He fired a shot in my direction, and I ducked behind one of the statues but it was shitty cover. As I fired in his general direction, I prayed to God that Kaya was deep in the gardens somewhere and headed for the other side. I knew there was a running trail on the edge of the gardens, a pond, and then beyond that, there was a parking area.

Maybe she had gotten to a car.

Maybe the team would find her.

Anything that meant she was far away from here. Safe from the hands of a madman.

"Igno, just come in with me. I can guarantee your safety."

"Can you? Then the Rogues have gone soft, and I plan on killing every one of you assholes I come across. Including my daughter."

"She's not a Rogue agent. She has nothing to do with this. She just wanted to get to know her father."

"Bullshit. Her mother was a Raven. I know all about Kaya. I have intel too you know. I have men inside of the government."

I knew that much was true. Connor Lohman had gotten out and someone had helped him.

"Why don't you tell me who your spy is?"

"Don't think so man. How about you watch as my daughter dies."

Then he went into the maze, and I ran after him. "Lock, if you can hear this, we're in the maze. I need help getting Kaya out."

But there was nothing on the comms, just static. My whole team was involved in the firefight. I booked it into the maze on my own, praying, hoping that Kaya made it out safely.

My lungs burned and my legs felt like lead. My world spun around me a little, but I fought to stay vertical. And then there she was. "Kaya, Jesus Christ, are you okay?"

She turned to face me. Her eyes went wide. And maybe I imagined it, honestly, I probably did because she was still angry with me, but I could have sworn there was a smile in her eyes. She was happy to see—"

A crack of gunfire pierced the air again, shattering the peace and calm around us. Before I could even call out her name, Kaya went down.

And my world fell apart.

———

Kaya

My mouth tasted like it was stuffed with cotton and sour fruits. Why was it sour?

My tongue tried to push away the offending taste. I tried to reach for my mouth, but someone was there stopping me. Preventing me from pulling these disgusting things out of my mouth.

"No, no. Don't. You need to rest."

That voice sounded like heaven and everything that I could ever want. I blinked awake, not believing what I saw in front of me. "Jasper?" My voice was rusty and raw.

"Hey stop, don't talk. Just relax, okay? You're going to be all right."

Despite his protestations that I shouldn't talk, I tried to speak, tried to understand what the hell had happened. I was on the ground in his arms.

Was I shot? Someone had shot me. "Ig-Igno. Did we get him?"

I'd heard the gun fire, and I was trapped. Because on the other end of the maze stood my father, gun pointed right at me, or right at Saint, and I was in his way. But he still raised the gun and fired, and I went down.

But was I shot?

Nothing hurt. Okay, my head hurt but in that dull, throbby, too-much-alcohol kind of way.

Saint's voice was low as he shook his head. "He escaped. But we're looking for him. The important thing is you're safe.

"Where was I shot?"

Saint shook his head. "No, you weren't shot, Sprite. Igno fired, but Gabe took the bullet. Yours truly, only got grazed in the shoulder. Everyone made it home okay. We were lucky."

My eyes popped open. Yes, I remembered! Out of nowhere, I'd been knocked down by a massive man. I'd knocked my head on the ground, and then something heavy was on top of me and I couldn't budge. "Oh God, is he okay?"

"Just fine, kid." Gabe was in a bed next to mine. And he, like me, was already trying to pull out his IVs. He growled, "I'm fine. I've taken a bullet before."

"You took a bullet for me."

"That I did."

"But why?"

Despite the nurses fussing over him, Gabe was undeterred. He pushed himself to sit up and then groaned, clutching his side. "It was through and through. Jesus, everyone fucking relax." But when his gaze settled on me, it was grave and heavy. "Because I gave you my word. I told you that I would protect you while you were inside. I gave Saint my word that nothing bad was going to happen to you. I had to keep it."

He rose to his feet and then tilted right over onto his ass.

The nurse had her arms folded and just stared down at him. "I tried to tell you. You've had some heavy-duty drugs. Stay in the fucking bed."

Gabe scowled up at her. "You drugged me?"

"With all due respect, sir, we all are aware of how you handled being injured last time. So, of course, I had no choice but to drug you."

He frowned up at her. "You're fired."

"Fine. You forgot last time, too. It always happens."

He grumbled as two orderlies came to help him up. I turned my attention back to Saint. "Was I drugged, too?"

"You've had a mild sedative, but still you shouldn't get up just yet. Anyway, I want you to know that I'm sorry. Kaya, I'm so, so bloody sorry. I should have never let you go in there alone."

It all came crashing back to me. Saint abandoning me, leaving me to my own devices, leaving me to Gabe. Although in the end, Gabe came through.

"What are you doing here Saint?"

"I fucked up, Kaya. I made the wrong choice, and that is eating me up inside. I should not have let you go. I had to come for you. I'm sorry I hurt you. I'm so sorry."

"What are you sorry for?"

He searched my gaze then. "I love you, Kaya, and I cocked everything up. I don't expect anything from you in return because I fucked up for real. But I had to know you're okay. And you need to know that I love you."

Tears clouded my vision. "I don't think I will ever believe you again."

"I know." He nodded, scrubbing a hand over his face. "I know I don't deserve you. I just wanted you to know before I walk out of here today." He turned his attention to Gabe and said, "You and I, we're not done. We have some things to work out, but thank you for saving her life."

Gabe was already laying back in his bed. "Spare me the melodrama. We both need sleep."

———

Saint

Kaya wouldn't even look at me. My heart squeezed and stuttered. She didn't want me there by her side. Every ounce of pain I was feeling now, her coldness, I deserved every moment. What had I expected?

You can't just tell her you love her. You need to show her.

Even if I did show her, she wouldn't believe me.

But love isn't for her. It's for you. The only way to become whole is by loving her. Make it happen.

And I would. I would give her everything. I turned my attention to Gabe once more.

"Don't be stupid next time."

Gabe just scowled with his eyes closed. "You're fired too."

"It's a good thing you can't actually fire anyone around here. Once you join the Rogues, you're always a Rogue, isn't that right?" I said, looking at the nurse, who just smiled back at me.

"I should change the bylaws," he grumbled.

I just stared at him lying in the recovery bed. We were not okay. I would continue to have problems taking orders from him, but he'd done the right thing by Kaya, and I owed him for that. Even if she didn't want me.

When I turned to leave, I found Gemma waiting outside the door. "You know, I came here to tell you that I was going to have to kick your arse. Really, I was determined. I even packed my brass knuckles." Sure enough she pulled brass rings from her back pocket. "But seeing your face, the truth in your eyes, you don't need me for that. You look pretty miserable already."

"Thanks. I feel fantastic," I said sarcastically. "Just bloody amazing."

"Did you tell her that you love her?"

"Of course, I did. But that doesn't change anything. I abandoned her when she needed me. I walked away. I don't deserve her."

Gemma threw her hands up. "Oh my God, you two are a pair. Seriously, a real fucking pair. Pain in my ass, the lot of you. You need to talk and get your shit together."

I glanced back at Kaya. Her eyes were closed now as she fitfully adjusted her position on the bed. "She's not talking to me. And that's okay. I deserve her silence."

Gemma grabbed my sleeve before I left. "So what, you're just giving up?"

"Of course not. I have every intention of fighting for her. This is only the beginning. Right now she needs to rest. But sooner or later she'll realize that I'm not giving up. Not ever. Our souls are locked together. I was the idiot who didn't recognize that, but now I do. I'm not going to rest until she knows it too."

Two weeks later...

Saint

I should have expected to see my father. He was still a voting member at large, and he did like to make life very, very difficult for the board members who'd ousted him. He always liked to show off what stock he'd bought after he'd been stripped of the original shares and they'd transferred them to me.

I knew I had a way out of this mess with the company. Finally, *finally*, I could make choices and decisions for myself.

Let's hope you make a better choice. No more breaking up with Kaya.

First I had to get her back.

She still wasn't speaking to me. Which was fine, even though it had been two weeks since she was safely rescued. Occasionally, I saw her on the Rogues campus. Saff had her training. She wasn't officially a Rogue, but I could see where she was going with it. Not that I was stalking her or anything. I was merely checking up on her progress.

Gabe wasn't pleased about the idea of Kaya and me ever getting back together.

He probably could attempt to get me with some of that *you're both agents* nonsense, though he'd had the no-fraternization policy revoked himself less than a year ago. And hell, she wasn't even trained, so that would be a bullshit argument. It didn't matter what anyone said though, I wasn't giving her up. Even if nothing I did brought her back, I would still give her everything because I truly loved her.

I would just be where she needed as long as she needed me. Even if I got nothing from her in return. But first, I had to deal with this family business shite.

Freedom would be a beautiful thing.

When all members were seated and the meeting called to order, I addressed the room and the voting members on the phone. "Thank you all for joining me for this session."

Bryson Date, an associate of my father's spoke up. "This is very unusual. Why are we all here wasting time on a meeting without a formal agenda?"

"Well, seeing as there is only one item to discuss, there's no need for formalities. I would like to inform the entire board of my decisions moving forward as CEO of All Saints Tech."

My father leaned forward. I couldn't wait to see his face when this dropped on him like a ton of bricks.

"Regarding the voting shares I wield entirely for the Saint family, effective today, I am transferring equal share distribution between myself, my brother, and my sister."

Several board members muttered under their breath, their low whispers and hums becoming a cacophony.

"You do recognize you'll get paid less." My father sat forward as he said that.

I smirked. "Money is not my concern. My concern is doing the best for this company and the employees counting on us. I chose some great investment opportunities for our future, and this board can have confidence in those decisions."

Bryson interrupted again. "But how will you reach a consensus?"

"While the three of us may have different ideas, I will still be interim CEO. But the day-to-day operations of the company will now be led by my sister."

Bryson pushed to his feet. "You can't do that. There are people who have more tenure than her that deserve the role."

"Maybe, but we don't have to consider tenure, and it's time that we change that idea."

I saw several board members nod in agreement, and one of them spoke up. "That change may be for the best."

My father pushed to his feet. "This is an outrage. You cannot split the shares. You will forfeit everything."

"Well, that's where you are wrong old chap. We can according to legal. And while we're at it, I know that the clause that stipulates I need to marry remains in effect. And I shall, within thirty days' time."

How do you plan on pulling that off?

I hoped to Christ that was more than enough time. I'd have to figure it out.

All the responsibility is not yours.

I knew it wasn't, but I still needed to keep my word. Of course, one of my siblings could marry. The code allowed for such a thing. But I just knew Kaya was the one and this was our time. I would have to convince her that we belonged together.

My father shook his head. "You cannot make these changes."

I turned to him with a smile, the first moment of happiness I'd felt looking toward him in a long time. "That's the thing, Father. I just did."

I turned to Adrianna and Trevor. "The three of us will run the company together. Trevor and Adrianna will handle the day to day, and I will continue to be the face of the company. I understand there are some obligations to be met, and we will honor those. From this meeting forward I will no longer have singular voting rights. The three of us will run this company together as my grandfather intended."

I deliberately met the board member's gazes, letting them know that they were not shoving us aside and that we were there to stay.

My father pointed at me. "You're doing this on purpose. You are deliberately making efforts to devalue this company. My voting shares are not being sold. You aren't getting rid of me."

I smiled at him bitterly. "Father, my whole goal in life was to keep you away from making any decisions that would affect all of us again. If I have not successfully done that this time, I intend to keep trying. I let my obligations keep me from happiness once before, and I won't ever do that again. The decision has been made, and no vote by the board can change it."

CHAPTER 50
KAYA

I FINALLY HAD my life back, and I poured myself into school. I had viable reasons, but so far this term was shit, and I'd been hustling over the last two weeks to catch up.

To avoid your empty heart?

Fuck, I wasn't thinking about him. Or how much I missed him. I needed to focus and fight for my normalcy.

Most of my classes were fine. I had good study habits, and I was able to play catch up pretty easily. The one class I couldn't fake it in was photography. Xander had asked to see me after class, and I knew he couldn't be happy with me. My classmates were all busy out scoping places to shoot and meeting their assignments, where I was barely passing the course and turning in assignments. I got some shots in Scotland, so that was helpful. But God, I needed to realign my world back on track to get this done this semester.

Easier said than done when I was missing someone fiercely and felt like a piece of me was missing. God, I missed him. That deep, hearty laugh, his teasing smile and warm embrace. His hugs were just a cocoon that I wanted to stay in, but that wasn't an option.

I missed everything about him. I was walking through a fog,

going through the motions to just get by. Part of the problem was that all of this felt, not boring exactly, but like it was somebody else's life. I'd been living on adrenaline for two months, and now I was just supposed to go back to taking classes and be completely normal. How did people do that?

Not to mention, I'd met all these other people. Created attachments with a sort of family. I hadn't been alone. I hadn't dealt with that feeling of having to stay separate from everybody all the time. For two months I'd had a family. Not just Saint, but Westin, and Saff, and Lachlan, and of course, Gemma.

Gemma was the kind of friend I hadn't paid enough attention to before. She was my friend and I loved her, and she'd even let me move into her flat until I could find a place of my own. We were obviously close, but I'd kept her at arm's length until she had helped me through the fire that was Jasper Saint's world. And that world felt like my world now. It felt like where I belonged.

This world had started to feel awkward and uncomfortable. I still loved school, but I needed to get my focus back.

Gemma and I were walking across campus, and she said, "Oh shit, incoming. Andrew."

I immediately turned on my heel to go the opposite direction, but Gemma grabbed my elbow. "You are going to deal with him because we are not missing Xander's class."

I frowned. "Are you kidding me right now?"

"Look, the sooner you deal with him, the sooner you don't have to deal with him anymore. Ever." She had a point there.

He was coming down the stairs as we were going up. "Hey, Kaya, can I talk to you?"

"I don't have time today, Andrew. I have a lot going on."

"Look, I won't take up much of your time. I just... I fucked up, okay?"

"Yup, I got it."

"Maybe I shouldn't have told the world that we were dating.

That was a mistake. A miscalculation. But you're right, there's no reason why we can't be friends, and I should be happy with that."

I frowned at him. "Wait a minute, you spoke to the press, questioned the validity of my engagement, told thugs where to find Gemma, and you think we're going to be friends?"

His brow furrowed. "Well, I mean, yeah. But you said some things that were really harsh to me, too."

I turned to glance at Gemma, and she shook her head and rolled her eyes.

I looked Andrew straight in the eyes and said, "You're a fuckwit. We're not friends. And I don't think we ever were. So, if you don't mind, I have—"

A man jogged down the stairs and handed me an envelope then turned and jogged away. What the hell?

Andrew still shifted from foot to foot in front of me, but I ignored him. Gemma leaned over my shoulder. "Come on, open it. What is it?"

"Oh my God, give me a moment, would you?"

I handed my bag to her and then slowly unfastened the envelope seal, reading over the document. It didn't make sense until she loudly interrupted. "And you're saying he doesn't love you?"

Inside the envelope was a deed for a property, the building right next door to my former flat that had been destroyed by Igno. Saint had purchased a whole entire building in my name.

Holy shit. Why had he done this? I searched for a note and found one inside the envelope.

"I know all you wanted was peace and all I ever gave you was chaos. I hope you will accept this gift to give you a safe home. It's the building next to your original flat. I can't replace it, but hopefully this will do. I thought you might have fun designing it with Gemma and maybe Saffron and Tabatha, too. With all my love, J.S."

I stared at the deed. I owned a whole building.

Jasper Saint had given me a whole building of flats.

He wanted me to have a home.

Not one that was located inside his, but one that was mine. All mine. But that idea made my heart break even more.

I'd been stubborn thinking I was so right to stay away. But he hadn't come to me either. Instead, he'd gone out of his way to *show* me love, not just tell me.

I missed him.

God, this made me love him even more. And all I wanted was to get him back.

———

Kaya

All through class I was distracted. Xander even had to call on me once or twice to ask my opinion on a fellow classmate's photo just for my brain to stay engaged in the conversation. After class, he called me up to his desk. Gemma's eyes just went wide, and she looked a little freaked out. Then she abandoned me. Gave me a little wave and mouthed *See you later*.

Wow. So much for loyalty.

"Professor Chase," I started as I approached his desk. "I know I've been distracted. I know my last set of photographs wasn't up to par, but I promise I will do better. Everything is settled down now. Back to normal."

He sat on the edge of the desk, his long legs out in front of him and crossed at the ankle. When he said nothing, I continued rattling on.

"I've been working really hard. I just haven't been able to focus the way I wanted to, so please don't fail me. I would love to take the class again, but honestly, I'd rather take some of the more advanced classes, and I don't want to repeat this intro again if I don't have to, and..."

He shook his head slowly. "Are you all right?" His voice was low and soothing. And he didn't sound the least bit annoyed. His dark blond hair was artfully tousled, and his silvery gray eyes were level on mine.

"Um, yeah, I think so."

"Good, that's all that matters. From now on you'll be focused?"

"Yessir. I'm here. I swear."

"That's all I wanted to know."

"That's it? I'm not in trouble?"

He lifted a brow and then pushed himself to his full height. I staggered back because, Lord Almighty, he was tall. There was a knock at the door, and I turned to see his wife, Imani, strolling toward us. She gave me a wide beaming smile and then a softer one for her husband. "I'm sorry, am I early? Didn't mean to interrupt."

I couldn't help but smile at her. "No, of course not, sorry. I'll just be going."

I looked up at him again. His gaze was fully on his wife, and he looked... *wolfish*. It was the only way to describe it. He honestly looked like he was all teeth and wanted to eat her whole.

God, to have someone look at me like that.

You had someone who looked at you like that.

Okay, that was true, but he couldn't just fix things by buying me something.

It's not about buying you something. It's about giving you the home that you wanted.

When I thought about it like that, my heart broke in two. I wanted a home with him. I wanted him to love me. I wanted all of it. God, I missed him so much. It had been two weeks since I woke up in medical at Rogues. He hadn't called. He hadn't texted. Not that I wanted to hear from him, but still.

You do want to hear from him.

Every night when I went to bed, I heard his voice in my head, whispering how much he loved me, and then I would replay how he broke my heart. I would replay how it felt to have him walk away. I couldn't risk that again.

Is this thing that you're doing much better? Are you happy?

Well, that was easy. I was not happy. I had a hole carved out of my soul.

But how dare he just buy me a flat? Well, a whole building really. I couldn't be bought. How dare he give me the perfect gift? A home. I didn't ask him for anything.

You know the answer to that. You know why.

As I walked past the cafe, Gemma called up to me. "Hey Kaya, where the hell are you going?"

"I have to see a man about a deed."

"Ugh, thank God. Honestly, you've been moping for weeks now. I didn't want to say anything, but moping does not look good on you. It's not your color."

"Gee, thanks."

"I keep it real. Go on, mate. Go have the shag of a lifetime."

"That's not why I'm going to see him."

"Sure, it's not. But it's going to be a consequence of you telling him that you're angry, that you miss him, and that you love him too. You recognize that, right?"

"You know, I never did like you."

She grinned and then gave me a quick hug before sauntering off. "Have fun."

I rolled my eyes and then headed straight for the Tube.

When I reached All Saints Tech, my stomach felt tied in knots. I hadn't been back there since Saint and the Rogues team had walked into my father's compound. Interestingly, that was one of the few things I did not think about. Like my brain was trying to protect me from having to relive all of that betrayal and hatred. One of the front desk security guards waved me in, recognizing me. I guess my access wasn't revoked after all. Maureen met me in Saint's reception area. "You are a sight for sore eyes."

"Hi, Maureen. I know I don't have an appointment, but is there any chance—"

"Now child, I know you're not asking me for permission to go in and see your fiancé. That's a standing order. Let me just go tell him there's an emergency. A problem with our Jamaican acquisition."

"Jamaican acquisition?"

"Yeah, that's our code phrase for *Kaya's here and you need to see her right away.*"

"Oh, I didn't realize I had a code phrase."

"You do."

"Right. Thanks Maureen."

In three minutes, several people piled out of his office and Maureen came out again too with a wide smile. "He's all yours."

I had no idea what I was going to say. Maybe I was going to slap his stupid little deed down on the table and tell him to shove it. Maybe I was going to cuss him out. He deserved it.

Maybe he does, but you're not going to do that either.

Right. I wanted to see how long I would last before I kissed him.

Ah, that's more like it.

I was doomed.

When I stepped in his office, the faint whiff of his cologne was like coming home. It filled me with thoughts of warmth and happiness and being wrapped in his arms, and all I wanted to do was soak in it.

Saint was at the bar, pouring me a tonic water with lime. Lots of lime. "Is this still your drink of choice?"

I held out the envelope with the deed inside. "Why did you do this?"

"I think the answer should be obvious. I love you."

I held the paper tight in my hand. Tears welled in my eyes and began streaking down my face. "You hurt me."

"I know. And I know I don't deserve forgiveness, but I'm asking for it anyway."

"You can't just buy me."

"Oh, trust me, I know, but I could give you a gift. Something you wanted. A home of your own. All I wanted to do was make you happy."

"Why did it have to be like this?"

"Because I'm a fool. I was so terrified of loving you that I just pushed you away. I was afraid it couldn't be real."

"This isn't fair. You're not playing fair, Jasper."

He placed the glass he'd just poured on the coffee table before stalking toward me. "I'm in love with you. I don't intend to play fair. Your move."

He was close. So close that I could smell the sandalwood and vanilla. It wrapped around me, cocooning me, lulling me into a trance. It pulled me into his gravitational orbit, refusing to let me go. I was ensnared in the trap and there was no escaping.

Oh yeah, like you're working real hard to escape.

"This isn't fair."

"Yeah, you said that already." His breath was a whisper on my cheek.

"You can't just seduce me."

"Who said anything about seducing you? I'm just standing here, willing you to stay. Willing you to be mine. What's your answer?"

Even before I'd gotten on the Tube to come here, even as the past two weeks had droned on with the pain of losing him never numbing, I'd known this moment would come. So I said the only thing that I could.

"Yes."

CHAPTER 51
KAYA

I woke enveloped in Jasper's arms, the heat of him surrounding me like a furnace.

I attempted to get out of bed, but he drew me back and leaned into my neck, the scruff of his beard igniting my skin. He growled, "Where are you going?"

His voice was a deep rumble that made my pussy clench. "I'm going to get water."

"I'll get it."

He moved to get up, but I stopped him. "No. I'm already up."

He rubbed his hips against me. "So am I."

I laughed. "Oh my God, Jasper Saint!"

His chuckle was low. "What? I am up."

"You stay, I have to pee anyway."

"Fine. If you insist. But hurry back, or I'll come looking for you. And whatever room we end up in, I'm going to get creative."

"This is supposed to make me hurry back, right?"

"Oh, you dirty girl. If you end up in the kitchen, I will get creative with oil."

I flushed deep. "Oh my gosh, yes, I hear you. Maybe I will get lost in the kitchen."

He lifted his brow. "Woman, you're going to kill me. I mean, I'm willing, more than willing to satisfy. But you are going to kill me."

"I know. Now can I please get up?"

He grumbled and groaned but finally rolled over, letting the morning air cool my naked skin.

"I'll be right back. Stop sulking."

He made an adorable pout, sticking out his bottom lip, and I couldn't resist leaning in to nip it. "Why are you so damn good-looking?"

He threw an arm over his head. The sheet hung low on his waist, abs on full display, tattoos on his pecs, all tempting me. He grinned. "It's a curse, I swear."

I shoved at him, and this time climbed out of the bed.

When I was done in the bathroom, I meandered my way down to the kitchen, not bothering with clothes. Saint had started keeping the temperature warmer in the flat after he'd seen me shivering in my sweats one day. I got my glass of water, and as I drank it, I eyed my mother's box dubiously.

As I drank, I lifted it with my left hand, holding it up to the light. The only way into this thing was a saw. But if we did that, the internal mechanism might lock forever. It could not be broken into. Absentmindedly, my fingers played over it as I started to hum the lullaby I'd heard in Croatia and tried to find a way into the puzzle.

I had run my fingers all over this thing. Yelled at it, clutched it with both hands, even Harry Pottered that shit, but nothing worked. Not a damn thing. But as I looked at it in the light, something strange happened. I kept humming, and it almost felt like the box was heating up. I frowned and tried again, using both hands this time, moving this way and that, assessing it, trying to break my way in. When I stopped humming, the box cooled. When I hummed again, that strange heat was back and it felt like it was vibrating.

And then something clicked.

Oh, holy shit. Something was happening.

Oh my God. Oh my God. Oh my God.

I kept singing, and the latch slid a little more. I hummed and hummed, and hummed, trying to remember the words of the lullaby. And then finally, the latch fully gave way, exposing what looked like a keyhole. I was so surprised I almost dropped it. I put the box on the counter gently and tugged at the key around my neck, pulling it off.

I licked my bottom lip before wiping my hands on my jeans. Jesus. This was how everything fit. With trembling fingers, I slid the key in and waited. With a slight wiggle, it clicked then turned. The box opened and I gasped, shocked by what greeted me inside.

Brilliance. Pure brilliance. Diamonds, glittering back at me. I'd opened my mother's puzzle. I had finally opened it.

Holy fuck me. There were at least two handfuls of diamonds in there. Large handfuls. This was what my father had been looking for. This was what he'd been willing to kill for. Was this what a hundred and fifty million dollars looked like? Give or take a few million that mum had given to Connor Lohman. Holy Jesus.

"Woman, I warned you what would happen if you took too long. Now I'm going to have to show you. I've never used olive oil as lube, but I am willing to give it a—" He abruptly stopped talking and his face morphed into a look of concern. "What's wrong, baby? Sprite, talk to me."

I didn't know what to say. I couldn't breathe. "I... Oh God, I opened it."

Saint rushed to my side and stared at the box. Then he stared back at me, back at the box, and back at me. "Holy fucking shit. How the hell did you do that?"

———

Kaya

"You don't have to do this," Jasper said. "No one is expecting this of you."

"Relax, I want to do this. I didn't even realize there was a part of me missing until I came here. There's a history of my mum here. And even though I've always been anti-chaos, I think that was partly me running away from who I was meant to be. I don't know... I feel a little bit like I'm stepping into a legacy at Rogues, stepping into who I'm supposed to be and not hiding it the least."

Saint took my hand, threading my fingers between his. "I know, but being a Rogues agent also means dealing with Gabe. And you already know he's going to put you in danger. I don't like it."

"Well, I'm not an agent yet, right? I'm just going in to have a conversation."

He pursed his lips. "Fine." As we walked from his bungalow on the Abott Manor property, I still marveled at my surroundings. The manor house was like stepping into Downton Abbey. It was lush and green with gardens and land as far as you could see. It was surrounded by woods, from what I understood, also owned by Abbott Manor. There was enough distance that nobody should come looking or asking questions about what was going on here.

When I'd been there before, I'd had a little time to explore the property. I knew that there were tennis courts, a swimming pool, basketball court, cricket field, and an indoor squash court somewhere. Subterranean levels were the training rooms. Sparring. Weapons training. Unless it was long range targets, then they came out to the fields and the woods. Gabe had made it very clear, Saffron too, to not wander into the woods because there were constant training ops there. But I was curious to see more. To see where my mother had spent so much time.

Jasper said, "I know he saved your life, and I'll forever be grateful to him for that. But he was also the one who put you in that position, so he's not my favorite person at the moment."

"I know. But remember, I made the choice. He gave me the say and I decided to walk in. Am I not your favorite person too?"

"Now that you mentioned it, you're not. But this isn't about favorites. You are *my* person. That's all that matters."

I grinned up at him. "I love you too."

He leaned down to kiss me, and his lips were soft. "I don't like this. But I support you, okay?"

"That's all I can ask for. And thank you."

He started us walking again. "How about the diamonds? You're not going to give them all to Rogues are you?"

"I honestly don't need any of them. I kept a couple to make some diamond earrings for Gemma for her birthday. And I gave ten to Lydia and Michael. They were good to me. Took care of me when they didn't have to."

"Well, they were your parents."

"Yeah, I know. But when you go into care, it's like a box of chocolates. You never know what you're going to get. And they were lovely. The house was a little loud, constantly filled with chaos, but it was also filled with love. They cared about each and every one of us kids that came through there. It wasn't always easy, but we were warm, and safe, and fed. I just want to show a little appreciation."

"You're a good person, you know that?"

"I'd like to think that maybe Mum would have wanted me to thank them. Maybe this is her way of thanking them for me too."

"I'm sure she would have loved it."

When we stepped into the enormous doors leading to the back of Abott Manor, Saint squeezed my hand just a little bit harder. We made a left toward Gabe's office and found it crowded with the people I'd started to look on as my new family. Saffron was there, Lachlan, Gabe, obviously, and Gemma too.

"Gems, what are you doing here?"

"Relax, no one's ever going to make me a badass hand-to-hand combat person. But apparently, if you're going to learn to be a badass, it's going to require some new security protocols for me."

"Oh, I wish I'd known you were coming. We could have come here together."

"Nah, it's cool. James picked me up."

Gemma winked at me, and all I could do was shake my head. Same old Gemma.

Gabe indicated one of the seats directly across the desk from him for me to sit down. I started to move, but Saint stopped me. I lifted a brow at him. With a sigh, he walked toward it and pulled out the chair for me a little, and then I sat.

He took the seat next to me. Lachlan and Saff joined Gemma on the couch. I couldn't help a flush as I thought about the things I'd done last time I was on this couch.

"Okay, as much as I love to see everyone, what's all the drama about?"

Gabe cocked his head. "For starters, you opened the damn box."

"I did."

Gabe lifted a brow. "All right, do you know how you did it?"

"Honestly, I couldn't tell you. Finger placement, and then I was humming to it, a lullaby from my childhood."

"Can you do it again?"

"I can try, but we probably want to take all the diamonds out of it first just in case."

Gabe handed me a pouch to put the stones in, and I reengaged the locking mechanism. Then I held the box and met Saint's eyes as I hummed the lullaby. When the latch gave way, just like the last time, I used my key to open it.

"Your mother was clever."

"Yeah, she was." I turned to Saff. "I didn't know she was a Raven. I didn't understand any of it until Igno told me. Do you have any paperwork on the Ravens? I'd like to read more about it."

Saff nodded. "Of course. They were pretty badass chicks."

"Not that I have big shoes to fill."

Saff just grinned and looked at me. "I think you're going to be just fine."

Gabe studied me. "So, what are you going to do with the diamonds?"

"I don't want them."

Saint muttered, "And she doesn't need them either. We're still getting married."

Gabe lifted a brow. "Oh, I wasn't aware."

"Yes, my brother and sister and I will split our company voting shares. I'm willing to give the lion's share to them. And while we split the day-to-day duties, they'll be the ones really running All Saints Tech. That way I can focus more on Rogues."

Gabe nodded. "Excellent decision."

"While she's training, I'm going to be here."

I rolled my eyes. "I appreciate the loyalty, but you don't need to do that."

"Yes, I do."

Gemma chuckled in the corner.

I placed the box in front of Gabe, then placed the pouch of stones next to it. "Let's lose the diamonds."

He whistled low. "So that's what a hundred and fifty million looks like?"

I shrugged. "Give or take. I might have dropped a few along the way."

He smirked then. "Dropped a few?"

"You know, these things happen."

"Of course, they do." He winked. "Well, your mother was an agent. A damn good one too. I'd love to offer you the opportunity of formally training with us. See if being a Rogue is something you want to think about doing." He shrugged. "I know you're in school and probably want to finish. Lots to consider, but it never hurts to be trained anyway."

"That is accurate. I never want to feel helpless again. While my mother trained me in a lot of disciplines, I still have large gaps. I'd love to learn more."

He nodded. "Excellent. Saff and Tabatha will take care of most of that." His gaze softened then. "Just one more thing... There's the matter of your mother."

"I don't know where she is, Gabe."

He smiled. "I know you don't. But I do."

CHAPTER 52
KAYA

Saffron swept my leg. I fought to hold on, bearing down on my core, but I couldn't because she was already spinning out of the way. And as my head turned to follow her movements, I went splat on my ass. Again.

There was no beating her. I had tried every which way from Sunday, and I couldn't. She was so damn fast. And to make matters worse, we weren't in the familiar area of the manor. We'd gone off site today near Primrose Hill. To the rest of the world, it looked like the lot of us were just doing a kind of a workout here in the open, and I had no idea what the catch was. So I was on edge, waiting for the other shoe to drop.

From the sidelines, Saint called over. "You have to stay focused, Kaya. Pay attention to what's going on around you, to how she's moving, what she's doing. She's telegraphing her movements. You just need to pay attention to her."

"Don't you think I'm trying?"

From somewhere behind me, Tabatha was having a field day with Lachlan. Tabs was short like me. Curvier though. And she was running circles around Lachlan.

Jesus, she and Saff were like something out of a Wonder Woman manual.

Saffron tagged Saint in, and my fiancé strode toward me. "You don't have to do much, Kaya. Just stay on your feet and try to put me on my behind."

"I can use any tactic?"

He lifted a brow. "Sure. Anything except a groin strike. Why not?"

Lachlan laughed. "I say a groin strike is fair game."

Saint just shot him a withering look.

"All I have to do is put you on your behind?"

"Yes."

I checked first to make sure everyone else was engaged. Then as Saint approached, I did the easiest thing I could. I lifted my shirt. He stopped in his tracks. I was wearing his favorite sports bra that pushed my tits up under my chin. And then from there, it was easy to sweep his leg.

From the ground, he grumbled. "Not fair. You know that's not what I meant."

I grinned. "You said by any tactic was fair game."

Behind us, Lachlan and Saff and Tabatha were laughing their asses off. Saint looked less than pleased, but he took my hand when I offered him help to stand. "You, woman, are diabolical. You won't get by so easily next time."

I squealed and darted out of the way when he dove for me. Something from my peripheral vision caught my attention and I spun, hands up, ready for anything. There was a woman watching us on the fringes of the track.

Saint jogged up to me. "Now you're distracted." And then he saw what I was looking at, and the oddest thing happened. He squeezed my shoulder. "Go on, she's been watching for a while."

I frowned at him. "What?"

"Gabe made an arrangement. That's why we're here. The rest of us are just here for backup in case Igno has someone watching."

I wanted to run right over. I wanted to throw myself in her arms and hug her tight, but I couldn't make myself move. "I don't think I can."

Saint's hand massaged the base of my neck, and I had no choice but to relax as his heat seeped into my muscles. "Look, this is all you've ever wanted. And Gabe had to pull some strings to make this happen. It's his way of saying he was sorry for putting you in danger."

"This is really happening. She's here?"

"Yeah, she is. If you want to talk to her, all you have to do is walk over."

I glanced up, and Saffron gave me a soft smile. "If she didn't want to talk to you, you would never even have seen her."

I frowned at that, wondering how often she'd been watching me, how many times she could have reached out or spoken to me. And then the fear that had rooted me gave way to compulsion, as I charged forward, wishing that I looked different, that I was stronger or more confident, or at least had makeup on, for the love of Christ.

As I approached, I noticed that she looked exactly how I remembered her. The years hadn't done anything to her in the sense of time. Her smile was tremulous. Like she was unsure if she should come up and hug me. I stood awkwardly the same way, three feet away, unsure of what to do with my body, my arms.

"You've grown into a beautiful young woman, Kaya."

Just hearing her voice, I started to shake. The worry and the fear and the loneliness taking over my body all at once, raging through me, making me long for the days gone by.

She rushed forward and wrapped her arms around me. "Oh, there, there, my sweet love. There's no need to cry. I'm here now."

She was here, alive. And suddenly it didn't matter why she'd been gone all these years.

I wasn't sure how long she held me like that or how long the tears fell because I was in my mother's arms again.

She led me to a bench and we sat. As I wiped my tears with the backs of my hands, I said, "I'm sorry. I just... I didn't expect to see you again."

Her gaze searched my face. "I'm sorry about that, Kaya. I'm really, really sorry. There's so much I wanted to tell you over the years."

"Where have you been?"

"Never far away. Not from you."

"You let me believe I was alone."

"I'm sorry for that, but I couldn't risk your father finding you. Finding out I've been hiding you. I was terrified for your safety. I couldn't come to you."

"You climbed in that car with Connor Lohman, and you didn't even text me or let me know you were okay. You just vanished, Mum."

She was crying now too. "I know. I know. And I regretted that decision every day. But any contact with you would have put you in graver danger. Lohman betrayed me that day, and coming back to you or contacting you would have been risky. I know you must have thought I abandoned you. Or worse, that I died."

"I'm not sure what's worse."

"Baby, if I could have seen you, I would have. As it was, I worked hard to make sure you were never alone."

"Never alone? Mum, I was in foster care. Because I had been abandoned. You were gone."

"Baby, that first place... I couldn't leave you with them. So I sent the social worker to you."

"You sent her?"

"Yes."

"That social worker... It was as if somehow she'd been watching and knew how bad it was, because she didn't asked many questions. She told me to pack my things and get ready to move."

"I know," Mum said. "The next family was better. They were kind. A lot of kids. I figured it would be easy for you to get lost and not have to think too hard, and maybe that's what you needed."

"You placed me with them?"

"Let's just say that over the years, I got to know Lydia and Michael well. I just wanted to make sure you were protected."

"Protected? I needed you, not a stranger."

"I know, but when you couldn't have me, Lydia was a good mother to you."

I watched her, knowing that she'd considered the pain we both had to go through. She had paid attention to it. She'd done this purposely.

"You did all this to protect me?"

"Yeah, of course. My past caught up to me when I ran into Lohman on the street. And I had to make moves I hadn't intended on ever making."

"And what about Rogues? Why didn't you take me to them?"

She chaffed. "I know how they work all too well. You were a child that wasn't supposed to be, and they would have exploited you. And I couldn't possibly risk that."

"So you just let me think I was alone all this time?"

"You've never been alone. Once you had Lydia and Michael, your foster siblings, and Gemma, I knew you'd be okay. I never did like that Andrew boy, but there was nothing I could do to make him walk away from you."

My eyes went wide. "You know my friends?"

She nodded slowly. "Only from a distance. She's a good friend to you. I've always been watching sweetheart."

My mind was going to explode. All these things I never thought or considered.

"What about now? Are you coming back? Are you going to be a Raven again?"

She shook her head. "I can't. Igno is still out there, and he still has it in for me. If I'm captured, it's a little too dangerous for my team, and well, Igno will stop at nothing if he knows I'm alive. It's for your safety if I stay away. But if you need me, I'm never far away."

EPILOGUE
SAINT

I tried not to fidget. Not that I was at all nervous about my first ops assignment as team lead. I was fine. I could do this. It was a simple mission. Retrieve Nile Marks, an informant on the cartel, apply pressure on him to spill his guts, and then return him.

What I was concerned about was that Kaya was in the field. Well okay, technically not *in* the field. She was running comms in the van, but she was with the field team and they were still in danger.

I knew Lock would have her though, and Rook too. I still wanted to glower at him every time he was near her. She was mine. She had always been mine. But maybe I'd needed Rook sniffing around her to see what was right in front of my face.

Over the comms, I heard Lock's voice. "All right, we are in position. Rook, go to position two. Raven, confirm comms."

When Kaya's voice came over loud and clear, I couldn't help but smile to myself. "I hear you loud and clear, King. Heir, comms check?"

Saffron's voice was low since she was at the bar watching our target. "Roger, loud and clear."

"All right, Heir, you're on."

"Perfect. Now sweetheart," Saff said, "I don't want you to come over and break his nose, but I do want you to get a little jealous."

I smirked. "King, don't break anything."

All I got as response was Lock's chuckle. I could hear the background noise from the bar. "Raven, can you reduce the noise for me?"

There was no response from Kaya. I pressed my comms button again. "Raven, do you copy?"

Oh shit, what was wrong?

I hit my comms button again. "Raven, do you—"

"Copy," she answered. "I just... interference."

Interference? What had gone wrong?

Saff's voice came over the line again. "Copy... position..."

Kaya interrupted. "Interference. Jamming... fix..."

Fuck. I had a button to call if something went wrong. Was this that moment? Sure, it was an emergency to me. Kaya was potentially in danger. I knew I was being monitored and if push came to shove, I could always call on Gabe, who would know what to do. But I needed to be the one to make the decision. "Team A, come in. Switch channels. Do you copy? Switch channels."

Suddenly, Kaya's voice came in loud and clear. "I got it. One of our antennae looks frayed."

I frowned at that. "What do you mean, frayed?"

"I got out of the van and climbed on top of it to check."

"You did what?" I growled.

"Saint, we don't have time for this. Heir, do you copy?"

Saffron came through. "Yes, now I copy. We are in position. Making my approach. Rook, do you copy?"

No response, but it was too late. Saffron approached the target, and I could hear the script we'd come up with. I could hear her going through it line by line and the target responding. On her worst day, Saff was stunning, so he was probably counting his lucky stars.

Lock played his role to a T. "Hey, she's my woman. What the hell are you doing?"

The other bloke tried to back up as Lock approached. There was a scuffle, and then Lock delivered one of two response calls. The primary was supposed to be, 'If you ever touch her again, I will sever you from your spine.' The other one was, 'Baby, come on. We're going home right now.'

He delivered the first, and I breathed a sigh of relief.

After that, Saff was supposed to apologize to the guy, tagging his skin with a tracker. Once they were out of the building and back in the comms van, he would get a phone call, requiring him to go outside in order to hear. His truck was parked out back, and when he moved, Rook was going to get him.

Saff's voice came over the line. "Target tagged."

Kaya responded. "Acknowledged. Rook, are you in position?"

Nothing came on the line.

"King, verify Rook's whereabouts." Kaya was calm and handling herself well.

Saffron reported that she was back in the comms van and Lock was checking on Rook.

What the fuck was Rook doing? What was he up to?

When Lock's voice came back online, his words were tight, like he was speaking through clenched teeth. "Mission abort. Mission abort. Rook has been taken."

To be continued in The Rook

As a special gift to my readers, I have a special bonus for you of Saint and Kaya. Click here to get your exclusive bonus epilogue for The Saint!

———

Thank you for reading *THE SAINT*, book 3 in the Gentlemen Rogues Series. I hope you're ready for a wild ride, the Rogues just get sexier from here!

First rule of being a Rogue, hide in plain sight. Second rule of being a Rogue, never get involved, the mission above all.

But less than forty-eight hours on my new assignment and I'm ready to break every rule in the book.

Lissa Montgomery, the one woman I cannot tough or fantasize about.

Read about Lissa and Rook in ———>THE ROOK!

WHILE YOU WAIT, dive in to Liv and Ben's story with **The See No Evil Trilogy:**

I've been a prince in exile, but I'm finally going home, tarnished crown and all. This time, I won't let anyone keep me away...Not Ariel, the woman I left behind. Not the killer on my tail. Hell, not even my cousin—the king—can stop me...

➜ Yes, you can pick up **Big Ben, The Benefactor** and **For Her Benefit** now!

> "*...a **dramatic, suspenseful and amazing read** that*
> *you just can't put down. I loved it!*"
> ————**Goodreads Reviewer**

Can't get enough royals? Meet a cocky, billionaire prince that goes undercover in **Cheeky Royal!**

He's a prince with a secret to protect. The last distraction he can afford is his gorgeous as sin new neighbor.

His secrets could get them killed, but still, he can't stay away...
Read Cheeky Royal Now!

Turn the page for an excerpt from Cheeky Royal...

UPCOMING BOOKS

THE ROOK
THE SPY
THE VILLAIN

ALSO FROM NANA MALONE
CHEEKY ROYAL

"You make a really good model. I'm sure dozens of artists have volunteered to paint you before."
He shook his head. "Not that I can recall. Why? Are you offering?"

I grinned. "I usually do nudes." Why did I say that? It wasn't true. Because you're hoping he'll volunteer as tribute.

He shrugged then reached behind his back and pulled his shirt up, tugged it free, and tossed it aside. "How is this for nude?"

Fuck. Me. I stared for a moment, mouth open and looking like an idiot. Then, well, I snapped a picture. Okay fine, I snapped several. "Uh, that's a start."

He ran a hand through his hair and tussled it, so I snapped several of that. These were romance-cover gold. Getting into it, he started posing for me, making silly faces. I got closer to him, snapping more close-ups of his face. That incredible face.

Then suddenly he went deadly serious again, the intensity in his eyes going harder somehow, sharper. Like a razor. "You look nervous. I thought you said you were used to nudes."

I swallowed around the lump in my throat. "Yeah, at school whenever we had a model, they were always nude. I got used to it."

He narrowed his gaze. "Are you sure about that?"
Shit. He could tell. "Yeah, I am. It's just a human form. Male. Female. No big deal."

His lopsided grin flashed, and my stomach flipped. Stupid traitorous body...and damn him for being so damn good looking. I tried to keep the lens centered on his face, but I had to get several of his abs, for you know...research.
But when his hand rubbed over his stomach and then slid to the button on his jeans, I gasped, "What are you doing?"
"Well, you said you were used doing nudes. Will that make you more comfortable as a photographer?"

I swallowed again, unable to answer, wanting to know what he was doing, how far he would go. And how far would I go?

The button popped, and I swallowed the sawdust in my mouth. I snapped a picture of his hands.

Well yeah, and his abs. So sue me. He popped another button, giving me a hint of the forbidden thing I couldn't have. I kept snapping away. We were locked in this odd, intimate game of chicken. I swung the lens up to capture his face. His gaze was slightly hooded. His lips parted...turned on. I stepped back a step to capture all of him. His jeans loose, his feet bare. Sitting on the stool, leaning back slightly and giving me the sex face, because that's what it was—God's honest truth—the sex face. And I was a total goner.

"You're not taking pictures, Len." His voice was barely above a whisper.

"Oh, sorry." I snapped several in succession. Full body shots, face shots, torso shots. There were several torso shots. I wanted to fully capture what was happening.
He unbuttoned another button, taunting me, tantalizing me. Then he reached into his jeans, and my gaze snapped to meet his. I wanted to say something. Intervene in some way...help maybe...ask him what he was doing. But I couldn't. We were locked in a game that I couldn't break free from. Now I wanted more. I wanted to know just how far he would go.

Would he go nude? Or would he stay in this half-undressed state, teasing me, tempting me to do the thing that I shouldn't do?

I snapped more photos, but this time I was close. I was looking down on him with the camera, angling so I could see his perfectly sculpted abs as they flexed. His hand was inside his jeans. From the bulge, I knew he was touching himself. And then I snapped my gaze up to his face.
Sebastian licked his lip, and I captured the moment that tongue met flesh.

Heat flooded my body, and I pressed my thighs together to abate the ache. At that point, I was just snapping photos, completely in the zone, wanting to see what he might do next.

"Len..."
"Sebastian." My voice was so breathy I could barely get it past my lips.
"Do you want to come closer?"
"I--I think maybe I'm close enough?"
His teeth grazed his bottom lip. "Are you sure about that? I have another question for you."

I snapped several more images, ranging from face shots to shoulders, to torso. Yeah, I also went back to the hand-around-his-dick thing because...wow. "Yeah? Go ahead."

"Why didn't you tell me about your boyfriend 'til now?"

Oh shit. "I—I'm not sure. I didn't think it mattered. It sort of feels like we're supposed to be friends." Lies all lies.

He stood, his big body crowding me. "Yeah, friends..."

I swallowed hard. I couldn't bloody think with him so close. His scent assaulted me, sandalwood and something that was pure Sebastian wrapped around me, making me weak. Making me tingle as I inhaled his scent. Heat throbbed between my thighs, even as my knees went weak. "Sebastian, wh—what are you doing?"

"

Proving to you that we're not friends. Will you let me?"

He was asking my permission. I knew what I wanted to say. I understood what was at stake. But then he raised his hand and traced his knuckles over my cheek, and a whimper escaped.

His voice went softer, so low when he spoke, his words were more like a rumble than anything intelligible. "Is that you telling me to stop?"

Seriously, there were supposed to be words. There were. But somehow I couldn't manage them, so like an idiot I shook my head.

His hand slid into my curls as he gently angled my head. When he leaned down, his lips a whisper from mine, he whispered, "This is all I've been thinking about."

Read Cheeky Royal Now!

NANA MALONE READING LIST

Looking for a few Good Books? Look no Further

FREE
Shameless
Before Sin
Cheeky Royal
Protecting the Heiress
Big Ben
The Heir

Gentlemen Rogues
The Heir
The King
The Saint
The Rook
The Spy
The Villain

Royals
Royals Undercover

Cheeky Royal
Cheeky King

Royals Undone

Royal Bastard
Bastard Prince

Royals United

Royal Tease
Teasing the Princess

Royal Elite

The Heiress Duet

Protecting the Heiress
Tempting the Heiress

The Prince Duet

Return of the Prince
To Love a Prince

The Bodyguard Duet

Bodyguard to the Billionaire
The Billionaire's Secret

London Royals

London Royal Duet

London Royal
London Soul

Playboy Royal Duet

Royal Playboy

Playboy's Heart

London Lords
<u>See No Evil</u>
Big Ben
The Benefactor
For Her Benefit

<u>Hear No Evil</u>
East End
East Bound
Fall of East

To Catch a Thief

<u>Speak No Evil</u>
London Bridge
Bridge of Lies
Broken Bridge

The Donovans Series
<u>*Come Home Again (Nate & Delilah)*</u>
<u>*Love Reality (Ryan & Mia)*</u>
<u>*Race For Love (Derek & Kisima)*</u>
<u>*Love in Plain Sight (Dylan and Serafina)*</u>
<u>*Eye of the Beholder – (Logan & Jezzie)*</u>
<u>*Love Struck (Zephyr & Malia)*</u>

London Billionaires Standalones
Mr. Trouble (Jarred & Kinsley)
Mr. Big (Zach & Emma)
Mr. Dirty (Nathan & Sophie)

The Shameless World

Shameless
Shameless
Shameful
Unashamed

Force
Enforce

Deep
Deeper

Before Sin
Sin
Sinful

Brazen
Still Brazen

The Player
<u>Bryce</u>
<u>Dax</u>
<u>Echo</u>
<u>Fox</u>
<u>Ransom</u>
<u>Gage</u>

The In Stilettos Series
<u>*Sexy in Stilettos (Alec & Jaya)*</u>
<u>*Sultry in Stilettos (Beckett & Ricca)*</u>
<u>*Sassy in Stilettos (Caleb & Micha)*</u>
<u>*Strollers & Stilettos (Alec & Jaya & Alexa)*</u>
<u>*Seductive in Stilettos (Shane & Tristia)*</u>
<u>*Stunning in Stilettos (Bryan & Kyra)*</u>

~~~
~~~

In Stilettos Spin off
Tempting in Stilettos (Serena & Tyson)
Teasing in Stilettos (Cara & Tate)
Tantalizing in Stilettos (Jaggar & Griffin)

Love Match Series
**Game Set Match (Jason & Izzy)*
Mismatch (Eli & Jessica)

ABOUT NANA MALONE

USA Today and Wall Street Journal Best Seller, Nana Malone's love of all things romance and adventure started with a tattered romantic suspense she "borrowed" from her cousin.

It was a sultry summer afternoon in Ghana, and Nana was a precocious thirteen. She's been in love with kick butt heroines ever since. With her overactive imagination, and channeling her inner Buffy, it was only a matter a time before she started creating her own characters.

Now she writes about sexy royals and smokin' hot bodyguards when she's not hiding her tiara from Kidlet, chasing a puppy who refuses to shake without a treat, or begging her husband to listen to her latest hair-brained idea.